Also by Glen Huser

STITCHES
TOUCH OF THE CLOWN

Skinnybones and the Wrinkle Queen

# Skinnybones and the Wrinkle Queen

## GLEN HUSER

GROUNDWOOD BOOKS
HOUSE OF ANANSI PRESS
TORONTO   BERKELEY

Groundwood Books / House of Anansi Press
110 Spadina Avenue, Suite 801, Toronto, Ontario M5V 2K4
Distributed in the USA by Publishers Group West
1700 Fourth Street, Berkeley, CA 94710

We acknowledge for their financial support of our publishing program the
Canada Council for the Arts, the Government of Canada through the Book
Publishing Industry Development Program (BPIDP) and the
Ontario Arts Council.

ONTARIO ARTS COUNCIL
CONSEIL DES ARTS DE L'ONTARIO

Library and Archives Canada Cataloging in Publication
Huser, Glen
Skinnybones and the Wrinkle Queen / by Glen Huser.
ISBN-13: 978-0-88899-732-6 (bound).–
ISBN-10: 0-88899-732-9 (bound).–
ISBN-13: 978-0-88899-733-3 (pbk.).–
ISBN-10: 0-88899-733-7 (pbk.)
I. Title.
PS8565.U823S55 2006     jC813'.54     C2006-901870-7

Printed and bound in Canada

My appreciation to family and friends who read the first drafts of *Skinnybones and the Wrinkle Queen* and offered many helpful comments.

Once again a special thanks to my editor, Shelley Tanaka, for her insightful suggestions throughout the revision process.

For Gail,
and in memory of William,
fellow travelers on the road to the Ring.

# 1

Choices. It's probably Mr. Mussbacher's favorite word. During the drive across the city to the south side where the Shadbolts lived, he'd used it at least ten times.

"You *do* have choices in life, Tamara," he'd said, glancing at me as we waited at a traffic light. "Only you can choose to turn things around. Only you can choose to meet people half way…"

I nodded my head a lot but I didn't say much. There was a light snow falling, and he kept clicking the windshield wipers off and on.

Changing foster homes was starting to happen for me on a regular basis, sort of like changes in the weather. I didn't remind him about all of the things where I didn't have any choice at all.

Take parents. Not my choice. Who would choose Wilma for a mother? A new baby every two or three years. Maybe she had some kind of a deal with Social Services to keep the foster homes of Alberta busy.

And my dad? Again — not my choice. Wilma said I got my cheekbones from him so I guess he wasn't a total disaster. If you're going to be a model, cheekbones are a real bonus. Be nice if he'd stuck around to see how they turned out.

Foster families? You're crazy if you think you have any choice about them. The Tierneys — I couldn't run away from them fast enough. Good thing their house and bottle-recycling business was right next to the transit line. You can get far away pretty fast on the light rail transit.

And the Rawdings with their lists of rules all over the place, taped to the fridge, on the inside of the bathroom door: *Don't use more than 6 squares of bathroom tissue during a visit. Don't open the refrigerator door unless you have permission.*

Didn't have to run away from the Rawdings. One thing about foster parents is a single phone call can spin you on to the next family on the Social Services list.

"The Shadbolts." Mr. Mussbacher double-checked a file between us on the car seat. "Shirley and Herbert. They're a new application. You'll be their first."

"Whoopee ding."

Mr. M. shot me an eyebrows-pushed-together squinty-eyed look.

"Give it a chance, Tammy. Tamara," he corrected himself as we pulled up in front of a house with walls covered in that kind of stuck-on sand with tiny bits of broken glass in it.

After Mr. Mussbacher had done his little half-hour visit at the new place and left, Shirley Shadbolt had gushed, "I want you to feel like you're one of the family." She speared a giant waffle out of a waffle iron and added it to a platter warming in the oven. "You can call me Shirl."

I smiled. It was one of the other things Mr. Mussbacher had urged me to do on the drive over. Smile more.

"You have a chance to make things a lot easier for yourself," he kept telling me. "I know things didn't work out with the Tierneys and the Rawdings, but things might have gone a lot better if you…"

"Smiled more." I mouthed the words with him. Actually, I think I was smiling when I dropped Mrs. Rawding's bone china teacups on the parquet floor in the living room after she'd banned me from the TV room.

For someone who wants to be a model, TV is one of life's essentials. You don't allow anyone to mess with your viewing privileges. Of course, one of the things a model-in-training learns right from the start is how to smile even when there's nothing to smile about. I've practiced a lot and I'm pretty good at it. I just haven't maxed my killer smile on Mr. Mussbacher or the loser families he's found for me so far.

I smiled for Shirl, though. Who says I'm not ready to work on a new beginning?

"You'll be able to tuck into that waffle in just a couple of minutes, honey. Herb and the kids and me — we had ours already, but, hey, I'll have another one to keep you company." She placed one of her pudgy hands over mine.

"Not for me," I told her, still smiling.

"No waffles!" Shirl looked like I'd walloped her one in the chops.

"I have an allergy to flour."

What I mainly watch on television are programs showing the latest fashions or giving grooming tips. I know fashion shows don't fill all the time slots in a TV schedule, so sometimes I find myself watching the health news or the soaps or the sitcoms if I'm really desperate.

It was while I was watching *Health Hotline* one afternoon at the Rawdings (before I was banned from the TV room) that I saw this program about celiac disease. If you have celiac disease, eating anything with wheat flour is not good for you. So I filed that away for future reference. Having an allergy is easier than just saying no to the tubs of starch people keep trying to push at you.

Being thin, of course, is right up there with smiling for models.

"Mr. Mussbacher didn't say anything about an allergy. No wonder you're as skinny as a drinking straw." Little creases of worry crinkled up Shirl's forehead. "Why don't you check the fridge and find something to tide you over until lunch?"

"Sure, Shirl."

You can picture the fridge. Mayonnaise and tubs of sour cream, bricks of butter, some pieces of leftover pizza, jars of jam. In the crisper, there was part of a cabbage turning black around the edges and a few carrots that had sprouted whiskers from old age. I pulled the carrots out — and a jar of olives.

"Oh, honey, is that all you're going to have?" Shirl looked distressed.

"What's for lunch?"

"I thought I'd bake some macaroni and cheese. It's a favorite…"

That's what I was up against.

Her two chubby gremlins, Lizzie and Lyle, had wandered down to the kitchen.

"Macaroni!" Lizzie twirled one way and then unwound by twirling back again. "I love macaroni!"

"I want ketchup on mine," Lyle whined.

I smiled at the three of them and began scraping the whiskers off a carrot.

"You have a choice of schools," Shirl told me as she helped me unpack my things. "We're right on the boundary line between Stanley Merkin Junior High and Blatchford. It's got elementary and junior high."

"I'll take the one with no ankle biters," I said.

Speaking of choices, something I've discovered I do have a choice about are the half-days of school worth missing. I even keep a weekly plan. I mark the teachers and courses I dislike the most on my school timetable and then match it up with the TV schedule. Herb's got satellite TV so, like I say, lots of choices.

Things have been working out pretty well at this foster home. You can get *Fashion Forecast* on Wednesdays and Fridays, and those are afternoons when I have hour-long blocks of L.A. and Social from Mrs. Whipple.

Actually, I don't really dislike Mrs. Whipple. It's just that she's so boring, by the time you've got through L.A. and you're heading into Social, you're practically in a dead coma.

Plus she has no fashion sense. She and Shirl must be related. Miss Whipple has this middle-aged tummy that makes her look like she's a few months pregnant, and she wears skirts that are always tight there. And blouses that are a size too small, with bunched-up Kleenexes always falling out of the openings by the cuffs. Very sad. Out of kindness, I won't say anything about her shoes.

How is it possible to get away with missing so much school, you ask? Lots of practice. A few excuses by letter, a few by phone (it only took me a week to get Shirl's voice down pat) and, of course, you can't be too predictable. Once in a while you need to sacrifice a Wednesday or Friday and maybe stay home a morning instead of an afternoon, even if it is slim pickings on the TV. Monday is Herb's day off, so that's out, but the rest of the week is up for grabs. Shirl works every weekday at a daycare, and the gremlins go there after school so there's never anyone home on the other days until after five.

Fast forward to a Friday in May when, after missing two Friday afternoons in a row, I make the mistake of showing up at Stanley Merkin and find myself plunk in the middle of some brainless project Miss Whipple's dreamed up, partnering our class with the Sierra Sunset Seniors' Lodge, a three-block walk from the school.

"Oh, Tamara," Miss Whipple spies me as I come in just a bit late. "How are you feeling, dear?"

The whole class is in a bustle, with odd-shaped packages on their desks. Some of the kids are still packing theirs; others are writing notes and putting them in envelopes.

I try to remember what excuse I phoned in on Wednesday. Stomach cramps? Pinkeye?

"A lot better, thanks," I smile.

"I'd forgotten you missed the first session of the Seniors Project," she says breathlessly, "but never mind. I brought extra things — for just such a circumstance."

I raise my eyebrows a touch. Enough so it looks like a question, but not true interest.

"Everyone is taking a little gift for his or her senior buddy," Miss Whipple explains. "Now, I know you aren't buddied yet, but I think Mrs. Golinowski at the lodge has one more senior she wants to match up. A lady who wasn't feeling well last week. Now, let's see, you could take her a set of these slippers I knitted."

She hands me a couple of hideous lavender-colored wooly things with pink bows on them.

"Lovely," I say.

"And here's a gift bag and some tissue paper. You could write her a little note to go with them."

The gift bag looks like it's been used a few times. It has pictures of fishing rods and fish hooks and dead fish splattered all over it. The tissue paper is orange. I try not to throw up.

"You'll have to hurry," Miss Whipple chirps. "We're just about ready to head out."

If I happen to live long enough, please shoot me before putting me in the Sierra Sunset Seniors' Lodge. It looks a bit like one of Shirl's overcooked waffles. Just magnify that a few times in your mind and stick a tiny window in each little square. All the windows have the same curtains and blinds.

Inside there are old people in wheelchairs who look at you from odd angles, like they're trying to see the world through those little peepholes they put in apartment doors.

In the lounge, there are more wheelchairs and more old people. Some are sitting on plastic chairs at tables or moving around with walkers. There is a smell that is a mixture of many things. Disinfectant, meatloaf, dueling colognes, talcum powder, unflushed bathroom.

I'm not the only one in my grade nine class looking like I could bring up my lunch at any minute.

Miss Whipple is having a little chat with someone from the lodge staff, a woman in a mint-green pantsuit and the kind of shoes people use for creeping around hospitals. She is beckoning us all toward the center of the lounge.

"Welcome again," she says in that kind of loud voice people use when they forget that not everyone in the world is hard of hearing. Even though I'm at the back of our group, I can see she should have some serious electrolysis work done on a dark eyebrow that caterpillars from one side of her forehead to the other.

"Most of you will recognize your senior buddies from your first visit, but if you can't locate the person you were with, check with me or one of the other staff members." She looks at her clipboard. "Now, let's see. Oh, yes, is Tamara Tierney here? Tamara?" Eyes beneath the endless eyebrow searching. I wiggle some fingers at her. Everyone begins drifting away to find their senior buddies.

"Now, I've matched you up with Miss Barclay," she says, patting me on the shoulder, "but you need to know, dear, that she can be a bit difficult at times, and she may not be too friendly right to start with."

Great. Match me up with the house crank.

I follow Mrs. Golinowski to a far corner of the lounge. I wonder if she knows what her double-knit pantsuit looks like from the rear?

There is an old woman (surprise!) sitting in an armchair against the lounge wall. She is wearing a dress the color of overripe tomatoes with a big, sparkly brooch pinned to it. She has dyed black hair and the meanest eyes I've ever seen in a human being not on TV.

And about a million wrinkles.

# 2

Nothing is longer than a day at the Triple S ranch. Unless it's a Triple S night. If you do manage to get to sleep, that's when half the population of the lodge decides it's time to decongest and visit the washroom. Coughing and flushing is loud in the land.

Sometimes reading helps me get back to sleep. Charles Dickens can be as effective, at times, as a sleeping pill, although I have to say *A Tale of Two Cities* isn't quite as sleep-inducing as *Bleak House*, the one that got me through April.

Of course, as soon as I turn my light on, the Triple S patrol's poking its nose in.

"You all right, dearie?" That'd be Latoya. Latoya thinks a light in the night means you want to talk. I ignore her.

"Did I show you this picture of my boy?" Latoya

wears some sort of lab coat with pockets big enough to hold a collection of photographs and cards and jokes her husband prints off from his computer.

"George," she grins proudly, poking the snapshot in front of my nose. A dark-haired boy with a self-conscious grin and bad skin.

"When he outgrows that acne," I tell her, "he'll be better-looking."

"Oh, he's good-looking now. The girls…" She waves the snap as if she were warding off a swarm of gnats. "Would you like a little something to help you sleep, Jean…er…Miss Barclay?"

Good, she's remembering that I don't consider myself on a first-name basis with any of the help.

"No," I say. "I think I'll just read for a while. That generally does the trick, providing I'm not interrupted."

"I like to read myself." Latoya begins fussing with my pillows. This close, I can see that she has skin blemishes that look like they've been with her since her own adolescence. Maybe George is doomed.

"When I'm getting my groceries at Safeway, I like to pick up a magazine. *Star* is good. *National Enquirer.* Some people think those stories are, well, you know, made up. But it's funny how many turn out to be true. Just yesterday I was reading about that there Jennifer what's-her-name…"

Finally she retreats, her shoes making little squelchy noises on the tile.

I am awake for two hours. It may be necessary to find the bottle of brandy Eddie got for me, if there's any left. It's been a week full of restless nights.

In the process of looking for it, I knock over a pitcher on my bureau. It makes as much noise as the fall of the Bastille. And, of course, Latoya comes squelching back in. Lord, help us!

It seems like I no sooner get to sleep than the woman who does the cleaning is clattering around my room, pulling the drapes, fiddling with the Venetian blinds, running water in the bathroom, slopping mops around.

A mass of energy this one, always rushing about. What's her name? Betty?

"What are you doing?" I am surprised that my voice emerges wispy and a little cracked. I meant it to be strong and forceful.

"Just finishing up, Miss Barclay." She flits around the room, picking up anything that's not nailed down. Betty likes to see all the fake-woodgrain surfaces shiny and clutter-free.

"They brought you a breakfast tray," she says. "Latoya left a note that you had a restless night."

"Don't touch that book!" The cleaning dervish has *A Tale of Two Cities* and is trying to find a place for it on my bookshelf. My voice sounds more like the school-teacher voice that never failed me whenever I was in front of a herd of teenagers.

Reluctantly, Betty replaces it on the pristine surface of my night stand.

"You need any help getting up?" she says.

I don't know why she always asks. When you've had one hip replaced and the knee on the other leg recon-structed, one thing you can always use is help getting out of bed.

"Where's Eddie?" I say as she exposes the atrocities on my breakfast tray and pours coffee out of a little thermos jug. Eddie, one of the custodians, is my source for cigarillos and brandy, and I think my stock of both is getting dangerously low.

"Friday's his day off. Friday and Saturday," Betty says, propelling her cleaning cart out the door.

Wonderful invention, the thermos. What amazes me is that it never works here to keep coffee hot. Not that one would really want to call whatever they serve here coffee. Worse than the stuff in school staff rooms.

As I drink the lukewarm liquid and nibble on the toast — good dollops of marmalade can help one for-give the lack of heat — the director pokes her nose in. Mrs. Golly-something. Mrs. Golly-woggle?

"Good morning, Jean," she says, managing to keep

her Cheshire cat grin even when she's talking. "How are we feeling today?"

We, indeed! "I'm not sure how *we* might come to a consensus," I say.

She has run-together eyebrows that take on a little puzzled wrinkle in the middle, but the Cheshire grin doesn't disappear.

"Today's the day the grade nines from Stanley Merkin are coming over. And they have little surprises for everyone!"

I can think of nothing to say to this escapee from Wonderland. Stanley Merkin! So they finally named a school after one of the most pathetic trustees to ever sit in a public school boardroom. Couldn't manage to get an intelligible sentence out of his mouth if his life depended on it.

"You might want to dress up a bit, and I'll send Rita in to do your hair if you like." Mrs. Golly-whatever looks like she could use Rita's services herself. Red hair with gray roots sticking out in odd snatches here and there.

Stanley Merkin! I shake my head sadly.

Rita isn't the sharpest cookie-cutter in a baker's kitchen, but she's pretty good at setting hair, and she's never stingy with the hairspray. She can spray your set so that it lasts the better part of a week.

"Do you ever think of going to something a bit lighter than jet black?" Rita asks me. "A lot of seniors, you know, go for something a little closer to…"

"I have always had black hair," I tell her, "and I plan on going to my grave with that shade, thank you very much." Long ago, I made the decision to never have gray hair or wear the color purple.

Rita helps me get dressed for the afternoon. I've decided on a red outfit I bought three years ago when I was on an opera tour in New York. BHR. Before Hip Replacement.

"My, that's a lovely brooch!" she says, pinning it in place.

"It belonged to my mother," I tell her. "She always wore it with her black crepe dress to the opera."

"The opry," Rita says. "Fancy that." She gives my hair one more spray.

"Not the Grand Ole —" I start to set her straight but she's off to set and spray the next person on her list.

Hyperactive Betty gives the walker a little dusting off as she sets it up. Good to have the cage all shiny. When we reach the lounge I make her fold it up and lean it low against the wall beside my armchair. Every time I look at the contraption, it makes me shudder, so I can imagine what it might do to some teenage kid.

It's wise to have your back to the wall. You don't

teach junior high for forty-one years without learning a thing or two about the adolescent homo sapien — one of which is to keep your back covered. Don't let them circle you.

When they arrive and I see them milling around in the lounge, it all comes flooding back. The awkwardness, body parts out of sync, tortured hair, acne, tentative mustaches, boys' voices cracking, girls laughing too loudly. No matter how they dress themselves, teenagers haven't changed all that much since I stood in front of my first class in 1935.

Now, their teacher — that's a different matter. That creature fluttering around, patting kids on the arm, giggling nervously, dressed like some frazzled housewife. When I took my Normal School courses we learned a few things about discipline, decorum and dress. If I were in charge, this lot would be settled down in one hurry, or be answering to me after class.

The old woman with blue-rinsed hair in the armchair next to me is gushing over a gift her — what was it Mrs. Gollywoggle called them? — her "buddy" has brought her.

"Oh, bless your heart!" she's exclaiming before she's even ripped off the recycled — could it be Christmas? — yes, Christmas wrap! Christmas in May.

"Bless your heart!" Little tears are springing to her

eyes. The buddy boy is turning bright from embarrassment. Can't say I blame him.

She's got the gift wrap off now and she's holding up a teapot. Just what we need around here — another teapot. This one is in the shape of a squirrel. The tea spout is actually the squirrel's tail. Think about that for a minute. Blue-rinse is making little squeals.

The boy, shuffling from foot to foot, says, "There's a card, too. I made it on my computer."

It appears that everybody's been matched up and Mrs. Golly-whatever is padding across the room with what I expect must be the leftover teenager for me. Life is filled with such joys!

"Miss Barclay!" the Cheshire cat exclaims. "I want you to meet Tamara, your Stanley Merkin buddy. Miss Barclay's only been with us since January but she already feels like one of the family. I think the two of you are going to get along, well… like a house on fire."

The girl is taller than Mrs. Gollywoggle. A lip-glossed smile is frozen onto her face. She's wearing eye makeup that Nefertiti of Egypt would have thought excessive and her hair, a magenta color, has been clamped here and there with little clips — like a permanent curl treatment being caught in mid-session at the beauty parlor.

Although she's as tall and slender as a Zulu princess,

she's wearing a too-tight little jacket and some kind of tank top that looks like it's been fished out of a lost-and-found box. It's difficult to tell if what she has on is a skirt or just a lacy slip. And shoes that a chorus girl might wear. Heaven help us! I can't withhold a chuckle.

"Tamara!" I say.

Skinnybones.

# 3

I guess when you're the Wrinkle Queen and you're pushing ninety, you can give up worrying about your fashion presence. No facial in the world is going to make Miss Barclay's skin look younger. She makes me think of a funny old bird with hawk eyes, one claw curled around the arm of her chair, the other clutching a shiny red purse. Her black hair is like some kind of plastic sculpture. It would take a good whack with a hammer to crack it.

"Hello." I smile my *Vogue* model smile. Just a little tip at the corners of my lips. I hand her my gift.

Her hawk eyes are focused on the recycled wrapping paper.

"Fishing tackle?" she mutters. "Just what I've always wanted."

I don't say anything but I tip my smile up just a bit more at the ends. Gwyneth Paltrow.

One end of the package opened, the old woman's bony fingers clutch at the orange tissue paper. Suddenly she pulls it all out and the purple slippers are revealed in their full glory.

"My God," Miss Barclay says, her voice raspy but a strong whisper. "What on earth...?"

"Slippers," I say, and try to keep from laughing.

"They're the ugliest things I've ever seen," Miss Barclay says and then looks at me. "No offense."

I try to be quiet, but it doesn't work. I burst out laughing.

"I was forced to bring them," I manage to say, finally catching my breath. "They look like purple hairballs some cat threw up."

For the first time, I see Miss Barclay smile. Wrinkles rearrange themselves around her eyes and the edges of her lips.

"Forced?"

"I didn't have a buddy gift. This was a spare one Miss Whipple had."

"Miss Whipple?"

"Our L.A. teacher."

"That one in the navy skirt? With the stomach?" Miss Barclay arches a painted eyebrow.

31

"That's her," I say. "Miss Whipple."

"That's what I taught. Language arts. English, we called it, before they decided to rename everything." Miss Barclay holds up one of the deformed purple slippers like it's a rotten fish. "Forty-one years."

"You're a teacher?"

"Was." Miss Barclay's voice is suddenly clipped. Sharp. "Past tense."

"What do you want to do with this stuff?" I point at the mess of fishing-tackle paper, crumpled tissue and the lumps of purple wool.

"Maybe we could take them into the courtyard and bury them," Miss Barclay says.

"Good idea."

"Or I could save them for Latoya." She looks slyly at me. "Latoya would like these."

"Latoya?"

"Night staff." Miss Barclay shudders, sending a ripple through her tomato-colored dress.

Mrs. Golinowski has been going around the room from one buddy set to the next, and now she is in front of us.

"What have we here!" She scoops up the purple slippers. "Aren't these cozy! Why, I could just steal them. You'd better keep a close eye on these, Miss Barclay."

"I'll post a guard." Miss Barclay's voice is thin and

dry as chalk dust. I look at my watch. Still a whole half hour to go.

"Miss Barclay," Mrs. Golinowski leans towards the old woman and announces loudly, "why don't you take Tamara on a little tour of the lodge." She turns to me. "I'm sure you'd like to see the cafeteria and the craft room and the multi-denominational worship center."

I smile.

The eyebrow leaves us and makes its way to another group.

"Do you want to go for a walk?" I say.

"I *would* like to get out of this bedlam." Miss Barclay waves a claw at all the kids and old people in the lounge. "Can you set up that contraption for me?" She nods towards the walker leaning against the wall.

Walkers, I know, are for old people to hang onto so they don't lose their balance. Kind of a folding cage on wheels. Miss Barclay looks fierce as she struggles down the hall. I follow half a step behind with the crumpled gift wrap and slippers.

At the end of the hall there is a T-intersection.

"You don't really want a tour, do you?" Miss Barclay's walker has come to a stop.

"Whatever." I shrug my shoulders.

"Here's the reading room." She points at a door in

the middle of the T. "Let's just hole up in here for a while. You can tell me about what they're teaching in so-called Language Arts these days."

I hold the door open for her. The room looks a little bit like a library. At least there are shelves with books on them. But the books look like the kind left over from garage sales.

"Mostly trash." Miss Barclay waves a hand towards the shelves. She eases herself into a vinyl-covered chair. The chair is faded orange and has been patched with silver duct tape. You can imagine what the Wrinkle Queen looks like in the middle of it with her bright red dress.

"I think there are a few copies of Dickens and Austen. I have my own books in my room though." She points at another vinyl-covered chair. "Sit down."

I nudge the slippers and crumpled paper under the chair.

"Is that what young ladies are wearing today?" She's giving me the once over. Once and back again and then again.

"Is that what old ladies are wearing?" She can see I'm staring at her nosebleed-red polyester, and this fancy brooch flopping on her skinny chest.

"*Touché*," she cackles.

"Actually, I'm going to be a model," I tell her. "If you think what I've got on today is crazy, you should watch *Fashion Forecast*. This is nothing."

"I see." She fishes a pack of cigarettes out of her purse. Long brown cigarettes like thin cigars. Maybe they're made special for witches.

"Are you allowed to smoke in here?"

"Do we care?" She flashes her false teeth at me, lights a match, gets the brown coffin nail going, and then, for a second or two, stares at the fire burning down the matchstick. When it reaches her fingers, she drops it into a piece of ceramic sculpture on an end table.

"Such rules are a transgression against our civil liberties," she says. "Did you know that in *Götterdämmerung*, the last of the great operas in Wagner's Ring Cycle, the whole stage is filled with smoke and fire? So wonderful. Exhilarating. I suppose that's the next thing they'll be banning."

"Gotter what?"

"*Götterdämmerung*. The twilight of the gods. If I guess correctly, you've never seen an opera."

"No," I say. "And it's not high on my list."

Miss Barclay sucks on her mini-cigar and then exhales a few dragon puffs of smoke.

"This is the year," she sighs. "The year they're doing

the whole cycle in Seattle. *Das Rheingold, Die Walküre, Siegfried* and *Götterdämmerung*. And I'm stuck here. I might as well be six feet under."

"Couldn't you just go? You're not locked up, are you?"

"Next thing to it."

"I'd go," I say. "If I really wanted to. If I had the money. Nobody would stop me."

She takes another long drag on her weird cigarette. It gives her a small fit of coughing and, still hacking, she whispers, "I believe you would."

# 4

She's tough, Skinnybones. A fledgling walküre. No one will stop her from flying.

The gollything comes flip-flopping by the reading room door just as I've finished my cigarillo, thank the Viking gods of smoke and fire. She wrinkles her nose and looks accusingly at me.

"Something stuck on the radiator, I think," I say. "Maybe Tamara wouldn't mind helping me back to my room."

"I think you'd just have time." Gollywog beams her my-I'm-glad-you're-bonding smile, and Tamara smiles back at her.

"Someone should help her," she whispers as we round a corner and head down the stretch of hall to my room.

"Mrs. Gollywatchit?"

"She could use an extreme makeover."

"Extreme is the signature word," I agree.

"Are you expecting company? There's a man waving at you," Tamara says.

She's right. It's my nephew, Byron. And to think the day had been going so well for a change.

"I'm okay from here," I say. "Thank you again for my lovely gift."

Tamara pats the hideous package she's tied to the side of the walker.

"You're so very welcome," she says with mock seriousness. "See you next time."

I watch her for a minute heading back down the hall, moving like some exotic zoo animal.

"Hi, Auntie." Byron has strolled down to meet me. So attentive, Byron Barclay, ever since that day when I was sure death waited for me and I signed a paper giving him power of attorney. Is it possible to sue a doctor who suggests an eighty-nine-year-old heart might not make it through surgery? Any mind would have to be morphine-addled to put her affairs in the hands of a high-school dropout who has worked most of his life servicing soda-pop dispensing machines.

Six months ago, when the pain was so bad it made me dizzy, I was sure my boat was headed out to sea, all primed with tar, ready for the torch. I said things; I signed things. But the funeral barge wasn't set afire. And, God, it's hard to have to hobble back to shore and find Byron waiting for you.

In fact, he always seems to be lurking these days. Like a turkey vulture.

"Alberich," I say.

"Alberich?" He shakes his head, puzzled, and then smiles. I can tell he thinks I've gone off into loony land. I don't bother telling him that Alberich is the ugly dwarf guarding the gold of the Rhine maidens in *Das Rheingold*. That he's Alberich and the gold is mine.

"Have you given any more thought to selling your house, Auntie?" He's followed me into my room and drops into the visitor's chair.

Poor Byron, he's lost pretty well all of his hair like my brother did, and he's red in the face, as if the very business of living embarrasses him. He mops at the perspiration on his forehead.

"I can't think why I'd sell it," I say. "I expect I'll be back there soon. Once this hip is working."

He doesn't look at me. He stares, instead, at the bureau by my bed, as if it were a heap of Rhine gold.

Minnie, an afternoon worker, comes in and helps me into bed. She sends Byron out into the hall while she gets me out of my dress and into a wrap.

"You're tired, aren't you, Miss Barclay?" she says.

I like Minnie. There's no nonsense about her. She does up the last couple of buttons on my housecoat and tucks a quilt around me. "You want me to send him away?"

"No. I can do that."

She smiles. "I'm sure you can."

"Think of it," Byron says when he comes back in. "It's a seller's market right now. You'd really come out on top."

"I'll think about it," I say. I *am* tired and, more than anything, I'd like Byron to go. I close my eyes.

"And your car," he says. "I'd like to put an ad in the paper. I just had it tuned up and it's running like a charm. Anyone who test-drives that Buick —"

"I'll think about it."

"Think about it," Byron echoes, tiptoeing to the door.

The last trip I took with the Buick was to drive to Seattle to see *Die Walküre*. Gladys Enright went with me. It would have been better to have gone by myself. Gladys dithering and twittering around. The type that would say sorry to a coffee table if she stubbed her toe on it. Never learned how to drive. Always had a husband who did it for her until he died. Once he was gone, Gladys would declare, "Too late to teach an old dog new tricks."

It was at the end of that trip that I began to notice the hip pain, and by the time I got home, it was agony to work the pedals. But it was Gladys, an old dog with no new tricks, who had the heart attack and died three weeks later.

Will I ever drive again? The doctor says no. "It's not just your legs. You have lapses, times when your mind just shuts down for brief periods. It's really not safe for you to drive."

The thought makes me furious. Why does life tantalize us with possibilities, only to turn coy, withdrawing?

Anger shoves aside the fatigue that had been settling over me like a blanket. I grab the little stand-up calendar on my bureau.

It's the second week in May. Only a couple of months until the great Ring Cycle of operas will be beginning in Seattle.

In my mind, I can hear that astounding beginning, the first bars of *Das Rheingold*, like the world being born anew. Music at first as slender and thin as light through water and then building, leaping, enfolding, cascading. That incredible beginning playing through my mind, and I can only think it is from the splashing of the Rhine maidens that there are trails of dampness along my cheeks.

41

# 5

When I get back to the common room, my class is grouping at the front door for the walk back to school. It has begun to rain. I can see the hour and a half I spent on my hair — all the anti-frizz serum and mousse and hair glue and sculpting gel — gone to waste.

What will the Universal Style people think of someone coming in looking like a half-drowned rat?

"Tamara," Miss Whipple calls, "walk fast or run if you want so you won't get too wet. Just be careful at the intersection. Be sure and push the pedestrian crossing button."

A lot of the kids are running and even Miss Whipple jiggles along in front of me. I can't run in the shoes I have on so I'm the last. Me and the blob of a kid who gave his senior buddy a squirrel teapot. Timmy. I don't think Timmy has ever run anywhere in his life. He's beside me, matching his stride to mine.

"You want my rain cape?" he says. It's kind of a clear plastic baggy thing. "I don't really need it with this old jacket…"

"Hey. Sure. Thanks." I give him my best smile. There might be hope for my hair yet.

"No problem."

During Social, the last class in the afternoon, I take the flyer out and look at it again. Since I picked it up at the community center where Shirl's daycare is, I've come close to wearing out the sheet. But even now, this thousandth time I've looked at it, I feel a tingle along my spine.

### UNIVERSAL STYLE

*Dream of becoming a model?*

*Dream no longer. Universal Style's proven program of model training offers you a ticket to major work in the field. Study the arts of personal enhancement, make-up, movement, photographic posing, and runway protocols with a team of outstanding fashion professionals.*

*"I thank Universal Style for helping to make my dreams come true," states Kelly Kidd, recently awarded the Modeling Association of North America's Outstanding Newcomer Award. "They gave me my start and I've been soaring ever since."*

Just below the phone number and a Whyte Avenue address, there's a picture of Kelly Kidd. Light seems to shine off her cheeks and hair. She has a perfect smile.

The only appointment I could get was for 4:30, so I had to make up a story for Shirl who gets home at around 5:15 and expects me to be there.

"I'll be late," I told her. "Grad committee. You're always wanting me to join stuff so I joined the grad committee."

"Oh, honey, I'm so pleased." She patted my knee with one of her pudgy hands. "See, I told you you'd be fitting in before long. Herb said so, too."

There's an hour between the end of class and my appointment. I don't have to wait for the bus to Whyte Avenue and, in fifteen minutes, I'm at the place where the interviews are being held.

It's a three-story office building with To Let signs in half its windows. Inside, there's a central court with a couple of tables, coffee and soft drink dispensers. I have enough change with me for a Diet Sprite. While I'm sipping on it and reading an *Elle* magazine I scoffed from the Stanley Merkin library, a man and three children, all girls, grab the other table.

"I wanna Coke," the youngest kid whines.

"Okay," the man says, "but let me comb your hair first. Stand still, Caroline!"

The girls are all wearing party dresses and hair ribbons, white stockings and baby-doll shoes. One of them has discovered the railing that goes along a winding staircase to the second floor. She's trying to do something gymnastic on it.

"Caitlyn!" the man hollers when he notices what she's up to. "Look at what you're doing to your hair ribbon!"

She's managed to snag it on a piece of the wrought iron.

"Candace, can't you keep an eye on your sister?"

The older girl shrugs, scowls and blows a big bubble of gum, letting it pop and collapse against her face.

"I told you no gum!" The man's voice is getting higher by the minute. "Not 'til after the interview." He looks at me and shakes his head.

"I wanna Coke." With the combing finished, the little girl is hopping from one baby-doll shoe to the other, chanting.

"We better wait..."

That's when we see him. The model man coming down the stairs. Definitely Calvin Klein material. All in black except for a white shirt. Silk? Open at the neck. The bit of chest you can see looks like it's been polished. His hair has blond highlights. As he gets to the bottom of the stairs, I can see he has smoky-blue Jude Law eyes.

The bubblegum girl licks the last bit of gum off her lips and smiles at him.

He flashes a smile back at all of us. A white-strip smile that could blind you.

"Mr. Andrews? I'm Brad Silverstone," he says. "We're ready for you and your lovely daughters. If you'll just follow me."

Then he notices me with my *Elle* magazine.

"Miss Tierney?"

I nod and give him my best smile.

"Good. As soon as I've completed my interview with the Andrews…"

"I wanna Coke…"

"Hush, dear." Mr. Andrews fluffs the ruffles of Caroline's dress as they follow Jude Law Model Man up the stairs.

When they come down a half hour later, the Coke kid is howling her head off.

"I don't wanna be a model," she shouts.

"You think they'd be just a bit grateful," the man says loudly to no one in particular when they get to the bottom of the stairs. "It's all for them…"

"I'm going to be a veterinarian," the gymnast kid says to me as I slip *Elle* into my backpack.

Model Man is at the top of the stairs beckoning to me.

"What a crew," he chuckles, holding the door to his office open. There's a glittery star on the door and a sign: *Universal Style — Training for the Stars of Tomorrow.* "We're checking to see how much interest there is in setting up a modeling program for children. Maybe having one of our summer institutes just for kids. I'm not sure." He looks up at the ceiling as if asking for help from above.

He clears some papers off a chair for me and then grabs one for himself behind a green card table covered with brochures and files.

"Now, you, Tamara," he smiles his white-strip-ad smile, "we can work with. And you've got bone structure, young lady, that many would die for."

He asks me some questions and begins filling in a form. I tell a lie when he asks me my age.

"Eighteen," I say.

He raises his eyebrows.

"In a couple of weeks," I add.

"Great."

When he's finished filling in the form, he gives me the details of the course.

"It's a week-long intensive in the summer and you can choose from a few dates and a couple of locations," he says, after outlining the program. "We'll run you off your feet but, at the end of it all, you'll have a Universal

Certificate and, in the fashion world, that means something. I notice you had last month's *Elle* magazine. Page seventeen — one of ours. Finished the course last summer."

"In Calgary?"

"No. Our Vancouver campus." He leans back and brushes his fingers through his streaked curls. They fall perfectly back into place. "We arrange everything. We can even set up billeting and meals if you need those features."

"And the price?"

"Incredibly inexpensive," he says, "considering what's in the package. Exclusive of the billeting, it's twenty-five hundred. That's with a five-hundred-dollar deposit. Up the deposit to a thousand, and we drop the course price to a bargain twenty-three fifty."

I do have a bank account. One of Mr. Mussbacher's projects. "Helps develop responsibility and a sense of money management," he reminds me from time to time. It's right up there with smiling.

I have $43.12 in my bank account.

"I'll have to think about it, Mr. Silverstone."

"Call me Brad." He flashes the teeth. "We're in town for a couple of more weeks with our recruitment program. All we need is the deposit — cash or a cashier's check — to get you registered."

He hands me a booklet.

"This'll give you more details of the program." His hand brushes mine as I take the booklet, and I'm surprised at the tingle it sends along my arm.

"Hope you can swing it," he says. "To tell the truth, it's like I can see you on page seventeen already." He winks at me.

On the bus going home, the numbers swim in my head. Twenty-five hundred. No point asking Shirl and Herb for it. At the end of every month, Herb does a lot of moaning and sighing over bills and pops Rolaids by the handful. Shirl gives him shoulder rubs and says she's got a plan for cutting down on groceries next month. The plans never seem to work, though.

Who in the world has twenty-five hundred dollars? The question aches inside me.

And then I think of her. Miss Killer Tomato and her diamond-studded opera brooch.

The idea's crazy, of course. She looks tougher than the Wicked Witch of the West.

And yet the idea doesn't go away.

# 6

To tell the truth, I'm surprised Skinnybones is there with the next Stanley Merkin invasion. Someone who skips school when she can, I've been thinking. Wouldn't have pulled the wool over my eyes, though. She'd have been down to the office with her parents — foster parents, whatever — faster than you could say "forged excuse."

Not only is she here, but there's something different about her. Like a tough cookie that suddenly reveals it has a marshmallow center.

"How have you been, Miss Barclay?" She smiles and hands me a small tissue-wrapped package tied with silver ribbon. "This time I brought you a real gift."

"Too small for slippers," I say.

It is a silver filigreed bookmark with a dragon design. Not real silver, of course. Some kind of plastic silver but very nice.

"A dragon." I rub my fingers over its head and wings, its coiled tail. "Did I tell you about the dragon in the Ring operas?"

"No." She hasn't quit smiling. "But I'd love to hear about it. Do you want to go to the reading room again?"

Definitely changed. She rattles on about her English class and how she's reading *Great Expectations* with a literature circle group. All of this chattering has brought a slight flush to her face and a bit of a shine to her eyes.

Then she tells me about the modeling school interview.

Twenty-five hundred dollars.

That stops the conversation. She's quiet while I light up another cigarillo.

"Miss Havisham," I say.

"Miss Havisham?"

"In *Great Expectations*. Pip believes the crazy old lady gives him the money he needs to get on in life."

"We've only read about the first thirty pages," Tamara sighs.

"Do you think I'll give you the money?"

"It would just be a loan. I'd pay you back as soon as I start getting modeling jobs. They gave me an extra brochure. I'll leave it."

"I may be a crazy old lady but I'm not that crazy.

Besides, Miss Havisham didn't give Pip the money. Sorry to spoil the book for you."

"I didn't really think you would." She drops the smile.

"It's in July, this course?"

"They offer it four times during the summer. I'm going to see if I can get an after-school job and go to the last one."

"It'll have to be an after-school job robbing banks," I say, and she does laugh — a small, polite, marshmallow laugh.

Mrs. Gollywatchit pops her head suddenly through the door.

"Jean Barclay," she booms, her transcontinental eyebrow doing a little dance. "You know that smoking is forbidden in this building. What an example! Put it out immediately."

"Oh, my." I extinguish the cigarillo against the ceramic gizmo on the reading table. "It slipped my mind. So many things to remember."

Tamara snorts.

"Your class is getting ready to leave," she says to Tamara, who has wheeled my walker into place.

"Is this your last visit?" I ask her when the Gollything has gone.

She shrugs. "I think we come again next week. Miss

52

Whipple's scheduled an extra visit because a TV station wants to film us for some special they're doing."

"Maybe you'll be discovered."

"You never know." But there's a touch of defeat in her voice.

"Don't forget your dragon." She tucks it into the modeling brochure before we leave and slips them into my purse.

Back in my room, I use them to replace the postcard I've been using as a bookmark in *A Tale of Two Cities* although, later, I fall asleep reading and my place is lost anyway. Miss Pross and Madame Defarge battling it out — how is it possible to fall asleep in the middle of that?

Sometime in the night the book and the brochure have landed on the floor and Latoya is asking me where I want them put.

"I'll take them. I'm awake now with all this fuss."

"How 'bout a hot drink?" Latoya plumps the pillows. "You been sleeping since just after supper but I kept you a snack and a cuppa decaf from the nine o'clock snack wagon."

"Just the coffee. Now, where are my glasses?"

It takes her half an hour to clean the glasses, heat the coffee and fill me in on what George the Acne Kid has been failing to learn at school and her husband has been confiscating at airport security.

"You wouldn't believe the things people try to take onto a plane," Latoya sighs. "Incredible. Things clipped onto rings where their body has been, well, you know…pierced. Nipples and even…"

"Latoya!"

"But I let you read now," she says finally. "Call me if you need anything."

The brochure, I notice, is filled with the kind of advertising gimmickry I always pointed out to students in my English classes. Skinnybones — such a willing victim. As if a five-day course could turn her into a cover girl for *Vogue*.

And the expense. Such preposterous expectations. Twenty-five hundred dollars. Choose where you'd like to be parted from your money. Calgary…

Or Vancouver?

I look at the back of the brochure more closely.

*In August, Universal Style offers its course in Vancouver, Canada's most beautiful city, on a campus located a short walk from the Pacific waterfront.*
   *August 6-10. August 13-17.*

Vancouver.

Just three hours from Seattle.

Serendipity is not something I've ever believed in.

Alignments of the stars are fine enough in a piece of literature or high opera but in real life I've always believed we forge our own pathways. The horoscope page of the newspaper would be the first thing I'd use to wrap leftover fish for the garbage.

And yet, here it is before me, August days and pinpoints on the globe somehow connecting the dreams of an ancient woman (yes, admit it in the dead of night) and the terrible yearning of a skittish, wild colt of a girl. Life whirls and the planets spin and possibility lies in wait for lines that will connect the dots, the way Wagner himself must have connected the dots of music notes from his pen to the trails of staves across a manuscript page.

"Why not?" I hadn't meant to utter the question aloud. But Latoya's out of earshot.

Why not?

Maybe Skinnybones will get to take her modeling course. Maybe Jean Barclay will get to see one more Ring Cycle.

# 7

The old dragon. Guarding her money. What would make her part with any of it? Maybe I could be her personal shopper, do her hair and make-up every week. Play Rummy? Read aloud to her?

Twenty-five hundred dollars. It'd take a lifetime to work it off. Of course, there can't be too much of the Wrinkle Queen's lifetime left.

When we get back to Stanley Merkin, we still have a period before dismissal. Once or twice a month on a Friday, Miss Whipple lets us have the period for what she calls USSR. Uninterrupted Sustained Silent Reading. Must have been something she started doing long before the real USSR fell off the map. When she announces we'll have USSR today, the class cheers.

"Remember, sustained and silent," she says and makes a point of getting out her own free reading book.

I've no sooner got *Great Expectations* open and I'm reading about one of Pip's visits to play with Estella when there's a call on the intercom for me to come down to the office. Everyone in class puts their sustained silent reading on hold to watch me for the few seconds it takes to get out of my desk, across the room and into the hallway. Someone hisses loudly, "Admit to nothing!" as I close the door.

A secretary tells me to go into the counselor's office. Mr. Gossling. I saw him when I first came to Stanley Merkin. A one-man welcoming committee for foster kids. Bald head and a goatee and a bolo tie. It's hard to forget those skinny braids slipping through a brass cow's head.

Today he's not looking so welcoming. And he's wearing a real tie with a western sunset on it, a pinkish-orange sun sinking behind a cactus plant.

There are other people at the conference table. Mr. Mussbacher. I give him my Mona Lisa smile. And Shirl. Good heavens, what's she doing here? She's a little redder around the eyes than usual. And puffier.

"Sit down, Tamara," Mr. Gossling says. "I think you must know why we're here…er…having a meeting today."

Huh? All I know is when you get a group like this together, it's probably time to play the foster-home game. Spin the wheel. Which family's up next? Or maybe it'll be a group home this time.

Mr. Gossling opens a folder. It's my personal file with a neat line drawn through the name Schlotter on the tab and replaced with Tierney — the last name of my second foster family. It's the only thing I took with me when I left them two years ago. I can see that, along with other stuff — grade records and official forms — there's all the absence notes I've been writing since I came to Stanley Merkin.

I decide to look down at my hands. One of my projects over the past few months, since coming to stay with Shirl and Herb, has been to get my nails into shape. That can be hard work for someone who's been a nail-biter all her life. It's taken a ton of polish. And wearing band-aids on the tips of my fingers every night for about ten weeks. Of course, Shirl kept accusing Lizzie and Lyle of taking them.

"I'm not surprised you're ashamed, Tamara," Mr. Mussbacher sighs. "I thought you'd given up all that games-playing. I wouldn't be surprised if the Shadbolts decided to release you. What with this…fraud. And stories about having celiac disease. Do you have anything to say for yourself?"

This is where you do have some choices. I could throw a hissy fit. Haven't done that for a while. I'm a little out of practice. Hissy fits are always great, though, for stirring things up. Shirl looks like she could use a little zap of something.

Or I could cry. Haven't done that for a while, either. That time when Wilma came to see me two families ago. When I was still with the Tierneys. Can you believe I actually begged her to take me back with her? Welfare Wilma. She cried, too, and said it wasn't possible now that she was with Adam and there was the baby, Justin, and another baby on the way and hardly room for the three of them — soon to be four — in their apartment.

Crying can really mess up your eye make-up.

Or I could try the silent treatment. That makes everyone so angry they sometimes forget why you're there in the first place.

But what's really sticking in my mind is Miss Barclay and her diamond brooch. And how she asked if I was coming to the lodge again. I know whatever I do now, I can't do anything to mess up seeing her next week.

That means apologizing. I don't have much practice with that, but how hard can it be?

"I'm sorry," I say.

"What were you thinking?" asks the sunset tie. "What was more important than school?"

"Nothing," I mumble. And then I add, "I was… confused."

That'll light up buttons for both Mussbacher and Gossling. Confused. Social workers and guidance counselors love that word.

"Confused?"

Jackpot. They repeat it at the same time.

"About what's important," I say. "I didn't really like school when I first got here. But I'm liking it a lot more now."

"What's caused the change?"

The third degree — and I better not slip up. Don't say anything about modeling. They'd jump all over that, go on forever about learning to walk before you can run and how you need to finish school before you can even think of anything else.

"*Great Expectations*," I say. "I can't believe how good that book is. Every day we get to talk about what we've read in a literature circle."

"Weren't you reading it two days ago when you signed my name to this note?" Finally Shirl talks. Tears are beginning to come. "Please excuse Tamara. Her celiac disease has flared up."

"What is all this nonsense about celiac disease?" Mr. Mussbacher gives me his double-whammy look.

"I thought I had it," I say. "There was a show on TV about it and...well, I thought maybe I had it."

"She does shy away from anything with flour in it."

Shirl gives up a search for a Kleenex in her purse and grabs one from a box in the middle of the conference table. Counselors are always ready for criers.

"You want to have a doctor check that out?" says Mr. Gossling.

Oops. Going to doctors. One of my least favorite things to do and I can just imagine what kinds of things they might do to test your digestive system.

"I think it was…" Choose your words carefully, I think. "A false alarm. I guess it was a false alarm."

"What? You ate a doughnut and discovered it didn't kill you?" Mr. Mussbacher isn't buying it.

I smile at him.

"Mainly I just don't like real starchy food. It's always like…well, like lead in my stomach."

"Honey, you could've just said," Shirl sighs. "Heaven knows it wouldn't hurt all of us to cut down, eat more…vegetables."

It sounds to me like she's having a hard time getting that last word out.

"We may be getting a little off track here," Mr. Gossling says. "What we're really looking at is Tamara's truancy and, I must say, her rather amazing repertoire of petty subterfuges."

Now there's a mouthful. We all look at him. Even Mr. Mussbacher.

Mr. Gossling blushes, his forehead and cheeks taking on a bit of the sunset color of his tie.

"Since the Shadbolts are willing to allow Tamara to continue staying with them, I think what we need is an action plan."

It takes another three quarters of an hour to hammer one out. Shirl has to leave halfway through to get back to her daycare job. I have to agree to all the points in the plan. Mr. Gossling even has the secretary type it up and makes me sign it.

"It's a contract," he says. "You mess with this and you may not like the consequences."

I wait until I'm back at the Shadbolts' to read it through and really think about what I've signed.

*Personal Action Plan*

*I agree to the following:*
*1. I will attend classes faithfully and give each course my best effort.*
*2. Permission to remain home due to illness must be obtained through Mr. Gossling personally. Failure to do so will result in immediate suspension.*
*3. I will be proactive in assisting the Shadbolts with household chores, babysitting, etc.*

*Signed: Tamara Tierney*

"Proactive," Mr. Mussbacher explained, "means don't always wait to be asked to do things to help your foster family. Jump in and offer."

I go into the kitchen and poke through the cupboards. There's one shelf entirely filled with bags of pasta. Shells and bow-ties and stuff that looks like bird nests. Spaghetti, linguini, macaroni, lasagna noodles. Next shelf down there's pancake mix and Bisquick and packages of stovetop dressing.

Proactively, I put some water in a big pot, add some salt and, when it's boiling, dump in half a package of bow-ties.

What else does Shirl do to get supper on the go? There's half a jar of Cheez Whiz. I scrape that out into a pot and add a can of mushrooms. Sauce for the bow-ties.

And, hey, there's lettuce and tomatoes in the crisper. As I rinse the big wrinkly Romaine leaves, I hold up the last one. It's as wrinkled as the skin on Miss Barclay's hands.

Mr. Mussbacher's always talking about turning over a new leaf.

I turn it over and begin chopping.

# 8

Skinnybones in Seattle. In Vancouver. When I wake up, the possibility continues to tease, hovering like a bothersome cat. An amazing amount of determination for someone her age. And I have to admit she does have an arresting presence. Eyes that don't allow you to look away. But she needs shaping, smoothing. Heaven knows she's got more rough edges than a block of firewood.

I phone Byron and ask him to bring my travel diary from the house.

"Reliving some of your trips?" He handles the book with its tapestry cover as if it were something feminine and fragile. "New York. Santa Fe. London. All those concert tours."

"Yes, dear." We're in the cafeteria and I try my best not to rush him through his coffee and cinnamon bun.

"Logged a few miles on the Buick. Those trips to Seattle, and didn't you drive to San Francisco once?" He licks the icing from his fingers.

I wait until he's gone to open it. Reread the inscription written on the front page in calligraphy by the art teacher in that last school:

*For Jean Barclay on her retirement. The adventure begins...*

Then I flip to the back pages. Good. Ricardo's phone number is there. On the blank page just before the addresses and phone numbers, I begin composing a list, and by the time a student nursing-aid has refilled my coffee cup twice, I've got it finished.

*1. Get Byron away for two weeks. (A trip to the Philippines?)*
*2. Does Tamara know how to drive? If not, a crash (!) course. Where? From whom?*
*3. Tickets to the Ring. Phone Ricardo.*
*4. Story for Tamara to tell her foster parents (needs to be foolproof!). How often does the social worker check on her?*
*5. Money for Tamara's course. (Does she need a deposit?)*

Number five isn't a problem. One thing Byron doesn't know is how much money I've got tucked away here and there in my bedroom. If my heart had conked out during surgery, I wonder how much of it would have been found, hidden behind photos in my album and under the false bottom of my jewelry box. Inserted into telling chapters of books.

I've written the list but as the day wears on I think more and more about tearing it up. Would they call it kidnapping, whisking a teenager off to another province, another country? Have they ever sent an eighty-nine-year-old woman to jail? Am I way off-base in my reading of Skinnybones? Wishing too hard for her to have the flint and fire of a Rhine goddess? Maybe she's nothing more than a muddled adolescent with a crust of attitude.

It might be absolute craziness to give her that much money. I could hire a nurse or a companion to go with me, wheelchairing me in and out of airports. Could I stand another Gladys?

Even dear Byron might take me, at least as far as the opera house door, but he'd never agree to four days of Wagner. For Byron, there's only one kind of music — the kind blaring from his car radio whenever he takes me out for a drive. Blaring for the few seconds it takes for me to demand he turn it off. Country and western. God, I hate it. Twanging guitars, sniveling lyrics.

A couple of weeks with Byron might just do me in. That would appeal to him. He'd have the house and the Buick up for sale in forty-five minutes flat.

No. For this last Ring, I see Tamara with me. The great adventures unfold for those willing to think beyond the narrow confines of everyday existence. Tamara, I feel, has that sense of adventure, the single-minded determination of a Marco Polo to seek new lands, a Wagner to seek new music. Spiky little bundle of nerves and energy and fake smiles.

She does come with her class on Friday.

Her hair is blue.

Her smile is wide.

I forgive her inattention for the first few minutes while the TV crew is filming. She manages to get herself in front of the camera at least three times in different parts of the lounge.

"The reading room?" she asks, returning to my corner as the cameraman is packing up.

"No, I think the patio if it's not too cold. Mrs. Gollywatchit has her eye on us. If we're inside, I know she'll be checking every five minutes to see if I've lit up. And I must say I do like to puff on a cigarillo during our little chats."

I've brought my fur jacket with me. There's a slight breeze but not too bad. Tamara helps me get my cigarillo lit.

"Did you know Dickens wrote two endings for *Great Expectations?*" I ask her.

She looks at me questioningly.

"I've been thinking. Perhaps I was hasty…"

"I could work for you. I could —"

"I was thinking of something more like a trade-off."

"Trade-off?" She's become very still, Skinnybones. Almost as if she's afraid to breathe.

"I had a chance to look at your brochure and what caught my interest was the fact that in August the course is being offered in Vancouver the week after the Ring Cycle operas are staged in Seattle."

Her eyes are getting bigger. The mascara is heaviest, I notice, along the underlids.

"So here's the deal. I give you the money for your course but we go a week early. We go to Seattle and take in the whole glorious Ring Cycle of operas. For this you will serve as my companion. You will attend the operas with me. Not only will you attend, but you will appear to like them."

"Operas?"

"I know what an accomplished little actress you are, my dear." For an instant the fake smile becomes something of a grin. "You will appear to enjoy them because I, your benefactress, am enjoying them."

"And when the operas are over?" she asks. "You'll go home and I'll take my course in Vancouver?"

"Actually, no," I say. "At that point we shall reverse roles. I'll become your companion — your chaperone, if you prefer — in Vancouver. At least I'll retain the role of the person with the purse strings. We will drive back together at the end of the two weeks."

"Drive!"

"Can you drive, Tamara?"

The wheels are spinning, I can tell, in her mind. She's wondering whether to tell the truth.

"No," she says.

Good. She recognizes the folly of lying to me.

"But I could learn," she adds.

"You will learn. You're old enough, I know, for a learner's permit. And my license doesn't lapse until September. Before my legs failed, I drove regularly."

"I need to give the Universal Style guy a thousand dollars by Tuesday." Tamara watches me. "Or at least five hundred."

I meet her gaze. "If I give you the money, you are agreeing to commit to this project with a full realization that, as world adventurers, we will need to do whatever's necessary to achieve our goals."

"Whatever's necessary?"

"Short of murder, of course. Or grand larceny. There will be…" I search for the right term, "the creation of fictions. Small deceptions. If I read you correctly, you have some talent for those."

She's silent for a minute, her long fingers playing with a cardigan that looks like it's spent a month or two on a Value Village rack.

"What about you?" she says. "Are you a good liar?"

"Liar," I laugh. "Such a harsh term. I'm clever, Tamara. Top of the class when I got my Education degree. My legs have pretty well given out but I haven't needed any pins put in my brain yet. And, while my mind is still good, I long to sit one last time before the bonfire of the gods."

This time she does arch those painted eyebrows.

"Wagner knew," I laugh. "He lets us glimpse that other world. And what do we see? The reflection of the earth and humanity with all its spectacle and follies. And glory. The stories we come up with will be small, Tamara. Small coinage compared to the currency in which the immortals deal."

# 9

She's a witch with a list, the Wrinkle Queen. Sitting there at a patio picnic table at the Sierra Sunset Seniors' Lodge. Wearing dead rats and smoking her skinny cigars. Old and crazy.

She reads her list out slowly, stopping after each item as if she's waiting for me to applaud. Every time she pauses, smoke drifts out past her dentures. Sometime today she must have patted powder all over her face. It makes her look like a hundred-year-old geisha.

I can't help her with number one on her list. Getting her nephew Byron out of her hair for the time we'd be gone. Seems like Miss Barclay gave Byron signing power when she thought she was booking into the cemetery a few months back.

"Byron likes to keep a close check on me," she says. "The way you might keep an eye on gilt-edged securities.

I wouldn't put it past him to get some doctor to agree that I wasn't fit to travel."

"Where'd you get the idea about the Philippines?" I ask her.

"Byron's a man of few words, but I asked him once what he'd do if he won the Lotto and he said he'd get a boat and sail to the Philippines where you can live like a king on very little for a very long time. His idea of paradise, I guess. Now, Byron has a birthday at the end of July. I could give him an expense-paid holiday."

"Isn't this trip to the opera costing way more than it's worth?" I light another cigarillo for her. It tastes horrible but the sweet tobacco smell hangs in the air.

"You need a ninety-year-old's perspective to answer that," she says. "I've never had much patience with aphorisms and the people who spout them, but one for which I've gained increasing respect is 'you can't take it with you.' I have money, Tamara, the savings of a professional who traveled solo. Oh, not a great deal of money — but enough."

"Put a check mark by the Philippines," I say. "Wherever they are."

"And the driving?"

"Maybe Herb will teach me. Especially if I say I can help Shirl with running chores. I'll be sixteen in the fall and then I can drive by myself. Take Lyle to his Little

League games and Lizzie to her ballet lessons on Saturday. All part of being proactive."

The Wrinkle Queen gives me a questioning look.

"Part of an action plan I had to sign. Being helpful and proactive." I tell her about the meeting at school.

"Oh, my, you are a deceptive little beast, aren't you?" Miss Barclay's thin cackle gets lost as she breathes out smoke. "Of course, I'll have to see if Ricardo's bought any extra tickets this year. They sell out about a year in advance."

"Ricardo?"

"The owner of the bed and breakfast where I always stay."

Bed and breakfast? Must be some kind of motel. I remember the motel next to the Tierney's Bottles Up Recycling. Sleepytime Al's. It had a sign like Christmas tree lights that stayed on all night, only one of the letters had burned out so what you saw in the dark was *leepytime Al's*. Patty-May Tierney showed me where to look for bottles in the trash bins in behind. We'd sneak out at night and collect them before the old guys with Safeway carts came along.

The Wrinkle Queen smokes silently for a few minutes. I can see Mrs. Golinowski peering out of a hallway window at us. I give her a little wave and smile.

"I think your social worker may be the biggest

problem. Doesn't he check in with you every week or so?"

"Every month, as long as things are going okay. If I go missing from the Shadbolts, he'll have the police out looking for me." It was the police who picked me up three blocks from where Wilma was living when I ran away from the Tierneys.

Mrs. Golinowski is at the door now.

"Come on in now, you two," she hollers. "Tamara, your class is getting ready to go."

"Here." Miss Barclay reaches into her purse and, pulling out an envelope, presses it into my hand. I slip it into my backpack.

"Be sure and get a receipt," she says.

I wait until I get home to open the envelope. There's a thousand dollars in it in fifty-dollar bills. I've never seen so much money. It seems like enough to run off somewhere and start a new life. No Shadbolts. No Mr. Mussbacher. No Wrinkle Queen rattling on about operas.

But I don't.

On Tuesday I go to the office building on Whyte Avenue where Mr. Jude Law Model Man has his office. He looks surprised to see me and he gets pretty excited when I take out the money.

"Hey! Good for you, kid!" He opens a file folder and looks at a schedule. "Yup. There's still a couple of spots open in the August class. I'll just slate you in here and get you a receipt."

He has a deadly smile. My hand shakes as I take the receipt.

"You can pay the balance when you register in August. Now, let's see, here's a package about billeting and meals if you want to tap into that option, a map of Vancouver and the campus area..." He stops in mid-sentence. "Are you okay?"

"Yeah. Sure." But I do feel like I could keel over. "I guess I should have eaten more lunch."

"Watching your diet, eh?" he says.

I nod.

"You're thin, and I know people think a model can never be too thin. But as a photographer I can tell you that with a little more meat on your bones — say, ten pounds — the camera's really going to love you."

As he shuffles papers, I notice his hands. The fingers are nicotine-stained.

"Where do you work?" he asks.

"I'm not working right now. I've still got a few high school courses to finish." I don't tell him that it's all the courses in grades ten, eleven and twelve. "My family wants me to finish those before I begin working as a model. But they're very supportive. They're happy that I can start training this summer."

He fiddles with a cigarette he's freed from a package of duMauriers. I can see he's anxious to get outside for a smoke.

"Are you going to be there this summer?" I ask.

"You bet," he says. "I do the photography. We make sure everyone has a great portfolio by the time the course is finished."

As we leave the building together, I see my bus a couple of blocks down, yell goodbye, and make a dash across the street. From the bus window, I can see him leaning against a wall, smoking, and I know he's watching the bus.

"Everything okay?" Shirl asks when I get home. "How was your grad committee meeting?"

"Oh…you know. Committee meetings… No one could agree…"

"Tuna casserole for supper. And a big Caesar salad." Shirl is beaming. "We're eating healthy tonight, sweetie."

"Great."

As I head down the hall to my room, I can see the gremlins glued to the television. A cartoon moose is dancing around in a ballet tutu. Too bad. *Tips for Teens* is just about to come on.

What I really need is my own TV. It's not hard to imagine what kind of amazing big-screen television I could have bought with that thousand dollars.

Before they decided to take in a foster kid, my room used to be Herb's study. Most of the stuff — bowling trophies and the computer — he moved into the master bedroom. But I still run into bits and pieces, mainly stuff from a company Herb had selling some kind of magical car polish. I guess the bankruptcy company didn't want the five thousand brochures he'd had printed.

I put my *Universal Style* folder at the back of a desk drawer and cover it with a couple of stacks of Eterno-Shine brochures.

"The creditors did take Herb's lease car," Shirl told me just after I first came to live with them. "It was a cherry-colored Jetta that was absolutely dazzling when it had a couple of coats of Eterno-Shine buffing up the red. Thank heavens they didn't take my 1990 Plymouth."

When Herb gets home from work, I wait until he's settled in the living room with a beer and the newspaper before I go in and perch on the ottoman — close enough to chat with him, far enough from the TV to cut through the cartoon racket.

"Hey, Tam," Herb says through a beer belch. "How's it going?"

"Great. Everything's good at school." I pause. "And I'm thinking about working. In fact, I'd like to get set for a job I've heard about. But it involves driving." That idea just popped into my head.

"Driving?"

"Yeah. Making some deliveries."

"But you're not sixteen." Herb struggles with another Pilsner burp.

"In a couple of months, Timmy..." It's the first name that comes to mind. "Timmy thinks there'll be an opening and I want to, well, you know..." I give Herb my most heartwarming smile, "be an excellent driver."

"Delivering pizza?"

Herb's good at filling in the blanks.

"Yeah. His cousin's going away to university next fall. He's driving for them now. But, if I could drive, I could also help Shirl, driving Lizzie and Lyle to their lessons and things." I remember my original argument.

It's like a light clicks on. Herb's eyes all of a sudden have a bit of shine. Even his bald forehead takes on a glow.

"You've come to the right person," he says. "I actually worked part time for a driving school when I was going to business college."

# 10

I wonder how Skinnybones is sleeping these days? Tonight my mind is so filled with the scheme that I think I'll never get to sleep. There's that social worker, Mr. Muss-something. Bound to be checking up on her. But how often? And what can we tell him?

When I try to read — I've put aside *A Tale of Two Cities* and hunted up a copy of *Great Expectations* — I find it impossible to concentrate. Latoya comes in and, I can't believe it, but it's actually a relief to have her hovering around, chattering away some of these long minutes of the night.

"He's going to have to go to summer school," Latoya says as I close the Dickens. "George and English just don't mix. They're oil and water."

"He'd have made his grades if he'd been in my class,"

I tell her. "They used to give them all to me — the truants, ESL…"

"That's what he needs," Latoya sighs. "Someone to get him away from all those computer games. His dad says, 'George, no computer 'til you bring home the good marks' and then there's a big fight…ai yi, I'm right in the middle. He needs the computer for his homework and his dad says no computer…"

This could go on for a while.

"Summer school will probably be good for him," I say.

Byron has bought me a contraption with earphones that plays CDs, which I have trouble getting to work. But the thought crosses my mind now that listening to something might while away some of this endless night. And, slim chance, Latoya might be able to get it working for me.

She is eager to try, anyway, poking bits of sponge against my ears, popping open a little compartment.

"You gotta CD you wanna hear special?" She's flicked on the bureau lamp and is shuffling through a small pile of discs Byron brought from the house.

"*Götterdämmerung*," I say.

"What?"

"G-O-T-T…"

"Yes!" Latoya waves a CD case triumphantly. "Some

of the names they got for these groups, eh?" She pops the disc into the player and presses a button. There is a storm of static pouring into my ears and I yank off the earphones.

"Too loud?" Latoya giggles. "Let's see." She finds the volume button. "There, try it again."

Ah yes. Better. Exquisite. I love the opening music to this opera. The norns — the three fates — dark figures encamped on the walküre's rock, shrouded in fog, weaving into a rope the strands of the story past, the story to come.

Such music — the soft, undulating murmur of the mists of dawn, or is it the fire in the distance beginning to flicker?

And now, yes, they begin to sing. The three of them mourning Wotan's slaughter of the sacred ash tree.

I wake up before the Triple S morning staff begin their hustle bustle. The earphones have fallen off and the CD has, I'm sure, finished playing. For once the Triple S ranch is close to being completely quiet.

I think about the norns, the three fates, spinning the deeds of the world and the overworld of gods.

Somewhere in that spinning is an answer. We weave our own stories…but to find the right threads. A bit of light creeps beneath the Venetian blind. A simple, dim shaft of light tracing a line along the wall opposite.

And then the idea begins to form. Simple as a straight line.

Mr. Muss-something, Tamara's social worker, will be told. And the Shadbolts, too. A summer job for Tamara. Paid companion to an old woman who needs help at home for a couple of weeks, getting the house ready for sale — or some such story.

Yes. Morning light is becoming stronger. Insinuating its way into the room. The problem shifts to how to convince the Triple S that it's okay for me to be gone for two weeks. They don't need to know that the only one with me will be a skinny hard-nosed grade-nine kid. A practical nurse will be in attendance, of course, during my home stay, I'll tell them.

Timing. It will all depend on timing. Byron off to the Philippines, and then letters. A letter to the Triple S. A letter to the Shadbolts. A letter for Mr. Muss-whatsit.

# 11

"You'll need to type the letters," the Wrinkle Queen tells me. "Letter perfect. I'm presuming you know how to type."

She looks at me with her little witch eyes. It's raining buckets out so we're in her room. She's on her bed in a shiny quilted bathrobe. Me on a chair by the bed.

On the way in, I ran into Mrs. Golinowski, who practically hugged me when I told her I'd come to see Miss Barclay all on my own "just because she's so neat!"

"I can type," I say. "Just not very fast."

"They'll need to sound authentic. I'll dictate the drafts to you. Tell me everything I need to know about your foster family. And your social worker. Have you got a notebook?"

She watches me rummage through my backpack. Most of the stuff I've told her before but I guess when you're a hundred or so, stuff doesn't stick like it used to.

I open my binder and hold my pencil like I'm a secretary in a TV show. The Wrinkle Queen looks at me sharply.

"Dear Director — no, dear Mrs. Golly-whatsit…"

"Golinowski."

"Yes, Golinowski…Sierra Sunset Seniors' Lodge…" She pauses to see if I'm keeping up. "I have arranged for my aunt, Jean Barclay, to spend two or three weeks at her home, assisting with preparations for the sale of her house. A practical nurse has been engaged for the required time. If you would be so kind as to arrange for a taxi to take her on the morning of…check the calendar, Tamara. What's the Thursday before we go?"

"August 2nd."

"The morning of Thursday, August 2nd, the nurse will be there to meet her. I will be returning from a business trip a day or two later…"

She closes her eyes when she finishes rattling off that one. Her voice, which was strong a few minutes ago, shifts into a crackly whisper.

"Dear Mr. and Mrs. — what was it? — Shadbolt?…" She rattles off another letter, all the time watching me as if she doesn't believe I can write English. But she runs out of steam about half way through.

"Requires the services of a companion…" I repeat the last words. She's suddenly really tired. Her eyes close.

"Someone to assist her getting ready for bed," I suggest. "Etcetera."

The eyes snap open.

"Yes," she says. "Etcetera. New paragraph. We are pleased to pay Tamara a stipend of five hundred dollars per week."

"Sti-what?" She frowns at me. I guess it's too much to ask that she use normal language instead of sounding like she's swallowed a dictionary. She spells out the word impatiently.

"We expect Tamara's services will not be required for longer than two weeks…"

"Do you want to do the last letter?" I ask her when we've finished that one. "The one to Mr. Mussbacher? We could do it another day."

"No. Let's do it and get them all done. I'll need to look at the typed letters when you get them finished anyway. Like I say, they need to be letter perfect."

Imagine having the Wrinkle Queen for a teacher. Must have been a barrel of fun.

"Fire away," I say.

She looks at me oddly and gives her head a little shake. The rooms at the lodge always have their heat jacked up so it's like you're in a jungle. The Wrinkle Queen is looking totally wilted.

"Dear Mr. Muss…"

"Mussbacher."

"Mussbacher…"

"I think I can figure it out," I say. "I'll just take some parts from the other letters."

When she nods her head, I stow my binder in my backpack and check the calendar again. I have three exams next week but there's one study day.

"I can drop by on Thursday and you can see how the letters turned out."

Maybe she's gone to sleep. I'm ready to tiptoe out when she rears her head and says, "How's the driving coming?"

"I've had four lessons. Only killed one garbage can so far."

But she's got her eyes closed and she's muttering away again as I head out into the hall.

Actually, Herb's not a bad teacher. Very patient. Obviously not from the same school that trained the Wrinkle Queen.

We have a lesson tonight. Herb laughs at how fast I clear away the supper dishes. I've made it part of my proactive thing, and Shirl acts like she's died and gone to heaven when she sits down and has another cup of tea and watches one of the Oprah shows she's taped because it always comes on while she's getting home from the daycare.

The one tonight is on makeovers, and I can't help bobbing back and forth between the kitchen and the living room to see how Oprah's specialists change a dowdy-looking middle-aged lady with gray hair down to her waist and another woman who's overweight and goes around in sweats all the time. Quite amazing, and it wouldn't hurt for Shirl to take a few notes.

"Oh, my," she sighs when they come out at the end of the program. "You can hardly believe it's the same people."

"So, Tam —" Herb's given the gremlins their baths and got them into pajamas. "Ready for the garbage can derby?" He winks at me.

Tonight we're practicing parallel parking. Herb takes the wheel first. He must remember all the stuff he used to say when he was a part-time driving instructor.

"Pull up beside the vehicle just ahead — and you want to be pretty close. Not so close you're gonna scrape the door handle, but almost, and when you've got the nose of the car just about to where the parked car's windshield is, then…"

He shows me on three vehicles. And then it's my turn.

"Good. Right turn arrow on. Now put it in reverse and turn the steering wheel…"

This is scary. It would be so easy to connect with the other car. And if you do, does that mean they take away your learner's permit?

"Don't tense up," Herb is saying. "Just take it slow and easy. That's it…now straighten the wheels out."

He makes me do two more. When I finish the last one, I lean my head against the steering wheel.

Why does everything have to be so hard?

I feel Herb's hand squeeze my shoulder.

"You did good," he says. "Just fine."

Now I am crying. Don't be nice to me, Herb. In a few weeks I'm going to be papering your mailbox with letter-perfect lies and running away to the edge of the world with the Wicked Witch of the West.

# 12

Byron and I are sitting together in the Triple S cafeteria. He's speechless. He holds the vacation package in his hand and keeps looking at it, ignoring the candle that the cafeteria chef has lit on the pink-frosted cupcake.

"Happy Birthday!" I say, raising my glass of cranberry juice.

"But it's not for a month yet."

"I want you to be on the beach at Puerto Galera on your real birthday." I try to look him in the eye but, like his father, he can't keep his gaze steady for longer than one and a half nanoseconds.

"And there's more," I say. "When you come back, we'll put the house up for sale. And the car, too."

"Auntie!"

"Now, now." I pat his hand. "I know I'm not going to be able to live there again. And Lord knows I'll never drive again. You can be my agent in both deals. A good commission." I raise my glass again. "And, of course, it will all —"

"Thank you." He captures my hand with one of his own restless ones and, for once, he does lock eyes with me. He looks like my brother Raymond the Christmas morning he unwrapped a ham radio set our parents had bought him.

Yes, Byron, enjoy your little stretch of paradise. I plan to find my own. The same ocean, but half a world away with the lights of Seattle like the flashing gold of the Rhine. And, inside the opera house, the music swelling like a great wave, beautiful beyond bearing. No wonder Ludwig, the young king of Bavaria, was driven mad by it.

"Are you okay, Auntie?" He has blown out the candle and inhaled the cupcake.

"Oh, yes." I laugh.

As he leaves, Byron keeps looking back over his shoulder, as if he can't believe the fortune the last hour has brought him. He offered to take me back up to my room but I told him I'd be fine and I wanted, after all, another cup of coffee.

"Aren't you afraid it'll keep you awake?" he fretted.

"Byron, my dear…" I patted his hand again. "You don't think they actually have caffeine in anything they brew here!"

When he's gone, I work the walker out to the patio. The June evening is warm and no mosquitoes yet. It will be possible to smoke in absolute peace. I wonder what she's doing, the Tamara girl. Scrapping with her foster family? No — probably not. Not with the prospect of the trip to Vancouver and her modeling course hanging in the balance.

Eddie, the caretaker, spots me from a hall window and comes out to join me. He lights up a cigarette of his own.

"I have it for you," he says in a low, conspiratorial voice. "A bottle of brandy. A carton of cigarillos. How can you smoke those…?" He shakes his head and laughs sadly. "They should have killed you years ago."

"Perhaps they contain the elixir of life. The magic smoke of an immortal dragon."

"You sure that's all you been smoking?" Eddie makes a little twirling gesture by his ear.

"You're right, Eddie," I chuckle. "I am a bit crazy tonight. And I'm glad you've brought a carton. I'm going on a little trip and I like to be well supplied."

"A trip!" He looks at me with surprise. "Hey, look at you! A tour!"

"Yes, Eddie, a tour." I finish my smoke and he helps me up to my room, coming back in a couple of minutes with a small shopping bag.

"Usual spot?" I nod and give him his money after he stows the bag's contents in the back of the bureau drawer, third one down. Tonight a more generous tip than usual.

"Hey!" he smiles. "You have a wonderful trip. Mexico? Hawaii?"

"I'm still deciding," I say. "Pour us both a little drink of brandy. I feel like celebrating tonight."

Eddie retrieves the bottle from the drawer and pours shots into two plastic glasses.

"Bon voyage!" he says.

# 13

When I take the Wrinkle Queen printed-out copies of the letters, she eyeballs them and makes a few corrections.

"I used spell check," I tell her.

"No good with apostrophes or homophones," she says. "I'd think by the time you're in grade nine you'd know the difference between p-a-s-s-e-d and p-a-s-t. If you're going to be a model and move in the higher circles of society, you're going to have to learn to use language correctly."

"Maybe I'll just keep my mouth shut," I tell her.

"It's probably not a bad idea." She gives me one of her death stares. "Fix the mistakes, run the letters off again, and I'll sign Byron's name and they'll be ready to pop into the mail. Look in that top drawer, will you?" She gestures to her bureau.

I pull out a letter. It's got an American stamp on it.

"From Ricardo. He's got tickets and he's put them aside for us." She smiles and pats the letter. "You realize they're worth a small fortune, and we were lucky to get them at this late date. Bless Ricardo's heart."

"Yeah. Wow."

She looks suddenly mad and then sighs and leans back against her pillows.

"Maybe just a bit more enthusiasm," she says. She's sounding crankier by the minute, and she keeps rubbing the knee that had surgery. I guess when you're pushing a zillion, just about everything starts to hurt.

"I think I need to get up and walk." She struggles to sit up. She's wearing a pink dress today and probably hasn't noticed the coffee stains down its front. She tries to tell me how to support her as she gets off the bed, but I guess I don't do it right and she's moaning by the time I get her into a chair and set up her walker.

"You have the gentle touch of a prison warden," she mutters, waving a bony hand at her purse on the bureau. She's not going anywhere without her brandy and smokes.

It's going to be a trip to remember. Two weeks with a miserable old nag who's losing her marbles.

I smile at her.

It's raining today but we find a picnic table beneath

a roof overhang on the patio. Of course she has one of her skinny cigars out and is puffing away as soon as her slippers hit the patio blocks.

"We'll stay in a hotel," she says through a small cloud of smoke. "There's a place right on English Bay where I always stay when I'm in Vancouver. You can make a call when we go back to my room. I've got the number in my address book." Then she levels one of her glares at me. "You can practice being a companion."

I come close to saying something. Like how it'd take a four-year course to learn how to be a companion to someone like her. But I chew on my lip for a second, flash the smile again and say, "Good idea."

Lighting up her second cigarillo, she seems to be getting into a better mood, and even manages one of her cackly laughs when she tells me about giving her nephew his birthday present.

"You'll need a couple of good outfits for Seattle," she says, giving me the once over. "And do you think it's possible to do your hair in a way that doesn't look like you're auditioning for a horror movie?"

"Oh, sure." I have my permanent smile on now. "Maybe I can dye it black and spray it in place so it'll be hard as a rock for a month."

She looks at me with her witch eyes again but doesn't say anything for a minute.

"I have an account at Holt Renfrew. Go in and try on some dresses. Imagine…" She searches for words. "Imagine you are dressing to meet the prime minister at a banquet. You'll need a pair of shoes, too. Have the clerk put them away and ask them to give me a call."

Holt Renfrew.

Sometimes I used to walk by the Holt Renfrew windows in their big downtown store. When I was staying at the Rawdings and had a school bus pass. You could spend an hour going from one fancy dress shop window to the next. Security guards giving you the evil eye. There was one by Holt Renfrew who chased me when I stuck my tongue out at him.

She has one more smoke and a coughing fit that lasts for about half an hour before we head back up to her room. I find the number of the Vancouver hotel in the back of a special book she has with all her trips in it. The Wrinkle Queen has a cellphone! Life is so unfair.

"Ask for a smoking room," she says, "and I like something with a view of the bay. Here, let me talk to the desk clerk. I know the room I want."

When she's on the phone, she doesn't sound like she's a million years old. She sounds like she's used to having people listen to her and doing what she says.

The trip to Holt Renfrew will have to wait for a few days. I have a final tomorrow. English. I'll need to study a bit but it's actually my best subject. Math is the killer but it's two days down the line. Shirl has my exam schedule taped to the fridge door and insists on doing the dishes tonight. But Herb is out with his bowling league so I offer to keep an eye on Lizzie and Lyle while they have their baths.

"Where's Dad?" Lyle pouts.

"In jail," I say.

"Jail?" Lizzie is twirling around with a bath towel cape but this stops her. "He's not in jail."

"How do you know?" I pour a capful of shampoo for Lyle.

"How do you know?" Lizzie fires back.

"Because I had him arrested."

"Did not."

"Did too."

No wonder Herb escapes to bowling once a week. Of course, once they're in their pajamas they beg for a story.

"All right," I say. "The name of this story is *Great Expectations*." And I begin to tell them about Pip's trip into the graveyard to see his parents' grave when he runs into the escaped convict.

"What's a caped convict?" Lyle asks.

"It's someone who was in jail but ran away."

"Like Dad?"

"That's right," I say, "but he's not escaped. He's locked up until ten o'clock tonight. Then they'll let him out and you'll see him at breakfast tomorrow morning."

Miss Whipple has given us a study sheet. Item number one tells us to review a novel we've studied in class during literature circles. I fish *Great Expectations* out of my backpack and reread a couple of my favorite parts. I like Estella the best. I bet she would have had a perfect fashion sense. Beautiful. Moving through the world with everyone paying attention to her. And not having to really do anything except be nice to a crazy old woman with lots of money.

# 14

Waiting for Skinnybones. She phoned my cell this morning to tell me the letters are ready and she'd be over by three. It's four now.

I think of Byron off on his holiday. He came to see me before heading to the airport. Wearing a Hawaiian shirt and some kind of baggy khaki shorts with bulging pockets, and sandals.

"Now, you're sure you have everything you need, Auntie?" he gushed. He'd brought me a bag of toiletries, shopping from a list I'd given him. Even made a special trip to get me a carton of cigarillos. Better to have too many than too few.

"I should stop at the office and let them know where to contact me in case of emergency."

"Oh, no!" I startled him, grabbing his hand. "I've already told them you'll be gone, and I wrote down the names and numbers of your hotels when the travel agent got your package ready. Didn't want you to be bothered, dear, with all the getting ready you've had to do."

For a minute I thought he was going to shed a tear, but he gulped and gave me a hug.

"Love you, Auntie."

Never in his life has Byron said he loved me. I think he was as surprised to hear the words coming out of his mouth as I was. Until he was about seven, he used to run and hide whenever I visited my brother. Not that I minded. He was a slow, stuttering child with a perpetually runny nose and a whiny, plaintive voice.

"Have a wonderful trip," I said. I walked him to the front door, afraid he might stop in at the office at the last minute.

That was midmorning. Where is Skinnybones? It's important to get the letters mailed as soon as possible.

Finally she's here, rushing in a bit breathlessly, dropping her backpack.

"Sorry," she says. "I was at the library using the computer. I had the letters done by two-thirty but I ran into some kids from school."

"You surprise me, Tamara. I thought you avoided the madding crowd." Obviously responsibility is not this one's middle name. I gesture toward the walker. "Let's go outside for a bit."

"Just Timmy and a couple of other kids who were in my lit circle," she says defensively. "We had caramel lattes at the Second Cup."

"Caramel lattes? I thought you models had to watch your weight."

"Brad Silverstone says I need to put on a few pounds."

"Well, I guess he's the expert. Grab my purse, will you? I've got stamped envelopes in there."

"Just a week and two days," Skinnybones reminds me as she organizes her long arms and legs into a pose at the end of the picnic table. She's wearing jeans that look like they've been retrieved from a rag bag and then dragged over a costume jewelry counter, snagging all kinds of odds and ends. Chains. A couple of brooches. My Lord, is that an earring hanging onto a thread by her ankle?

"Did you get to Holt Renfrew yet?" I can feel the smoke from my first cigarillo of the afternoon seeping through me like the fog of the norns.

She doesn't say anything for a minute, and I notice the flush of embarrassment reddening her cheeks.

"You didn't go, did you?"

She glares at me.

"I went. Bunch of stuck-up…"

"What happened?"

"Oh. Some guy came running over when I was walking by the jewelry counter, like he was afraid I was going to walk off with half the stuff. I was just trying to find the dress department."

She's suddenly become fixated on a bauble sewn onto her jeans.

"You didn't give up."

"No. He kept telling me where the other stores were. The Bay. Zeller's. So I accidentally-on-purpose knocked over an earring display and he started yelling at me. I had to wait outside by the door for about an hour until he was over on the other side of the store with a customer and then I went back in and there was this guy selling ties and shirts and he took me over to where the dresses were and this lady with silver hair."

"Phoebe."

"Yeah. Phoebe. She was friendly but you should've seen the look on her face when I told her I needed dresses for the opera. You know the way someone looks when they're trying not to laugh?"

"You have a thinner skin than I thought, Tamara."

"What do you mean?"

"Never mind. I do hope you managed to get something to wear."

"One black dress; one green. Nile green, Phoebe called it. Black pumps. She picked them all out."

"Phoebe has a good eye."

Tamara gives me the letters and I fish a pen out of my purse. When I'm through signing them and she seals the envelopes, I review the things she needs to remember to do — post the letters, pack her suitcase and be ready to come over on the morning of the 2nd, take my CAA card and pick up the maps we'll need.

"When you're at my place, I'll get you to phone the Lodge and ask some little question — maybe something about my medications — just to get them properly lulled."

Two of the nurses who have been out for a smoke get up from a table across the patio and head back into the Triple S. In my purse is the flask of brandy Eddie got me. I slip it out along with one of the little paper cups from the washroom dispenser.

"I feel like celebrating," I say. "You don't drink, do you, Tamara?"

"I've given it up." She gives me one of her chippy smiles.

The Courvoisier tastes like liquid fire. "There's a soda pop machine inside if you'd like something."

The caramel latte has filled her up, she declares. She runs her fingers through her hair. For once it isn't sprayed purple or magenta or green. It's reddish brown and has a bit of curl to it.

"I like your hair," I say. "It looks…well, normal. Is auburn your true color?"

"The real me." She smiles her phony smile. She's anxious to be on her way, I can tell. I get her to take me across to the dining room since it's almost time for dinner. She waves the letters at me as she heads out the door.

Mrs. Gollywatchit is burbling around the dining lounge. Must be picking up some overtime.

"Jean! So nice to see you're well enough to be taking your meals with us again." As she pulls out a chair and sits down, she gives my shoulder a pat. "I think that Stanley Merkin girl has given you a whole new lease on life."

"You really think so?"

"And you get to access more of the special programs. Today we have the Dixie Belles and Beaus."

She's not kidding. A band is setting up in the corner where an old out-of-tune upright piano is always parked. By the time Mrs. Gollything gets up and moves to another table, an accordion and a banjo and a couple of sopranos who should have given up singing forty years ago are urging everyone in the Rancho Cafe to "roll out those lazy, hazy, crazy days of summer."

It's a worthwhile thought, I decide. Roll them out. The crazy days — I'm ready. Not even the Triple S meatloaf with gooey mashed potatoes and flavor-leached peas can squelch that little trickle of excitement. I don't care if it may only be a residual glow from the Courvoisier.

# 15

With school out and Shirl and the gremlins at the day-care, there are times when I feel like phoning the Wrinkle Queen just to talk to someone. How's that for desperation?

Herb and Shirl said they'd keep an eye out for odd jobs for me and I did get some hours helping in the kitchen where Shirl works, and babysitting Herb's boss's kids for a couple of weekends. They made Lizzie and Lyle look like angels.

But most days I'm home alone — all day — with no one arguing about what to watch on TV. Herb's satellite dish, tilted up on the roof, gets about a thousand channels. On Monday, his day off, he hangs onto the remote like it's a lifeline, cruising from one sports channel to the next.

"That's interesting, Herb, watching golf," I say. "Sort of like watching grass grow."

But we make a deal. I make him lunch — a grilled cheese sandwich or maybe a bowl of soup — and he agrees to take an hour off from his sports watch to give me a driving lesson after lunch.

On that last Monday before blast off I ask him, "You want fries or salad with that?" I use a voice like the waitress at Humpty's.

"Fries," he sighs. "But don't tell Shirl."

"Our secret," I tell him.

During my driving lesson, he has me try out a traffic circle. In my hurry to take advantage of an opening in traffic, I rub the car's back wheel against the curb.

"Take it easy," Herb says. "We'd like a little rubber left on that tire."

But I parallel park twice with no problems.

The letter comes on Wednesday, in with utility bills and a fat envelope of stuff from Reader's Digest. It looks funny sitting there on the hall bureau. I think of the times I had to type it — three before I got it perfect — and Miss Barclay's old fingers with their bright red nail polish carefully forging Byron's signature. And then the letter going to the big downtown post office where the stamp gets canceled and it's sorted (by people?

machines?), and then coming all the way back here. In a way, it seems like the post office is one of our partners in crime.

"Tamara!" Shirl nearly explodes with excitement when she reads it. "I think you might have a job for August — at least for part of August."

"What do you mean?" I pause from helping Lizzie mix up a batch of Kool-Aid.

"Well — this letter. It seems that old lady you were visiting with your school…"

"Miss Barclay?"

"Yes. That's the one. She's taken kind of a shine to you and would like you to go to her place and work as a — you know — paid companion. This letter's from her nephew."

Lizzie manages to spill a small lake of Kool-Aid as she pours out tumblers for herself and Lyle.

"You want some?" she asks me.

"Why don't I just lick up what you spilled."

"No, I will," Lyle squeals and actually does start licking the table top before I manage to slap a dishrag over the mess.

Shirl has wandered into the kitchen with the letter.

"Have a look at this."

I read the letter over. Very good margining, I think.

"Wow. Five hundred dollars a week. A thousand bucks," I say.

"And you wouldn't actually be working for a lot of the time," Shirl points out. "You'd just have to be there."

"It would be nice to have some extra money. I guess if you and Herb don't mind."

Shirl gives my arm a little squeeze. "You've just grown up so much in…well, just in this last few weeks. I think it's ever since you did your action plan."

Mr. Mussbacher phones that evening. I guess he got his letter, too. He and Shirl yack about the whole idea for a few minutes and then she turns the phone over to me.

"Is this something you want to do?" he asks me.

"Yeah," I say. "I could really use the money for clothes."

"Nothing for fun?"

"Well, maybe a few movies…and there's a couple of CDs."

Mr. Mussbacher laughs. "I think it would be fine. I'll go over when you start, to make sure everything's okay."

"Oh, I'm sure it'll be okay."

"I'd like to see this lady you've made such a conquest of."

He's not going to be talked out of it so, the next day, I make a quick trip over to see the Wrinkle Queen between *Fashion Forecast* on Channel 84 at 1:30 and *Style Time* on Channel 68 at 4:00. I need to find out what we should do.

The nurse warns me that the old lady's having a bad day. Hasn't even gotten out of bed. When I go in her room, it looks like she's either sleeping — or dead. But I guess she hears me come in. Her eyes flutter open. Her licorice-black hairdo is kind of squished to one side and it looks like the wrinkles have multiplied in the last few days.

She stares at me as if she's never seen me before in her life.

"What do you want?" she croaks.

"Miss Barclay?" I try to take her hand.

"Go away." She curls her fingers, making two fists that look like dead chicken feet.

"It's me. Tamara."

"Tamara?" But a light goes on somewhere, and she tries to sit up.

"It's okay. Why don't you just stay lying down — and rest."

She's mussed her covers, and I do what I can to straighten them.

"My social worker says he's going to stop by and see

how things are going my first day with you. When you go to your house."

"My house?"

"You know. Like we planned."

She's managed to hoist herself up a bit, and one of the fists has opened up and become fingers again, and she's waving them at the purse on her bureau.

Her brandy? A cigarillo? I hand it over to her and she opens it, her hands shaking and, after pawing through, pulls out a lipstick. In a couple of minutes, she's smeared her lips with the shade of fire-engine red she always uses.

"He's coming over?" Her voice still sounds like she's about to croak. "Did he say when?"

"I guess once I get to your place."

"We'll have to put on a little show for him." Her mouth has worked itself into a kind of lopsided smile. I can see quite a bit of the lipstick has gotten onto her dentures.

As usual it's about a hundred degrees in her room. I can feel sweat along my forehead and neck, but the Wrinkle Queen looks as dry as dust.

"My driving's coming along real good."

"Coming along well."

"Whatever."

"I think I'll do the driving," she says, her eyes narrowing. "That Buick is worth a lot of money. It's not just some rattletrap. You can spell me off if I get tired."

The nurse wasn't kidding. Definitely a bad day.

"Sure," I say. "Or maybe we could just hire an ambulance and a tow truck to go along with us."

She scowls at me.

"Might not be a bad idea," she says.

# 16

The letter to the lodge that Skinnybones mailed has arrived. Mrs. Gollydoodle is the one who comes to talk to me about it.

"I'm concerned," she says. "You've been in bed for two days. I don't think you're in any shape to go home and be sorting through household stuff."

"Nonsense," I say. "I feel fine. I was just under the weather. Byron's done so much for me that I owe him this. I feel fine today — and there'll be a nurse. Would you like her to give the office a call?"

"Well…" The wall-to-wall eyebrow has a furrow in it. "Actually, I would like her to…"

When she's gone, I close my eyes.

What's happening to me? I can't believe the last two days have run away on me like an escaped convict.

Somewhere in the middle of it Skinnybones perched by my bed like some little fledgling buzzard. Probably wondering whether or not she'll have to give back the money if I croak.

But I'm not about to croak. When Betty comes in, I have her give me a hand getting dressed. It's important to be seen up and about.

When I try to stand, though, I come close to toppling over.

"You want me to put in a call for a nurse?" Betty asks.

"Don't be silly." My voice sounds like it's coming from someone else — someone whose volume button is turned down. "I just need a minute."

What I really need is ten minutes. And dust-buster Betty isn't happy about how long it's taking to get into stockings and undergarments.

"What dress would you like?" She has disappeared into the closet.

"Something red," I say. When I look in a mirror I'm horrified at what's happened to my hair. "Do you know if Rita's in today?"

Betty promises to check. When she's gone, I manage to get to the bathroom and pour myself a couple of fingers of brandy. Life begins to seep back into me.

Is this what I'm reduced to, sitting on the only seat

this kind of room has to offer, shakily imbibing from a pathetic paper cup with a waxy taste to it?

My mother always said she didn't want to grow old. Maybe she was the lucky one, shuffling off her mortal coil five days after we'd gone to see *Madame Butterfly* at the Jubilee Auditorium. Young enough that she'd hardly begun dyeing her hair. Still looking regal in her long black first-night gown with its low-cut back and bit of a train. And her diamond brooch.

Someone banging on the bathroom door.

"Miss Barclay, are you in there? It's Rita. I could fit you in right now for a quick comb-out and spraying."

With my hair back in place, I feel more like a human being and, after lunch, I run into Eddie, who invites me down to the boiler room for a smoke.

"I don't know how you can stand those cigar things," he says. "Nobody in the world smokes them far as I know. They smell foul. They ain't got no cork tips."

"But they make a statement."

"Matter of opinion," he chuckles and taps some ashes off his filtered du Maurier into a coffee can filled with sand.

They are a special breed, custodians. I have always liked them. Like the seers of mythology, they are sources of knowledge and profound speculation. Water pipes gurgling in place of sacred springs.

"So that's your trip! You're goin' home for a couple of weeks," Eddie says. "Do some downsizing, sorting out. You sure had me going for a bit there, though. Mexico!"

He has an old maroon-colored easy chair by the sand can that he's given over to me on my visits. Easy to get into but the devil to get out of.

"You tell that skinny little girl that's been coming by for visits?" Eddie eyeballs me. "What if she stops by while you're gone?"

"I'll let her know, Eddie," I reassure him.

Eddie's there to help me when the taxi comes on Thursday morning, carrying the small bag I've packed, collapsing my walker and getting it into the trunk.

"There's a little something extra I tucked into your handbag," he whispers to me before closing the cab door. As the taxi heads across town, I check the bag and find a mickey of brandy. It's not Courvoisier, but it's not bad.

"Bless the custodians of the world."

"Ma'am?" the taxi driver looks back at me for a second.

"Nothing. Keep your eyes on the road."

The house in the Crescents hasn't changed in the six months I've been gone. One thing about Byron, he's kept the grass trimmed and bushes pruned. Hoping to see a For Sale sign sprouting on the lawn momentarily, of course. It had been white stucco until Papa died and then Mama had it painted a rich reddish-brown, what they've taken to calling terra cotta now.

"If we're going to live in this godforsaken country of snow and cold, we can at least have a house that's warm in color." Mama lived in Georgia until she was sixteen. Every few years I've freshened the paint, but it's always been Mama's color.

I hadn't thought about the steps. They're not going to be easy to negotiate.

"Hey, you!" I holler at the taxi driver who's trying to make a quick getaway after setting up my walker and carrying my bag to the door. "Come back here and give me a hand up this front stoop."

He looks like a storm cloud but he does it.

"Some people say please and thank you," he mutters as I search my purse for a house key.

Some people show respect for elders, I think. It's unfortunate that there are no detention halls for rude and surly people. I wouldn't mind having this one cool his heels while he copied out a couple of dictionary pages.

The house smells musty. Unlived in. When I pull the drapes, I can see it could use a visit from dust-buster Betty. Maybe Skinnybones can spend a bit of time with a dust cloth and a can of Lemon Pledge. It wouldn't hurt her to be doing a bit more than practicing her smile and trying not to be unpleasant for all the money I'm giving her.

In the kitchen, the coffee maker is in its usual spot on the counter, flanked by empty tins of the soda pop Byron peddles. The coffee canister, of course, is in its place on the second shelf by the window. My legs protest as I reach for it and I nearly end up dropping it on the counter. Interesting how the simplest maneuvers become major adventures once your health begins to betray you.

The phone rings in the living room — about seven times before I manage to get to it.

Skinnybones.

"I nearly did myself in getting to this blasted device," I inform her. "I would have thought you might have remembered that I keep my cellphone close at hand." Actually, I'm not sure where the contraption is at the moment, but that's not something she needs to know.

"Mr. Mussbacher is driving me over," she says.

This is going to be a long day, I think. I can hear Tamara breathing into the pause.

"Tell him I have the coffee on," I say.

# 17

We're driving through a ritzy part of town close to the river where there are fancy old houses with shutters on the windows and porches with pillars. One of them must be the Wrinkle Queen's, but which one?

"You've turned things around, haven't you?" Mr. Mussbacher sounds pretty pleased with himself.

"All that smiling, I guess." I wonder if my dad looked like Mr. Mussbacher. He has good cheekbones. Too bad about the mustache, though.

We pull up to a bungalow the color of dried blood, and I see her at the window watching for us. I bet she's already killed a few cigarillos.

She has. She tries to wave away a cloud of smoke as Mr. Mussbacher carries my suitcase in. She's all smiles for him and her voice drips honey. Should be on TV or in the movies.

"Now there's coffee but I apologize for the fact that there's no milk, if you take it with milk," she's saying. "I haven't had time to have groceries delivered. And, besides, I wanted to check with Tamara about what she'd like to eat while she's staying with me."

"Just sugar," Mr. Mussbacher says.

"We have plenty of that." She laughs.

You're not kidding, I think. It's knee deep right now.

"I'm so looking forward to having Tamara stay with me."

She pours coffee into a bone china cup with a Royal Albert design. The same design that was on Mrs. Rawding's cups, the ones I dropped on the floor before I went to live with the Shadbolts. *This fine china is not to be handled!* Mrs. Rawding had written in a little note on one of the saucers.

"I think what I like best is that, above everything else, she's an excellent reader. I like to read but my eyes tire and then Tamara reads out loud to me."

"*Great Expectations*," I add. It was one of the details we'd worked out last week. Social workers, guidance counselors and teachers go soft when you mention a love of reading.

"Well, I think it'll be a good experience for her," he says, holding his cup very carefully as he sips from it. He gives Miss Barclay his card in case she needs to call him, and makes sure we have her doctor's numbers and other emergency numbers on a paper beside the phone.

"If it's not working out or you're uncomfortable with any of this, give me a call," he says to me on the front porch as he's leaving. "We'd need to get in touch with her nephew so he could set up alternate arrangements."

As the car disappears around the curve of the crescent, a delivery van pulls up. The Holt Renfrew packages. Talk about timing.

The Wrinkle Queen is exhausted. Being polite has probably been quite a strain on her. I help her to her bedroom so she can lie down for a while.

"Why don't you make a bit of lunch," she says. "You'll find all kinds of tinned goods in the kitchen pantry."

Sure enough, there's a whole little room just off one corner of the kitchen, its walls lined with tins and jars and cartons of just about everything imaginable. A little different from the cans of Chef Boyardee the Tierneys stockpiled on Discount Tuesday or the two-for-one Safeway Select pasta Shirl's scrunched into the cupboard by the stove. Stuff I've never heard of. Caviar. Melba toast. Capers. Beef Bourguignon.

Hey, mushroom soup. Well…wild mushroom soup. That seems safe, and a package of crackers. Not regular crackers that you crumple up in your hand and drop into a bowl of Campbell's cream of mushroom. Cocktail crackers, it says on the box. Sounds like something Miss Barclay would like.

There's a regular set of normal dishes in the cupboard. When I've set the table and heated the soup, I check on the Wrinkle Queen. Snoring away in her bedroom.

I decide to let her sleep. In a room off the living room, there's a TV, and I've only missed ten minutes of *Fashion Forecast*. They're broadcasting from Milan, Italy. Some designer who's into feathers and leather. A good model can wear almost anything in the world and act like she's strutting around in jeans and a T-shirt. Like a leather bra with pigeon feathers sticking out of its sides. Or suede hot pants fringed with rawhide laces dripping bangles and beads.

"Tamara."

Hold onto your dentures, Queen Elizabeth. My show's almost over. She scowls at me when I come into the bedroom a couple of minutes later.

"Lunch is all ready," I tell her. I've never figured out why it's always tougher for her to get off a bed than get into one. You'd think the force of gravity would be with her.

"Oh, good," she croaks when I get her to the table. "Wild mushroom soup and…cocktail crackers."

"Would you like Melba toast?"

"No. But I wouldn't mind a proper spoon. You should never serve soup with only a teaspoon. And the soup bowls should have plates underneath them…"

She's not happy until I've got the big spoons and plates and rounded up cloth napkins that look like big hankies. But she slurps a spoonful of soup and sighs. "Why can't the Triple S figure out how to make something this good?" Cracker crumbs make a trail down her fuchsia-colored dress.

"Now try on those new dresses," she says after I've cleared away the lunch dishes. "I'd like to see what you've got for my money."

Her money. Is she ever going to let up? I model the green dress with the full skirt first.

"I'm trying to imagine what it'll look like on you when your hair doesn't look as though you've stuck your finger in a light socket," she mumbles through a cloud of smoke.

"Well, work on it," I suggest, "but don't give yourself a stroke while you're doing it."

"Now don't get touchy," she glares at me. "There's no point in you wearing a two-hundred-dollar dress if your hair looks like a magpie's nest."

She puffs away for a few minutes on her cigarillo as I go and look at myself in the hall mirror and do a twirl.

The dress does look awesome. Especially with the dress pumps. Forget about the old bat carping.

When I change and come back out in the black sheath, she says, "You're a little young to wear black. But it's a good fit. Now go into my bedroom and look in the top right hand drawer. There's a jewelry box I'd like you to bring to me."

So the dragon has some treasure in her cave.

The box is antique-looking — fancy gold trim and shiny bone stuff on the outside.

"My mother's." The Wrinkle Queen's voice has gone suddenly soft. When she opens the lid, it plays a tiny, tinkly bit of music. "The waltz from *Coppelia*."

"Pretty."

"Nothing terribly valuable in here." She rummages through it. "But, yes, this will do quite nicely with the green dress — and the black, too, for that matter."

It's a triple strand of pearls.

"Cultured," she says.

"What?"

"Cultured pearls. Quite good quality. Leave them out and we'll pack them."

The pearls glow in the window light, and the beads feel wonderful as I run them through my fingers. To tell the truth, I wouldn't mind borrowing some of the other pieces from the old jewelry box. A silver bracelet that looks like a snake. Big chunky gold earrings. But Miss Barclay bangs the lid down, stopping the tinkly waltz in the middle of a note.

She has a matching set of bright red luggage (surprise!), and she loans me the second-biggest bag so my green dress won't get crushed.

Her own opera dresses are long silvery things. One has about a zillion little glass beads sewn all over it. And another has a pattern of swirls that makes you dizzy when you look at it. The Wrinkle Queen treats them like they are precious pets and has me make little nests for them out of tissue paper. She throws in one of those wraps made out of dead rats, too. This one is white.

"Likely it'll be warm in Seattle," she says, "but every once in a while it gets a little cool and drizzly. That reminds me, we should take umbrellas."

She points at a list I'm making. I write "umbrellas" beneath "opera glasses." They have special glasses for looking at opera? Who would have known?

It takes us most of the afternoon to pack. Mid-afternoon I phone the nursing home and tell them I'm Miss Barclay's nurse, Stella Havisham, and everything is a-okay. Just a quick question. Should she be taking an aspirin a day along with her other medications?

Then, at 5:30, when I know everything will be in an uproar at the Shadbolts with Shirl hustling to get supper, and the gremlins fighting over which cartoons to watch, and Herb hunting up a beer and trying to find all the pieces of his newspaper, I give them a call.

Herb answers.

"Everything is going great," I tell him. "Miss Barclay's ordering a pizza for supper and then we're going to watch a video. It'll be fun. Say hi to everyone from me. I'll phone you in a couple of days."

Miss Barclay actually does have a couple of shelves of videos — ones she owns, not just rentals she's forgotten to take back. But, instead of watching a movie, we decide I'd better practice driving the Buick. She hasn't made any more noises about doing the driving herself.

This isn't like Herb's Plymouth or Mr. Mussbacher's Toyota. The Buick has white leather seats and lots of shiny chrome and so many dashboard dials it looks like the flight panel on an airplane.

Once she's managed to get into the passenger seat, the Wrinkle Queen pats the dash like it's some kind of pet.

First I have to back it out of a garage that must have been built when cars were skinnier. I actually scrape the side view mirror — the one on the side where the Wrinkle Queen is sitting — against the door frame.

"Are you sure you've been taking driving lessons?" she asks. She's already lit up a cigarillo.

"Herb didn't teach me how to back out of a closet." I feel like grabbing the cigarillo and chucking it into the lane. "Would you mind opening your window? I wouldn't want to die from second-hand smoke poisoning before we even get started."

"Then turn off the air-conditioning," she snaps.

"You turn it off. I'm driving."

Neither of us say anything as I steer the car down the alley and out onto the street.

"You can just drive slowly along the crescents here," she says finally. "No need to get out onto Stony Plain Road any sooner than we have to. When we get back, you can park in front of the house. I hate to think what might happen if you attempt to get this vehicle back into the garage."

The Buick is twice as big as Herb's car. Candy apple red. Give it to the Wrinkle Queen, she means business when she says she's not into old lady colors.

We're back by ten o'clock. And, yes, I did get out onto Stony Plain Road, the one we'll take out of town tomorrow morning, to get gassed up. It was kind of scary but traffic wasn't too bad on a Thursday night.

I can see the Wrinkle Queen is going to be a pain to drive with. I guess you can't call it backseat driving because she's in front. Sideseat driving? Some of what she has to say, I need to hear. About one percent. Like which side street will give me a light onto Stony Plain. But the other ninety-nine percent I could do without. Look out for that street fountain…now be sure and signal…I didn't see you shoulder check…yadda yadda yadda. She's yammered on so much that she's practically dead from exhaustion by the time we get back to the house.

Still, she has some of her brandy in a little glass that looks like it should be hanging from a chandelier. I let her pour me a taste, too. It's pretty awful, but I pretend I like it.

We clink glasses.

"To Wagner." The Wrinkle Queen raises her glass. "Dreadful man but the source of the most wonderful music ever written."

"Dreadful?"

"Womanizer. Racist. Egomaniac." The words sound almost like praise the way she says them.

"To the journey," I say, "and may all our expectations be met."

"Remember, dear." Miss Barclay drains her glass. "Dickens was being ironic. Maybe, like wearing black dresses, you're a little too young for irony."

# 18

It seems like I've just fallen asleep when I'm awake again. But it is three o'clock, I can see by the relentless red digits of the clock on my bureau. It's not easy getting out of bed, but I manage — I don't want to wake Skinnybones. She'll need her energy for that drive.

There's a kind of wonder to the night. Witching hours, I guess. The light of the street lamp shining through the living-room sheers onto the Persian rug. Without even thinking about it, I make a tour of the house. Very slowly. Using this wretched walker contraption. But slow is fine at night.

Skinnybones is fast asleep in what used to be Raymond's room, the one I turned into a study with a pull-out couch. Asleep, she looks as if she were twelve instead of nearly sixteen.

Lord, Jean Barclay! What have you gotten yourself into?

In the kitchen, I treat myself to a smoke and another bit of brandy — mindful of its sleep-inducing attributes. When I do get back into bed, the clock reminds me, minute by minute, of the slothlike passage of time. 5:17. And then I do drift off.

Someone touching my hand stirs me. At first it seems like it might be Mama, waking me to go to school. That's how she'd do it. Even when I was older and going to Normal School. Just tapping my hand.

"Time to get up."

"Mmm. What time is it?" Can that be my voice?

And it isn't Mama. It's someone else.

"Seven o'clock."

I see it's the girl. Skinnybones. Her hair all spiky.

"There's coffee on."

She's a bundle of energy. Almost doing a little dance as she gets me into the clothes I had her lay out on my bedroom armchair last night.

"Settle down," I tell her. "No one's going to run away with the road. Where are my cigarillos?"

She's a terrible driver, I realize, when we get out onto the highway. Poking along ten kilometers below the speed limit, drifting over lane lines, driving half way onto the shoulder at times.

"You might want to get over and let that dump truck by," I suggest.

"God. He's got other lanes!"

"But you're driving in the fast lane and you're going slower than the rest of the traffic. Now get over." I haven't lost it, the voice that could send students hurrying from the classroom into the hall or down to the principal's office.

She changes lanes abruptly without a proper shoulder check, and a huge semi blares its horn at her, frightening her so badly that she scoots totally over onto the shoulder and stops. I expect she's going to cry but instead she just grips the steering wheel and clenches her teeth and utters a couple of choice oaths. It seems like a good time to light a smoke and settle my own nerves.

Finally she turns and glares at me.

"I can only drive if you quit nagging me," she says, dropping her words like stones, each one thudding. "Otherwise, I can't concentrate."

"All right," I say, "but if you're going to kill us, I'd prefer you did it on the way back, after I've seen the Ring."

"Right."

The traffic going west thins out as we get farther away from the city. Most of it is coming into Edmonton.

And she does seem to steady, the more kilometers we log.

"Where did you put those tapes?" Over the years I've put together a collection I like to listen to on a car trip. Mostly Wagner, but some Puccini and Verdi, too.

"Under the picnic hamper in the back."

She's not happy about pulling over and rummaging in the back seat for them, but she doesn't say anything.

"Ah, there we are." It's the top one in the carrying case. "*Das Rheingold*. Act one. Imagine the scene, Tamara. Water nymphs frolicking in the river water. Music so exquisite it breaks your heart."

She thinks I don't see her but I do. Rolling her eyes.

"And then the music will change. A dark, ominous undercurrent filled with menace. That's because Alberich, a dwarf who lives under the river, comes up and begins flirting with them, but they reject him. Alberich spies the gold, though, glinting in the sunlight through the water."

For a minute, I close my eyes and see that image, one of my favorites in the whole cycle. When I open them again, I catch Skinnybones stealing a quick glance. Checking, no doubt, to see if I'm still alive.

"The Rhine maidens tell Alberich if he can renounce love forever, the gold will be his along with magic powers that will allow him to shape it into a ring."

"Lord of the rings?"

"Well…a different story but not all that different." I push the tape into the slot on the dashboard.

As we drive, the morning sun makes its own dappled patterns through the trees and across fields, somehow a perfect fit with the Rhine music.

Yes, it's all worth it. When you get closer to the end of your life, the decisions you make are shaped by a sense of urgency — a kind of urgency that plays out in slow motion. Last chances, I guess.

She's liking the instrumental music, I can see, but when the first Rhine maiden begins to sing, she grimaces, glances at me in amazement, and then begins to giggle.

"Now be patient," I say. "Opera singing isn't something you latch onto the first five minutes you hear it."

There's a small park with picnic tables just off the highway not far from Hinton and we make our first stop there. Tamara looks suspiciously at the outdoor toilets. I don't think she's ever seen the like before.

"We are explorers on the road of life," I tell her. "You can't expect there to be hot and cold running water at all the stops along the way."

I'm intrigued to see what she's packed in the picnic hamper for us to snack on. A tin of deviled salmon. Olives. Melba toast. Brandied peaches. A thermos of coffee for me. Perrier water for herself. The hamper is equipped with silverware, glassware and napkins — all the essentials for picnicking during the opera intervals in Seattle.

It's a perfect day and, for once, Skinnybones is grinning like a normal teenager instead of practicing her smirky model smile. She laughs as brandy syrup trickles down her chin. Midmorning light filters through the evergreen branches, hopscotching over the glass and silver.

A family at the next table is eating heart-attack food from cartons. Two little boys watch us solemnly, their open mouths spilling bits of hamburger bun and mustard.

I catch Tamara's eye. She raises her bottle of Perrier in a little salute, and I reply with a slight tip of my coffee cup.

Conspirators.

# 19

I like driving. I mean, I'd probably love it if the Wrinkle Queen could stop griping about how I'm doing for three and a half seconds at a time. Is there anything worse than old L.A. teachers? I finally had to tell her to shut up.

What's so great is tearing along the highway and everything flashing by, like in a movie. Green fields and bunches of trees and farms. Some of them even have red barns like you see in picture books when you're in grade one. Red barns and real cows and horses!

One time Wilma told me she lived on a farm when she was a little girl. With her grandma. Grandma Schlotter. Feeding chickens, collecting eggs. But then the grandma died and she went back to living with her dad and his third wife in a part of Edmonton where there was a drug house two doors away. Her dad died when she was twelve — got drunk and fell off a fire escape. And her mother — well, Wilma wouldn't really talk about her. She'd just say, "She's dead to me."

So somewhere I might have a grandmother, but I have a feeling she's not living on a farm raising chickens.

When the Wrinkle Queen gets through pouting about not being allowed to sideseat drive, she decides to put on a tape of her opera music. But first, of course, she has to tell me this story about dwarfs and mermaids and a magic ring. I'm thinking this guy Wagner has been drinking more than Rhine water himself. And when the Wrinkle Queen actually quits yattering and turns on the music, it turns out the mermaids are all yodeling and shrieking at one another. God help us.

We get a break from it all when we stop for lunch. Of course Miss Barclay isn't into anything normal like going to Wendy's for a bit of salad. Instead we park ourselves at a picnic table where I get to unload the stuff I packed from the pantry. We snack on petrified toast named after some opera singer who lived a hundred years ago. Petrified toast with some kind of fishy sandwich spread. Good thing I brought a jar of olives.

The Wrinkle Queen looks like she's died and gone to heaven, puffing away on one of her skinny cigars underneath a pine tree where a squirrel is running around, up and down branches.

Back on the road after lunch, I get to hear more of the story of opera number one. The king of the gods and his wife wake up and find out that a couple of giants have built a castle for them.

"Wotan has promised his sister-in-law Friea to the giants in payment for the castle," Miss Barclay is saying. "But then he insists it's only a joke and there's a huge fight. That's when Loge the god of fire shows up…"

She rattles on for about fifteen minutes. I'm beginning to see mountains in the distance. It's like the farms — hard to believe they're real. They grow bigger all the time as we get closer, and by the time we actually get up beside them and there are rocks right beside the road that are a hundred times bigger than the Buick, she has the music going full blast again.

And there are animals like out of a National Geographic special. Elk walking along the ditches, checking out the cars on the road. In a couple of places, mountain sheep with their curved horns, way up on the tops of cliffs.

"This is the part where Loge the fire god tricks Alberich into putting on a magical helmet, and he turns himself into a toad." The Wrinkle Queen cackles like she's come up with the trick herself.

"We're going to have to stop in Jasper," she says. "Like the rest of me, my kidneys are a bit worn out."

To tell the truth, the Perrier water has done a job on me, too. There are washrooms in a big old train station which also has a bunch of Greyhound buses and tour coaches parked outside.

And one RCMP car.

There's nobody in it, though, and when I go back into the station to wait for Miss Barclay to come out of the washroom, I see them. Two mounties buying coffees and joking with the girl at the concession stand.

"Mounties," I hiss into her ear as I try to hurry her with her walker toward the door.

"Jasper always has mounties," she says smugly. "They hire them as a tourist attraction."

Of course, the Wrinkle Queen, dressed head to toe in ketchup red, isn't about to fade into the crowd. I'm sure one of them is watching us from the door as I collapse the walker and stow it and get back into the car. It's a relief to get out onto the main street and see that there's no police cruiser in my rear-view mirror.

We haven't reached the town limits when she has her opera music blaring again.

"In this part," she says, "Wotan collects all of the dwarfs' gold and forces Alberich to give him the ring."

But in a few minutes she's fallen asleep in her seat and is snoring softly. I find the volume button and turn it way down.

I'm driving through country with lakes and streams and little waterfalls. Trees. Mountains topped with snow. It looks like pictures on a wall calendar. I'm wondering if Wilma ever got to see this — or was it just the two places in her life. The chicken farm and downtown Edmonton.

Before I was put in the first foster home, we lived close to the hockey arena. Wilma would let people going to the game park on the lawn for five dollars. One night we were able to get six cars into the yard and Wilma took me and my two half-brothers, Todd and Taran, for pizza. Going out just like a normal family. But when we got home, Todd's father, Dwight, was there and he and Wilma went to a party and didn't come home for three days.

They got back right around the same time the social workers got there.

I wonder sometimes how Todd and Taran are getting along. Mr. Mussbacher says they've always just been in one foster home, a family with three boys of their own, the dad coaching little league hockey, the mom volunteering at their school. Maybe some day they'll have steady jobs and cars of their own and will be able to go to a hockey game and pay a family five dollars to park in their yard.

Do models have cars? Mostly I think of them being

driven around by other people. Photographers and limousine drivers. Or maybe movie star husbands.

The Wrinkle Queen is moaning and talking in her sleep.

"Don't you dare…" she says.

Probably reaming some kid out for not doing his homework.

Imagine having her for a teacher. I try to think of what she would have looked like twenty-five years ago when she quit teaching. I bet she had the same black hairdo, just fewer wrinkles. Wearing her killer tomato dresses and too much make-up.

For a minute I think she's going to wake up, but then she starts snoring again. Whew.

The kilometers slip away under the tires of the red Buick, bringing me closer and closer to Vancouver and Jude Law Model Man. "The camera will love you." I think of him saying that to me. And I think of how awful it would have been to be born without good bone structure.

I imagine Jude taking my picture from a hundred different angles in the modeling studio with its gilt-edged mirrors and flowing draperies, potted palms and furniture that looks like it might have belonged to French kings back in the days before they got their heads chopped off.

The Wrinkle Queen sleeps right through to Mount Robson.

"Pull in to a gas station here," she mutters, half awake. "We'll fill up and I need to use a washroom again."

I can see that she's cranky as a hornet trapped on a windowsill.

Yes, Vancouver, I think.

But first there's Seattle. Somehow I'm going to have to live through that.

# 20

The car seat is cramping me.

"We'll stop for the night in Kamloops," I tell Skinnybones. "I need to lie down."

When she helps me out of the car, I feel like I'm going to collapse, even with my hands riveted to the walker. In fact, I start to go down and she grabs me and holds me from behind.

"Take a deep breath," she says, and I hear a little bit of fear in her voice.

The motel has a picnic table sitting in a patch of brown grass by the parking lot. She gets me over to a seat there and then finds the cigarillos in my purse. The flask of brandy, too. It takes a few minutes before I feel like I'm not going to topple over.

There's a woman watching us from the door of the motel office.

"Tell her to come over here. I'm not going to try to get my walker into that roadside closet."

The woman comes out reluctantly.

"If you just come into the office…" She has that kind of graying hair made frizzy that a whole breed of middle-aged women seem to embrace.

"As you can see, mobility is somewhat difficult," I tell her. She's gone slack-jawed. "I'll thank you to take my credit card, make an imprint, and then bring the receipt out here for me to sign."

"How many nights?"

I can't help a little laugh that emerges as more of a snort. Would anyone stay longer than one night in a place like this?

"Just overnight," Tamara says.

"Where you folks headed?" Frizzy asks, eyeing the credit card.

"To Vancouver." Tamara walks with her back to the office. "My grandma and I…" The rest of the story is lost as the screen door bangs shut.

It's Skinnybones who brings the bill back out for my signature.

"She needed to know our home address and I couldn't remember what yours was so I gave her Shirl and Herb's."

The motel room is as cold as a morgue.

"My god, Tamara, turn off that air-conditioning or I'll perish." It's a hideous room with what looks like paint-by-number sad clowns on the wall, a chipped arborite counter with a TV set and an ice bucket. There are cigarette burns on the bed quilt.

"I asked for a smoking room," Tamara says. She's got the TV on, of course, flicking from channel to channel. I lie down and close my eyes. She has sense enough to turn the sound right down so it's only a murmur, almost soothing.

Is this how it's going to be every day? My legs aching, my balance gone, energy pressed from my body? I wonder if Byron is lying on a beach in the Philippines right now. Sun beating down on him. No aches or pains.

If it's going to be this hard, maybe I'm not meant to get to Seattle. Is there only so much music one is allowed in a lifetime?

"Tamara." My voice sounds like it's being dragged over sandpaper. "Bring me my purse. I'm going to take a couple of Tylenol."

They ease the aches but they don't help me sleep. One of the curses of old age — sleeping during the day, being awake all night. Tamara is tired, though. After we've had a bite to eat, she falls asleep watching TV.

"Get into bed," I say. "We'll get up early in the morning. It's still a ways to go, you know. And the

Coquihalla Highway can be a challenge. Even if it's the middle of the summer, there can still be sleet and you can expect fog on those high mountain passes."

She's still tired in the morning when we turn in the key. A man — Frizzy-hair's husband? — is at the door of the office, yawning. He's in an undershirt and dirty suspendered trousers. Balefully he watches us as we ease the Buick out onto the main road.

"Don't pay him any mind, Tamara. One of Alberich's minions. Mindlessly mining gold."

It doesn't take long to get into the heights. Then it begins to rain. Large trucks throw up a spray, blinding the windshield.

"Keep the wipers on, girl." I don't mean to be screaming at her but I am.

I think about plugging another tape into the player, but the time doesn't seem right. We're on the top of the world, in with the rain while it's still in the clouds. There are actually tears streaming down Skinnybones' cheeks but I'm not sure she even realizes she's crying. She's gripping the steering wheel like it's the wheel of life, the ring of the universe.

As we get closer to Hope, the rain stops and the sun comes out.

"Let's stop in Hope and have some breakfast," I say. She doesn't argue.

I pat her hand as we wait for our scrambled eggs.

"You've got fortitude," I say. "It takes guts to drive the Coquihalla when the road is disappearing into the clouds. I'm sure, at one point, I saw the rainbow bridge the gods used to enter Valhalla."

"The castle of gods and fallen heroes?"

"That's the one." Steam rises from our breakfast platters, carrying with it the warm buttery smell of the toast.

"The next challenge will be driving through Vancouver. Now, the good thing is it'll be early afternoon when we get there." I slather the toast with marmalade. "Not rush hour."

When we get onto the long stretch of valley road, I tell her a bit of the story of the second opera, *Die Walküre*. The love story of Siegmund and Sieglinde and the magic sword Wotan has left for Siegmund in a tree. Skinnybones doesn't seem too interested but she perks up a bit when I get to the part about Sieglinde being married already, and the discovery of the lovers that they are actually brother and sister.

"Incest set to music," she observes.

It's smooth driving now, and the music in this act is beautiful beyond belief. It's probably a good thing that Act Two, with Brunnhilde and the walküres riding through the sky, is loud, rousing music, or we'd both be falling asleep.

"Are we getting close to Vancouver?" she asks as the tape goes silent, switching to the other side.

"That was Abbotsford we just passed. Less than an hour now."

How many years is it since I first drove this road? That summer — 1959? 1960? — when I bought my first Buick and I drove Mama to the coast for a holiday. The year before she died. That was before they built the Coquihalla, and we'd driven the Fraser Canyon road to get to this stretch.

In a way, my fingers itch to feel the arc of the steering wheel beneath them. The power of metal churned to life, the exhilaration of hurtling over asphalt. Mama loved it, too. I think both of us made some little walküre cries as we careened along cliffs, and Hell's Gate boiled below us.

# 21

The Wrinkle Queen's gone off her rocker, doing little whoopee singalongs to the *walküres'* shrieks as they gallop — get this — through the sky. The last time she saw the Ring, she tells me, they were on plastic horses suspended by superstrength fishing line, breezing across the Seattle stage.

How did I manage to end up driving along the road from hell with a madwoman?

My own private Miss Havisham.

She's lost in thought now as the skyline of Vancouver appears.

"Do we have to go through Vancouver? Couldn't we go around it somehow?"

"I always go through Vancouver on my way to Seattle," she snaps. "It's how I always go."

So there are other roads, I think. But it's probably too late now.

"Have you got your map?" I ask her.

"You just need to follow the highway signs," she says. But she does pull a map out of the glove compartment.

In a few minutes we're on a gigantic bridge with wall-to-wall traffic, never mind that it's not rush hour. It's traffic that's rushing somewhere, all going way too fast.

"You need to be in the curb lane to exit," the Wrinkle Queen says.

"How can I get over there if there's no break in the traffic?"

"Turn your bloody blinker on!"

She rolls down her window, sticks her scrawny arm out and begins frantically waving her hand. About twenty cars are honking their horns at us.

"There's a break," she screeches. "That minivan is letting us in."

I move over.

We're off the bridge but I think we're going north. Toward the mountains.

"Isn't Seattle south?" I say. We're on another bridge now.

"For God's sake, weren't you watching the signs? We need to get over to Number 99."

"Pardon me, but I was watching the road." We're on a highway that makes you drive a long way before you can turn around. About half an hour later we're on the same bridge going south.

"There's the highway sign," the Wrinkle Queen says. "Just stay on this until we get to the Lougheed…"

It takes about an hour to get through Vancouver. We even have to go through a tunnel that seems to go under the city forever.

"Keep your left blinker on!" she yells at me. "That way people can tell where the edge of your car is."

They still honk their horns at me, though. Maybe it's a B.C. thing.

When we get through the tunnel and outside Vancouver, she tells me to find a place to gas up where there's a restaurant. After what we've been through so far today, I feel like I might need a sugar fix, but I order a Perrier. Once we've told the waitress what we want to eat, the Wrinkle Queen makes a beeline for the bathroom, and she's in there so long I finally go looking for her. I can see her red shoes in the crack beneath a cubicle door.

"Miss Barclay?"

"Thought I'd better have a couple of sips of brandy,"

she says, banging her walker into the stall door as she comes out. "It's going to be me driving for a while until we cross the border."

"You're kidding."

"I'm not," she snaps. "I don't even know if they allow fifteen-year-olds to drive in the state of Washington. We can't take any chances."

So there she is with her claws glued to the steering wheel as we pass the Peace Arch. She barely comes up as high as the dash, and the official at the crossing booth looks down at her in amazement. She gives him one of her big lipsticked smiles and hands over her passport.

"Purpose of your visit?" he says.

"Pleasure," she croons. "I'm taking my granddaughter to see the Ring Cycle of operas in Seattle."

He's not happy that I don't have a passport, but he waves us through.

We drive a few miles past the crossing booths and she pulls over, groaning.

"I hate my legs," she cries. "Just reaching the pedals has given me pain I didn't know was possible."

I help her around the car to the passenger seat and, when she gets settled, she drains the last of her mickey of Courvoisier and pops some Tylenol.

Needless to say, she's asleep before we reach Bellingham, the first big town on the road. In fact she sleeps all the way to Seattle. When we reach the out-skirts, though, I pull into a gas station. You'd think this would wake her up but it doesn't. I still have to pat her hand a couple of times.

"Where are we?" she croaks, her eyes suddenly wide and frightened.

"Seattle. But we need to look at the map to figure out where we're going."

The gas station has a cafe, and we spread the map out on one of the tables.

"We're here." The Wrinkle Queen taps one of her scarlet nails on the map. "And we're staying at Pagliacci's Bed and Breakfast." She flags the waitress and asks to borrow her pen. "It's not hard to get to." She traces the route. Her hand isn't very steady and the line looks like wool that's unraveled.

I memorize the places I need to turn.

"Okay, test me," I say. "I don't want Vancouver happening all over again."

"I told you to follow the signs."

"Yeah. That really worked."

I only make one wrong turn, and it's easy to go into a keyhole, turn around and get back onto the right road.

The Wrinkle Queen seems to be sucking in energy from Seattle. No chance of her drifting off to sleep. Her head with its smushed black hairdo is turning this way and that, and she's chattering like one of those talking dolls.

"Yes. We're getting close now. There's the Space Needle. And the opera house. Just a block or two now."

When I find the bed and breakfast, she's practically leaping out of her seat. We're on a semicircular driveway in front of what looks like an old walk-up apartment building. It's covered with pink stucco and looks like a dried-up birthday cake. It even has those little white Christmas lights on a kind of fancy iron fence on the top of the building.

There's a man at the front door waving at us. His bald head shines beneath the porch light. He's wearing a shirt that looks like it's covered with big red poppies, some cut-off jeans and sandals.

Maybe when you have a beer belly that big, you quit worrying about what you look like.

Miss Barclay has the window rolled down.

"Ricardo!" she calls out. "We're here!"

# 22

"Ricardo!"

"Jean!" he says and stoops to give me a hug. He's wearing some kind of after-shave that smells like vanilla, and I remember it, the vanilla.

"Where's Bernard?" There were always the two of them. Ricardo trying his best to look like a Mexican houseboy, Bernard looking like he'd just put aside his newspaper at some posh men's club.

"He's gone." Ricardo clasps my hand. "We lost him last November."

I give his hand a squeeze. "I'm sorry."

Skinnybones is standing at the back of the Buick, trying to disappear into the shadows of a holly hedge.

"Meet my companion." I beckon to her. "Tamara, this is Ricardo. Runs the best bed and breakfast in Seattle."

Ricardo is a hugger, and he enfolds Skinnybones.

"Hardly anything to hang onto here. We'll remedy that with a few good Pagliacci breakfasts."

Tamara mumbles something, but I don't think it's actually words.

"I've saved the Butterfly Room for you," Ricardo says as he helps me in. "When you told me about your surgeries, I thought — something on the main floor. I know you used to prefer the Parcival Parlor on the third but, as you know, we don't have an elevator. I was always after Bernard to get one installed. Now maybe I'll just do it myself and, if you come next year, you can be back there with the swords and the grail."

"The Butterfly Room will be just fine," I tell him.

Of course, it's more than fine with its little Japanese lamps, decorative fans on the walls, some pieces of antique, lacquered oriental furniture, and bedspreads that look like they've been fashioned from the kimonos of geishas.

Ricardo pushes a button on the radio, and the flower duet from *Madame Butterfly* fills the room like filtered light. I grab his arm, and he helps me to a chair.

Skinnybones has headed out for the rest of the bags.

"How would you and Tamara like a bite of supper?" he says. "I know this is a bed and breakfast, but for special guests I've been known to put together a supper tray. Some pâté, pickled artichokes, fruit. Coffee. It would be my pleasure."

Ricardo, Ricardo, I think we need you at the Triple S ranch.

"Do you have any Courvoisier?"

"All this and Courvoisier, too!" He laughs as he leaves.

"He's a bit…gay," Skinnybones says, dragging in her suitcase.

"I beg your pardon?"

"Well…you know…"

I can't help laughing. "Tamara, my dear, are you really thinking of knocking on the doors of the world of high fashion?"

She blushes and begins unpacking.

"His name's not really Ricardo," I tell her. "He told me once he felt there was a Latin trapped inside him, so he had it legally changed."

Along with the Courvoisier, Ricardo brings a bottle of wine and a soda spritzer. He takes over the little table in the room, pulling up chairs, moving aside the bonsai tree in a porcelain pot, unfolding cloth napkins.

"I'll join you if you don't mind," he says.

"Mind!" I give his hand a pat.

Tamara eases a couple of pieces of artichoke and some crackers and cheese onto her plate. Ricardo spritzes some soda into a glass, adds a cordial and a slice of lemon for her. I can see she's enchanted with these maneuvers. With her fork, she spears an artichoke, tastes it very tentatively and then looks to see if we're watching. A bit of the marinade slicks her smile. Ricardo catches my eye and winks.

"Have you heard anything about the cycle yet?" I ask him between nibbles of baguette slathered with Cognac pâté and sips of a very good California red.

"They're calling this one a Green Ring. Earthy with lots of light and greenery." Ricardo swirls the wine in his glass. "We already had our tickets reserved before Bernard passed on, so a good friend of ours, Adrian, is joining me. I think you'll like him. And Tamara, did I hear you say you're studying to be a model? You definitely need to meet Adrian. When he isn't teaching, he does fashion illustration. He's very good."

When he takes the tray, he leaves a bottle of Courvoisier on the table.

"This is some hotel," Skinnybones says, checking out her hair in a fan-shaped mirror on the wall. The spikes have wilted a bit over the course of the day. She seems to be trying to revive them with a bottle selected from a congregation of toiletries she's gathered on one side of the dresser top.

"Do you think I'd better phone Shirl and Herb?"

she asks, unpacking my cosmetics and putting them on the other side of the dresser. In a minute she's wandering around the room with the cellphone cupped to her ear.

"Yeah, great," she says, catching my eye. "We watched a video and today she's been teaching me all about some classical music she's crazy about...you know, like opera...we might listen to some tonight...the medications aren't hard to keep track of...No, she seems just fine. I haven't had a chance to get bored...I made wild mushroom soup for supper..."

But the day — that drive through Vancouver and then Seattle — has pretty well done her in. She watches a few minutes of TV from her bed, and then she's as dead to the world as Brunnhilde in her long sleep on the fire-shielded rock in *Die Walküre*.

I pour some brandy into a Japanese sake glass and sip it slowly. It seems to ease the pains in my hip and legs, and a small breeze comes in through the window Ricardo opened, a balm to the soul. Another glass and the aches of the world ebb away — the deaths of Mama and Raymond, the betrayal of that music professor who said he wanted to marry me. Gerald. Gerald with his sandy-gray hair and Clark Gable mustache. Gerald of New York, behind the lectern in that summer course in music appreciation. The light of August afternoons falling across his face. 1967. Half a life ago. Odd that it still surfaces. Like rheumatism.

And now Bernard gone. He can't have been old. Sixty-five? A bit older than Ricardo.

I know Ricardo doesn't like anyone smoking in the rooms and, since it's late, I try not to make any noise getting out of the room and moving the walker down the hall to the back door and into the courtyard.

Ricardo is sitting out there, barely visible in the soft light from a couple of Japanese lanterns. Having another glass of wine. He lights my cigarillo from a tea candle sputtering in a small porcelain bowl.

"I think this is when I miss him most," he says. "Eleven-thirty at night, when we'd finished up all the B and B work of the day and we'd sit out here and have a glass of sherry. Bernard would have a cigarette and we'd compare notes on the guests or just sit and listen to a bit of music." He sighs and gestures toward the wine with a questioning look.

I shake my head.

"Now tell me about Tamara. How do you happen to be traveling with her?"

"A paid companion," I confess. Ricardo, I know from experience, is one of those people who can sniff out fabrication like a hound on the trail of blood. Of course I leave some parts out.

"She's been a bit troubled at home, so I think this trip is probably good for her and something of a relief to her family."

"Wants to be a fashion model?" Ricardo says. "One of the great cellophane dreams. I'll light candles for her at St. Joseph's."

"Light a candle for me, too," I say. "I'm the one chaperoning her through that course she's going to be taking."

# 23

Trust the Wrinkle Queen to check us into some flaky hotel where she's totally best friends with the gay guy who runs it. We're in a room that looks like it's been put together after a week of shopping in Chinatown. You can't turn around without bumping into a spread-out fan or some little stunted pine tree in a china pot with pictures on it.

Ricardo treats Miss Barclay like she's one of the royals. But he's a gay guy who can do hair, too.

"I was a stylist for fifteen years," he says, "before I met Bernard and we bought this apartment building and turned it into a bed and breakfast."

Once he's got all the breakfast chores out of the way, and the laundry machines are going full blast, he sets to work on us in the kitchen, washing Miss Barclay's hair, curling and combing it, spraying it back into place.

Then it's my turn.

"Jean says something to go with an Audrey Hepburn dress." He waves his scissors in the air and makes snapping noises with them. "How about a little trim? I can give it body and it'll look very natural, very Sabrina."

"Whatever. But don't chop off too much."

The result is pretty cool, actually, and he tells us to be sure and come into the parlor so he can see how we look all dressed up before we go to the opera.

"You need to meet Adrian. And we'll have tea and English sandwiches before we head out. It'll fortify us for the first act."

Ricardo's friend Adrian is thin and middle-aged. Going gray. Trendy glasses. Simple black suit. He's shy, too, and lets Ricardo, stuffed into a tuxedo that might have fit him a few years back, do the talking.

"Doesn't Jean look stunning?" he says.

The Wrinkle Queen is in her beaded dress, which is way too long for her. She's done some serious shrinking in the last few years, I'm thinking. We've hoisted it up at the waist and added a wide belt from one of the other dresses to cover where we've pinned it.

"I've always loved that beaded dress." Ricardo serves tea from a silver tea set and bone china cups. These aren't Royal Albert, though. Just white with gold trim. "And Tamara! Adrian, who does she remind you of?"

"Audrey Hepburn?" Adrian manages to say through a mouthful of cucumber sandwich.

"Yes! And I won't tell you who did the hair!" Ricardo's practically bouncing in his monkey suit and he's got a camera out, taking pictures of everyone.

After he's done in about half a roll of film, he phones for a taxi.

"Adrian and I will walk over but we'll let you take the picnic hamper."

It's probably filled with stuff like smushed-up liver and diskettes of crusty bread and black fish eggs.

When the Wrinkle Queen tells the taxi driver where to take us, he shrugs his shoulders and says, "Jeez — why is it always me who gets the four-block fares?"

"What!" she screeches at him. "You, I believe, are a public servant. Such insolence! I want your number."

"Don't get your pantyhose in no knot," he says. "Four blocks is more than enough for driving you any-where."

"Tamara," she's still screeching. "Get his number…"

"I haven't got a pen with me," I tell her. It's really kind of funny. "Do you have a pen I can borrow?" I ask the driver.

He's laughing now. "Sure, honey. In your dreams."

"No tip," Miss Barclay tells him as she fishes in her purse for her American money. "Exact change."

"Aw, gee," he says, "and I was hoping to retire on that one."

"Taxi drivers," she fumes. But the whole argument seems to have charged up her batteries. I practically have to race after her, barreling along with her walker. I feel like Red Riding Hood carrying the wicker basket filled with goodies.

You don't have to be a rocket scientist to figure out it's going to be kind of a weird crowd who will pay to listen to people screeching at one another in a foreign language. There's old men who look like mad scientists in tuxedos, and a lot of old ladies, not all that different from the Wrinkle Queen, in fancy dresses that might have been in high fashion when Cher cut her first record. And then there's some polished-up types in expensive summer clothes who look like they've just stepped off the pages of *Vanity Fair*. Throw in some guys with long hair and worn-looking jeans and Value Village suit jackets. And, hey, there's some kids my age with spiked, colored hair, and they're wearing studs and leather.

If I could catch the Wrinkle Queen's eye, I'd glare at her. I could have gotten by without being Audrey Hepburn.

She's busy arguing with an usher about our seats, though.

"I suggest you check your picnic hamper," the usher says through a frozen smile as she's taking us down the aisle.

"I suggest you mind your own business," Miss Barclay tells her.

"You can't set it in the aisle," the usher says.

The Wrinkle Queen gives her a look that says, "What's your point?"

I balance the basket on my lap as if this is something I always do when I go to the theater.

As the lights dim, Miss Barclay hisses at me. "Set it on the floor. The lunch gestapo have gone."

It's dark. The conductor comes out and bows, although you can hardly see him because the orchestra's down below the stage. Everyone claps and then he turns around and waves his wand and the music begins. It's the same music we listened to in the car but here, in this gigantic cave with a zillion people all hushed and hardly breathing, it does make the hair stand up on the back of your neck.

And somehow they've made the stage look like there's light shining through river water, and the Rhine maidens manage to fit their yodeling into all the right spaces in the music. When I look sideways at the Wrinkle Queen, I can see she's right up there with them in her own glitzy outfit, ready to guard the gold and scare off love-hungry dwarfs. Every once in a while she clasps one of her bony hands to her breast as if her heart is going to bounce out of her dress at any minute.

When I was in grade six, I went with my class to the Jubilee Auditorium in Edmonton to something called Symphony for Kids, but it was nothing like this. At the Jubilee, Patty-May Tierney made a little pattern of gum wads on the back of the seat in front of us, and every time the tuba played she held her nose like someone had farted.

Here there's a woman in front of us with a little diamond crown on her white hair. Maybe she's a princess. An old princess with an old prince in a tuxedo beside her? Watching everything through little binoculars you hold with a fancy handle. Opera glasses. The Wrinkle Queen is still mad because I left hers on her bedroom dresser when we were packing.

Miss Barclay sighs when the music fades and then everyone is clapping madly like someone won the biggest race in the world.

"Oh, my, that was absolutely divine!" She flings her mohair shawl over her shoulders.

The usher scowls as I carry the picnic hamper past her when we go outside during the interval. Ricardo has been keeping watch and waves us over to a spot where Miss Barclay can sit down.

"I love the Rhine maidens," he says, helping me unpack the basket. "They look like they're fresh out of a circus act, and that's what Wagner needs — a Ring with a resounding three-ring approach."

"You're right," the Wrinkle Queen laughs. "A touch of Barnum and Bailey but just a touch. Let the music do its work."

They yammer on about the first act, and Miss Barclay and Adrian light up their cigarettes. I was right about the picnic food and, of course, there's wine. Ricardo put in a thermos of lemonade for me, though. It's icy cold and not too sweet. As I sip it, I look around at all the people in their fancy outfits, and the sky shining with a bright gold sunset coming.

It's hard to believe I'm sitting here, in the middle of all this.

I close my eyes.

What is it you're supposed to do? Pinch yourself?

# 24

I have to sleep a fair amount during the day to have the energy for the operas in the evening. Ricardo has taken it upon himself to show Seattle to Skinnybones. They come back in the afternoon chattering about the Pike Place Market, the downtown stores, an excursion along Puget Sound.

On Tuesday, when there's a break in the cycle and the opera house is dark, I go along with them to a fashion show at Adrian's college. Students attending a summer institute are putting it on, mainly for tourists in town taking in the Ring.

The fashions are wild. Men in fishnet and silvery plastic; girls wearing hardly anything at all. But I can see Skinnybones is enthralled. In her mind she's strutting right down the ramps with them.

"God," she pokes my arm, "that one's got bow legs."

"A hazard," I agree, "when you're wearing no more than a couple of doilies and — what is it? — a tool belt?"

After the fashion show, there's a reception. Fruit punch and pastries. Blackberry tarts! I'd forgotten about west coast blackberries. Tamara is flapping at me with a paper napkin, trying to get rid of crumbs that have fallen onto my dress.

As the crowd thins out, Adrian invites us to his office. His studio walls are covered with fashion sketches, figure studies and bric-a-brac. Skinnybones is drinking it all in like some kind of elixir.

"Would you like me to sketch you?" Adrian asks.

"Oh, wow!" Today is a spike hair day, and she's wearing a little top that exposes a fair amount of stomach, and those jeans with scabs of costume jewelry. Adrian places a sheet of paper on a big easel and positions Tamara. He adds some bracelets above the hand that he wants her to rest on her hip.

"This'll take about half an hour," he says, brandishing a piece of charcoal. "Why don't you and Ricardo nip out onto the grounds. You can smoke there, Jean."

There's a ramp for wheelchairs and it's easy to move the walker along it to a bench beneath a huge tree that would never grow in Alberta.

"I think it's wonderful." Ricardo says, "that the two

of you have found one another. It's great that her parents are so accommodating."

I can guess what Skinnybones has been telling him while they've been riding up and down the Space Needle.

"Your generosity…" Ricardo is smiling at me as if I were Eleanor Roosevelt or Mother Teresa. "I mean, to experience the entire Ring — what an introduction to the world of opera and, well, really a whole universe of art and culture that wouldn't be accessible to… Her parents are not especially well off, are they? Pretty blue collar?"

Ricardo's on a roll. The Seattle sunlight and the cigarillos are soothing, too.

"…and sponsoring her for that little course in Vancouver that she has her heart set on. Adrian thinks it may not be much of a school, but what's important is how much it means to her."

Skinnybones emerges from Adrian's studio with her portrait. She's beaming. He's made her appear even taller and thinner, if that's possible. But she does look like something from a Saks ad.

When we get back to Pagliacci's, Ricardo lets her pin the sketch on the wall of our bedroom between two Japanese fans.

He invites us for dinner but today's excursion has

played me out, and it seems like I'm falling asleep even before Tamara has rolled back the kimono bedspread.

When I wake up, the sun is still shining, though, filtering through a bamboo blind. Maybe it's not too late to join them — or at least for an after-dinner coffee.

As I try to get up, though, I see a note propped against the lamp on the night table. It's in Tamara's scrawl: *You were sleeping so I didn't wake you up. Ricardo is taking me to Pioneer Square and we're going to grab lunch there. He says to ring the kitchen and Matt will have a tray for you. He's the cleaning guy. See you this PM.*

God, I've slept through until noon. And no one around to help me get up. I decide it's time to have a little talk with Miss Skinnybones and remind her about the duties of a paid companion.

I can hear someone vacuuming in the hall. When the noise stops, I call out, "Hey, you!" I have to yell three times, though, before the housecleaner comes.

It's a tall, gangly young man, barely out of his teens, I'd guess, with a mop of straw-colored hair and a ring through the side of his nose.

"Miss Barclay?"

"I could use a hand getting out of bed."

He's strong and does a passable job of getting me sitting up on the side of the bed.

"My walker," I say, and he gets it set up and helps me

to the bathroom. Skinnybones has hung an outfit on the bathrobe hook. Not what I'd choose to wear today, but I don't really want nose-ring poking through the closet for something else.

"Ricardo left lunch for you in the kitchen," he says. "You want it here — or there?"

"In the courtyard, if you don't mind."

I can't believe it, but after lunch I fall asleep again in a wicker chair beneath a monkey puzzle tree. It's Skinnybones' scratchy hand that wakes me.

"Do you want to get dressed for the opera now?"

"Where have you been?"

"Pioneer Square. I left you a note." She looks like she could use a nap herself.

"Very thoughtful," I say. "The note was a great help to me getting out of bed and getting dressed."

"You seem to have managed."

"Damn right," I say and light a cigarillo.

She's impatient when she does help me get ready.

"What's the big show tonight?" she asks, trying Mama's diamond brooch in different places on my white knitted gown.

"Quit fiddling," I tell her. "It's too important a piece to wear on a belt. Pin it where it's supposed to go, close to the neckline on the left side."

With a sigh, she positions it and closes the clasp.

"It's *Siegfried* tonight. Wonderful music, but Siegfried is supposed to be a lithe, handsome, Germanic superhero, and they'll likely cast him with some middle-aged overweight tenor. He's the son of the brother and sister who fell in love in the last opera."

"Inbreeding," Tamara declares. "That's how you get idiots. We learned that in Health."

"Except for gods and heroes. Above the law — even the laws of genetics," I say as she redoes my eyebrows.

That evening, though, before the curtain goes up, there's an announcement that the singer playing Siegfried has had an accident and will be unable to move around the stage. He'll sing, but there will be a stand-in actor playing Siegfried.

When he appears, it's as if a sigh ripples through the whole auditorium. This is what a Siegfried should look like.

Tamara looks at me open-mouthed.

"He's lip-syncing," she whispers.

"It works," I say.

*Siegfried* is my favorite of the four operas, but I fall asleep midway through Act One. Tamara rouses me by poking my arm and hissing that I'm snoring. Ricardo fetches me a cup of coffee during the first interval, but I fall asleep again in Act Two, waking only toward the end when Fafner the dragon is killed.

"You're just under the weather today," Adrian says when we go outside for a smoke during the second interval. "It's so hot I think we all felt as if we were right there in that blacksmith's forge. You weren't the only one falling asleep."

"I hate people who sleep at operas," I tell him.

# 25

So get this. Sitting in the Seattle Opera House with the Wrinkle Queen snoring away in the next seat. Her mouth open. Little piggy snorts, and then it's like she quits breathing and I can see the two guys sitting next to us looking worried, like they're wondering if she's died. They're watching her more than the dragon that's ranting around the stage breathing smoke and fire. They look at one another and laugh softly when she lets out another piggy snort and we know she's still alive.

Thank God there's just one more opera to go. *Götterdämmerung*. Twilight of the Gods. The Wrinkle Queen says this is the one where the whole stage is on fire at the end.

Sometimes I think she might not make it. After sleeping through *Siegfried*, yesterday was a day off and she slept through most of that and didn't seem to know where she was when she woke up.

I got scared and called Ricardo. He gave her some brandy on ice and sat and talked with her for about half an hour, and she turned back into the Miss Barclay we all know and love. Telling me to get out that swirly dress that makes you go cross-eyed when you look at it, make sure it's not creased and press it if it is, and see that there's smokes and brandy in her purse.

She says she's determined to buy lunch for everyone tonight during the interval.

"I'm tired of packing that picnic basket around," she grumbles (as if she ever carried it). "We'll have Champagne."

Ricardo helps me pin the dress around the waist before he combs her hair.

While he's busy with the brush and hairpins, I decide to give Shirl a call.

"Honey, how're you doin'?" Shirl says. I can hear the gremlins in the background. "I'm glad you called 'cause I was going to call you later."

"Oh."

"Yes. Lyle…" She's covering the receiver and yelling. "Lyle, you let your sister have that…I don't want to tell you again…

"Oh my," she says. "We miss you, Tamara. Anyway, I don't know if you remembered but it's Lizzie's birthday on Sunday and I was thinking it'd be so nice if you could come home — even for a couple of hours — if Miss Barclay can get along without you…"

"Oh…hey!" I say. "Lizzie's birthday. Let me check with her." I cover the receiver and count silently to twenty.

"Shirl?"

"I'm here, sweetie."

"Miss Barclay planned for me to go with her to visit her nephew on Sunday. He lives out of town and she wants me to drive."

"You're driving her around?"

"Well, it's not far. But a little far to take a taxi."

"But —"

"It's okay. She's still got her license, and I have my learner's permit. Maybe I can come over a little later in the week. I'd like to get a gift for Lizzie and I haven't had time to go out shopping."

"Sure, honey…"

"Give those two my love, and say hi to Herb."

When I push the end button on the phone, it's very quiet. Ricardo is looking at me. I realize he's listened to the whole conversation — my end of it.

"They don't know, do they?" he says.

"No," I can barely hear my own voice.

"Ricardo…" The Wrinkle Queen is sputtering.

"Not my business," he says, giving Miss Barclay's do a final spray. As he leaves, I notice him shaking his head.

"You stupid girl," she hisses at me.

"I didn't know..."

"Stupid. Call a taxi. I'm not about to miss *Götterdämmerung* because you haven't had sense enough to..." She doesn't finish the sentence. "I think I want my white stole tonight."

"You want a fur wrap!" I yell at her. "When it's ninety in the shade?"

"Don't you question me," she says, her voice stronger than I've heard it in days. "I happen to be the benefactress, a detail you would do well to remember. All of this cozying up to Ricardo and gallivanting around Seattle. What did you expect? That he wouldn't figure things out?"

"What was I supposed to do?" I ask her. "Stay here and listen to you snoring away all day long?"

"Stupid! Stupid! Stupid!" She's chanting.

"Oh, drop it."

"What did you say?"

"I'm calling the taxi."

Needless to say, things are still tense at the opera house. The Wrinkle Queen doesn't fall asleep in this one. She's too mad. There's the big bonfire with Brunnhilde on her horse riding through the flames. And then the sky castle of the gods disappears. Everything's back to water and the Rhine maidens.

Ricardo and Adrian don't come to find us. No Champagne is ordered, and the Wrinkle Queen has a double brandy during each interval. I end up carrying her white rats, and I feel like everyone in the auditorium is looking at me.

When the final curtain comes down, she glares at me.

"What?" I'd like to throw down her stole and stomp on it.

"You've done your best to spoil it. But you haven't. You can't kill the music. You can't destroy the Twilight."

I look up at the ceiling of the auditorium and whisper, "Give me a break. Twilight!"

"Don't you be muttering under your breath around me." She thinks she's whispering but it's loud enough for everyone around us to hear. "I've put up with your lack of consideration, clothes strung all over the bedroom, all that clutter of stuff on the bureau...your hair in my hairbrush..."

"Yeah, well try putting on make-up with a glass full of false teeth sitting on the —"

"For what I'm paying you..."

"Big deal."

"It *is* a big deal. I'm footing the hotel bill, Ricardo's *my* friend, and you get him to take you out sightseeing with no thought —"

"I suppose we should have dragged you half dead out of your bed?"

"You should have stayed with me. That's what a paid companion —"

"Give it a rest."

We don't speak to one another on the cab ride back to Pagliacci's.

At least we're leaving in the morning! I shout in my mind. Leaving in the morning!

The bedroom seems impossibly hot and, after the Wrinkle Queen finally falls asleep, hot and noisy with her snoring. I slip into jeans and decide to sit out in the courtyard for a while. I've plunked myself into the big peacock chair before I see Ricardo sitting in the darkness off in a corner.

"Hey," he says. "So what did you think of *Götterdämmerung?*"

"Lots of fire. Lots of loud singing."

He looks at me, his eyebrows raised.

"Okay, so it was amazing," I add. "Miss Barclay loved it, I think. She's been dreaming about it for months."

"Why..." He searches for words. "Why didn't you just arrange with everyone for you to come with her?"

"I guess...she didn't think they would let her leave the nursing home for such a long trip. Her nephew... She has some bad days when she's kind of out of it."

"And what will you do when she has one of those days?"

180

"I have her medications."

Even in the dark, I can see Ricardo shaking his head.

"And your family?"

"They're not my family."

"Can I persuade you to call them and let them know what's really happening?"

I close my eyes. I don't want to look at anything or anyone right now. Especially Ricardo, who's been treating me like his own kid. Do all gay guys treat you like you're their best friend, part of the family?

"It would all be finished then," I say. "I'd probably be put back in government care. Go into some crappy group home."

Ricardo has moved to one of the chairs closer to where I'm sitting.

"It's only a week, Ricardo, the fashion course. Just a week and we'll be back. Nothing's happened to her so far. She'll be fine. She'll just rest in the hotel while I'm off at the course during the day."

"You want it that bad?" he says.

I nod my head.

"I was going to do some phoning," he says. "Instead I think I'll do some praying."

# 26

She's packing. Skinnybones. Running around in shorts and one of those little bits of an undervest that teenage girls wear these days. But I don't feel like getting up. All those hours, all those incredible hours of music and drama, I wrap to me. I won't let it be over.

"Are you okay?" she says.

"I…am…wonderful. I've seen the Ring. All of it."

"Except ninety percent of *Siegfried*, which you slept through."

"Ah…well. At least I got to see what a real Siegfried should look like. Those legs! Now I can die."

She laughs. She's in a good mood. I get her to help me up. She has my candy-striped blouse and a red flared skirt set out for me. And my straw hat with the red ribbon. Does terrible things to Ricardo's hairdo, but…

"Tell Ricardo I'd like to settle the bill."

He comes in. Smiling. And gives me a kiss on the cheek. The old marshmallow. I give him a hundred-dollar tip.

"No," he says. "I couldn't."

"You can and you will. You've done our hair and fed us and gone out of your way to keep this juvenile off the paths of delinquency."

Adrian, too, comes over to wave us goodbye. Tamara holds up the scrolled portrait, tied with a ribbon, for him to see before she stows it in the trunk.

And then we're driving north. I'm very tired and I don't say anything when Tamara finds a radio station playing that kind of frenetic music kids listen to today. As long as she keeps the volume low. After all, the Ring is over. Brunnhilde has forgiven Siegfried and plunged into the fire. The smoke has cleared.

I sleep until we get close to the border. Skinnybones remembers to pull over well ahead of time so I can get into the driver's seat. But it's drifted away from me. What to do.

"Put it in gear," she says. "Keep your foot on the brake."

My foot doesn't do what I want it to do. My leg is numb.

"It's okay," she says. "If they ask, I'll tell them I'm just driving for a little while until you're feeling better."

But the crossing patrol doesn't ask, and I fall asleep again until we're in Vancouver. On Granville Street, heading downtown.

"Where's the hotel?" Tamara asks. "We need the Vancouver map."

She pulls over and parks on South Granville.

"After the bridge, turn left onto Davie Street," I say. "We need to go along Davie and then turn left again on Thurlow."

"Why is it always left," she groans. "I hate left turns."

"Then it's a right on Beach, and that's actually just a few blocks along Thurlow, if I remember. The hotel's right on Beach."

It is one of the older hotels — old even when I first began coming to Vancouver on vacation — with south-facing windows peering out of a veil of ivy.

"Did I remember to tell you I'd like Suite 307?" I ask the desk clerk.

"Yes, ma'am," she says. "It's all ready for you."

"Lots of memories," I say. The elevator with its wrought-iron door, the cream-colored hallway with its wainscotting and worn Victorian rug.

"Look," I tell Tamara when she's got our bags in. "You can look out the window and see the ships anchored in English Bay."

"It's great," she says. "You want to get some supper now? I'm not hungry."

I can see she has other things on her mind.

"Nor am I," I tell her, "but I could use a smoke."

"It's a smoking room. No problem." A bundle of nerves, she can stay seated for no longer than ten seconds at a time. She paces back and forth, flips through magazines the hotel has left on the coffee table, flicks the TV channels relentlessly, checks out the window every couple of minutes.

"Settle down. You're making me dizzy."

She grabs the Vancouver map and drops into the wingback chair.

"Okay if I go and see where that school is?"

"You go ahead. I'm fine." To tell the truth, more than anything in the world, I'd appreciate being alone right now. This suite is filled with ghosts. Mama liked to sit at that little writing desk. And Myra, who taught social studies and traveled with me a few years before the big C did her in — she'd sit in the wingback chair in the corner, reading or doing a crossword puzzle before we'd head out to a play or for dinner. It seems like her words hover in the room. *That was quite the effect, a lightning storm across the bay — perfect backdrop for* The Tempest. *Can you think of a four-letter word for perspicacious? Would you like a nightcap?*

But despite feeling exhausted, I can't fall asleep now. The remote to the TV is within reach and I click the power on. The picture congeals into one of those dreadful reality shows that everyone seems to watch in the lounge at the Triple S ranch. I quickly find the arrow for changing channels. Someone is making over a hideous room — wait, the makeover's already happened. Whose idea was it, I wonder, to glue a floral bedspread onto a wall and surround it with bamboo framing? On the next channel, there's a riveting game of lawn bowling in progress.

At least there's concert music on Bravo. I close my eyes. Mendelssohn. So different from Wagner. I wonder if any of the music Tamara has listened to in the past week has managed to penetrate. She'd probably never admit it if it did, spiky as she is — and with that kind of shell around her.

She reminds me of that boy I taught back in the mid-1960s. Graham? Gordon? Answered an essay question on a grade nine final with a long poem that sounded like it had been written by Dr. Seuss. So clever. So bad. I remember laughing until my sides ached.

She's back. Skinnybones. Trying not to make any racket as she comes in. Likely hoping I'm fast asleep so she won't have to talk to me. When she sees I'm awake, she says, "Hey — thought you'd be dead to the world. After the day you've had."

"Did you find the school?"

"Well…yeah," she says. "But it doesn't really look like a school. More like a church."

"A church!"

"I think it probably was a church, and maybe it's still partly a church. I mean, there's a bell tower and it's got those churchy windows that go to a point at the top. There's a big bulletin board at the front, though, that lists all the things going on. Yoga classes. Ceramics. Alcoholics Anonymous. And Universal Style."

# 27

The Wrinkle Queen laughs when I tell her the modeling course is being held in an old church. A laugh that's half laugh and half cough — and, of course, she's sitting up in bed, groping around for her cigarillos.

I don't tell her that someone in the alley behind the church tried to sell me some dope.

She's awake half the night smoking and coughing, turning the TV on and off. I think her hearing's going. Someone pounds on the wall of the room beside us to get us to turn the sound down.

"Will you listen to the racket they're making next door," the Wrinkle Queen says. "I wonder what they're doing in there?"

All of this, of course, means that I'm awake half the night, too. In the morning I have ghost eyes, dark circles on the white sheet of my face. A great look for my first day.

The Wrinkle Queen's asleep when I leave. To top everything off, it starts to rain when I'm a block away from the hotel, and by the time I get to the church, I'm soaked.

There's a janitor watching me as I come in.

"Universal Style?" I say, pushing my wet hair off my face.

"Downstairs." He points toward a hallway.

There's a stairway at the end of it, and the first door I see in the basement has the same star and sign that was on the Whyte Avenue office door in Edmonton: *Universal Style — Training for the Stars of Tomorrow.*

When you go through the door, there's kind of a little foyer and one of those church hall kind of tables — the ones with collapsing legs.

Jude Law model man is sitting there. Brad Silverstone.

"Hey, Tamara! Great, you got here okay." There's a couple of registration packages on the table. He fills in a receipt when I give him an envelope with the rest of the money.

"Just one more to come," Brad says. "Ethan. He's from Edmonton, too."

A girl with long blonde hair pokes her head around the door.

"Alicia," Brad calls to her. "Take Tamara in and introduce her around."

"I'm an assistant," Alicia tells me. "They gave me a deal on my registration, and believe you me I needed it after working at the McDonald's in Nelson for the past year. First we'll get you a name tag."

Through the foyer, there's a big room. Alicia takes me past some orange room dividers where there's a couple of old sofas with coffee tables in front of them plus three tables you can sit at.

There are ten people. Three boys and seven girls. They have names like Madison and Mason and Brittany and Zachary.

I sit down at a table where a young man is sitting by himself. His name tag says Christophe. He seems scared to death to look at me or anyone else, and I'm thinking I kind of know how he feels. I wish I had dry clothes.

"Hi," I say.

He blushes and says, "Hey." And then he adds, "Can I get you some coffee?"

"Is there any juice?"

He lopes over to a counter under the basement windows and grabs a carton.

As I'm peeling off the plastic straw, Brad Silverstone

brings in Ethan. He looks like he's at least forty-five. Everybody's jaws drop.

"Never too old to pursue a dream," he giggles.

Not only old, but he has bad teeth.

Brad points to some metal chairs over by a bunch of gym risers set end to end to make a kind of runway.

"Can I get everyone over here?"

A couple of middle-aged women have straggled in from the staff room to join him.

Brad introduces them.

Ava, with bleached blonde hair in a mountain of Dolly Parton curls and a load of make-up that reflects the light from the overhead fluorescents, will be doing sessions, we are told, on skin and nail care, make-up artistry, hair styling and color analysis. She has a little, high-pitched voice, and it seems like she has to stop and draw a breath two or three times a sentence.

All of us are trying not to look at one another, but the red-headed girl named Mason must have caught someone's eye, because she's giggling and trying to cover it up.

Waltraud, the other instructor, glares at Mason. She's a thin, stringy brunette in ballet workout clothes.

"In my classes you will improve your poise and movement. You will learn how to exercise and what to eat. Dressing and runway technique. It takes work to be a model, and you *will* work, and not be laughing so much. If you think it's a joke, you will be thinking again."

Mason has quit giggling.

Now Jude Law Brad takes over. He's in a T-shirt and blue jeans so tight it's hard to imagine how he got into them without doing damage to body parts.

"Photography. Creating videos. Fashion shoots," he says. "I'm the man with the camera. Believe me, when this week is finished, you're going to have an amazing portfolio to take with you. And we'll do individual videos, too — ones you wouldn't be ashamed to screen in L.A."

He likes to talk, Brad, and he has a way of making people feel comfortable. Our first class of the day is with him.

"I want you to feel totally at ease in front of the camera, so choose one or two things to wear from the racks — maybe something amusing — and just have some fun. We have a few props over in the corner of the room."

There's a big folding screen, a kind of long, padded sofa, one of those giant exercise balls and a wicker chair like the one Ricardo has in his courtyard.

The racks are filled with all kinds of clothing — some vintage, some that looks like costumes from a theater — and there are boxes of hats and shoes. I'm still feeling damp so I take a jacket and vest from a man's pin-striped suit, a dress shirt and a funky tie with colored triangles on it, along with a pair of baggy jeans. One of the smaller rooms off the main hall is a dressing room for the girls, and I quickly change out of my wet clothes.

Brad is shooting pictures of Madison when I come out. She looks like a movie star. Actually she looks like quite a few movie stars, in a dress not too different from the ones the Wrinkle Queen took to Seattle. Brad is loving taking pictures of her on the peacock chair and the sofa. In some, he has her hold a cocktail glass with a bit of juice in it.

When it's my turn, he says, "The return of Annie Hall! Not bad, but let's find you a bowler hat, and let's loosen the necktie, make that collar as rumpled and interesting as possible."

It seems like he takes a hundred pictures of me lying on the floor or the sofa, or draped over the big purple ball, or dancing with a hat rack.

We spend the rest of the morning with Ava, as she does make-up demonstrations on one of the girls, Lesley, and a boy with bad skin, Tyler. The sunless tanning cream she uses on Tyler, though, turns his whole face orange.

"The problem with sunless creams," she squeaks and draws in a deep breath, "is that skins react with different degrees (another breath) of sensitivity."

Desperately, Ava squishes some dark coloring into his hair to try to make his skin look lighter.

Mason is having a small fit of giggles that is catching on and rippling through the class. Tyler is starting to look like a pumpkin whose top leaves have been blackened by a killer frost.

Even though most of the students are grabbing lunch at a sushi restaurant on Davie, I decide I'd better make a quick trip back to the hotel to check on the Wrinkle Queen.

She's managed to get up and get dressed and is in the wingback chair, smoking and watching TV.

"You should have been here a few minutes earlier," she says. "You would have seen yourself on television."

# 28

Watching TV news is something I've done very little of in the last few years — even less at the Triple S ranch where the televisions in the common room and the lounge are as old and tired as most of the people watching them. When they actually work, they're tuned to *Wheel of Fortune* or reruns of the *Mary Tyler Moore Show*.

I've always preferred a good book. Among the items Skinnybones and I failed to pack, though, was anything to read. When I went down to the cafe for breakfast, I noticed a couple of shelves of reading material in a nook in the lobby, but most of it was ancient Reader's Digest condensed books, which I refuse to read, and some copies of Doubleday Club selections from the 1940s. I didn't read Frank Yerby and Frances Parkinson Keyes then and I don't plan to begin now. Luckily there was also a copy of Henry James' *Portrait of a Lady*.

But a couple of chapters of that was enough to make me turn on the TV in the suite. Some dreadful morning show with a woman, face frozen into a smile, big capped teeth, interviewing a movie actress who is in Vancouver making a film. A horror movie, from the sound of it.

"Hollywood North!" the interviewer laughs through her teeth. "Watch out for the gore in Gastown!"

After commercials, the station brings on the noon news. I'm about to click it off when the screen is filled with a face.

It's a school picture of Skinnybones — her hair in some crazy lopsided hairdo that looks like it's being held in place with butterfly paper clips — smiling what she believes to be her killer model smile.

"Have you seen this teenager?" a voice is saying. "Police are uncertain when fifteen-year-old Tammy Schlotter, who also goes by the name Tamara Tierney, and an elderly woman to whom she was a companion…" Now my picture comes up. It's thirteen years old — the one I have on the piano in the house. "…eighty-nine-year-old Jean Barclay disappeared from Barclay's Glenora home.

"At this point, police are uncertain if there is foul play involved. The disappearance of Barclay's vehicle, a 1997 red Buick, from her garage is another piece in the puzzle of the missing teen and senior. Anyone with any information is asked to call the RCMP at…"

"Maybe you'd better phone the Shadbolts," I tell Tamara when she comes back at lunchtime.

"No," she says, flinging off the crumpled clothes she's wearing, pulling on a shirt and the costume-jewelry jeans from the closet. "Have you had lunch?"

"Late breakfast. I'm not hungry. Maybe if you call and explain…"

"You think they'd let me stay here and finish the course?" Suddenly she's laughing and then swearing under her breath. "I wasn't born yesterday."

"Close," I remind her.

"You should be worrying. What do you think they're going to do to you?"

"You know, dear, I really don't care."

Now she's looking at me with fire in her eyes.

"Of course you don't care. You got to go to all your stupid operas. I've only started my course. It's not fair."

"Whoever told you life was going to be fair?"

"Oh, can it."

She's pacing around the room, muttering.

"I'll call Shirl and Herb tonight," she says, "just to say we're okay, but I'm not going to tell them where we are."

When she comes back from afternoon classes, she decides to make the call before we go out to eat.

"Hi, it's me," I hear her say. "I'm fine. Remember, I said Miss Barclay wanted me to drive her to visit...yes, well, guess what?...her nephew lives in Jasper and he wanted us to stay with him for a couple of days...No, he's not here right now. He's taken her out for supper. I didn't feel like going...Call you when they get back?...Sure, if I'm still awake...His name? Magwitch. Phillip Magwitch...Bye, now...My show's coming on...Bye..."

As she gets my walker ready and finds me a sweater, I tell her, "If the fashion modeling thing doesn't pan out, you should consider writing fiction. Only you may want to try coming up with names Dickens hasn't already used."

The car has been baking all day in the hotel parking lot and she turns the air-conditioning on full blast as soon as the key's in the ignition.

"Something less than a windstorm would be nice," I say. "You have some idea where we're going for dinner?"

"There's a restaurant on Fourth Avenue." She looks at me out of the corner of her eye.

"Fourth? You want to get into bridge traffic?"

"It's not hard," she says, waiting for a break in the Beach Avenue rush-hour traffic. "I checked the map. We're really close to the Burrard Bridge."

On Fourth Avenue Skinnybones gets to try parallel

parking. A lot of angry drivers pull out around us during the process.

"Maybe Herb needs to give you a few more lessons," I say.

She scowls as we go into the restaurant.

"So, how was your afternoon class?" I ask her when we've placed our orders.

"The woman who's having us do exercises is a Nazi. Her name is Waltraud and there's this guy in the class, Ethan, who calls her Well-trod because she looks like she's been around the block a few times."

The server is quick to bring us our drinks. With a double brandy in hand, I can even forgive her for sprinkling her waitress chatter with "you guys" and "no problem."

"Brad, now, he's a different story." She's rooting for something in the bag she's brought with her. "You know, the one I told you who looks like Jude Law? He took photos of everyone this morning and printed up five for each of us."

She pulls the photos out of a manila envelope. Skinnybones *is* photogenic, kibitzing around in an outfit that looks like a mixture of something Cary Grant would wear and Charlie Chaplin's Little Tramp costume.

"He's a good photographer," I agree.

"Tomorrow we're all supposed to bring something really dressy to put on for the photo shoot. What do you think — the green dress or the black?"

She chatters on about the class, but I can see, at the back of it all, some fear that the forces of social care and moral retribution might well swoop down on us before the week is out.

"Who did you talk to on the phone?" I ask her.

"Shirl." Tamara toys with the croutons in her Caesar salad. "I guess Mr. Mussbacher went by your place on Saturday just to see how things were going and discovered there was no one home. Had the police come and open the place up. Check the garage."

I signal the waitress and tell her to bring me another of the same.

"A double Courvoisier?"

"That's what I said."

"No problem," she gushes.

# 29

The Wrinkle Queen is pretty well blitzed but I suggest a drive out to Jericho Beach and she agrees. I think she's sick of being in the hotel all day. While we sit at one of the patio tables outside the restaurant and she has her smoke, I check the map for the best route to the beach.

The rain of this morning has cleared away, and the few leftover clouds seem to have stuck around as props for the sunset. I know about Jericho Beach because during coffee break Christophe told me he's been going there every evening since he's been in Vancouver. It's a good place to walk his aunt's dog.

I find a bench for Miss Barclay, but she's having trouble keeping her eyes open. It looks like she's okay sitting up, though, with one of those big Vancouver trees on one side of her and her walker on the other.

There's a guy walking a dog along the beach and, as he gets closer, he waves.

I walk down to meet him. It turns out Christophe isn't so shy when there's just the two of us and an old German shepherd. Huckleberry.

"Named by my aunt." Christophe smiles. "Her last name's Finn."

"Hi, Huckleberry." I scratch behind his ears and he licks my hand. "Huckleberry Finn. Huckleberry hound."

Christophe is from Kamloops.

"Cowboy country," he says. "I'm scared of horses, though. They're even scarier than Waltraud."

He tells me about the dress-up outfit he's taking to class tomorrow. His grade twelve grad suit.

"It's not really Armani but it looks like it. Are you through school?"

"Not yet," I say. "I've got a few courses to pick up yet."

"Shall we walk?"

Huckleberry's ears perk up.

"Okay — but not far. I need to keep an eye on my…my grandmother. She's on the bench having a cat-nap. A little too much brandy with supper."

Christophe picks up a piece of driftwood and chucks it far out onto the sand. As Huckleberry goes bounding after it, he touches my hand and turns toward me.

"You're her, aren't you?" he says. "The runaway girl with the red Buick?"

"What?"

"It was on the news." He doesn't lose contact with my hand. "At my aunt's, we always eat at TV tables in the den. And tonight…" He picks up another stick for Huckleberry. "Tonight there was a story about a teenage girl from Edmonton who's gone missing with an elderly woman."

"Shit."

"Seems the girl phoned and said they were in Jasper but gave some false names. So…they're trying to decide if she's been kidnapped or if she did the old lady in and took her car, or if the two of them are just doing their own Thelma and Louise thing."

"I guess everyone will know by tomorrow."

We head back to the part of the beach just down from the bench where Miss Barclay is snoozing.

"Maybe not," Christophe says. "Most of the kids in the class probably aren't news watchers. And Brad…I think he's likely too busy playing with digital images on his computer, or out having a good time. Now Waltraud…maybe. Although I expect she's more into bondage videos. And Ava? What would Ava be watching on TV?"

"A Dolly Parton special?"

"Yes!"

Christophe and I high-five each other.

"I won't breathe a word," Christophe says. "I want you here all week."

We walk back to the bench. Miss Barclay is awake now, smoking. Huckleberry sniffs her red patent-leather shoes and then pees against the leg of the bench.

"Where did that pathetic creature come from?" she says.

"I hope you don't mean me," Christophe laughs and nods to the Wrinkle Queen. "I'm taking the course with Tamara."

"A chance meeting." She gives me one of her looks. "I'm afraid I'm tiring, my dear. I think we'd best get back to the hotel."

Christophe opens the car door for her and puts the walker in the back seat.

"Cool wheels!" he whispers to me before he and Huckleberry begin running back the way they came.

He winks at me when I come in fifteen minutes late the next morning. I decided to drive and park in the church parking lot rather than carry the opera dress seven blocks, but I hadn't thought about what Vancouver traffic can be like during rush hour. The Wrinkle Queen, of course, was sleeping when I left, so I wasn't able to check with her about taking the car. For only seven blocks, though, I figured nothing could go wrong. Besides, how would she even know?

Ava is in full swing, going on about color combinations. She has Ricci, a girl with pasty skin and hair that's been dyed blue-black, in the make-up chair.

"Now this works wonderful," she's saying in her Minnie Mouse voice, as she drapes a chartreuse green scarf against Ricci's neck and over her shoulders. "See how it brings out the green in her eyes." She pauses to suck in air. "And, you know, if we add a bit more green eye shadow, the effect is even more dramatic."

When we get into our formal outfits, Waltraud has us do different runway combinations. Solos, in twos and then trios and four abreast. Brad has some techno music with a thudding bass on the boom box, and he's busy taking a thousand pictures. When the catwalk drill is finished, he has us pose against colored panels he's brought in.

"Always arch your neck, Tamara," he says to me, "and tip your head a bit to the left. That's it. Perfect. Now let's try one of you holding an American Beauty rose. Yes, inhale, even more deeply — and a little less smile…"

I ask him to take some pictures of Christophe and me together — as if we're on a prom date. The bit of face cream and color Ava has put on Christophe's face makes him glow under Brad's lights. He's shiny and handsome with that kind of shy look that would be great in a GQ ad.

"Send your resume to Calvin Klein," I tell him when we're finished.

"Yeah, right." He laughs softly. "Let me get out of my monkey suit and I'll walk you to your hotel."

"We don't have to walk," I tell him. "We can drive. The car's right outside."

But when we go outside, the parking lot is practically empty and the Buick is gone.

# 30

Skinnybones has her fashion school Twinkie with her when she comes back at lunch time. Thankfully, no overweight police dog. Both of them look like they've stared over some ledge and seen the end of the world.

She's late, which I find annoying, but there's still time to drive me to the beauty parlor over on Burrard where I've set up a full afternoon of appointments. Massage. Nails. Pedicure. Hair. She can leave the car and pick me up after class.

"Can't," she says when I tell her the schedule. "No car."

"Now, Tamara," I say, "that's not even remotely funny. If you're trying to irritate me, you're doing a good job. First of all you're half an hour late and now…"

"It's gone."

"What do you mean?"

"Someone stole it from the church parking lot." She sits down on the chair by the door and begins to cry.

This is totally unnerving.

"What was it doing at the church parking lot?"

The Twinkie tells me the rest of the story.

"I knew you had nerve." I light a cigarillo. "But I never pegged you for a moron. You're not even supposed to be driving on your own."

"I'm better on my own," she sobs. "You just make me nervous."

"And how could someone take it? You have the keys."

"I thought I had the keys but when I checked, I didn't. I was rushing to carry my outfit into class. I must have forgotten…"

So this is it, I think. The twilight, the world burning, Valhalla crumbling.

"I'm going to phone the police," I say as I finish my smoke. "That Buick is worth a fair chunk of money."

"If you phone, it'll all be over." Tamara's voice is small.

"Read my lips, Tamara," I say. "It *is* over. They're going to be taking us home."

"You want that?" she flares. "You want to go back to sneaking around to have a smoke, stupid idiots trying to get you to make Valentine cards and paper snowflakes like you're in kindergarten…"

I pull out another cigarillo, and the model boy rushes over to light it.

I remember when I bought the Buick. On sale just before a new year's releases. Fully loaded. An opera recording never sounded as good as it did on that car's sound system. I can recall driving down Jasper Avenue in Edmonton and some twit with a deliberate five o'clock shadow and hair sticking up in Vaseline peaks was playing rap rubbish tuned to illegal sound decibels, and I turned the "March of the Toreadors" up as high as the volume would go and opened my window. He stared at me like he'd encountered an alien force.

"So you want me to just let it go. Let some Davie Street druggie drive away in my Buick and no consequences."

"Yes!" she screams. "If it'll buy me time. We don't need the car right now."

"It'd probably be better to go to the police," the young man says. His face is red with the embarrassment of the scene. "In the long run —"

"I don't care about the long run," she yells at him. "I just want to do the course. I want to be a model."

"I know," he says softly, and squeezes her shoulder.

"Pick up the phone," I tell her, and I'm pleased my

voice is strong, not the betrayal it sometimes is these days.

"No," she whimpers.

"Pick up the goddamn phone. And call a taxi. I am going to the Aloe Vera on Burrard Street. I am going to get my hair done. I am going to have a manicure. And a pedicure. And a massage. And then I'm going to go to the lounge in the nearest hotel. I can do it without your help, Tamara. In fact, I think it would be very good if we don't see each other for a while."

It's the Twinkie who phones and then helps me to the elevator and out onto the street.

"Do you want me to call the police?" he asks as I get into the taxi.

"No," I say. "In for a dime…"

He gives me a little salute as the cab pulls away.

The masseuse at the Aloe Vera is sweet and gentle. I can imagine her as Suzuki, the maid in *Butterfly*.

"That feel good, eh?" she says after working on my shoulders. "Lotta stress there."

"You've got that right."

The girl who does my nails isn't quite as gentle, but at least she isn't a chattering twit like the hairdresser.

Agnes-Anne.

"So you're from outta town." Agnes-Anne clicks the blades of her scissors like they're some instrument in a mariachi band. "A lot of our outta town customers come back when they're in Vancouver. Probably it's because Aloe's what I call a one-stop come in and relax and drop parlor. Get everything at once. Not many shops'll bring you a cappuccino while you're getting your hair dried but we've been doing it — golly — almost since we opened. You wanna try this new shade of black? Perfect for your complexion. Midnight cherry — just a touch of red in it. And I can see you like to wear red so it all works."

She begins brushing on the Midnight Cherry goop.

"You couldn't have picked better weather," she says. "Just ideal for the beach except for that little bit of rain we had yesterday morning and we needed that to refresh the flowers and grass. I always say let it rain a little bit in the morning and get it out of the way for the rest of the day. You been spending time at the beach?"

"I was planning to," I tell her, "but I misplaced my surfboard."

When she's finished, though, I like what she's done, working a couple of subtle curls into the upsweep. And it is a rich shade of black. A beautician gives me a facial and then reapplies my make-up.

"All ready for a big date?" she says with hardly a trace of condescension.

"Something like that."

"You want me to telephone for a cab?"

"No," I say, "I'm just going next door to the hotel."

She helps me get my walker out to the street. I've never been more ready for a brandy and a smoke, and the bar sign in the window of the hotel is a friendly beacon. There's a wheelchair ramp so I don't need to negotiate stairs.

I'm almost to the door when it happens. The wheel on the walker catches against a ridge on a planter and, struggling to keep my balance, I go plummeting into a mass of castor beans in full bloom. Before the pain sweeps over me, I see those big blossoms waving like red flags above me.

My color, I think, and then everything goes black.

# 31

I've never seen her so angry. While Christophe takes the Wrinkle Queen down to the cab, I head for the bathroom. My eyes are red and the skin around them is puffy. Washing my face in ice cold water helps, and then I do my make-up.

"We have time to grab some sushi on the way back to class," Christophe says when he returns.

He has elegant hands, Christophe. Elegant the way he holds a California roll. Elegant, I've noticed, with his thumb tucked into the front pocket of his jeans, or his fingers smoothing the lapels of a suit jacket.

"What if the car is just driven a ways and abandoned?" he says, his hands cupping a small bowl of green tea.

"I can't think about it," I say. And it's true.

Everything has become too complicated. "Do you remember what we have first this afternoon?"

"More runway routines with Drill Sergeant Waltraud. Then, if the weather stays nice, we're doing an outside shoot with Brad down at the beach. Wait till you see me in a bathing suit." He wiggles his eyebrows at me.

The runway routines take about an hour.

"Concentrate," Waltraud snaps at me. "You're out of sync with the rest."

I try, but it's not easy. Too many things have been happening.

Has there been anything in the newspaper, I wonder.

For the beach shoot, a sportswear shop has given us clothes left over from last year's line. I find a red sun dress that works with the sandals I'm wearing. The Wrinkle Queen would like this one.

As we trek down to the beach parks along English Bay, it feels like the field trips we used to take in elementary school. Ethan is cracking people up by walking funny, goose-stepping, power jogging. It's a brilliantly sunny afternoon, and, with Christophe beside me, it's possible to forget everything that's been happening. At least for a few minutes.

But when Brad is taking some shots of me in a gazebo, I hear a loud booming sound coming across the water. Probably from construction work going on somewhere, but it makes me think of the cannon fire Pip hears at the beginning of *Great Expectations* — the convict ship's signal that prisoners have escaped.

Can they put the Wrinkle Queen and me in prison? The thought of her in jail is kind of funny. Heaven help the warden and the guards.

"That's it," Brad says. "A nice natural smile. Now lean your elbows against the railing."

They have special jails for kids. Young offenders centers. Do they have special jails for old people? Senior detention centers?

Maybe that's what places like the Sierra Sunset Seniors' Lodge really are.

Christophe is posing on some rocks. He's wearing baggy shorts slung low on his torso. I can tell he works out.

"Do you think she'll be okay?" he asks on the way back to the church. "Getting to the hotel from the beauty parlor on her own?"

"Sure. She said something about going to a lounge after. If she's not at the hotel when I get back, I'll go over to Burrard Street and look for —"

Christophe suddenly grabs my arm. "I think maybe there's someone waiting for you at the church."

In the driveway by the front entrance there's an

RCMP cruiser and a mountie leaning against it, watching all of us straggling back from the beach.

My first impulse is to run, but then I think, if the police have tracked me this far, there's really no point. It's all over. I don't plan to go out of my way, though, and lie down at the mountie's feet. As we go in, he eyes each of us, and then he's talking to Brad.

When I come out of the change room, Christophe is writing something on a scrap of paper.

"Here's my aunt's number here in Vancouver. Below that's my number and address in Kamloops." His fingers don't leave when he presses it into my hand.

"Tamara." It's Brad waving me over to the staff room.

The mountie is there.

"This is Sergeant Gibbs," Brad says. "He'd like to talk to you."

"Tammy Schlotter?" He's checking something on a notepad.

"Tamara," I say.

"You've been leading everyone on quite a merry little chase, haven't you?"

"Pardon?"

"We've checked the hotel where Miss Jean Barclay's registered, but there's no one there."

"She's out," I say. "Getting her hair done."

"Well, we need to first of all get together for a little talk with you both and find out just what in tarnation's been going on. And, second of all, get you pointed back in the direction of Edmonton, where there's a few people waiting for you — all of them just a bit hot under the collar." There's sweat on his forehead, and he mops it with a big handkerchief.

I don't say anything. And I don't look anyone in the eye. Not Brad. Not the mountie.

"Best get your things and we'll take a little drive over to that hairdressing place."

Christophe asks the mountie if he can come, too, but the mountie says, "No, this isn't no joy ride."

I sit in the back seat. Sergeant Gibbs has a little roll of flesh that bulges along the back of his neck, above his collar. I feel like reaching out and giving it a good pinch.

"This where you said? Aloe Vera?"

When he asks, they tell him Miss Barclay was finished over an hour ago. Said she was heading over to a hotel. We go to the hotel next door and check the lounge, but the Wrinkle Queen's not there.

As we're leaving, the doorman says an old lady in a red dress had a fall. Paramedics rushed her down the street to St. Paul's.

Miss Barclay's there. In Emergency. But barely conscious. A nurse stands by while the mountie talks to her.

Is she going to die? In that skinny hospital bed that looks like a trolley, she looks so small, like there's hardly anything holding her together.

"Don't die," I whisper. I feel tight inside, and dizzy.

"Miss Barclay?" The mountie's surprisingly gentle as he takes hold of her hand.

"Uh?" Her eyes don't seem to focus. Her face is all done up with fresh make-up and her hairdo, although it's lopsided, is blacker than ever against the white pillow. There are some bits of plant caught in it.

"We're going to have to get Tamara home," he says. "The nurse says you're going to have to stay in the hospital for a few days at the very least..."

"Tamara?"

"I'm here," I say.

"We'll check you out of the hotel," Sergeant Gibbs tells her. "You'll be well looked after here. And Tamara is going home."

I touch her hand the way I did when she was sleeping and I needed to wake her up.

"Miss Barclay," I say. "We almost did it."

She closes her eyes.

"Is she going to be okay?" I ask the nurse.

"The doctor says she wrecked the knee that had been

reconstructed. He's going to have to do revision sur-gery."

At the hotel, I pack a bag for the hospital. Just her toiletries and her nightgown and robe and a couple of day outfits. Sergeant Gibbs watches as I repack her gowns in tissue paper and then get my things together.

"What's going to happen to me?" I ask him.

"Social services will be dealing with you." He gives me a look, probably the same one he uses on dope ped-dlers and murderers.

"And what about Miss Barclay's car?"

"Her car?"

"It was stolen this morning."

"Did you file a report?"

When he finds out we didn't, he swears under his breath. Then he's using the phone, calling the airline, booking a later flight.

By the time we get to the airport, after taking Miss Barclay's bag to the hospital and stopping at the police station to report the car theft, Sergeant Gibbs is so mad his face has turned a blotchy red.

"Is it okay if I make a phone call?" I ask him.

"Who to?" he snaps.

"Just Christophe. My friend from the course."

"You've only got a few minutes before boarding."

"That's all I need."

At a pay phone, with Gibbs standing close enough that he can probably listen in if he wants to, I call the Vancouver number that Christophe has written down on the scrap paper.

"She fell in a planter and broke her knee all over again," I tell him.

"Oh, God."

"But in a way I'm glad…I mean not glad that she broke her knee. But glad, in a way, it's over."

"The course?"

"Yeah. If it hadn't happened today, it probably would have tomorrow. I don't know if you can get to be a model in five days anyway."

"You can be a model," Christophe says. "You're beautiful. I just wish you were older than fifteen."

"My birthday's in September," I say. "I'll call you after September seventh and I'll be sixteen."

"I could call you."

"You could if you knew where I'll be," I say.

# 32

"It's healing nicely," the doctor says. "You should be able to fly home in a couple of weeks." He's a tall man with a shock of white hair. Or is it just blond? Who knows with men coloring and streaking their hair these days? He doesn't look old enough to have spent seven years at medical school.

"You're getting in and out of the wheelchair okay?"

"I could use a shot of Demerol before and after," I tell him.

"Now, now." He laughs softly. "We don't want to turn you into a drug addict."

What I could really use, I think, is a mickey of brandy and some cigarillos. One of the orderlies has been bringing me cigarettes but he refuses to go to the liquor store. He's good about wheeling me down to the sidewalk for a smoke during his break.

Hernando.

"Very bad for your health," he tells me at least once a trip.

I'm expecting him this afternoon, but the man standing at the door is a mountie. The same one who came a couple of days ago and asked me questions about the car.

"Any news of the Buick?" I ask him.

"They found it half way to Langley. Pretty well trashed," he says. "A write-off."

"I guess no more can be expected in a city of criminals."

"You got that right." He looks at me knowingly.

"Do you mind?" I gesture toward the wheelchair. I can sense his strength as he helps me off the bed and into it — strong arms of the law.

"Do you have time to wheel me down to the parking lot? We get to smoke out there. Mixes nicely with the car fumes."

He pulls out a package of Nicorette gum and pops one into his mouth as I light my cigarette.

"That was pretty…ill-considered," he says. "Taking a minor into the States, letting her drive your vehicle, lying to her guardians. If it were up to me, I'd have you charged. You were a schoolteacher, weren't you? What kind of woman…"

He's getting red in the face. I think he would like to see me behind bars.

"Is she back home?"

"Signed, sealed and delivered," he says, moving the wheelchair to a spot of shade.

"You couldn't let her finish her modeling course?"

The traffic of Burrard Street hums alongside us. One of the horde of Vancouver homeless pauses and eyes my cigarette longingly. I flip one up out of the package for him and he shuffles over, self-conscious in front of the mountie, to retrieve it.

"It was only three more days. What would it have hurt?" I add.

"I don't get either of you." He shakes his head. "And especially you. Deceit. Public mischief…"

"Our own private mischief."

"Watch what you're saying, lady. It may not be too late…"

"She had a dream. And it was so close…she was reaching out and touching it. So close."

"But it was wrongheaded," he says, "and you letting her drive…she could have been killed."

"We're all on a life journey and the ending's the same," I inform him.

"Yes, lady. But you're a hell of a lot closer to the finish line than that little girl is…"

"Spare me the race car metaphors."

I can see him rolling his eyes.

"You flatfoot." My voice has gone low and raspy but I think he hears me, no trouble. "What do you know of roads taken — and roads not taken?"

"I'd better take you back in," he sputters. "I wouldn't want to be the first officer in B.C. history charged with decking an old dame in a wheelchair."

# 33

---

Mr. Mussbacher is furious. If he was a cartoon, there'd be smoke coming out of his ears and nose.

"You've done it," he says. "You've screwed everything up. The Shadbolts were good to you. How could you do this to them? They want you to pack up your things and get out as soon as possible."

"Get out...to where?"

"I'm working on that."

I try to pick a time when nobody'll be home to go and get my stuff but, wouldn't you know it, Shirl is home taking her holiday weeks, and the gremlins are there, too. They run over and grab my legs.

"Tamara," Lizzie yells. "Mom, it's Tamara."

"Where've you been?" says Lyle.

"Oh...you know. Vancouver. Seattle. Over the rainbow."

Shirl rushes into the living room.

"Tamara! We were so worried about you. How could you do such a...such a thoughtless thing?"

"I'm sorry," I say.

"Using us!" Tears are welling in Shirl's eyes. "Using that poor old woman! It might've killed her."

"I just came to get my things," I say.

"I don't want Tamara to go." Lyle is still hanging onto one of my pant legs.

"She's been bad!" Lizzie twirls around. "Hasn't she, Mommy?"

"You two go and watch TV. I want to talk to Tamara."

We go into the kitchen and sit at the table.

"Herb and I decided we can't take you back," Shirl says. "There needs to be trust in a family."

"I know," I say. "I don't deserve to be taken back."

"Do you even want to?" She's searching for Kleenexes.

"Yes." I surprise myself when I say this. But it's true. I want it — my TV-less room, the gremlins, Herb showing me how to check engine fluids under the hood, Shirl hopelessly trying to put together low-carb meals.

When I've got my things into three shopping bags and a cardboard box, Shirl insists on driving me back to the shelter, Lizzie and Lyle piling into the back seat of the Plymouth.

"I shouldn't be at the shelter too long," I tell her.

226

"Mr. Mussbacher says there'll be a spot in one of the group homes probably next week."

"A group home." Shirl says the words like they are daggers to her heart. I feel the same way but I keep my mouth shut.

Three days later I'm playing Nintendo with a little girl who's just come into the shelter on the weekend when Mr. Mussbacher shows up with Shirl and Herb.

"You get an extra turn," I say to Emma-Lee.

Mr. Mussbacher takes us all into one of the shelter's little meeting rooms. As he hunts for an extra chair, Herb and Shirl and I spend a few minutes not looking at each other. I can see, though, that Herb's face is red like he's embarrassed out of his mind, and Shirl is nervously turning a tissue into confetti.

Back with a chair, Mr. Mussbacher drops into it and says, "I don't know why, but the Shadbolts say they're willing to take you back."

Now I do look at them. Maybe, somehow, we find our families. It just takes a few tries. Tears are starting to stream down Shirl's face. Mine, too.

"I don't deserve it," I say.

"No," Mr. Mussbacher says, "you don't. But there are people in this world who aren't quite as selfish as you are."

Mostly, for the half hour we meet, Mr. Mussbacher rakes me over the coals until even Shirl and Herb are ready to step in to shut him up. At the end of it all, I have to agree to go to group therapy for six months, to do five hours a week community service at the Sierra Sunset Seniors' Lodge for that same amount of time, plus never miss a day of school for the rest of my life.

Probably the worst of all this is the group therapy. There's seven of us — two crystal meth addicts, one kid that's into slicing bits of skin off himself (I think he's trying to disappear), a girl who's a compulsive shoplifter, a nymphomaniac, a boy who gets his kicks setting fires, and me, the pathological liar.

"Actually," I tell the group, "I'm not really a pathological liar. That's someone who lies simply for the satisfaction of getting away with the lie, or to enjoy the special attention a lie might bring. Like lying to everyone and telling them you have cancer."

Dr. Gregorichuk, the group facilitator, nods at me to keep talking.

"What I really am is an expedient liar. Someone who lies to get something important to herself. As a means to an end."

"That's astute," Dr. Gregorichuk says, "but is it any easier to recover from?"

"Once a liar, always a liar," Jerome the arsonist says.

Hey, pal, thanks for the support. I think maybe I'll make him a gift package of all the matchbooks Herb's collected from different bars over the years. They're sitting forgotten in a bag in the bottom drawer of the desk in my room, behind another stack of Eterno-Shine brochures.

Christophe has called twice since I phoned and left a message with his mom in Kamloops. He says Brad has asked him to help with the school next summer, and that if I can come, they'll let me start all over again — no extra tuition — since I missed over half the course.

I love his voice on the phone. It's the kind of voice that's a perfect match for what you see in your mind. And what I see is Christophe's beautiful body on the rocks on English Bay. Little drops of water across his chest and stomach, that GQ smile.

I was dreading the hours I'd be putting in at the Seniors' Lodge, but they're not that bad. At first Mrs. Golinowski wouldn't even talk to me, but after a couple of weeks of the deep freeze, she came up with this idea for me to produce a seniors' fashion show. I have to say it beats laminating fall leaves for place mats and helping old ladies in and out of the washroom.

The best part of being at the home, though, is getting to spend some time with Miss Barclay. Her nephew, Byron, went and got her from the hospital in Vancouver the third week in September. I brought her some flowers to welcome her back.

Red carnations.

# 34

She has one of those Safeway bouquets of carnations. Red.

"Why, Tamara," I say, "how thoughtful. Look, Byron, carnations."

He scowls at her.

Later when she's gotten me into my wheelchair and taken me down to the patio for a smoke, I tell her, "He's mourning the Buick. I told him the insurance money was all his but I think he'd still like to put a good helping of arsenic in my cocoa."

"Cocoa!" Tamara snorts. "I've never seen you drink cocoa."

"You're right," I say. "But don't ever let Byron near my flask of Courvoisier. Not that it's easy to get these days. Eddie's giving me the cold shoulder, and I think the Gollywatchit has a squad search my room every few days. I expect she thinks I'm into drug-running now."

"In two years," Tamara offers, "I'll be old enough to buy your booze and cigarillos."

She has a bag with her and she pulls out several small photos that have been framed with cardboard props at the back so they'll stand up.

"Oh, my!"

"Here's one of us all at the opera," she says. "Remember when Ricardo asked that guy to take our picture? This one's in Ricardo's yard. This is my favorite one that Brad took when I had my Charlie Chaplin hat on. And in this one I have on a red sundress and I'm in the gazebo on English Bay."

"Thank you, my dear," I say. "These will have a permanent place on my bureau. When I can't sleep I'll be able to turn my lamp on and see them. And remember — everything. Have you heard from Ricardo? Is that how you got the Seattle photos?"

"When the Shadbolts let me go back with them, before school started, I was pretty well grounded. I started a letter to Ricardo and by the time I was finished, it cost three times the regular postage to send it. But he wrote me back and sent a bunch of photos. I'll bring the rest the next time I come..."

She's chattering on about the news in Ricardo's letter, but I drift away from the words, drift into the evening itself.

There is something about September, I think, that makes us hang onto life the way the leaf of a prairie maple hangs, fragile and golden, onto its branch. All the powers of imminent winter cannot force it to let go until it is finally ready. Around us, there is the waning autumn sunlight and the smell of smoke in the air and the sound of birds — their clamorous honking as they head south.

"You know, Tamara," I say, "there's a marvelous opera festival in the south. In Santa Fe. You haven't really lived until you've listened to *La Traviata* in the opera house that opens onto the New Mexico hills."

"Is it far from L.A.?" She smiles her model smile at me.

"You could probably drive it in a day or two."

She laughs and hugs her arms around her knees.

Skinnybones.

# "Stop pushing me away, Raine, because I'm holding on."

Kyle's blue eyes blazed. "You seemed ready to trust me there for a while. Then I got too close, and you fell into the trap of pushing rather than facing it. Well, I'm not letting go, Raine. What does it take to make you accept that?"

"I'm not sure what you're saying," Raine said, trembling in response.

"The hell you're not!" Kyle leaned close, voice slow and emphatic, and tantalizingly gravelly. "I'm saying that I won't let you get away with evasion. Is that plain enough? We have something between us that might be worth building on."

"Might being the key word."

"Take a chance, lady."

He was asking her to step out of a world where she knew all the boundaries. He was asking her to risk everything on love.

**Deborah Davis** calls herself a romantic and a dreamer. At twelve years of age, she began writing about "the people in my head," stories that she would never let anyone read. Now, of course, she wants people to read about the characters that have become so real to her they often take over the story. Deborah, who enjoys reading, sewing and sketching, lives on a very small farm in Kentucky with her husband of twelve years. They enjoy a full family life shared with brothers, sisters and their children.

# The Healing Effect
## Deborah Davis

# Harlequin Books

TORONTO • NEW YORK • LONDON
AMSTERDAM • PARIS • SYDNEY • HAMBURG
STOCKHOLM • ATHENS • TOKYO • MILAN

Original hardcover edition published in 1987
by Mills & Boon Limited

ISBN 0-373-02917-9

Harlequin Romance first edition July 1988

# CHAPTER ONE

RAINE JACOBS huddled beneath the lightweight tarpaulin that a state trooper had given her, keeping one end of it carefully tented over the child who lay motionless on the ground. She'd sacrificed her coat to cover him and her teeth were chattering relentlessly, jarring the pain in her temple. The cold, hard pavement bit roughly into her knees. Yet, aside from holding the folded compress to her head, she paid no attention to her own discomfort. Her stricken eyes were on the boy.

He could be little more than two years old. Shaking, Raine stared down at the frosty lashes and brows, the tiny round mouth that was softly slack and colourless from shock. The side of his face had been struck during impact and the raw scrape on his cheek was already swelling. Carefully avoiding the angry red area, Raine made small soothing noises and stroked his hair—as light and fine as cornsilk—back off his brow. He was unconscious. He couldn't feel or hear her. But it was something to do, something to ward off the terrible, numbing horror.

The other victim lay a few feet away, swathed in a blanket from the police car and surrounded by hunched figures, so that Raine could see only the lovely, delicate face with its blue-veined lids. The flaming cap of short curls, as vivid a colour as her own, contrasted pointedly with ghastly pale skin. The highway patrolmen had administered first-aid, but Raine understood that the girl needed trained paramedics...and quickly; her condition was grave. A siren was droning in the distance...the ambulance on its way, please God. Until it arrived, keeping the accident victims warm and dry was the only remaining recourse.

The deadly weather continued to assault them. The morning's drizzling rain had turned to sleet, solid sheets of ice freezing on the pavement. It was a nasty day to venture out...late November, dark with chill and damp, but who would have foreseen the danger in that sudden temperature drop? Lamentably, not Raine, who had left Gavin Reynolds' office a short time before, deeply preoccupied with matters that now seemed pitifully trivial. Apparently, the other driver was just as unsuspecting. Brakes ineffectual at the glassy intersection, her battered little Volkswagen had shot through its red light so unexpectedly that Raine was left virtually defenceless in its path. She'd glimpsed the girl's frantic, screaming face a split second before impact, then something had struck her head. She couldn't even recall getting out of her Mustang, although she could see it parked at a haphazard diagonal across the road, the front fender and one headlight smashed. She had no idea how the white handkerchief had come to be in her hand and pressed to her temple. She only knew her sick panic upon seeing the dilapidated blue Volkswagen overturned, patrolmen and motorists struggling to free its trapped passengers.

An officer broke from the nearby huddle and walked over to Raine, going down on his haunches beside her. 'Miss Jacobs?' When she turned, he searched her face for signs of shock, but found little to help him decide. The wide grey eyes glittered with unshed tears, and the lovely mouth was tightly compressed, her complexion perfect, but drained of colour, so that her beautiful, brilliant hair looked even more exotic. None the less, she seemed to have achieved a careful, brittle kind of control. 'Your copy of the accident report.' She looked faintly questioning, and he passed the slip of paper across. 'You'll need to notify your insurance company, of course, but you won't be held responsible.'

His weary eyes wandered towards the prone figure to his left, and he marvelled that two young women who were strangers to each other shared the same odd colouring. Raine glanced at the page, perfunctorily at first, then more closely. Melanie Thompson. Twenty-one years old.

'We took as much information as possible from her driver's licence and vehicle registration,' the officer said, in answer to her unspoken thought. 'And there was an insurance card to provide the rest. That report will be self-explanatory to your agent. The girl ran a red light. More than likely, her brakes failed on the ice. But, whatever the reason, she was at fault.'

Raine nodded distractedly, unconcerned with the damage to her car, with the question of blame. 'When will her family be notified?' she asked, the words hurting her tight throat. 'I feel that I ought to speak with them.'

The man frowned thoughtfully. 'Since the girl doesn't live here, it will mean tracing them. That may take a while. Depends whether the address on her licence is up to date.'

They heard a moan then, a tiny whimper of sound from the child, and both adults looked down. Raine waited, holding her breath, but the closed eyelids didn't move. The officer reached for the boy's pulse, his brow furrowed, eyes saddened. 'At least he's holding on.'

'His leg is broken, isn't it?'

The patrolman shot her a considering glance, then sighed heavily, shifting his gaze away. There was no use trying for optimism when they could both see the un-natural jut of the child's left hip, the way the small sneakered foot turned inward. 'Looks that way. The ambulance should be here in no time.'

'Where will they be taken?' Raine couldn't recognise the steady huskiness of her voice, when she was quaking dismally inside. 'What hospital?'

'Physicians is my guess. It's closest.' He seemed ready to straighten, but paused, frowning again. 'You really need a couple stitches yourself. Wouldn't you like to call someone?'

*Who?* Raine almost asked, unconscious of the pin-point of bleakness that leapt into her eyes. She'd be with Gavin now, had he kept their lunch date, but he'd begged off again, his drafting board littered with sketches for the new McKenna ad campaign. And her partner Felicity couldn't leave their shop. There was no one else, no other close acquaintances at all in her busy, independent life.

'No,' she raised amethyst-grey eyes, willing her statement to carry the necessary resolve, 'I'm fine.'

'What arrangements do you want made for your vehicle?' he conceded after a moment.

'If it will still run, I'll drive it.'

The patrolman might have protested had an ambulance not wailed up to the intersection then, requiring his help to disperse the small gathering of bystanders. Raine held tight to the little boy's unresponsive hand, while the young woman—his mother, she presumed—was transferred to a stretcher. The speed at which the attendants worked was proof of Melanie Thompson's critical condition, their exchanged looks of near-futility chilling Raine to the bone. Someone came to check the child and, seeing his obvious fracture, called for help. Two men lifted him on to a stretcher, hands beneath him at four separate points to keep his tiny body flatly aligned. Raine leaned over him as the cot's folded wheels were extended, silently willing his survival.

She was staring into his small still face when the light lashes fluttered briefly, showing her blue, blue irises ringing pupils that were wide with fear and confusion. The tiny round chin quivered and a whimper escaped. 'Mom-ma . . .' Little fingers tangled desperately in the red-gold shimmer of Raine's curls, and then she understood. Only half-conscious, he'd been misled by the colour of her hair.

'Shhh, darling.' She nearly choked on her tears, stroking his silky brow. 'Mama's here.' The toddler gave another tiny moan, then his fingers relaxed their grip and his heavy lashes swept downward.

She was back in the Mustang, hearing the engine splutter and flare, staring blankly after the disappearing ambulance, when the big officer walked over to detain her. He asked a few more questions, looked again at her

head. She understood that he was satisfying himself
whether her mind was clear. 'All right, Miss Jacobs, but
take it slowly.' He finally stepped away. 'I'll follow you
as far as the hospital in the cruiser. You feel light-headed
in the *slightest*, nauseous, anything, I want you to pull
over.'

But she reached the emergency entrance without
mishap, and woodenly returned the officer's brief wave.
She'd been inside, in the waiting lounge, for over an
hour before her eerie false calm began to unravel. The
hospital odour of antiseptics and disinfectants assaulted
her nostrils, dredging up unpleasantness from the past,
until she could have wept her bitter unwillingness. Not
the old hurts, not now, when she had more than enough
strain to cope with. Normally she avoided hospitals like
an anathema, and her vigil seemed pointless enough as
it was. Yet the thought of the injured girl and child kept
Raine in her seat. Both of them remained critical,
Melanie Thompson comatose and the little boy taken to
emergency surgery shortly after arrival, with no word.
No one else had arrived to enquire, and Raine found
that she could not leave them that way, not without
someone there who cared about the two of them.

So she waited, flicking beautiful, distressed eyes about
the large room, distractedly flipping pages in a magazine, and the interminable hours blurred. At one point,
the receptionist brought a fresh compress, trying again
to persuade her that the small cut really did need attention, but Raine had refused treatment. Now light-
headedness hovered over her like a soft blanket, and she
shook her bright head to stave it off, causing the dull
ache in her temple to throb with renewed vigour. She
supposed that she might have sustained more damage
than she had previously been willing to admit. She felt
just slightly demented, as if she might produce one of
those rages that redheads are famous for, and that she
personally indulged in only rarely. Undeniably, the
waiting was a strain.

Much later, she thought of calling Felicity, or Gavin, but still she didn't move. At nearly ten o'clock, Felicity would have RaineBo Shoppe safely locked up for the night, leaving her whereabouts a matter of deduction. The apartment they shared was the least likely possibility these days. Although Felicity still paid her half of the expenses, she had all but moved in with Brian Keaton. An aspiring musician, he managed a stereo shop down the mall from their boutique, and from the moment that he had sauntered into their new location to grin a welcome, Felicity was involved. Deeply. Jealously. She'd be backstage somewhere now, absorbing Brian's throaty lyrics and surreptitiously guarding him from the young groupies who had begun to follow the fledgling rock band from one nightclub engagement to the next. The effort of contacting her loomed out of proportion and kept Raine still.

Her reluctance to phone Gavin was not so easily analysed. The cancelled lunch had little to do with it; at twenty-nine, Gavin was well on his way to a brilliant advertising career, and he hadn't reached that point by giving personal commitments precedence. He was probably still working, at home now. Raine had no doubts that he would come if she called him. But, somehow, asking Gavin to venture out on a night like this, strictly to oblige her need for comfort, didn't fit the relationship they shared. Admittedly, the accident had left her badly shaken, aware of the tenuous substance of life, but seeking a shoulder to lean on would be indulging a vulnerability that she didn't want to feel.

Eventually she found the ladies' room and stood staring into the mirror, as if the reflection she saw there was a separate young woman, slender in her exclusive wool wrap coat, its collar retaining the child's faint baby-powder scent. Her heart-shaped face was shockingly pale above the soft cowl neck of a white sweater, her temple bluish and flecked with dried blood. After dabbing at the area with a damp paper towel, she withdrew a hairbrush from her slim leather bag and carefully pulled it through the tangled mass of hair. Its red-gold volume seemed to overwhelm the face in the mirror, rippling vibrantly against colourless skin. Her eyes were shadowed with pain, the irises a clear grey tinged with amethyst. For a moment she failed to recognise that haunted expression as her own.

*Get a hold on yourself, Raine.* Abruptly, she dipped her head to splash cold water on to her cheeks and eyes. The combination of icy moisture and increased blood to her head helped. She reached for a fresh paper towel and the strange sensation passed. With a slightly shaky hand, she re-applied lipgloss and blusher, then turned a delicate gold wristwatch into view. She had killed exactly ten minutes.

She paused to drink from a water fountain in the hallway, barely conscious of an empty stomach until it began to flutter nervously upon re-entry to the waiting area. The receptionist, looking her way, gestured, and Raine compliantly stepped up to the desk, her stomach muscles tightening even further. 'There's news?'

'Yes.' But not good news...the controlled expression and subdued tone of voice warned Raine of that. There was a long, searching look from kind eyes, then the older woman subtly squared her shoulders. 'I'm sorry to have to tell you this, but as I understand the situation, there's no reason why you should blame yourself.' A pause, coupled with the qualifying statement, compelled Raine to take a steadying breath. 'Melanie Thompson died a few minutes ago.' Raine was vaguely aware of sympathy edging the professional tones. She gripped her bag hard in front of her, needing to hold on to something. 'There was no pain,' the woman reassured her quietly. 'In fact, she never came out of the coma. She just slipped away easily.'

The silvered head bent over some papers on the desk, and Raine realised that she was being given a chance to control the tears that had welled up. Fiercely, she blinked them back, an anger born of injustice flaring swiftly in their place. 'And the child?' she choked.

'In Recovery now, and holding his own.'

'Meaning that I'm an outsider and can't be told too much.' That was unfair, but she couldn't seem to help herself. 'It's been hours. The family must have been notified. Why hasn't someone arrived?'

'There is no family.' The admission seemed involuntary.

Raine's grey eyes widened in dawning horror. 'No,' she resisted flatly, unable to believe the implications of that disclosure. 'No, there must be someone.'

'I'm sorry, but no, there isn't.' The receptionist sighed helplessly. 'We had a call from the police. They'd discovered that Miss Thompson grew up in a girls' home upstate, an orphan.'

*An orphan.* The words seemed to sear and burn through Raine's head, telling her more about Melanie Thompson's existence than she could easily endure. Carefully, she blocked off that avenue of thought, grasping at a new one. 'What about the child's father?'

'They don't know. The girl wasn't married, and the boy shares her last name. Stephen Thompson, it is. At least he's no longer a John Doe. With his mother unconscious, we had no way of knowing. I suppose the police turned up a birth record.'

Stephen. Somehow, having a name put to him made the little boy's plight all the more intense. Raine thought of the beautiful young woman that Melanie Thompson had been and felt a vast sadness mingle with her pain. There was a bitter sense of history repeating itself, because now the orphaned girl's baby son was motherless. Although Raine had been told not to experience guilt, she knew that a few minutes in timing might have made all the difference. She felt horribly persecuted by the force that people called fate, as if her whole outlook on the future had been darkened. As if she would always be bound by this crippling regret.

'What will happen to him?' Her voice sounded hoarse to her own ears.

'The authorities have already been notified.'

'God!'

'He's very young, Miss Jacobs.' The woman levelled a realistic look. 'He'll go to adoptive parents. After a while, he won't remember his life up to this point.'

So the flame-haired girl would gradually be erased from his young mind by some living, loving couple who had gone to a great deal of trouble and expense to get him. A more adorable child would be hard to imagine; his relocation could be swift, depending upon the laws involved. It was all a very comforting picture that had been painted, but Raine failed to be comforted. A young woman had died . . . his mother. And it was the here and now in the small boy's life that worried her, not some happy ending in the future. Right now, he was hurt and he was alone. Raine, who knew what it was to be small and abandoned, was burdened with a deep empathy that all the reasoning in the world couldn't lessen. Her heart went out to a two-year-old who hadn't the benefit of her own lengthy adjustment. She knew just how hard the coming days would be for him, and she wondered whether she could walk away.

Acknowledging the receptionist's quiet suggestion that she should go home, Raine refused the offer of a cab. A couple of miles, a few minutes, and she'd be inside her bedroom, almost as if this hellish day had never happened. Her head was pounding savagely, though, and the cut on her temple would only be responsible for the least of her scars. There was no escaping a personal involvement when a child had lost his mother and a young girl her life. Only Raine walked away, a part of her none the less destroyed.

From somewhere she found the strength to move. The air was still freezing outside, peppering her face with minuscule crystals of sleet. Automatically, she turned up her collar beneath a sheaf of vivid curls, then returned her hand to its pocket, staring into the night with bleak eyes. Amply spaced overhead lights failed to bring her car immediately into view, and arriving in such an agitated state she had forgotten to take notice of her parking space. For a moment she was seized with the uncontrollable urge to cry, just slide down to the kerb and sob, but control the urge she did. Swallowing hard, she resolved first to get herself home, then she'd probably shatter into countless fragments. There was only so much pressure anyone could take. Blindly, she ducked her head over her handbag, delving through its contents for keys that remained elusive. In a moment she would scream. Finally her fingers closed on the jingling assortment and she stepped quickly from the kerb.

Now, when she needed her voice, that faculty had deserted her. A horn blast whipped her head up, serving also to lock every other muscle, including those in her throat. Lights assaulted her vision, and she stood frozen, impact evident and reflexes nil. Yet no hurling weight struck her down. The car swerved madly, filling her ears with the angry screech of tyres, then a gritty sound as rubber hit a patch of ice. Raine watched, unharmed, as the dark blue Porsche slid to a halt only a few feet away.

The driver's door opened and slammed. A man was striding toward her, his imposing figure clearly illuminated by the security lights. Raine had time to register faded jeans and a leather bomber jacket, longish blond hair that looked as if fingers had recently raked through it, and a startlingly handsome face made rigid with displeasure. Then a pair of stark blue eyes pierced through her, their message crystal clear. She had been foolish. Unforgivably clumsy. Whatever she might have said dissolved on her tongue. She was trembling with reaction when antagonism surfaced, as swift and potent as a dose of amphetamines.

The man's height and proximity forced Raine to stare up, the shared look revealing fury on either side. She could see the texture of his tanned skin, stretched taut over a framework of strong, classic bones. The creases at the corners of eyes and mouth looked cynical without benefit of a smile. He exuded aggression through every pore.

'Are you all right?' His voice was low and gritty. And peremptory, telling her plainly that he had better use for his time. Well, so did she.

'I'm fine.' She managed to convey the mental rider no thanks to you. By rights, she owed him an apology, yet the way he came stalking up to her put an end to that. Her nerves were tautened by that near-collision, and they simply wouldn't stretch to accommodate a nasty scene. She aimed an unreasonably hostile stare, willing him to turn around and go back to his car before her knees buckled.

But he gave no indication of moving, blue anger glittering in his eyes until Raine felt as if her very skin were being burned. He meant to see her chastised, the curling of his clean-chiselled mouth fair warning. 'Didn't your mother teach you to look both ways?'

'I don't have a mother. And there are speed limits in parking lots,' she continued tightly, 'or hadn't you noticed?'

'Speed isn't the issue here.' He looked positively dangerous. 'It's *carelessness*. Yours, not mine.'

'Spare me the lecture.' Raine felt on the verge of hysteria, and just reckless enough to fight back. This arrogant, scowling male was more than she could handle calmly...the perfect ending to an unreal day. She hugged her leather clutch-bag closer, unwilling to let him see that her hands were shaking. The air was very cold and their breath mingled visibly. She took a small, unconscious step backward. Menacingly, he followed.

'Lady, you're getting off easy.' With a kind of angry fascination, Raine watched his jaw clench over the harsh words. 'That was the most stupid stunt I've yet to witness!'

'You weren't a witness. You were a participant. And my part in this is no more stupid than your streaking out of the parking lot like it was a raceway pitstop!' She had no evidence of that, the defensive comment based loosely on the model of his car and the sheer look of him. Nonconformist, and no gentleman. Otherwise, he wouldn't be badgering her when her bones felt like water.

His sensual mouth twisted in cynical attack. 'And you...do you normally wander into traffic with your head down? I turned the corner and there you were, vision perfectly obstructed by all that hair.'

Raine thrust a hand through the red-gold mass in sheer reaction. 'I was operating on the assumption that the pedestrian has the right of way. Or does a car like that come with special privileges?'

She made the mistake of tossing her bright head in the direction of the abandoned Porsche. A pain stabbed her so suddenly, so viciously, that she nearly crumpled. Her gasp must have alerted him; by the time she raised a hand to her head in reflex, he was already reaching to steady her. She was torn only momentarily between grasping for support and resisting, then a treacherous wave of dizziness forced her decision. Weakly, she leaned her forehead against his hard shoulder, barely aware of the steely arms that encircled her swaying body. Then she *was* aware, the whirling sensation evaporating behind closed eyes. The male scent of aftershave and leather penetrated her senses, the worn surface of his jacket cold against her face. Full realisation hit and she drew back abruptly, wincing as her head again protested sharp movement.

'I'm sorry.' Her apology was stiff.

'Don't be.' Her face had dewed with a fine perspiration, in spite of the extreme temperature, and seeing it, his eyes narrowed. Carefully he turned her towards the light, his hands sliding up her shoulders to cup her head. Raine felt the hair glide away from her temple and heard his grunt of comprehension. 'You told me you weren't hurt.'

It was the obvious irritation in his gravelly voice that made her retort, 'Don't worry, you didn't do it.'

'I can see that. Why hasn't this cut been treated?'

'It's nothing.' Unnerved, Raine struggled beneath his hands. 'Let go of me.'

'Just be still.' He held her motionless, speculating over the cut. 'You need a stitch.'

'No.' Raine set her mouth firmly, conscious of the high-handed manner in which he was holding her. She was no child. And neither was she any concern of his. Just a former obstacle in his path.

'One stitch,' he bargained drily. 'The cut will heal faster, and it probably won't scar.'

'A scar wouldn't show...not with all this hair.'

He showed precious little appreciation for her taunt. 'A scar isn't the worst that could come of that knock on the head. You may be hurt more than you think. A concussion is always possible.'

'I'll live.' The moment she'd said them, she was sickened by the callousness of her own words. She just wanted to get away. Away from the hospital, away from this man. She was falling apart, that brittle, sharp voice in no way her own. She aimed a pointed glance at the brown sinewy hand that cradled her chin, and he let his arm drop, at the last moment pinioning her wrist. 'Look,' Raine was fighting for every nuance of control, 'thank you for your concern, but will you let go of me now? I won't collapse.'

'Are you sure?' he came back with swift irony. His fingertips pressed firmly into her pulse for several seconds longer before he raised both palms in a hands-off gesture.

Raine lifted a silent grey stare, sufficient, she hoped, to send him towards his vehicle, yet he made no move to go. Furthermore, he was still watching her, those blue eyes too intense, too frank, for comfort. The assessing gaze fell to the rise of her breasts, and even though she was covered by heavy clothing to the point of disguise, Raine felt her cheeks begin to burn. She'd had enough. Groping for the keys that had never been removed from her bag, she heard his derisive snort.

'You aren't thinking of driving?'

Raine raised her head, resisting the urge to fling it and risk another near-disaster. Her mouth was mutinous. 'I am.' Without another word, she tucked her bag under her arm and strode off in the direction that she hoped would take her to her car. She was immediately aware that the heavier thud of male footsteps had joined the click of her high-heeled boots on the pavement. She skidded slightly on a slick patch and his fingertips bit into her elbow. She glared sideways. 'I don't recall asking you to walk me to my car.'

He ignored that, his face taut. 'You're in no condition to drive.'

'Listen.' Raine came to an abrupt halt half-way along a row of parked vehicles and turned to face him, her chin angled upward in frustrated defiance. 'I appreciate the fact that you didn't run me over when I gave you every opportunity. But that doesn't make my life yours. Do you understand? Now, aside from a headache that you aren't improving, I'm fine . . .'

'Lady, you aren't,' he ground out.

Raine's jaw tightened. She maintained eye contact with a steadiness she didn't feel. 'Surely I'm the best judge of that?'

'Normally, I'd say you are.' A cutting edge of contempt nullified the concession. 'You aren't showing a lot of sense at the moment.'

Raine stared into a face made all dark planes and angles by conflicting lights. She had never seen such eyes. Neither had she been the object of such open animosity. She wavered beneath his electric regard, feeling as if the odds were stacked high against her arriving home with her fragile composure and her sanity still intact.

'I'm a doctor, if that makes any difference to you.'

'Should it?' He didn't look like a doctor . . . sexy, a little rakish in the casual clothes, and too damned aggressive to be in such a people-orientated profession. She saw the handsome features harden.

'For some people that announcement generates a certain trust, yes.'

'I trust my instincts, Doctor.'

'Wow!'

Raine let the taunt hang there, catching sight of the Mustang farther back and moving towards it with renewed haste. Her pace didn't affect him, his long strides an easy match. She determinedly kept her profile to him, drawing her collar closer against a blast of icy wind.

'Will you listen to me?' he bit out suddenly. 'I had a good look at you back there, and I'm telling you you're in no shape to drive. Your pulse and your breathing are irregular... You nearly fainted in my arms——' there was a glimmer of white teeth, more grimace than anything else '—and we both realise that was a result of your sudden movement, and not my masculine presence.'

'Maybe my body objects to being a moving target.'

He gritted his teeth, the clenched jaw evidence of a temper held barely under control. 'You stepped off the kerb without so much as a glance in my direction. That only adds weight to my argument. Disorientation is common following a blow to the head, and it's a good indication that you are at least slightly concussed.'

'Fine. *I believe you.* Now I'm going home.'

'I'll take you.'

'I don't think so.'

His fingers were at her elbow again, only this time they bit in with a pressure that was just short of cruel. 'Tell me something.' He pulled her up short and there was no way that she could avoid the vivid gaze that burned into her. 'Just how much is standing your ground worth to you? You get behind a wheel tonight and you risk blacking out. Someone could be hurt.'

Pain uncoiled like a vicious serpent in her chest. 'Give me ten minutes' headstart and it won't be you!'

She knew it was a tasteless remark, born of pure reaction, and that he had no way of understanding the events and tensions leading up to it. His face told her that she had done a thorough job of maligning her own character. Emotions flickered in rapid succession. Disgust...scorn...anger. Glittery, profound anger. It seemed an extreme response, even allowing for her reckless taunt.

'Do you think I'm talking just to watch my breath freeze? I'm unsure yet of your grip on consciousness. If you were a wiser lady, you'd check into the hospital for observation and let someone stitch that cut. Barring that suggestion, you might at least take a taxi home. Endangering yourself is sin enough, but purposely operating a vehicle when you are less than alert is vicious. You put every motorist on the road in a potentially dangerous situation.'

Raine stood frozen beneath the lash of his tongue, and apparently he took her silence for continued defiance, thrusting a hand through dark blond hair in a gesture of leashed violence. 'Damn it!' he ground out, oblivious to her flinch. 'I just spent six hours in surgery with a two-year-old who has a crushed leg, courtesy of a traffic accident. He almost bled to death from torn veins and arteries. The bone is severed just close enough to the hip socket to make a clean knit doubtful, which leaves him facing four weeks or more in traction, followed by a body cast. There may be more surgery down the road. Even then I can't guarantee that he will walk properly. And that isn't the worst of it.' Blue fire seared her. 'His mother was killed...So don't tell me you're fine, lady. I'll take you home, or I'll call you a cab. But I won't let you behind a wheel.'

His cruelty took her breath away, and yet how could he know? The strong face was a study in bitterness. If he thought her an insensitive young woman in need of a good shock, then she had only herself to blame. But it hurt...*he* hurt. Desperately, she broke from him, unable to endure the unknowing condemnation that he'd set down. If she had wanted the truth about the child before, now she had it in a completely unsoftened state and she wasn't sure that she could handle the facts. Not only had the boy been robbed of his mother, he was probably crippled as well, or at least seriously impaired. And past experience told her that a handicapped child faced a life spent on the fringes of normal existence. She remembered a boy at the state home whose crutches and leg braces had barred him from nearly every activity. He was passed over for adoption again and again while healthy children were chosen, until the age factor had ruined his chances altogether.

Would Stephen face the same desolate future? He was such a truly beautiful child, all blond fluff and enormous blue eyes. Raine gave a strangled moan, engulfed by emotion. Wildly, she looked for her car, that had seemed close at hand only a moment ago.

'You really don't give a damn, do you?'

'I do!' Quite simply, her control broke. One moment she had stumbled against her car, fumbling to open the door, and the next moment she was wrenching around to face him, her grey eyes frantic with pain and outrage. 'I do care!' she flung out, scarcely aware that she had let fly with a balled fist until she felt her knuckles strike the leather of his jacket and sink impotently into the fleece lining beneath. She landed several erratic blows before he caught her fist in mid-air and held it tightly. Still she struggled wildly, her body arching away from his with a burst of adrenalin that neither of them had expected.

'Stop it!' he admonished tersely, his breath somewhere near her ear. Raine sacrificed her bag in order to lash out with her other hand, and he caught that one too, the interception accomplished before any solid connection could be made.

Reaction dictated that she keep fighting. He had no choice but to force her flailing body against the car, pressing full-length against her. She could feel every taut muscle in his torso and thighs as he held her pinned to the vehicle, his weight crushing the doorhandle into the small of her back. Her face was pressed into the leather hollow of his shoulder, while his chin rested with subdued force on top of her head.

She wasn't sure how long they stood in that position. The hysteria drained from her, replaced by seeping cold from the hard metal at her back. His warmth and weight still held her, both arms outstretched and restrained at her sides. Gradually, her sobbing breath quietened. He eased his upper body away, staring down sombrely.

'Don't look at me like that,' Raine ventured in an unsteady voice. 'I haven't really lost my mind.' She was frightened by her own vulnerability, and the declaration carried less conviction than she would have liked. His silence was not reassuring. Focusing on some point beyond her ear, he went perceptively stiff.

Raine twisted her head, following the look, and what she saw had her wondering abstractedly whether her skull had indeed remained intact. The driver's window of her car was destroyed, an intricate spiderweb crack marking the spot where her temple had struck. It was difficult to equate the damaged glass with the small cut that marred her skin... Alarmingly easy to visualise that radiating fissure on the bone surface. No wonder this persistent dull throb plagued her.

'I don't know why I didn't notice that before,' she murmured inconsequentially.

'If your head is responsible, then I'd hazard a good guess that you were stunned.' His voice was grim. 'It finally occurs to me that you wouldn't be here at the hospital without reason... and we've already established that cut as the least of your worries.' His blue eyes drew her with magnetic force. 'I'll admit that I came on strong, but a reaction as extreme as the one I just witnessed can't be provoked out of thin air.'

'Delayed shock?' she suggested evasively, her throat dry.

'I'll give you that much. Do you want to tell me what happened?'

Raine bit into her lip, carried away by her own involvement with the child who had triggered harsh outbursts from both of them moments before. She could see the doctor's mind at work, assimilating information with swift precision. 'I think you've worked it out for yourself,' she husked, unable to keep a haunted quality from her eyes, any more than she could hide the resentment that surged. 'I was the second party to that accident. You must think it's a little unfair...I walk away with this tiny cut, and the two of them don't walk away at all.'

'I didn't say that.'

His quiet tone in no way mollified her. 'You must be *thinking* it,' she persisted flatly. 'I know I am.'

He pulled away then. Raine watched him retrieve her bag from the pavement where she'd let it fall, hating herself for immediately missing the heated pressure of his body. Her keys were on the ground, too, but he kept those, opening the nearly frozen door with a bit of necessary force. Raine climbed inside automatically, stiffening with surprise when he held on to her key-ring. He crossed in front of the car after closing her door, and levered his lean frame into the passenger seat.

'What are you doing?' Raine asked, thinking the close confines of the vehicle too small to house the two of them and the charged emotions that pulsed between them.

'Sitting, namely.' Again a hand was thrust through his dark blond hair, making the summer-bleached ends stand out. His mouth twisted. 'I think you need to talk, and it might as well be within shelter. Why you let me yell at you, I don't know, but I'll understand now if you tell me to go to hell.' There was anger in his eyes, yet she could see that it was self-directed.

'There's nothing to talk about.' *Liar*, her heart protested and she went on to prove the point involuntarily, 'Melanie Thompson's car skidded across an intersection...I didn't stop in time.'

'Didn't or couldn't?' he asked after a while.

'What does that matter?' she countered bleakly, wondering whether she'd ever be able to define the difference in her own mind. If she hadn't been absorbed in her shopping plans, if she hadn't automatically let off her brakes when the light turned green, would the accident be a near-miss instead of reality? Hindsight was proving a painful sense.

'Nothing, except to you. The phrase "if only" can destroy lives. I've seen it happen,' he expounded, making Raine wonder what tragedy infused his voice with the dark note she was hearing. The very fact that he was a physician no doubt brought tremendous pressures to bear.

She nodded soundlessly, then laid her head against the back of the seat, warily watching muscles contract along the polished line of his jaw. His profile was near-perfect as he stared through the frosted windscreen with thoughts of his own. His presence diminished the Mustang's interior to intimate proportions, and she questioned the forces that had brought him into her company and her private dilemma. Blindly, she focused on one taut thigh, straining against faded denim, then realised that her hand lay within inches of touching it. Jerkily, she raised the hand to tuck an imaginary loose strand behind her ear.

'You haven't told me your name.'

That was, perhaps, the last thing she had expected him to say, and she blinked her confusion. 'It's Raine... Lorraine Jacobs.'

'Mine is Kyle Benedict.' Turning his head, he offered her a self-derisive smile, the blue eyes otherwise unreadable. 'Did anyone ever tell you, Raine, that guilt is a wasted emotion?'

'That's beside the point.'

'Agreed. I'm feeling my share of it right now, for obvious reasons.' His gaze didn't waver. 'You hardly needed my callousness. *I'm sorry*, though I doubt apologies mean a lot to you under the circumstances. I came out of surgery with the kind of chip on my shoulder that every doctor is taught to avoid. You made a convenient scapegoat.'

'I understand.'

'I don't deserve that, but I'll take it.'

He shifted position when she didn't answer, delving into a tight jeans pocket to produce a handkerchief. Raine had taken no notice of the tears until he wordlessly pressed the folded cloth into her hand. Then his gentleness had the perverse effect of turning the silent trickle into a sob. Embarrassed, she turned her head away. There was an almighty struggle between pride and release, but the former won out. She wiped her face, very conscious of the shrewd eyes that followed the movement.

'Your head is bothering you.'

She would have been foolish to deny his observation, when at any moment the pounding inside her skull would surely force its way through. The effort of holding back tears only added to the pressure. 'Doctor Benedict...' she fended, her voice strained.

'Kyle,' he corrected, frowning. 'Why don't you admit that you're hurting, and let me take care of you?'

'Because I only want to go home.'

For response he flipped on the interior light and leaned abruptly towards her. 'Let me have another look.' He gently swivelled her head, his face so close that she felt the clean warmth of his breath. For the first time, she realised how weary he looked, the eyes that were bearing down on her quite bloodshot, if incredibly alert.

'Doctor...'

*'Kyle.'*

'Kyle,' she conceded, 'you seem as exhausted as I feel... And, frankly, I can't go back in there now.'

His glanced locked into hers with considerable impact. 'I can't persuade you?'

'No.'

He wasn't pleased, but neither did he press the matter, as Raine had half expected. 'We'll take my car, then... what I said before still stands,' he countered her movement of protest. 'Driving tonight would be a risk. Even if your reflexes were in full force, there's still that broken headlight.' So that hadn't missed his notice, either. Her rueful expression confirmed his point. She had forgotten that the Mustang had only one functioning light. 'You need a lift home,' he reasoned. 'And, while I'm there, you at least need a dressing on that cut.'

'I can manage a Band-Aid on my own,' she pointed out futilely.

Kyle Benedict eyed her with a strength of will that she couldn't match. 'Don't be stubborn.'

Even as Raine wondered how he had managed to override her better judgement, she was voicing consent. And before she had time to reconsider, the switch of vehicles was made. She found herself settled in a low-slung leather seat, reflecting inconsequentially that she had never before ridden in a Porsche. Dark gleaming blue outside, it was stark black inside, right down to the smoke-tinted instrument panels, conveying the impression of power and, somehow, danger. Not exactly what she would expect in a doctor's car, although as soon as the thought formed she dismissed it as being absurd. Belonging to the medical profession didn't automatically tie a man to a Mercedes. Neither did any of the other generalisations apply towards Kyle Benedict. She was retaining her former opinion... he didn't look like a doctor, and it was more than just the muscle-hugging jeans that made picturing him in that role difficult.

A small, contradictory voice reminded her that he had dealt with her hysterics efficiently enough. She could almost feel the pressure of his hard body now, grateful for the shadowy darkness that enveloped them both. She was unsure how successful an attempt to hide her confusion might be. What was his interest in her, anyway? Just an all-inclusive compassion for humanity? She stole a glance in his direction, only to find that the dimness protecting her also concealed his expression from her view. The small glow from the dash did nothing beyond etching out the hollows and angles of a face that she could close her eyes and see too clearly.

'OK?' he tossed softly sideways.

'Yes.'

He drove with a mixture of speed and skill that she found reassuring. Although road machinery had cleared away most of the ice, the odd slick stretches required his concentration, so that Raine was left to brood over the grey scenery. Some haunting rock ballad pulsed from the rear speakers, and she recognised the song as one Brian Keaton's band performed regularly. The music was soft and sad, intensifying her mood. Black shapes and grey highway blended together, rendering the upcoming intersection insignificant. Then the streetlights began and her thought processes clicked reluctantly into order.

The clean-up crew had been very thorough. Only bare signs of the wreckage remained...A striped cone that had been forgotten. Violent friction marks along the ice-sheathed kerb. Dry-mouthed, Raine watched a few fragments of broken glass glitter in the drench of headlights.

The signal had turned to red. Kyle brought the vehicle to an easy stop and turned in his seat before she'd found her composure, and the illuminating streetlights left no nuance of that initial shudder untouched. Subjected to his gentle probing stare, she met it unguarded. Surprisingly, he reached over to take her hand.

Blinking, Raine looked down at their laced fingers. She'd never felt more off balance in her life, and was suddenly fervently grateful for his strength. He had the hands of a surgeon, lean, well kept hands with long, fleshless fingers that, by tangling with her own, made the conventional gesture of comfort something intimate. She felt deprived when the lights changed and his palm once more cupped the gearshift.

'You'll have to give me directions,' he said a few minutes later. Raine had merely waved him to a left turn as they'd exited the hospital grounds. Now she made an effort to remedy the situation, sitting up to direct him as precisely as she could. There was a straight stretch towards the city perimeter, then a couple of turns into an extensive residential area developed to accommodate the expanding Philadelphia population. Apartment houses spread in an intricate pattern of streets and culs-de-sac, some of them well established and others bare of vegetation, waiting to be landscaped in the spring. Raine pointed out the familiar building. 'Number 218'.

Kyle whipped the Porsche into a space that her Mustang normally occupied. Raine didn't wait for him to come around, climbing out on her own while he extinguished headlights and engine. He caught up as she surveyed the frozen square of lawn and the one small tree, its bare branches ice-glazed and drooping. She saw that the management had cleaned the pavement and porch. A lit sconce flanked the outer entrance, and inside, the central area servicing a group of four apartments was equally well lit. Raine led the way to the second downstairs door.

Kyle silently took the key from her and fitted it into the lock. He found a light switch inside, then stood sideways in the doorway, waiting for Raine to precede him. She did so, not without a final fluttering of nerves. As Kyle looked around the small room, Raine did the same, unconsciously imagining her surroundings through a stranger's eye. Within a framework of standard white walls and light woodwork was a mating of styles that succeeded . . . her own overstuffed chintz sofa with Felicity's glass tables, her profusion of potted plants and Felicity's series of framed and matted *Vogue* prints. There was a prefabricated fireplace at one end of the room, and a breakfast counter separated the kitchen area opposite it. Four bentwood stools had been lacquered in a dark green colour taken from the floral chintz, and served to tie the two areas together.

'You live alone?' Kyle tossed out softly, his hands shoved attractively into jeans pockets.

'With a room-mate.' She gestured to a black and white photographic study that was propped on the mantelpiece. 'Meet Felicity Boian.'

Kyle thoughtfully contemplated the likeness. 'I'd call that strong beauty.'

Raine understood exactly what he meant. Felicity was not attractive in any conventional way, but the face was singularly arresting, all softly square angles, the eyes black as jet, with the same darkness echoed in hair and brow. The photo was one-dimensional, however, the

introspection captured there an incomplete represen-
tation of her partner's complex personality. Felicity's
brief romance with a young photographer had produced
enough moods on film to fill walls, and did, if her complacent account of the man's studio could be believed.

'Good friend of yours?' Kyle successfully read the
faint, indulgent curve to Raine's mouth.

'Yes, for years. We studied fashion merchandising together. Shared a dorm room. Now we're co-owners of
a boutique called RaineBo Shoppe.'

'And co-residents of 218B,' he commented drily.

'Which isn't as tedious as you seem to think. I have
the morning shift and Felicity works evenings.' And her
room-mate had become little more than an occasional
overnight guest, although she had no intention of voicing
that thought aloud. 'We barely see one another.'

'If it works for you...' He shrugged. 'Once I'd finished my residency, I was more than ready for some isolated space.'

'I'd say there's enough gravity attached to medicine
to make a clean break desirable at the end of the day.'

'That sounds good in theory...and it probably worked
before this was invented.' Mouth quirking, he lifted one
edge of his jacket aside to indicate the small beeper that
was clipped to his belt.

'Do you resent the claim on your time?' she asked,
and saw the half-grin fade to seriousness.

'Not when it's legitimate.'

'Like Stephen?' There was no mistaking his deep
concern and compassion for the little boy. On that level,
the two of them were solidly connected.

'Yes.' His eyes were disturbingly direct. 'Or you.'

For a moment, emotion caught in her throat, but she
told herself again that he was a doctor, and apt, as such,
to reach out to anyone who was hurt and shaken. She
met that criteria explicitly, her endurance at a dangerously low ebb, and he knew it. He was fulfilling an oath
here, nothing else.

'I shouldn't hold you to that house call,' she mused, suddenly focusing on the signs of strain that marked him. If she felt this depth of exhaustion from simply brooding in her chair, then how much greater was his own fatigue? Six hours in surgery, he had told her. His psyche remained dynamic, but his body was obviously tired.

'No problem,' he said simply.

No argument came to her tongue. After a moment, she thought to remove her coat, adding it to her bag in the nearest chair. Kyle handed her his jacket and she automatically folded it in half, feeling the warmth of his body in the sheepskin lining, contrasted with the cold leather shell. He wore a heavy fisherman's sweater underneath; she watched as he casually pushed the sleeves to mid-forearm, and absently noted the expensive precision timepiece that encircled his left wrist. He was watching her in turn, vivid eyes passing the length of her body, clad in its soft sweater and grey tweed trousers. Fashion favoured the oversized look this season, yet she had the impression that the surplus cut of her clothing was no disguise to him. Setting aside the fact of his profession, she realised that he had seen the female form countless times before...without concealment. That light of awareness was unmistakable.

Because she was uncomfortable with the notion that some barrier had been dropped, Raine led the way to her bathroom, opening a cabinet to take down antiseptic and cotton wool, along with an adhesive bandage. As an afterthought, she shook two aspirin into her hand. Kyle was already filling a small paper cup with water from the wall dispenser. She tipped the tablets to the back of her mouth and, with a hasty grimace, washed them down.

'Is that everything?' she asked, as Kyle flicked a competent eye over the supplies she had assembled.

'Should be enough. I'd feel happier with some suturing materials,' he added, his voice wry.

'I suppose you detest doing anything half-way.'

'Any good physician does. We're out to achieve the maximum healing effect, or at least we should be.' Raine didn't comment, and he picked up the bottle of anti-septic, deftly unscrewing its cap. 'You'll have to hold your hair out of the way.'

He caught hold of her chin, gently tipping her head to the angle he wanted. Raine put up a hand to sweep her hair aside and held it there, watching as he dampened cotton wool. 'Isn't this where you tell me that it's going to sting a little?'

'It's probably going to hurt like hell. This cut may look harmless, but it's deep.' He applied the antiseptic without hesitation, catching her head between both palms to still her involuntary jerk. 'Sorry.' His handsome mouth held a rueful twist, but sympathy didn't spare her his thoroughness. Finally he tossed the used cotton into a wicker waste-basket. 'I'll put a bandage on as soon as that dries.'

The short wait stretched. Just as he had eaten up the space in her car, Kyle now dominated the small bathroom, his masculine aura a deep contrast to the feminine décor. Avoiding his look, Raine turned her head slightly and encountered their mirrored reflection in-stead. Kyle was all lean, hard muscle, and beside him she looked intensely female. Fragile. Vulnerable. And not only her transparent emotions troubled her. The arm that still held her upswept hair left a small, firm breast explicitly outlined beneath the white angora. Raine dragged her eyes away almost guiltily, an intimacy about the dual image that she could in no way deny.

She stood very still while he stuck the bandage in place, absorbing the brush of his fingertips against her face with a peculiar hunger. She realised that she wanted his body pressing into her like before, the need for physical contact an actual ache. Yet she fought the impulse to lean into him, self-directed anger keeping her back stiff against the flower-sprigged wall. Who was holding Stephen? she derided her own need for comfort. Any sensual feeling towards the man in front of her was inappropriate, to say the least.

His task completed, Kyle turned watchful. Raine let her hair down slowly, floundering a little beneath his gaze. The situation was beyond her realm of experience. What to do? What to say? She still wanted to bury her face in the front of his sweater, a rather juvenile, stricken feeling that did nothing for her shaky composure. She told herself again his reasons for being there, but rationalisation didn't help.

'Raine...' Kyle's hands slid to her shoulders, his fingertips exerting a subtle pressure. 'You're only human.' The near-telepathy was a jolt. Her eyes flew to his, collided...held. His voice was rough. 'After what happened today, you're entitled to fall apart.'

'I thought I had,' she said shakily. 'You haven't forgotten our struggle earlier?'

'No.' His mouth twisted. 'I'd like to forget provoking you. You'd been hurt enough.' He shrugged, his look going deep. 'Enough to justify a few tears, if you trust me to let your guard slide. Your body could use the release, and I don't object to it happening now.'

She had no intention of giving in, yet her voice turned raw. 'That's a generous offer.'

He trailed a fingertip down her cheek. 'Maybe it's a selfish one.'

Her eyes were drowning so quickly. Kyle was pulling her close, and in spite of her notion of the inappropriate, Raine allowed herself to be drawn. Fatalistically, she pressed her face into his shoulder, breathing the warm male scent that came from him. His arms tightened, creating a safe, strong cocoon that was not without its contrary danger. Raine succumbed to the embrace without strength or desire to resist. If he wanted to hold her, then she needed it badly.

He was drawing slow circles in the small of her back. Unwillingly...blaming him for moving so skilfully past her defences, Raine felt the first shudder begin down deep. Afterwards, she wasn't sure that she could stop crying, yet Kyle took the flood in his stride, rocking her gently, as if he dealt with trembling, sobbing women every day. She made no immediate effort to move once the flow had ended, feeling light-headed and drained.

'I'll wait for you outside.' Kyle eventually disentangled himself after dropping a light kiss on top of her head.

*Considerate*, Raine thought, the first stages of self-consciousness setting in. She dried her eyes with a tissue, not daring to look at her face until she'd splashed on cold water from the basin. Aside from a pink nose and swollen eyelids, she was very pale, her irises a stormy grey that reflected her inner state. Stalling, she took a hairbrush from the vanity shelf and indifferently set about taming the riot of shimmering curls.

She found Kyle in the kitchen area, and saw that he was stirring a spoon around one of her china teacups. He seemed instantly in tune to her presence, mouth quirking slightly as he encountered her questioning glance. 'This is no medicinal potion, Raine... just hot tea.' He looked completely at home, and she found herself reacting to the role reversal, crossing the beige carpeting to climb uneasily on to a lacquered stool. She fidgeted with the woven place-mat as he liberally added milk to the tea. Still stirring, he carried the cup and saucer around, then pulled up a seat with casual grace. 'Feeling OK?'

Raine took a sweet, hot sip before answering, her beautiful eyes uncertain over the rim of the cup. She found that the tea exactly suited her taste, mellowed by milk and honey to the point of perfection. She was beginning to marvel at this man's instincts towards her. He affected her in a way that she dared not probe too deeply.

'Better,' she said carefully. 'Thank you.'

'Do you want to talk?'

He was watching her with an indefinable expression, and she set her cup down with a tiny jar. 'I'd like to know why you're being so kind to me.' She hadn't meant to ask that, but once the words were out she realised that she wanted his answer. 'Or do you always go right out of your way?'

'I didn't come here in a strictly professional capacity, if that's what you're asking.' His face had scarcely changed, yet she caught a glimmer of quiet challenge. 'I won't make a speech about circumstance drawing two people together, Raine. You know what went on as well as I do...what's still going on.'

In spite of a weak desire to drag her eyes away, Raine kept staring. She wasn't up to fencing comments, wondering just how important the traditional man-woman exchange of wit had to be. Having been in his arms, albeit innocently, could she really withdraw to the preliminaries again? Did she want to?

'Reality doesn't always fit the rules,' he drawled softly, causing her another tingle of disbelief. She found his voice as hypnotic as his eyes. That touch of gravel might have sounded harsh in another man, yet coming from him it had much the opposite effect, provoking a low-key sensuality that carried its own brand of shock. Raine had to remind herself that she had known Kyle Benedict for only a couple of hours.

'How did you do this?' She glanced about a little wildly, all her long-cultivated reserve rebelling against a man who had come too close too soon. Even her own voice conspired against her, low and almost panicky, flinging out a question better kept silent. It was as if they had skipped over whole pages of dialogue to get to the heart of a scene.

'I haven't *done* anything. Bandaged your head. Let you cry on my shoulder.' His faint mockery masked an underlying intensity. 'Why are you uncomfortable with that?'

Because I can't remember the last time I cried, she thought, or any time when I allowed a man to hold me the way you did. 'I barely know you,' she said huskily. She put an unconscious hand to her head. 'And I'm not a *clinging* person normally.'

'You don't normally have to deal with the kind of shock you experienced today. And maybe I've been doing some clinging of my own. Have you thought about that? Stephen affected me more strongly than any child has for a long time. I can't say why...there's something about him...' He trailed off with an impatient shake of his head. 'Anyway, you stepped in front of my car and interrupted some hazy plan I had to go home and get drunk. I should thank you for that. It was a foolish impulse that I couldn't afford to indulge.'

That was a stunning admission, and Raine blinked her momentary confusion before fixing him in a solemn amethyst-grey stare. 'So you doctors are human, too, is that the point?'

'If there is a point, I suppose so.'

She had offended him with a sarcasm that had been both unpremeditated and unintended. An apt attestation to her brittle state of mind. Biting her lip, she bent her bright head over her cup, slowly tracing a fingertip around its embellished rim. 'I'm sorry.'

'I hear you, lady.' Kyle's smile, though faint, was attractive. He put an unexpected finger beneath her chin and turned her face towards him. 'I think it's time for me to go.'

Swallowing on a kind of pain, Raine swivelled on her stool when he stood. She watched him cross the room for his jacket. 'I want to see Stephen tomorrow.'

He paused, one arm half shoved into a sleeve, and she saw a slightly guarded look fall into place. 'I expected as much.'

'But you don't like the idea?' Raine guessed when he didn't elaborate.

'Why tear yourself up?'

She stiffened, mutiny in the lovely lines of mouth and jaw. 'I can handle it,' she insisted tightly. 'In spite of what you saw happen tonight, I am rarely out of control.'

Kyle shrugged powerful shoulders into the jacket, impatiently turning down the collar. His eyes had never left her face. 'Raine, it would take a completely callous individual to walk into that boy's room, under your circumstances, and withstand the emotional pull. Hell, I couldn't do it,' he said tersely, 'and I see injured kids every day.'

'I realise that it won't be easy...'

'Then don't pursue it. I can keep you posted on his condition. There's no need for you to become involved.'

'I'm already involved!' With difficulty, she swallowed the aggression and softened her tone. 'Kyle...please.'

She endured a dark, brooding look from him that kept his thoughts an enigma. 'We'll talk about it tomorrow,' he finally offered, frowning. 'Come to my office around three. I'm in the Administrations wing at Physicians, first floor.'

Knowing that was the best compromise she was likely to get from him, Raine nodded a reluctant agreement. She watched him delve into a pocket for paper and pen and scrawl something, then rip the sheet from the pad, laying it on the glass-topped coffee-table. 'My phone number,' he told her. 'If you experience any dizziness or blurred vision, if that headache gets out of control, or even if you need a ride in the morning...call me. Will you do that?'

'Thank you.' She focused on the prescription form that he'd used, the black scrawl visible from where she sat, and knew that she wouldn't call. 'For everything,' she added softly, as he moved towards the door.

She sat for a long time after he had gone before finally remembering to go and turn the lock. The tea that he'd made her had gone lukewarm. Shrugging, she retrieved cup and saucer from the counter anyway, flipping off light switches in preparation for bed. She paused in passing the glass table, involuntarily staring at the square page. The number was bold and, in spite of the physician's reputation for illegibility, clearly discernible. On impulse, she scooped the paper up and carried it with the tea to her bedroom, wishing that Kyle Benedict...and her reactions towards him...had been as easily read.

# CHAPTER TWO

RAINE woke to the sound of ringing, and had sleepily knocked the telephone receiver out of its cradle before realising that her alarm clock, and not the phone, had been responsible for the noise. She leaned over to flip a button and to feel about the floor for the dangling receiver. After replacing it haphazardly, she subsided against the pillows, one arm flung protectively over her eyes. She had forgotten to close the blinds last night, and weak sunshine fell in a muted pattern across the bed and her face, prodding the headache that had lain dormant to new life. Without the dreams, she would deny having slept at all. She lay very still for a while, but that last tangled vision strayed elusively, leaving a faint, exotic sadness.

She threw back the covers then, racked by a surge of nervous energy. She wondered how she would last until the afternoon without news of Stephen. Business as usual, she conceded, fighting a slight dizziness as she swung her slender legs to the floor. Her head throbbed abominably the moment she assumed a vertical position, but soon subsided to a vague feeling of discomfort.

So she went through the motions of showering and dressing, applying a little more make-up than usual to hide the worst of the shadows beneath her eyes. After taking the last hot roller from her hair, she paused to test the bandaged area of her forehead with cautious fingertips, finding it sore, but not unbearably so. The headache was only a shadow of its former self; she noticed it most when she bent forward at the waist to brush the heavy fall of hair. Standing up again, she made one more sweep with the hairbrush and watched all the little

ripples form of their own accord. She kept her hair
simple, blunt-cut at just below the shoulders and parted
at slightly off-centre; but still any real attempt to manage
the vivid mass was a foregone failure.

Her grey flannel trouser-suit was cut on very modern
lines, and teamed with an orchid-pink silk blouse. At
final inspection, Raine hunted out an antique brooch
and pinned it to the high pleated collar, then stepped
into grey leather pumps. She could have used more
blusher to offset a lingering paleness, but she shied away
from the artificial look, especially in the daytime. She
preferred a more understated elegance to Felicity's brand
of bold vivacity.

On the bedside table, the clutter of her midnight cup
of tea remained and she carried it back to the kitchen,
then made herself another while mulling over Kyle
Benedict's house call. She struggled with the memory of
his touch, some deep unwanted wisdom telling her that
Gavin had never moved her to such a degree. Gavin. She
felt a gathering sense of disloyalty, although her mind
promptly countered emotion with fact. She and Gavin
had no ties between them; any understanding was im-
plied rather than spoken, but she couldn't quite bury the
feeling that she had betrayed him in some way.

Needing a distraction, she decided to arrange for a
taxi.

Kyle's office was masculine and very attractive, an
abundance of rich polished wood and earthy tones. Raine
crossed the thick rust-coloured carpet at his invitation,
sinking into a comfortable, upholstered chair and finding
a bare spot for her bag on the edge of his massive desk.
Her eyes wandered on with interest, inspecting an
autumn landscape by a local watercolour artist that she
admired, and several leafy plants in handsome con-
tainers. An aquarium, heated and lighted, held a wide
variety of species that deserved more time for observation than she could afford. She scanned a discreet
display of credentials, her respect for Kyle growing. Head

of Orthopaedics. That was a prestigious position for a man his age, presuming that her estimate was correct. She judged him to be in his mid-thirties, at most, although the intensity of his eyes somehow hinted at an experience more advanced.

He had examined her head briefly in the outer office, and she was still acquainting her mind to the difference in him. He fitted the role of physician better than she had been able to imagine last night, bringing a hard elegance to the image. His white lab coat was well-fitted and crisp over a checked shirt and knit tie, his brown corduroy trousers emphasising the lean strength of hip and thigh, without the body-moulding properties of his former faded denims. His dark blond hair had been brushed smoothly back at forehead and temple, causing the lighter ends to blend rather than stand out. Today, he was a very handsome, slightly preoccupied stranger.

He had sat back in his leather swivel-chair with lean animal grace. 'Well?'

Raine warily met his eyes. 'I haven't changed my mind.'

'Apparently not.' He expelled a taut breath. 'You realise that seeing this child could be pretty shattering?'

'You still think I'll fall apart, don't you?'

Kyle considered her challenge with a fathomless expression. 'I think...' He drew the moment out, tapping a pencil against his desk blotter several times before pitching it aside in a decisive motion. 'I think you'd be playing with fire just by going up there. If you were objective enough, you'd walk away, now, before you're tangled up any further. However——' his handsome mouth twisted '—human beings are rarely capable of that kind of objectivity. There are too many ruling emotions.'

'Yes,' Raine admitted, her grey eyes very clear. 'You aren't going to deny permission, are you, Kyle?'

'Maybe I'd like to. If I didn't know you'd take the decision as a lack of faith, instead of an attempt at protection.'

'My protection, or Stephen's?' She had to ask.

'Primarily yours. Stephen is too heavily medicated at the moment to be affected much one way or another.'

'How is he?'

His eyes narrowed thoughtfully. 'Good, all things considered. I intend to keep him under sedation for the next day or so, until the worst of the pain is past. His vital signs have been healthy, though. I'd say he's going to wake up one mad little boy.'

'One frightened little boy,' Raine corrected, a faint throb in her voice which she quickly quelled. 'Will you explain his injuries to me?'

Kyle sent her a frowning glance, as if considering her ability to handle the details, then, visibly resigned, chose to comply. 'Among the list of minors is a cracked rib and a slight concussion...a lot of bruises. There's a fairly ugly abrasion to the left side of the face that looks much worse than it really is.' Raine nodded silently, remembering the raw scrape that had marred Stephen's small face yesterday, and realising that it must have worsened with time. Still watching her closely, Kyle continued, 'A fractured femur of the left leg is our main concern. The jagged edges of bone were responsible for the torn blood vessels that we had to repair in surgery. The break is also high, and that complicates things considerably. I'll show you the X-rays, if you like.'

'Please,' Raine confirmed, swallowing on a dry throat.

Nodding, Kyle looked through a stack of brown envelopes and withdrew the appropriate one. Raine watched him clip the negatives to a board, which he then illuminated with a flick of a switch. 'You'll have to come around to my side,' he suggested offhandedly during the preparations, and Raine circled the corner of his desk.

'See how close the break is to the hip joint?' He indicated the fractured area with a pencil tip, careful not to touch the film surface. 'That creates problems in itself. If the bone won't knit properly under traction, it may mean more surgery later to insert a steel pin. The pin would stabilise the bone until a healthy fusion could be made.'

'Do you think that will be necessary?' she asked, dreading anything that would lengthen Stephen's stay in the hospital. A moment later she had to ask herself where else the child could go.

'I'm hoping the traction will be enough.'

'Why traction now? Why not a cast?'

'Because the muscle surrounding the fracture is traumatised...it wants to shorten and spasm, which draws the bone ends into an overlapping position like this——' He put his two forefingers together in demonstration, then moved them apart until they were tip to tip. 'This is what we want, to keep the bone ends together. Traction is the means. The weights in a traction system supply pressure to very gently stretch the limb into the right position and keep it there.'

He reached beyond her to a bookshelf, his arm and shoulder brushing her thigh as he withdrew a thick medical journal. A point near its centre was marked by a scrap of paper. 'I found this illustration earlier. I want you to see the system I'm using on paper before you see it on Stephen. This is Bryant traction,' he explained, holding the book open for Raine's inspection. She saw a diagram of a small child, both legs wrapped in elastic bandages that held triangular metal frames to his feet. Rope was tied to the frames, passed over pulleys above the child's bed, then attached to weights that hung over the foot railing.

'Is this painful?' she asked, voice flat but eyes dark with trepidation.

'No,' Kyle assured her. 'But sudden movement would be. That's why a small child with Stephen's type of injury is usually kept in a jacket restraint, and also why both legs are suspended. Any side-to-side movement of the body...any thrashing around...interferes with the even pressure of the weights, and can disturb a healing fracture.'

'I see.'

Kyle closed the book and laid it on the desk before swivelling slightly in his chair. Raine met the look that he angled towards her, with what she hoped was a reasonable sense of acceptance. Was he trying to weaken her plans to visit Stephen or did he simply mean to have her well prepared?

'As a physician, I believe in the most concise and honest explanation of a patient's injury that I can give, Raine.'

She couldn't keep a faint defiance from her voice. 'I thought you might be testing my nerve.'

'You haven't forgiven yourself for last night, have you?'

That seemed so totally off the wall that she could only stare at him in ill-disguised confusion. 'For letting me comfort you,' he elaborated drily, reaching up to grasp her hand. With very little trouble he manoeuvred her into a position facing him, so that she had to meet the impact of his eyes or seem a coward. The leap from a professional footing had been made so swiftly that something inside her did, in fact, retreat.

'Kyle...' she frowned, perching slowly on the desk edge, 'don't let's analyse.' His answering shift in expression was subtle, yet it disarmed her. She allowed her fingers to tighten briefly. 'I have to thank you for trusting me with Stephen.'

'Actually, the trust is conditional. I'm going with you.' Raine drew back a little, but Kyle wasn't backing down. 'Come on, lady. You don't need to be alone. And personal feelings aside, I have my patient's welfare to consider.'

She blinked heavy lashes, thinking that Kyle Benedict as an authority figure would make a formidable opponent. 'You're making it very obvious that you don't approve of this.'

'Damned right.' He laced his fingers deeper, a measured intensity in his lean face. 'Keep a sense of perspective on Stephen, Raine. He'll be out of our hands in a few weeks.'

\* \* \*

It became patently obvious a few minutes later that Kyle was not taking her to the Paediatrics unit. Comparing the blue lines along the floor of the corridor that they were travelling to an instruction graphic painted on the wall, Raine's suspicions grew to new proportions. Mouth compressing, she tugged on Kyle's sleeve. 'Where are we going? That was an empty elevator we just passed, and I know that Paediatrics in on the fourth floor.'

'We're making a small detour through Radiology.'

'Why?'

His expression was bland. 'Some unfinished business.'

'Kyle, no! Not me.' Raine took root to the spot, causing a minor traffic jam in the crowded corridor. Separate lines of people were already forming to go around them when Kyle grasped her arm and firmly pulled her aside.

'I insist,' he said, scowling mildly when a passing orderly tossed a speculative glance back over a shoulder. 'Raine, listen to me. I wanted to insist on an X-ray last night, but you were too upset to give in and I was too exhausted to argue with you. While I don't really suspect any trouble, complications from a skull fracture, even a hairline fracture, can be delayed. Do you understand? That makes any unclarified head injury a potential time-bomb.'

'Kyle, I feel fine,' Raine urged, unreasonably reluctant. Or at least the reason was known only to herself. The one time in her life when she had been forced to submit to a hospital's care carried the most unpleasant association.

'Then allow *me* to feel fine,' he challenged flatly. 'I promise it won't hurt.'

'That's the second time you've accused me of cowardice,' she said, violet sparks in her eyes. 'Actually, the thought of having an X-ray made doesn't frighten me any more than the idea of a stitch did last night. Has it occurred to you that I just do not want to bother?'

She realised the pitfalls of that statement as soon as it was made.

'Beautiful!' Kyle's mouth tightened grimly. 'You've just hit upon the one argument that a physician most hates to hear. I spent twelve years of my life learning to mend bodies, lady. All you have to do is lie on a table, and you don't want to bother?'

'This is *my* head,' she reminded him stubbornly.

'Empty though it may be.' He raked a hand through his hair at her taut expression. 'I'm sorry. This seems to be getting out of hand.'

'I agree.' Squaring her slim shoulders, Raine met the blue of his gaze. How traumatic could an X-ray be? She was twenty-four years old now, not five. 'It isn't the request that I object to so much as the manipulation.' Being tricked rang ominously of her past.

'I thought it might be the only way,' he admitted with a ruefully attractive smile. 'Will you come with me? I have a few connections with the radiology staff. Enough to have your head on film in about ten minutes.'

It was closer to twenty before a technician brought Kyle the finished products. He clipped them up on the spot, frowning thoughtfully over several views of her skull. 'It looks as if my bullying was unnecessary,' he finally made a diagnosis. 'That bump on the head of yours is no more than a bump on the head.'

'Do you feel better?' Raine couldn't resist the urge to taunt.

'Much, thanks.' Kyle took a quiet glance over her drawn face and began to replace the X-rays in their folder. 'You're still angry.'

Raine shrugged self-consciously. 'Not so much angry as impatient.'

'Try nervous,' he suggested shrewdly. 'You're trembling.'

'I'm shivering. That table was cold.'

'You could put your jacket back on.' Without giving her time to act on his comment, Kyle pulled her suit jacket from the back of a chair and held it out. Raine obligingly slid an arm into a sleeve, then turned her back to him as she completed the movement, feeling his hands settle the material over her shoulders. His fingers brushed her nape as he straightened her collar, and the touch felt warm and disturbingly welcome.

'Thank you.' Moving away, Raine found her handbag on the end of the examining table where she'd laid it. There was a small bathroom opening off to the left, and she walked in there to deal with her mussed-up hair, inordinately aware of Kyle's reflection behind her in the mirror. He was apparently amused by her yielding to the hairbrush; she saw that much in the faint twitch of his lips. Feminine vanity aside, she still wasn't stopping. That technician had done a pretty thorough job of tangling the already unmanageable mass.

'You have beautiful hair.'

Raine glanced up and met his eyes in the mirror. Like last night, she found that she had to look away. 'After an intimate look at my skull, I don't doubt that you appreciate the stuff that covers it. Does everyone have those little bumps and ridges?'

'Ever noticed a bald man?' he returned the dry quip.

'Can't say that I have.' She balanced her bag on the sinktop long enough to get the hairbrush back inside. When she turned around, her smile held a discernible edge. 'I guess there are no more reprieves for me, then.'

'A few minutes ago you were talking about impatience.' He knew instantly that she was referring to her visit to Stephen's room. 'No one is asking you to do this but yourself, Raine. I won't think any less of you if you back out now.'

'Ah, but *I* will.'

Raine was glad for the two student nurses who joined them in the elevator, their smothered giggles and transparent glances at Kyle distracting her from a rising sense of unease. The sudden stop intensified a vague queasiness in her midsection, so that she barely registered the opening doors. Kyle's hand in the small of her back propelled her forward and she stepped into the antiseptic air with a disproportionate sense of foreboding.

The Paediatrics ward was a relief. Seeing none of the sterile, utilitarian surroundings of two decades ago, Raine immediately had the impression of a big, sunshiney park. Bright yellow tiles and framed clown prints were everywhere. She saw a nursery rhyme scene painted across the nurses' station in bold primary colours. Glass nursery windows were curtained in ruffled yellow gingham, and Raine glimpsed a couple of rocking-chairs inside, one of them in motion. Half smiling, she watched a gowned and masked nurse croon to the baby she was feeding.

'Hi, Doctor Benedict.' A petite blonde, installed behind the central desk, had raised her head from a stack of clipboards and was watching their approach with friendly interest. 'You're early for rounds.'

'And you're working past your shift, as usual.'

'Charting.' The nurse made a cute face to convey her distaste for the task, then turned expressive green eyes to Raine.

'Raine Jacobs, Andrea Cummins.' Kyle performed the introductions with a crooked grin.

Andrea's pretty, vivacious face conjured up an instant liking. Raine imagined that the little ones on the floor loved her, when everything about her exuded warmth and enthusiasm. Even her appearance was intriguing, her white trouser-suit topped by a pink jersey cardigan instead of the normal lab coat, the sleeves pushed up comfortably to reveal a red and black Mickey Mouse watch. There was even a tiny toy koala clipped into a breast pocket and peeking over its edge.

'We're here to see Stephen Thompson,' Kyle explained, and to Raine's relief, Andrea didn't enquire about her own interest in the little boy. Nodding, she deftly extracted the appropriate chart.

'Here you are. We've moved him to 412.'

Kyle glanced over the page. 'His vitals are still good.'

'Yes,' Andrea agreed, grinning. 'He's a strong little guy. I'm probably going to fall in love with that one.'

'You fall in love with all of them, Andy.'

'Look who's talking!'

Their easy exchange went a long way towards putting Stephen's situation in perspective. Still, Raine was very glad that Kyle had shown her that diagram when she finally walked ahead of him into Stephen's room. Dropping her bag into a chair, she crossed to the stainless-steel crib where the child was sleeping, trying to ignore the contraption that held his tiny legs suspended. His fluffy head was turned sideways on the mattress and he sucked unconsciously on his thumb. The scrape that Raine remembered from the day before had swollen and coloured angrily. She saw adhesive tape around his ribcage, beneath the straps of the cloth jacket that restrained him to the cot. One small arm was taped to a board to protect an intravenous needle. Hurting, Raine watched the clear, steady drip.

Kyle, after making his own observations, moved unobtrusively to her back. She felt the warmth of his body before any contact was made, then he drew her lightly against him, both hands resting on her shoulders to knead the tense muscles there. Raine found the movement both soothing and disconcerting. Kyle's tenderness could easily crumble her defences, when seeing Stephen was making them fragile.

The baby jerked in his sleep and apparently sensed the restraint. Both adults went still, searching the little face for any signs of consciousness. The small mouth that had gone nearly slack worked frantically for a moment, then the thumb plopped wetly out. The soft lower lip jutted alarmingly and began to quiver. 'Shhh, darling,' Raine crooned softly, bending over the low bars to guide the curled little fist back to its destination. Stephen sucked greedily, then his blue eyes slitted open and he stared up with an uncertainty that made her throat ache.

'Mama,' he whimpered.

A pain shafted straight through Raine's heart.

'Don't say anything!' She whirled on Kyle when he had taken her to a conference-room that was blessedly empty and closed the door. She saw him leaning there with grim intensity, then the unbearable ache behind her eyes suddenly became his fault. The anger was an un-reasoning, defensive thing, a brilliant flash in her eyes striking out and searing him. 'A sense of perspective, right? Then don't touch me, and don't say anything, because I'm walking a very thin line.'

'Raine, come here.' He stopped leaning, made a move towards her, and she jerked away. 'For heaven's sake, stop it!' He caught her arm. 'This wasn't a test you had to pass. You were *fine*. You were beautiful. Now you're shaken and upset, with every right to be.'

She made a fist and thudded the wrist-side impotently into his chest. 'I feel so...damned...helpless! Kyle, what are we going to tell him about his mother?' She stared at him, stricken, and with a heavy sigh, he pulled her close.

'Come here. *Please*. If you don't need it, then I damn well do.'

Raine buried her bright head in his shoulder, too wounded to fight. She heard the unsteady thud of his heart between her own ragged breaths, and clung to his hard frame, in spite of any denouncements. The urge to cry became all but overwhelming, yet she raised a palm to scrub at the one tear that escaped, well aware that he possessed all the authority necessary to ban her from entering Stephen Thompson's room again.

Kyle wouldn't let her draw away completely, linking both hands in the small of her back when he realised her intent. 'Not yet.'

'I need to,' Raine retorted wearily, a new soft sarcasm edging the words. 'You're the man in charge here, aren't you? Something tells me the distraught pose isn't the best way to stay in your good graces.'

'Exactly where is that coming from?' His voice was equally soft, yet Raine knew that she had angered him. It was there in his eyes and in the perceptible stiffening of his body. 'If you want to stay in my good graces, then just be honest with me. Don't try putting on a cool front. Not now. Because I won't buy it, Raine.'

Raine bowed her head, struggling with the realisation that she had shown this man more emotion, more of herself, within twenty-four hours, than she had allowed Gavin Reynolds in well over a year. She wasn't a terribly physical person, yet Kyle had done little else but touch her in one way or another, and still she couldn't seem to get enough. Didn't all those elements add up to something dangerous? How could she tell him that the way he affected her was contradictory to everything she had believed about herself up to this point? There was no way of conveying to him that the cool front he'd derided could truthfully be called her natural manner.

Eventually she did the only thing that she could do. She side-stepped the issue entirely, steeling herself to confront a clearer one. 'Will I be allowed to come back tomorrow?'

Kyle stared into her uplifted eyes for what seemed an age, his handsome face taut. 'Raine...'

'Kyle, I know what you're thinking, and I wish you wouldn't.'

'Raine, do you know what you'll be getting yourself into if you keep coming back?' His hands moved up to her shoulders and tightened as if he wanted to shake her. 'A sick child can be heartbreaking. You've already felt the strain, and this was only the beginning. What about a couple of days from now, when he's awake and alert? He'll be hurt, he'll be bored, *frustrated*, you name it! He could take every ounce of mental reserve that you possess and still need more. And when you get right down to fact, you have no obligation, moral or otherwise, to become involved.'

'I have an obligation to myself,' Raine declared passionately. 'I wish I was capable of explaining my reasons to you, because I probably owe you that much. But I can't, and if I did I'm sure you wouldn't understand.'

'Then what you're asking for is blind trust?'

There seemed to be a hard, unyielding quality to him. Already Raine tasted defeat, but she made one last appeal, assaulting Kyle with her lovely shimmering eyes. 'Don't fight me on this. *Please*, Kyle.'

'You can't use a please and those eyes in one sentence,' Kyle said flatly.

'Is that a yes?'

'A conditional one only.' His impatient caution suppressed Raine's reaction before it properly began. 'No promises, Raine. Call it a probationary period, during which I reserve the right to call a halt if I see that either party is under undue stress. You agree to those terms, or nothing.'

'Lord, don't you love your power!' Raine got out, softly rebellious, and earned herself an attractive, but cynical smile. 'A minute ago you were telling me that there were no tests I had to pass...now I'm on probation. Obviously, there's no choice. Thank you,' she added with wry insincerity, 'for making this easy for me.'

Suddenly, all traces of humour in Kyle, mocking or otherwise, had flown. He put a finger under her chin and tipped her face, his eyes stripping away at the mutinous mask that she wore. 'Nothing can make this easy for you, Raine. You're too passionate towards your cause. I'd allow you free access to Stephen, otherwise, with no misgivings. But, as it is, all I seem to feel is a tremendous sense of unease.'

She had no answer to that, when the same restless feeling held her in its grip. She closed her eyes and remembered standing by Stephen's crib, his little hand curled in her palm, Kyle's hard body pressed to her back. But a sense of *rightness* evoked by the image was soon overshadowed by the disturbing element of truth. Neither boy nor man had existed for her before yesterday.

# CHAPTER THREE

RAINE made one last sweep over the glass display case with her cloth, then stood back to study the new arrangement of holiday sweaters inside. The cashmeres were done in an unusual array of colour, and she had enjoyed the challenge of matching them with an appropriate scarf or piece of jewellery, fitting blouses inside some and jackets over others. She had also unpacked some pine cones and flocked greenery to fill the shelf corners, and she was pleased with the result.

Walking to the front of the shop, she looked out and noticed that the mall's crew of workmen were there on ladders, hanging Christmas decorations under the staff designer's critical eye. She registered a slow ripple of surprise, again, that the holidays were upon them. Only a few days until Thanksgiving, and the weekend immediately following heralded the Christmas shopping season, five hectic weeks that brought in roughly half of the retailer's cash flow each year. Their own holiday decorating was scheduled for Friday, and Raine spent a few moments visualising how it could best be done. Simply and tastefully, if they achieved the intended effect. A great deal hung in the balance . . . not the least being their lease renewal in March. This first Christmas in Spirits Mall, more than any other, had to be perfect.

Even observing caution, Raine projected outstanding sales figures for the month of December. A previous freestanding location had set the groundwork for success, but business had nearly doubled since their relocation here last spring. The reasons were obvious. All the elements of mall shopping were working for them now: ideal placement in a large commercial area, abundant parking, the convenience of finding some ninety merchants under one roof, not to mention the added bonus of restaurants and cafés, cinemas, an arcade, a babysitting service…the list was impressive. Just their alliance with the mall brought them an entire cross-section of people who had never frequented the shop before, and they found that customers loyal during their three years on Pine Street were not at all averse to travelling the odd extra mile. Add to that Gavin's clever advertising tactics, and the future seemed irresistibly full of promise.

So why are you a bundle of nerves? she asked herself, as she unlocked the sliding gridwork that served as front door. She was aware that an underlying restlessness coloured her thoughts and actions these days, a restlessness that she felt most strongly during the hours she spent in the shop. She was still acutely conscious of the demands of her position, the responsibilities, yet the vitality and absorption that she normally derived from her career had diminished. And that emerging ambivalence disturbed her. It was an unstable way to begin trial by fire, which was what this point in time meant to RaineBo Shoppe and its ultimate success or failure.

Felicity came stalking in at one, the smoulder in her black eyes suggesting anything except a sunny mood, while the droplets clinging to her head and shoulders revealed that the weather was in total accord. Raine watched as she sifted an angry hand through her glistening hair, succeeding only in spreading the dampness, so that her style became even wilder. The curls, unlike Raine's, were artificial, but the lively mass of shoulder-topping dark waves made a wonderful frame for Felicity's strong features. She refused to touch her eyebrows, needing a definite shape to balance a full mouth and wide jawline. Her eyes were her most arresting feature, thickly lashed and so black that they might have been jet.

Raine laid her pencil down, brows raised in concern. 'What's happened?'

'Brian has happened,' Felicity answered tightly.

'An argument?' she ventured cautiously.

'Don't understate the obvious. We had a brawl.'
Felicity began stripping off a red batwing coat, to reveal
sleek black leather slacks and a voluminous red and black
tunic sweater underneath. Textured black stockings and
red leather pumps completed the look, stiletto heels emphasising Felicity's super-slim height as she stalked,
catlike, through the swinging service doors to dispose of
the coat. 'He's hired a new salesgirl,' she expounded
moodily upon re-entry to the floor.

'This is the busiest time of the year.'

'For heaven's sake, don't be sensible! She's a green-
eyed blonde, with possibly a better shape than even
yours. Her voice hovers about two decibels below un-
interested. And,' she disgustedly offered the clincher, 'she
can harmonise.'

'I see,' Raine responded carefully, reluctant to en-
courage a full-blown account of the injury. She knew
Felicity's capacity to become carried away.

'You don't,' Felicity maintained, 'but you will if we
take a casual stroll to the front door.' Finding her arm
taken and her body being stealthily dragged along, Raine
had little choice. From their vantage point behind a rack
of winter coats, they could easily see across the mall and
one door down, to where a lithe blonde was drawing the
full force of Brian Keaton's regard.

'Trouble,' Raine breathed succinctly.

'Right.' She could see her partner visibly struggling to
put the unpleasantness aside, and she thought it prudent
to initiate their move back towards the sales counter.
Store personnel had to be consistently pleasant, re-
gardless of personal problems.

'Her name is Nola,' Felicity volunteered. Raine
glanced round in acknowledgement of the comment, and
glimpsed an expression behind the black eyes that gave
her pause. Fear? Vulnerability? Her heart gave a small
answering lurch.

'You really see her as a threat, don't you?'

'Yes.' The reply was flat. Felicity changed the subject
as they approached the counter. 'Nice display.'

'Thanks,' Raine quirked her mouth in understanding. 'I'm thinking of buying the coral one for myself. Care to venture an opinion?'

'Since when have you needed my opinion?' Felicity sent her a speculative look none the less. 'What about that fuchsia one with the raglan sleeves?'

'With my hair?' Raine chided drily. 'No thanks.'

'Save it for me then, will you? I'll give myself another hang-on-in-there present. Thank goodness I'm not one of those women who eats her way through emotional disasters, or I'd be as big as a barge. With my luck, none of the weight could possibly go in the right places.'

Lunch for Raine was a salad in a small bistro-type restaurant in the mall's front wing, accompanied by the tall glass of tea that was all she really wanted. After pushing a few forkfuls of lettuce around the plate, she gave up altogether, opting to spend the rest of her break window-shopping the competition.

She passed the cinema entrance on the return trip, and out of purely idle interest stood watching as a young usher changed poster advertisements for the week. Walt Disney's *Pinocchio* had just finished a long run, the colourful announcement now removed from a wall-mounted frame and curling on the floor at the boy's feet. On impulse, Raine went over to his side.

'Would it be possible for me to buy that poster?'

The teenager blinked distractedly and spat a couple of thumbtacks into his palm. 'That one?' He thoughtfully screwed up his face, then shrugged. 'I wouldn't know how much to charge you, and the manager's gone to lunch…Hey, why don't you just take it, ma'am? You can have it.'

'Thanks, if you're sure.' He handed over the poster in answer, and, grinning, Raine started to roll it into a tube. 'I know a little guy who will love this.'

Felicity's reaction when Raine showed off the acquisition was inexplicably sarcastic. 'No chance it's going on your bedroom wall?'

'Mine?' Raine lifted delicate brows. 'No, it's for Stephen.'

'Of course.'

The droll tone, when repeated, was too much to ignore. Raine cast out a level glance. 'Is something wrong with that?'

'You tell me,' Felicity came back, too quickly. 'You've known him...what, seven days? Eight?'

'And?'

'And he isn't your child, Raine.'

The antagonism was so unexpected that she felt an answering jolt. 'He's no one's child. You, of all people, should understand how that makes me feel.'

Her voice had risen and heads turned. 'Excuse me...miss?' someone called from the dressing area and Felicity vaulted forward. Raine slowly rolled up her poster, all the joy gone out of it. From the corner of her eye, she could see Kim standing behind the cash register, with a look of surprise and uncertainty on her pretty face. Heart pounding unpleasantly, Raine took her poster and her jacket into the stockroom.

Felicity followed only moments later, her attitude a mixture of apology and defensiveness. 'I'm sorry,' she got out in the manner of one uncomfortable with admitting a mistake. 'I had no right to jump at you like that. I guess I'm letting my tension with Brian spill into other areas. But——' of course, there was a *but* '—you have to realise that your behaviour has been pretty hard to understand.'

Raine took her time putting her coat on a hanger before turning around. The anger was still there, but she willed it to subside. 'What's to understand?'

Felicity balked a little, then took a deep breath. 'This Stephen thing. A week ago you didn't know that Stephen Thompson existed, now he's practically a fixture in your life... You've spent every evening with him at the hospital, haven't you?'

'What if I have? He's two years old, Felicity. He needs reassurance, someone to entertain him. If I don't mind being that person, why should it bother you?'

'There are nurses.'

'For whom I am very grateful,' she agreed fleetingly.

Her friend looked uneasy. 'How much does this little boy mean to you?'

'A lot,' she was bound to admit. 'He's very special and very sweet.'

'Then isn't it obvious that you're going to be hurt? You told me that he should be out of the hospital in another four weeks. More to the point, our season starts Friday. How are you going to work a hospital visit into a twelve-hour day?'

The small silence that fell became an unintentional foreshadow of what was to come. She saw Felicity's face shift into tautened lines, but retorted, 'I don't object to a seven-day week, but I can't work beyond six o'clock or so at night. Not this year. I'd rather we hire an extra clerk to cover my evening hours. There's still time, if we start interviewing now.'

Felicity's expression could not have held more effrontery had Raine announced plans for a trip abroad. Which was, in a way, understandable. Past holiday seasons had seen total dedication from the both of them, a willingness to breathe, eat and sleep RaineBo Shoppe, if need be. Felicity had every right to expect the same now, except for one very important reason. Stephen. In spite of torn feelings, Raine knew that she couldn't give up her time with Stephen. The visits had somehow become too important to both of them. In fact, if she were honest with herself, she'd admit that the day only properly began when she walked into that hospital room. Whether that constituted the obsession that Felicity so obviously suspected, she could not have said.

'I don't have to ask why.' Felicity seemed to go rigid. 'Risking your emotions…those are none of my business, Raine, but when you neglect the shop, I have a right to protest.'

'Neglect?' Raine challenged flatly. 'You can hardly call it neglect when I'll be here more than sixty hours a week.'

'I just don't think it will work. Here we are, going into one of the most important seasons of our careers, and you've suddenly found outside interests!' She ground out her half-smoked cigarette with a shaky hand. 'I can't believe you'd jeopardise this business for the sake of a child that you'll never see again once the month is out. I thought you were committed.'

'I *am* committed,' Raine said, low-toned, resisting an impulse to point out Brian Keaton as the conflicting interest in Felicity's life, simply because her friend could barely see reason in that department. The word *never* used in connection with Stephen had caused her an instantaneous sharp pang, and she voiced the truth with a degree of self-discovery. 'The commitment is just no longer an exclusive one.'

'I see,' Felicity got out, an unhappy and fatalistic light in her black eyes. 'Meaning that the RaineBo Shoppe is in danger of taking a back burner.'

'If you believe that, then you don't know me as well as we both thought.' Raine grew impatient. 'I have no intention of neglecting my job, Felicity. If the need arises, I can always take the bookwork home with me at night, and spend the bulk of my time in the store selling. There's no reason why it can't work.'

Felicity's failure to respond to the reassurance left little doubt as to her feelings in the matter.

Stephen was Raine's compensation. The excitement in his brilliant blue eyes when he saw her crowded all memory of an unpleasant day from her head. The poster was unrolled and duly noted with a 'No-key-o!' and a delighted giggle. Raine had brought Scotch tape with her and set about fastening the colourful illustration to the wardrobe door, where Stephen could see it with a turn of the head, careful to keep it at his eye level. Standing back to judge the effect, she was treated to another of his throaty chuckles. The sound struck a joyous chord inside her. Lying flat on his back and immobile, Stephen had every right to cause chaos, yet, beyond the critical first few days, he had been unfailingly good-natured. Having steeled herself to cope with tears and tantrums, he was so much more than she had expected.

Funny that so small and immature a face could hold so much charm. He was unbearably appealing, with his bright blue eyes crinkling, and silvery cornsilk hair standing on end. She surrendered to the now familiar impulse, bending over the crib to kiss round cheeks dimpled from a wide grin. 'Hi, cutie.'

'Hi, you!' Stephen chortled, slapping a small hand to her face affectionately. The flat little palm moved from her cheek to her mouth and she took a playful nip at it, causing another deep giggle to erupt. 'Stay me,' he ordered—or asked, she wasn't sure which. 'Rubs me back.'

'Well, I can see right now that you're going to make a fine little chauvinist,' she scolded mock-sternly. 'Which is my fault for spoiling you, I'm sure. How's that, you little monkey?' Andrea Cummins had shown her how to reach under him for a back rub, how to feed him in his prone position, and other practical elements of his care. Raine was spending every evening with him, and she didn't in the least object to freeing the nurses of some of that responsibility. There was a call button within easy reach, and she was really happier to be left alone until the need to use it should arise.

Stephen was something of a sensualist, she'd discovered, which was not an uncommon characteristic for young children. He knew how to relax his body, lying supine during the back rub with lazily drooping eyes that said if he had been a little cat he would be purring. Raine bestowed a drily humorous smile upon him, finally withdrawing a hand that had grown tired under his slight weight. 'That's all for now. What would you like to do? A puzzle?' She had raided the toy shop for several of the wooden preschool variety, and found Stephen to be remarkably adept at handling the large pieces.

'No. Read,' he announced contrarily.

Another of his favourite pleasures. There was a new Golden Book in her handbag and Raine obligingly went to get it, offering Stephen a sip of juice through a straw before settling down in the bedside chair to act as narrator. She put a lot of animated inflection into her voice for his benefit, unfolding a barnyard tale with all the appropriate animal sounds. There was a typically raucous climax, then all loose ends tied up for the menagerie; the television set was switched on and the little boy's favourite *Sesame Street* filled the screen.

A whoop from Stephen announced Kyle Benedict's arrival some time later, simultaneously sending a spray of chocolate milk into space. 'Not with your mouth full,' Raine chided mildly, quickly withdrawing the carton and straw from his proximity. The hand that found a tissue and mopped at the damages betrayed the slightest tremble. A devilish grin from Kyle said that he saw it, and, furthermore, that the reason was no mystery. The grin immobilised her for a long moment, drawing her into the blue depths of his eyes.

Shattering. There was no better word to describe such sexual tension. After days of resisting the intangibles that battered at her instincts, Raine thought the attraction had actually passed into a psychic realm. He only had to walk into the room for all her nerve-endings to start pulsing. There was little chance of keeping an unaffected front.

'How's my little man?' he greeted Stephen.

'Big!' Stephen shouted gruffly, then shook with husky laughter at their shared joke. When the glee had partially subsided, he poked a stubby finger to his own apple-red cheek. 'Kiss me.'

It was a command not to be ignored. Kyle had to come past Raine and rested a hand at her waist in doing so. Her heart melted a little as she watched him lean over Stephen's bed and kiss the dimpled cheek that her own mouth had brushed at least half a dozen times that day. The gesture was completely natural and without self-consciousness. 'Who's been teaching you that?' he enquired, amusement in his tone.

'Me Raine,' Stephen replied, quite reasonably.

'Your Raine, hmmm?' Kyle straightened and cast a mockingly attractive look her way. 'Aren't you getting a little possessive, kid?'

Raine was unsure whether she had been addressed, or Stephen. 'It was only a figure of speech,' she said softly.

'If that's how you prefer to see it.' He was non-committal, but a fingertip flicked lightly at her cheek belied any real seriousness. 'Have you been here long?'

'Since six-thirty, or thereabouts.' A glance at her watch said that more than two hours had passed. 'I've been trying to get this little fellow to go to sleep,' she added drily. 'I can't get him up and rock him, that's for sure.'

'Tried a bedtime story?'

'Three at last count,' she admitted. 'Care to try your hand?'

'Do'tor Kyle read me,' Stephen echoed, successfully illustrating the fact that very little adult conversation went over his head.

'If I get to choose the book,' Kyle consented, a wry twist to his mouth. 'It had better be a quiet one. I think you're the only patient awake on the whole floor.'

Stephen looked pleased with that bit of information, and settled down contentedly, while Kyle flipped through his collection of books. He chose Beatrix Potter's *The Tale of Peter Rabbit*, pulling a straight chair close to Stephen's side and switching off all but the nightlight over the bed, while Raine shrugged away an impulse to protest the selection. She had attempted that story yesterday, with little success. Maybe a man's voice behind it would make a difference to the child's attention span.

Certainly, *she* had loved *Peter Rabbit* as a child. But, curling into her own chair in the corner, she reflected that she had never heard that or any other story read by a voice quite like Kyle's. Deep, gritty-soft, it sent minute shivers along her spine.

Barely two or three pages had been turned before she realised that something was wrong. A panicky look of restlessness seeped over Stephen's small features, and he began to wriggle within the jacket that held him pinned on either side to the mattress. 'Boo,' he said dejectedly, repeating the word that she'd heard him say before. Yesterday, Raine had taken it to be his best attempt at the word 'book', thinking that he disapproved the story chosen. He had been easily distracted by a switch of activity, and she'd placed no more importance on the incident. Now she wasn't so sure.

'Where boo?' Stephen whined, and Raine sat up straighter in her seat.

Passing her an enigmatic glance across the bed, Kyle closed the storybook and put it aside. Raine watched him lean down to the child's level and put a comforting hand over one small straining shoulder. 'Be still now.' The tone was a mixture of gentleness and authority. Stephen subsided a bit, fixing widened eyes toward Kyle. 'Where boo?' he repeated with childish pleading.

'Stephen, I don't understand.'

Frustration flooded the little face and made the full lower lip jut. 'Boo!' he howled, beset by the inability to convey his request in adult fashion. The tiny chest heaved upward, the cloth restraint clearly multiplying his complaints. Kyle's slight frown showed that he was as bewildered by the outburst as was Raine.

'Hey,' he chided mildly, moving his palm in a soothing circle over the little boy's chest. 'Calm down, little man. We'll find another story if you don't want that one. What would you like? *Cat in the Hat*?'

Stephen's head jerked from side to side, fiercely negating the attempt at diversion. His eyes, never so blue, were welling with angry tears. 'Don't want story!' he articulated gruffly, chin quivering. 'Want me boo!'

All protective instincts aroused, Raine uncoiled from her chair, taking a small teddy bear from the menagerie

that had been growing on the cabinet tops. Kyle stood
to allow her past him and remained standing at her back
while she bent over the little boy. 'It's all right, darling.
Here, I brought you Teddy.' She put the toy in Stephen's
arms, only to see it thrown hastily and firmly to the floor.
The little face was crumpling. Feeling helpless and inadequate, Raine did the only other thing that she knew
to do; she kissed him everywhere...on his trembling chin
and tear-streaked cheeks and on the little eyelids that
were squeezed tightly shut. A tiny fist came up, tangling
desperately in a brilliant strand of hair, and he opened
drowning eyes in one final appeal.

'I want boo, Mama.'

A breathless pain smote her, but somehow she
managed to calm him, stroking and gentling until his
tears took their toll. He looked shatteringly weary when
he finally fell asleep, and only then did Raine acknowledge the fiery ache behind her own eyes.

'I couldn't even hold him!' she said, low-toned, to
Kyle, glaring fiercely sideways, as if it were his fault that
Stephen couldn't be picked up and cuddled. And in a
way he was responsible. She was coming to hate Stephen's
traction system with all her heart, recognising that as an
illogical feeling, but one she couldn't curb. 'How do you
explain something like that to a child?'

'Be still,' Kyle murmured, his only response. His body
spread heat the length of her as he stood, gently prying
Stephen's fisted hand from her hair. The task took some
time, and she kept brilliant eyes on his face, the husky
tirade continuing.

'He is *two years old*, Kyle. He shouldn't have to hurt.
He shouldn't have to *feel* like that...And who or what
is "boo"?' The words became almost strangled. 'I've
never felt this helpless. I hate it!'

'Then walk away,' he said, deadly serious, the last silky
strand falling from his fingers and Stephen's.

Raine straightened on cue and jerked towards him,
disbelief glittering in a passionate face. 'That's the very
last thing I would do.' It was an effort maintaining the

low husky tone, when she wanted to shriek. 'Can't you understand?'

'You want to replace his mother.'

That was delivered flatly and succinctly, driving home a point that had safely eluded her grasp for days. He had taken all her torn, bleeding, emotive reactions to the accident and encased them in one compact statement. She closed her eyes against Stephen's dear little face and its shock of white-blond hair, still very plainly hearing his voice. He had called her 'mama'. A single crystal droplet began a slow course to the corner of her mouth.

'Raine.' Her name came on a ragged breath, and she had a notion that it came unwillingly. A moment later Kyle had framed her face in his hands. She opened her eyes and saw that his had darkened with some of her own torment. As a look, it was colliding and somehow naked. Instinctively, she lifted her mouth.

Nothing like the gentle, comforting brush that she had expected, there was instead a pulsing urgency to Kyle's mouth. A soft, slow-motion invasion of lips and tongue that burned heat through her. Like a young girl enduring her first caress, she convulsively began to tremble. There was no parallel in her experience and, steadying her swaying body as he pulled away, Kyle could hardly help but know.

Moments passed, with Raine shakily struggling for composure, seeing no indication from Kyle that he had been affected to anything approaching her depth. Perversely, she refused to break eye contact. She wanted to know that he had shared that explosive reaction. There was no excusing her own degree of participation otherwise, or the implication of misguided instinct.

He met the look head-on, blue eyes searing her almost as effectively as his mouth had done. She realised then that she hadn't misread him, and all her outraged nerve-endings quieted to their normal heavy pulse. A heightened awareness remained, her mouth throbbed, and she was suddenly looking anywhere except at Kyle.

'Come and sit down.' There was a dry note there, leaving her no secrets. Raine tucked a light blanket around Stephen's awkward little form, then padded on stockinged feet back to her chair in the corner. Kyle followed, setting his own chair close and reaching with familiar arrogance to take her wrist in his hand. His fingertips burned into her skin, but his expression was unreadable.

'What a time to take my pulse,' she said jerkily. 'Don't turn into Doctor Kyle on me now...I think I need someone to talk to.'

The soft appeal came without conscious thought, and she watched a shadow of a smile tug at Kyle's beautiful firm mouth. 'We're one and the same.'

'No.' She stirred a little, amethyst eyes momentarily lowered. 'There's a very definite professional face that you wear at times. Anyway, I might be asking help from the wrong counterpart. It's probably a professional opinion that I need.' He didn't respond, at least not in a verbal way, and she expelled a soft, troubled sigh. 'Do you think Stephen's remembered something?'

'Boo?' Kyle assimilated, eyes narrowed. 'I'm sure of it, although *what* it is, is beyond my powers of deduction. With a child's vocabulary, it could mean anything.'

'There's a link to the book. The same thing happened yesterday when I tried reading it, although Stephen wasn't really upset then. I was able to distract him pretty quickly.'

'There's every possibility that he's familiar with the story and that it brings back some memory to him.'

'Then you think this temporary amnesia, or whatever it is, could be slipping?' Raine heard a brief tremor beneath the question, its origin clear enough. She had come to dread the moment when Stephen asked for his real mother, instead of merely accepting her as surrogate. What words could explain death and its separations to a two-year-old?

Kyle frowned a little, and she found the gesture very attractive and faintly quelling. 'He's suffering from trauma, Raine. Strictly speaking, it isn't amnesia at all, but more a subconscious blocking of painful feelings. He had a shock that made his thought processes go a little fuzzy, and he's clinging to the confusion out of sheer self-protectiveness.'

Raine absorbed that information, absently noting a few minuscule dots of chocolate milk that had marked her white cord trousers. Still deep in thought, she curled her slender legs up into the chair. This corner had almost become home to her, the cramped confines no longer an imposition, and she wondered how she would cope if Stephen woke up right now and said, 'I want my mommy... you go away.'

With an odd accuracy, Kyle had divined the gist of her thoughts. 'Does he call you that often? Mama?'

There was almost a severity in his lean face and she answered with constraint. 'Aside from the first time you brought me to him, just tonight. And once, right after the accident, when he was being put into an ambulance. I leaned over him, and I'm sure he was misled by my hair. It's virtually the same colour as his mother's,' she expounded tautly. 'Mine is longer.'

'But there's enough physical similarity to make the delusion an easy one?' He frowned again, eyes shrewd. 'I didn't realise. That complicates things considerably.'

'And you hold me to blame?' Raine had to ask, a cold little knot of misery in the pit of her stomach.

'Things would be simpler without you,' he admitted, some quality of voice and expression giving the comment an unexpected double edge. 'Not that simpler is necessarily better. Right now, you're making life a hell of a lot more pleasant for Stephen, and that's something I could easily appreciate. Until the end of the story...when you and Stephen are separated, and both of you get hurt.'

Variations of that prophecy had come from so many people that Raine could no longer fail to take the issue seriously. Was she doing Stephen a greater cruelty than kindness by allowing him to become attached to her? The day would come when he was well enough to leave the hospital under supervision of the appropriate authorities, and she had every reason to expect that she'd never see him again. The idea was so intolerable that panic leapt up and made a weird, shimmery dance in front of her eyes, yet she had to acknowledge that a slow day-to-day phase-out would be just as painful. And to suddenly stop visiting at all didn't bear her consideration. So what was the answer?

Kyle, so beautifully male and enigmatic, offered no further help. Raine let a silence fall, and he turned his head to study Stephen's rhythmically breathing little form, obviously brooding over his own thoughts. Desire took its hold on Raine then and there, but as usual her timing was absurd. Her surreptitious glances told her that Stephen had Kyle's mind at this moment. She kept looking, and the dark, absorbed expression suddenly became definable. There was affection in it, and the wry indulgence that most men might show for a sleeping child, but an underlying vein almost of bafflement, as if something elusive hovered just at the edge of his grasp. She'd seen the look from him before, but until now had been unable to identify it.

Following the direction of his gaze, Raine swept a long glance over the little boy. The injury to his face had nearly subsided, leaving only a vague bluish tinge to the area around his left eye. He was a remarkably attractive child, his beauty in no way frail or transient. A thing of bone structure and inherent trait, it promised to endure into manhood, and possibly even to surpass the gawky stages in between.

Shifting her attention again to Kyle, she found his guard partially resurrected. A long look passed between them and she saw enough in it to bolster her faith in her instincts. 'Kyle... pass judgement on me if you like, but I believe you've become just as involved as I am.'

'Stephen draws me...' he admitted after a pause. 'I can't explain the feeling any better than that.' Mocking blue eyes raked her. 'I also have this nagging and probably ridiculous notion that I've seen him before, but the hospital records show no proof that he was ever treated here.'

'You actually went to the trouble of checking?'

Kyle shrugged almost irritably. 'I said it was probably ridiculous.'

'That little face would be hard to forget,' Raine reasoned.

'Is there a message in that for you?'

'Oh, don't,' Raine moaned, the bond of companionship beginning to shatter. 'I've discussed the possible consequences of my folly too many times already, and all unwillingly. I'd rather talk about Stephen.'

'I thought we were.'

Raine ignored that. 'Do you think rehabilitation will be a problem?'

Kyle was too much a professional to spare her feelings. 'Could be,' he frowned, leaning a bit closer. 'The worst that can predictably happen is that he'll have to learn his walking skills all over. And there will be a limp to adjust to. With any luck, he'll eventually outgrow that.'

But neither of them would be around to find out whether that happened. Sadness washed over her at the thought. She was already feeling the pangs of separation.

'Hey, lighten up, lady,' Kyle coaxed, his eyes holding her own. 'I admit that the one thing they teach you in the medical profession is to anticipate and prepare for the worst, but the thing you learn on your own is to believe in a miracle when you see one. Stephen's alive and he's doing fine. You can believe in that.'

'I know.' She tried to smile, and unable to quite manage it, laid her head back against the chair. 'There was a time when his physical injuries worried me most. Now that I know he's in good hands...yours...I'm more concerned with the psychological aspects. His mother was cruelly taken away from him; he's being kept here immobilised and among strangers; afterwards, he goes into either an orphanage or a foster home, to more strangers. How does a tiny child cope?'

'How does any orphaned child cope?' Kyle came back softly.

Raine's mouth took on a humourless curve. 'Ask one and find out.'

'You?' As always, his deductive powers were swift. She bit into her lower lip, already regretting the slip.

'It was just a silly comeback.'

'I don't think so.' Kyle's blue gaze bore into her. 'I've had a feeling that you share some unusual type of empathy with Stephen. That's it, isn't it? I'd like to hear what happened, Raine.'

Having got herself in that deep, Raine saw no graceful way to back off. But she wasn't bearing her soul, and the reticence in her grey eyes said as much. 'I don't remember my mother at all. My father let me tag along after him until I was five before he abandoned me. That's the story, Kyle. I'm not in the least bitter about it.'

She was unaware that every element of her expression contradicted that flatly issued statement. She thought only of putting the seal back on her past, quickly and effectively. But, of course, Kyle chose not to co-operate.

'What happened afterwards?'

'Kyle . . . please. What do you think? By the time the authorities had me sorted out I was well into the gangly little girl stage, all skinny long legs and missing teeth. Naturally, I wasn't adopted. I spent the next twelve years or so in assorted foster homes, until I was eighteen and old enough to be on my own. I used a government grant to put myself through fashion merchandising school, and the rest you know.' She laughed a little shakily when he didn't respond. 'I realise this all sounds like a bad melodrama, but you did trap me into it.'

'I was thinking of all the couples who missed out,' he told her seriously. 'You would have made a wonderful daughter.'

Raine searched his handsome face for mockery or patronisation, but found neither. 'Probably it was the red hair that kept scaring away prospectives.' A light comment was the only way she had ever known to deal with such moments. 'What about you?' she ventured evenly.

'I guess I owe you that much,' Kyle conceded, an odd glint in his eye. 'There's just my father and myself left of the four of us.'

'What happened?' she echoed his question of a few minutes earlier, before thinking. Proof that she was not without her own sense of curiosity.

'My mother died, when I was in college, of a bone disease that had been slowly killing her for years.' The statement came matter-of-factly; obviously an old wound that had had plenty of time to heal, it left only the vaguest pin-point of emotion in his blue eyes after the telling. 'She spent the last half-dozen of them in a wheelchair, but even then she never became an invalid. She was quite a lady.'

'You said four?' Raine prompted after a moment.

'Yes. My younger brother was killed in a riding accident a few years back.' The very lack of emotion in his voice and face gave evidence that there was a great deal of it. 'He was twenty.'

'I'm sorry.'

'So am I,' Kyle admitted. 'Which brings us to my father. Without going into detail, let's just say that he blames himself. Luckily, his business keeps him very busy. A brokerage firm. Benedict's.' He cocked a mocking brow. 'Ever heard of it?'

'Of course. As a matter of fact, they manage a modest portfolio for me that was *very* modest at the outset. I just began dabbling this past summer.'

'Care to invest in some hospital stock?'

'Now you're teasing me,' Raine grinned a little. A thought dawned on her and she rapidly sobered. 'Physicians is a privately run hospital, Kyle, and I know it's relatively expensive. If there's any question about the financial aspects of Stephen's care, I...'

'Forget it,' Kyle broke in with a brusqueness that half startled her.

'Why?'

'For one thing, because we've been round and round the subject of your involvement with Stephen, and that would be just another way of clouding the issue. But mainly, because the expenses have already been met.'

'By whom?' she wondered aloud.

'House rules, Raine...I can't disclose private details with regards to a patient.' The closed quality to his expression said that he wanted the subject closed, but she stubbornly went on.

'You forget that I'm familiar with the Child Welfare procedure. I expected Stephen to be transferred to a government-run hospital right away; it would have been more efficient and more expedient.'

'Except that I am his doctor, and his injuries dictate that he's better left in one place.'

'You aren't going to tell me, are you?' Keeping her tone even was difficult, when she was already imagining some secret sponsor who had his eye on Stephen, ready to spirit the child right out of her arms.

'No, ma'am,' Kyle drawled on a dry note.

'Fine.'

His blue eyes glinted with something she couldn't recognise. 'You have a redhead's temper under that layer of reserve.'

Reserve? The idea was almost laughable, when she'd behaved with anything except reserve towards Kyle right from the beginning. He'd cut straight through to the heart of her that first night. He was still doing it, actually, her recollection of that fiery kiss ample proof. No amount of reserve had kept her from the act, or now from the mental recounting of it, and no barrier blocked off the resulting wave of heat that suffused her skin.

Kyle's face, dangerously still, reflected like reaction. Raine swallowed slowly and moistened dry lips, unconsciously provocative, as the tension pulsed between them.

In the back of her mind, she heard Stephen's shallow breathing and the hospital's night sounds, but for the life of her she could look no further than Kyle's mouth. Masculine firmness with finely chiselled edges. Sensual lower lip. Wry curve. Every detail took on a clarity that she wouldn't easily forget.

Thrown into a weird kind of panic then, she almost bolted from her chair. Stephen's teddy bear was still lying on the floor where he'd thrown it, and she picked the toy up with jerky motions, returning it to its furry little friends. The half-finished book was likewise dispersed. Distractedly smoothing at a wrinkle in Stephen's blanket, Raine realised that there was nothing else to be done, and only then did she reflect that Kyle must think her a demented young woman to have launched into that burst of restless activity. Sliding him an almost defiant glance, she went suddenly still.

He was as she had left him, reclining with a deceptively lazy air, chair tipped on rear legs so that his fair head rested back against the wall. The relaxed stance ended with his eyes. Alert and watching her beneath half-lowered lids, they conveyed ironic humour and a kind of indulgence, but something else. *Hunger*, she thought, limbs trembling, and the word united with the ache in her own stomach in a way equally disconnected with food.

'Kyle, I . . .' Biting her lip, Raine let the sentence trail away. *I what*? I want you? No man has ever attracted and overwhelmed me the way you do, and the intensity is too much to be borne? *I am afraid*, a tiny voice inside her shakily supplied. But none of those admissions found their way past her lips. She simply leaned against the wall with her hands supporting her weight, and looked at him, unaware that her eyes were communicating everything.

'Raine, it's all right.' His sexy, grating voice smote her; he righted his chair and stood, but she knew instinctively that some part of him had been withdrawn.

'For now,' he added, the self-mockery in his face a fiercely attractive thing. 'But you can't run for ever.'

You're probably right, Raine silently acknowledged, as she watched him leave.

## CHAPTER FOUR

RAINE parked her car with a sigh of relief. At barely eight o'clock in the morning, Philadelphia's streets were already teeming with traffic, and her normal fifteen-minute drive to the hospital had taken almost twice that time. The air was unusually nippy, but the skies were beautifully crisp and blue...making a perfect setting for the Thanksgiving Day Parade that was scheduled to begin in an hour. Bundled adults and snowsuited children were already lining the parade route, anticipating the assembly of floats, gigantic balloon figures, and celebrity vehicles to come.

Delving about the back seat for the small bag containing Stephen's Thanksgiving goodies, Raine reflected that this would be the last full day she could spend with the little boy until Christmas was over. She wanted to make the time special. They were watching the parade on television this morning, then she was having a traditional turkey dinner with him in his room. There were new Golden Books to follow, along with a slightly more advanced preschool puzzle and pumpkin-shaped cookies from the mall bakery. She had brought her briefcase full of ledgers but, given Stephen's boundless energy, she might be taking the work home again tonight.

Satisfied that she had everything she needed, Raine locked the car and went inside. The hospital seemed to bubble with that particular enthusiasm that marked a holiday, the chatter a little brighter, the pace a little more brisk. She heard giggles as soon as she came out of the elevator, Stephen's deep belly laugh prominent among them.

'Excitement seems to be contagious!' Andrea Cummins laughed as Raine came into Stephen's room.

73

'If they act like this for Thanksgiving, what happens——' she staged a whisper '—when Santa Claus comes?'

Wet from the elbows down, Andrea was attempting to wash Stephen's hair in a plastic basin. Apparently, he'd made a game of thrashing his head about in teasing resistance. Raine could see damp splashes creating an arc where his neck touched the sheets, and felt grateful for the rubber padding underneath that kept his mattress dry. 'You look as if you could use some help with this little monster.'

'Great,' Andrea grinned, 'if you're sure you know what you're getting into.'

'I came prepared,' Raine made a vague gesture to indicate the jeans and Fair Isle sweater beneath her casual down jacket. An entire day with Stephen made adaptable attire a necessity. In spite of the traction and the jacket restraint that subdued his efforts, he managed to be one boisterous little boy, and she still hadn't forgotten the chocolate milk episode. Those white cord trousers were probably stained for life. 'I've got my sneakers on and my hair up——' she leaned over the crib in response to Stephen's wild whoops of greeting '—and I'm ready for you, young man.' Stephen seemed to find that inordinately funny, and she prolonged the erupting giggle by tickling his nose with the end of her ponytail. 'Hi, sweetie. May I have a kiss?'

Still grinning, Stephen promptly slapped a hand to either side of her face and tugged her head down, his sweet, sloppy kiss landing somewhere near her chin. 'Cartoons,' he immediately ordered, one stubby finger aimed towards the television set that had been mounted on the wall.

'Anything to keep you still,' Andrea teased, drying her hands on a small towel before switching on the set. 'There's Road Runner, OK?'

'Beep-beep!' Stephen mimicked in what they assumed to be agreement.

Meanwhile, Raine took it upon herself to keep the small hands from flailing about while Andrea rubbed in baby shampoo. They were doing fine until the sight of Stephen with hair slicked to his head like a fifties biker struck them oddly, then they both began to giggle. Stephen, intrigued by the outburst, swivelled his drenched head from one to the other, blue eyes round. 'Let me see!' Raine showed him a hand mirror, and the child's fit of laughter prompted Andrea to arrange a variation of soapy curls.

It was inevitable that someone should happen upon the unorthodox scene. Gavin had the honour, his dark brows rising in unconcealed disbelief as he halted just outside the door.

'Raine?' His voice got her attention, as well as Andrea's, and the two of them raised slightly guilty, slightly embarrassed faces.

'Gavin?' Raine responded dimly, aware in an instant of how she must look. Soapsuds specked the front of her pastel-patterned sweater, and a dark spot of dampness marked one thigh. A tendril of hair had escaped the ponytail, to drift across her cheek, and she pushed it slowly behind an ear, the carefree happiness fading from her expression, to leave a vague wariness in its place.

'I thought I might find you here.' He was still looking from one to the other of them, his brown eyes lingering last on Stephen's animated little face, which was topped by its crown of bubbles.

'Time to rinse,' Andrea told the little boy, her voice suddenly no-nonsense.

Raine put a hand beneath his neck for support while Andrea sluiced off the worst of the soap, using a plastic cup as dipper. 'You aren't working today?'

'It's Thanksgiving.'

Raine couldn't blame him for the slight sarcasm that underlined the words, although the question had not been meant in kind. Struggling for something to break the silence, she had simply come up with the wrong thing. She was doing that a lot with Gavin lately, an uncomfortable tension lacing any attempt at conversation, so that she found herself now weighing words. 'Of course it is. Are you going to your parents'?'

The tone was too bright, almost false. She could nearly see him wince. 'I thought I might. Can we talk somewhere?'

Andrea, back with a fresh basin of water, touched a hand to Raine's arm. 'I can manage from here on my own, if you need a few minutes.'

Bless Andrea, with her unobtrusive ways. Turning to Stephen, Raine gave him a reassuring smile. 'I'll be back soon, sweetheart. You can have your bath and your breakfast, and then we're going to watch the parade.'

She didn't miss the suspicious look Stephen threw the man who had broken up their fun and, apparently, neither had Gavin. 'There's a waiting-room around this corner,' she told him, and he followed her lead without comment. He looked as tense as she felt, a certain grimness around eyes and mouth. Given the early hour, the room was deserted of visitors and offered their choice of seating. Raine wandered over to a pair of upholstered chairs in the far corner, hands nervously taking up a magazine and rolling it into a tube even before Gavin was properly seated opposite her.

'Do you have any idea how hard you've been to contact the past few days?'

'You could have called the shop,' she pointed out, realising too late that the answer only irritated him further. Gavin rarely made personal calls on company time. And any attempt to telephone her after office hours would have been frustrated by the fact that she'd come straight here from work each evening. 'You haven't left any messages.'

'No.' Gavin let out a controlled breath. 'I wanted to talk to *you*, not the answering machine.'

'I'm sorry.' Raine softened, sighing. 'I've been really involved with Stephen.'

'Yes,' he agreed, the one syllable suggestive of many more. 'When you didn't answer at home or at the shop, I knew there was only one place to look at this hour.

Here. I'm surprised you haven't checked into a room,' he added, mouth twisting.

'What a coincidence, when I've often wondered whether your draftboard converts into a bed at night. It seems to be all you need.' The words out, Raine subsided in a kind of shame. Cattiness simply was not her style, yet she felt ready to slice away at Gavin with the newly awakened sharp edge of her tongue. And why? Because he had interrupted a playful and special moment with Stephen, or because accusation glittered in his dark eyes and threatened to dampen a day that had begun so brightly? She didn't want to fight with him, but it seemed to be a new talent of hers, prickly patches rising all over at the slightest incitement. 'Sorry,' she said again. 'I must have gotten up on the wrong side.'

'You can't expect me to believe that,' Gavin countered flatly. 'Not after what I just witnessed in that room. You were having the time of your life until I came along.'

'Hardly that,' Raine denied uncomfortably.

'I've never seen you laugh like that.'

'You've never seen me with a small child.'

Gavin rubbed fingertips into his temple, the gesture unconscious and weary. 'No, there's more to it than him. You're changing, Raine. I really can't put my finger on it, but you're changing.'

Startled, she didn't quite know what to say. 'I'm not sure what you mean.'

'I think you know. You don't have time for me any more, and the motivation isn't strong enough for you to *make* time.'

'Gavin, that isn't true.' A tiny inner voice contradicted the denial yet, unwilling to see him hurt, she said it anyway.

'Then prove it,' he challenged after a moment, his voice taut. 'I did have a reason for chasing you down this morning. You're invited home with me for Thanksgiving dinner, if you'll come. *Will* you come, Raine?'

Pressing back in her chair like a caged animal suddenly prodded, she looked at him with wary, darkened eyes. 'You know I can't do that. You heard me promise Stephen that I'd be back.'

'Then I'll meet you half-way. It's a long drive, but an hour one way or another won't make that much difference. I'll call my folks to tell them we'll be late. We can watch the parade . . . like you promised . . . then we'll leave.'

'You told them I was coming?'

'No, not with things the way they've been between us. But I come from a large family. One more is no trouble.'

'I'm sorry . . . I can't.' She made a determined effort to meet his eyes. 'I promised Stephen the entire day. The store will be chaos after tomorrow, and today is the last real chance I'll have to be with him, other than a couple hours in the evenings.'

'So where does that leave me?' he demanded, knowing that she had no answer.

'Gavin——' unhappily, Raine laid a hand on his arm '—please try to understand. Stephen needs me right now. He's just a little boy. Surely you can't begrudge him a few weeks of my company? Goodness knows——' her mouth unconsciously turned bitter '—I've lost enough of yours to McKenna's, or Lansers, or whatever the project of the moment happened to be.'

'This is different,' he argued tersely. 'After all, we have an understanding about our careers.'

'Then, if RaineBo Shoppe was taking all my time, it wouldn't matter?' Raine summarised, a new frowning edge to her expression.

'Don't put words into my mouth.' Gavin let his voice drop as a man walked into the room and settled into a chair near the doorway. 'It looks as if our conversation if over, anyway.' He stood then and tipped her face briefly when she followed suit, his kiss pointedly absent. 'Maybe we can celebrate the New Year.' The sarcasm was meant to hurt.

'Happy Thanksgiving,' Raine said tightly to his turning back.

Andrea had put Stephen into a fresh gown, towel-dried his hair into wispy ringlets, and was smoothing the last wrinkle out of his clean white sheets when Raine walked back into the room. As she drew closer to the bed and the little boy's irresistible soap-and-baby-powder scent reached her nostrils, her pasted-on smile relaxed into softer lines. His shiny pink little face beamed an innocent grin in her direction, small arms crossing over his chest with a patient air as Andrea added a sparkling white blanket to the bedding and tucked it around his legs. The nurse then straightened with friendly sympathy in her green eyes. 'Are you all right?'

'Was the tension that obvious?' Raine grimaced a little and received Andy's slight shrug in answer. 'I'm just stretched a little thin, I suppose.' She tried for a philosophical tone, but didn't quite make it. 'At least, that's what my friends keep telling me.'

'They'd have to see you with Stephen to understand.' Andrea busied herself putting away the bath things for a moment, then paused with the discarded sheets and blanket draped over her arm. 'Good-looking guy. Was he someone special? Tell me if I'm overstepping bounds.'

Raine shook her head at the other girl's wry qualifier, 'You aren't. There was a time when I thought he might be special,' she went on slowly. 'But things have been difficult lately.'

'Meaning that he isn't willing to stand by you when you need him?'

'Something like that. He doesn't feel that I need him enough.'

'The fragile male ego,' Andrea reflected softly. 'And do you? Need him?'

'Not the way he wants.' The acknowledgement took no thought at all, tumbling off her tongue as if it was something long ago admitted and accepted.

'Ah,' Andrea murmured sagely. She walked to the laundry bag that she'd left suspended from a doorknob and stuffed the used bedclothes inside. 'I believe Doctor Benedict is on the floor for rounds.' Though the comment was idly phrased, both girls were fully aware of the import behind it.

Raine raised her chin, bearing up under the friendly implication. Her smile was faint and a little dry. 'That's not fair, Andrea.'

'So I just discovered my boundaries.' The blond girl made an answering dry face. 'Sorry. It's just that if Kyle looked at me the way he looks at you, I'd make him the solution to all my problems.' Without giving Raine a chance to demand any elaboration, she blew Stephen a kiss and disappeared, laundry bag in tow.

Breakfast arrived shortly. Lowering the bedrail to perch on the edge of the mattress, Raine pulled the under-bed table containing the tray close to hand. 'Look, Stephen. Cornflakes...and bacon and scrambled egg,' she added, lifting the cover from a warming dish.

'Choc'late milk!' Stephen demanded imperiously, spying the brown and white carton she had been trying to conceal.

'Just a little,' Raine cautioned, well aware that he would consume the entire portion otherwise, leaving no appetite for the rest of the meal. Resignedly, she shook the carton to mix its contents, opened one end and inserted a bent straw. Stephen gulped contentedly, scowling when she took the straw away. 'Here, try some bacon.' Raine popped a crisp titbit into his mouth before the wail of protest could escape. While Stephen munched, she emptied a miniature box of cornflakes into his bowl and added milk and sugar. She barely got two spoonfuls into the baby bird mouth before its jutting pout forced a capitulation. The resulting grin dripped messily of chocolate milk, prompting an indulgent one of her own.

'Discipline, Raine, discipline,' Kyle's voice mocked her.

She half turned, to see him leaning against the door-frame, indolently handsome in sweater and trousers, hands in the pockets of his white lab coat, and blue flame flickering in his eyes.

'Easier said...' Smiling, she shrugged and left the phrase unfinished.

'I know,' Kyle straightened and walked towards them, his attention straying to Stephen. 'Who can resist those baby blues? Hi, sport! Happy Turkey Day!'

Stephen dissolved in giggles, as he was meant to do. It was a firm part of the ritual now for Kyle to kiss him, and he did so from the opposite side of the bed, angling a wry look at Raine as he drew away with a smear of chocolate milk on his lean cheek. She passed over a fresh napkin and watched him rub at the sticky spot. 'You'll do.'

'Thanks.' Kyle's fingers brushed her palm as he handed back the napkin, the familiar wicked grin hovering just below surface. Then his tone became official. 'OK, Stephen, I need to check your chewing reflex.'

Raine could almost see Stephen's little ears pricking as her own incomprehension cleared. Kyle moved the railing on his side of the bed and sat down, leaving only the width of Stephen's small torso between them. The stethoscope was taken from around his neck, earpieces put into place and the disc placed alongside the little boy's jaw. Taking her cue, Raine held out a spoonful of cereal and Stephen's mouth opened obediently.

Kyle listened, giving every appearance of stern absorption. 'Sounds healthy,' he decreed for Stephen's benefit. 'Want to hear for yourself?' Stephen nodded, enthralled, and the earpieces were shifted. Raine shovelled in a bite of bacon and watched him move the crumbly food about his mouth, listening furiously. The bacon was swallowed, a smile emerged, then the little mouth popped open for another bite.

Flinging Kyle a congratulatory look, she provided a forkful of egg, which was promptly ingested. Before Stephen showed any sign of boredom, over half the food on his tray had disappeared. Raine acknowledged Kyle's tactics with a grin while the child took the last swig of his milk. Kyle simply raised an enigmatic brow, making no attempt to rescue his expensive stethoscope from little

fingers. 'Want to hear your heartbeat?' he asked
Stephen, when Raine had wiped up and pushed the tray
aside.

'Uh-huh!' At the enthusiastic nod, Kyle placed the
flat part of the instrument to Stephen's small chest.
'Bum-bum-bum,' the child's chant rose in unison with
the sound he heard. Round blue eyes met the smile that
Raine bestowed, then lit with new interest. Pushing at
Kyle's hand, Stephen nudged the disc towards Raine.
'Hear Raine,' he ordered gruffly.

'May I?' Kyle's voice again mocked her, his eyes
sparked with blue flame. Raine caught her breath as he
leaned slightly across the bed, lifting the flat scope to
her throat. Movements slow and deliberate, he slid the
disc over the curve of her left breast. Stephen was totally
innocent of any undercurrents, his husky child's voice
chanting, 'Bum-bum, bum-bum.'

Raine found no defence against the tide of heat that
threatened to consume her. Bright spots of colour burned
high on her cheekbones as the pulse from Kyle's lean
fingertips beat into her breast. The mockery in his face
had changed to intensity. Stephen was oblivious,
chuckling his delight. 'You listen!' he offered the earpieces and, with a twisting smile, Kyle took them.

There was nothing Raine could do to slow the beat of
her heart to an acceptable rate. Kyle's eyes burned into
her, she stared back defiantly, then suddenly she had to
escape. Reaching to grasp his strong wrist, she tugged
the disc away from her breast, suppressing a shudder as
his hand slid across her stomach beneath the awkward
force. 'Stephen's the patient.' Her voice shook.

'Coward,' Kyle drawled softly.

There was a tap at the door then, announcing the aide
who had come to collect Stephen's breakfast tray. The
stethoscope was put to Stephen's heart, and the rest of
Kyle's examination performed. He finished by having
the little boy wiggle his toes to evaluate the circulation
in his feet and legs. 'Good work,' he praised the toddler's efforts, his deep grin one that Raine would have

given a great deal to merit. 'Now...isn't it time to watch the parade?'

'Yea-a-ah!' Stephen cheered.

Raine shifted position on the bed, while Kyle found the proper channel on the television and drew up a chair. 'Are you staying?'

'If there are no objections,' he said easily. 'My day isn't scheduled any further than morning rounds...which I just completed with Stephen.'

'Won't you be having dinner with your father?' Raine asked.

'No. My father usually eats Thanksgiving dinner out, with friends. We don't celebrate holidays in the family tradition any more, unless you count a shared brandy on the occasional Christmas Eve.'

'How very sad.' Raine responded candidly to his soft cynicism. 'If I had a family, no one and nothing could keep me from observing the family traditions. How can you be so careless about something like that?'

'Possibly because it doesn't mean the same to me as it obviously does to you.' The rebuke was mild. 'Don't imagine any great gulf exists between my father and me. We understand each other pretty well.'

'It seems to me that you should want to be with him,' she stubbornly went on.

The mockery was back, curving his mouth, 'I'm thirty-six, Raine.'

He may as well have said, 'I don't need anyone.' Feeling firmly put in her place, Raine fell silent. The Thanksgiving Day Parade came on the air in all its glory, prompting Stephen to do a great deal of shouting and pointing, his cries of 'Bullwinkle!' and 'Snoopy!' enough to send Raine over to shut the door. She wandered restlessly about the room for a while afterwards, ignoring Kyle's glittery, mocking looks. Finally, he dragged her empty chair next to his...a challenge that she couldn't ignore. She felt his breath against her temple as she sat down.

'Isn't it time you stopped running?'

Her eyes slashed sideways and locked joltingly into place, tiny flames of awareness, of alarm, licking across her skin. Before she could react, he had leant close to kiss her parted mouth. The salute was brief but frighteningly sensual, enough to dissolve bones. And Raine's response was instantaneous, a moist flowering that could in no way be misread.

'Try telling me this attraction is one-sided,' Kyle drawled softly, desire evident in the deep husky chords of his voice. His fingertips trailed along her jawbone and dipped into the soft hollow behind her ear, the gesture slow and deliberate.

'Kiss *me*!' Stephen shouted jealously, diluting an atmosphere that had grown dangerously intense. Kyle's lazy, heavy-lidded look was on her while she went to comply, but Raine could only feel grateful for the small boy's intervention. She had been much too far from any denials.

The morning went quickly, Stephen exuberant with his bounty of two guests for the day. Lunch was served and eaten, accompanied by an animated version of *A Connecticut Yankee at King Arthur's Court* following the televised parade. Kyle mysteriously excused himself afterwards, the absence lasting only a few minutes before he came back with the key to the mystery in his arms.

Her name was Jenny, Kyle told them. The little girl, who looked to be four or five, was held astride his hip, her left elbow encased in a pristine new cast and sling, while her right arm was hooked tightly about Kyle's neck with a fistful of his white lab coat in the little clenched hand for good measure. Raine had only a glimpse of the exquisite small face before it was buried frantically in Kyle's shoulder. Her heart turned over as he gathered the tiny nightgowned figure closer and made low, soothing noises, rocking gently. 'Don't be afraid, baby. I've got you.' His softest voice, combined with the cradling motion of his body, had a magical effect. The little dark head slowly began to swivel. A pair of the most beautiful velvet-brown eyes that Raine had ever seen peeped out from his coat front.

'Hi, Jenny.' She greeted the irresistible child with something of Kyle's tone.

Stephen, however, viewed the newcomer with less sensitivity. 'Look at me!' The gruff order found its mark. Jenny half turned in Kyle's arms, right hand still clutching at his collar. She stared at Stephen, trussed up on his bed, with first trepidation, then growing curiosity. 'What happened to his legs?' she piped in a shy, little-girl voice.

'Broke,' Stephen offered grudgingly, though the tremulous question had been directed to Kyle. The little boy had been given a brief, necessary explanation when he'd regained consciousness after the accident, yet that muttered word quickly drew Raine's enthralled eyes away from Jenny and back to Stephen. Rather than being pleased at a chance to make a new friend, he looked decidedly put out. Raine glanced questioningly at Kyle and he raised a brow in answer.

Taking his former position on the edge of Stephen's bed, Kyle settled the dainty, flower-sprigged little body on his lap. Jenny pressed back timidly, fingering one of her short dark braids. Kyle's arms tightened reassuringly around her middle. Raine sat on the opposite side of Stephen, judging his reception of the other child. His expression was not in the least encouraging—all pout and glower. She saw his blue eyes, suspiciously glittering, fasten on Kyle and Jenny, and his lower lip jutted as if pulled by a string.

He's jealous, she suddenly realised. The poor little fellow is jealous! She shot a lightning glance at Kyle, trying to convey the discovery, and saw that he had already guessed. Delving for the best way of dealing with the situation, she slipped Stephen's small hand into her own. The bright, possessive look he sent up and the fierce way he clung to her fingers confirmed her instincts. But Kyle was the real problem. After all, Raine wasn't the one holding Jenny on her lap. And no one was holding

Stephen, that inability to be cuddled probably the worst outrage of all, to his young mind.

Neither child spoke, and attempting to ease the moment Raine made an effort of her own. 'How did you hurt your arm, Jenny?'

There was a long, hesitating stare from enormous liquid eyes. 'Climbing a tree,' she got out, nearly inaudibly.

'Oh, no! Did you fall out?'

'Yes.' The little head bobbed vigorously.

'Tell Stephen why he'd better not climb any trees,' Kyle prompted gently.

The child's voice became very hushed and very grave. 'Because it's dangerous.'

'That's right,' Kyle agreed seriously, his eyes moving to Stephen. 'So are you going to climb trees, sport?'

'No,' Stephen denied, momentarily distracted, his eyes very round.

Object lesson dispensed, Kyle put out a lean hand to ruffle Stephen's silvery hair. 'That's my little man!' The hand quite naturally slid down to cup his shoulder. 'Jenny wants to stay with us for a while,' Kyle told Stephen, 'until someone comes to get her.' Man and boy exchanged a moment's silent communication. 'OK with you, sport?'

The little boy perceptibly began to relax. His glance flew to Jenny and he favoured the older child with a small experimental grin. 'O-K,' he rapped out then, staccato-style, blue eyes very keen.

Jenny nodded solemnly, sealing the pact, before stealing a long glance towards the cabinet tops spread with Stephen's childish paraphernalia. 'Can you do puzzles?' she ventured. 'I can.'

'Puzzles——' Stephen's eyes also darted '—an' colour books. Drink choc'late milk!' Clearly, he was mapping out an itinerary for the rest of the afternoon.

Now it was Raine's turn to communicate with Kyle. Heart in her eyes, she smiled her admiration for the way he had handled Stephen's misgivings, and Jenny's

shyness, for that matter. She could have watched him
cuddling the little girl for ages, a curious melting sensation in her breast.

But Jenny was ready to assert a little independence.
Raine helped Kyle set up the under-bed table as a playing
surface between the two children, piling pillows and
blankets in a sturdy chair for Jenny until she was seated
at an acceptable height. The children settled down am-
icably with colouring books and crayons, Jenny filling
her pages with meticulous clean-edged hues, while
Stephen happily drew his scribbles.

The afternoon passed in harmony. Colouring gave way
to inevitable puzzles. Raine brought out her pumpkin
cookies, and even made a face at Kyle when he accepted
his with a teasing, 'You made it yourself? No, not that
domestic, huh?' There were some forgotten party blowers
at the bottom of the goody-bag which provided the kids
with more fun once the last cookie crumb was cleaned
up. Then little eyes began drooping, and Kyle was ap-
pointed to read a story.

No wonder the children found Kyle's reading pref-
erable to her own, Raine reflected without censure. That
soft, deep sound with its raspy edges could have a
peculiarly mesmerising effect. Hypnotic. She sighed and
stretched as he turned a page, then had to bear up under
the mocking look he sent her. He wasn't in the least self-
conscious. The words on his tongue became every bit as
colourful as the illustrations that he periodically turned
to the children's view.

A born father. The phrase popped into Raine's head
unbidden and stayed there, conjuring up all sorts of related images so that she had to close her eyes in sheer
self-preservation. Angry with herself for allowing the
storybook day to take its toll, she delivered a sharp silent
lecture about the futility of unrealistic emotions to her
errant heart. But when she opened her eyes, the *family*
feeling persisted in the room. The sensation was so alien
to her and, paradoxically, so attractive that she felt
frightened.

'So this is where everyone went.' A strange woman's voice startled Raine from her tense reverie. Fortyish, very trim and attractively dressed, the newcomer smiled warmly from the doorway to encompass all occupants of the room. She was of diminutive height, with pale blue eyes and a short, pretty coiffure, her hair the rich blonde colour of toffee. The pleasant face was discreetly made-up and intrinsically maternal. She carried a burgundy suede tote bag, and a co-ordinating paisley scarf was draped with a wool coat over her arm. A half-formed impression entered Raine's mind but wouldn't crystallise.

Kyle clearly knew the woman well, his wry grin flashing a welcome. 'Meg, hello. Come in and join story hour.'

'Much as I admire that unusual voice of yours, Kyle, I'm afraid I haven't the time. I've come for this young lady,' she added, advancing into the room with a new smile for Jenny that expanded to include Stephen as well. 'And to see my other little puzzle champion. How's Stephen today?' she addressed the younger child.

Raine watched Stephen's beaming recognition with a puzzlement that was soon cleared. 'Meg Jackson,' Kyle made the introductions, 'I'd like you to meet Raine Jacobs, who is a special friend of Stephen's and now Jenny's. Meg is with Child Welfare,' he added to Raine. 'She's in charge of these two.'

Meg Jackson tilted her head, light eyes frankly assessing, though not offensively so. 'I believe I know Miss Jacobs from RaineBo Shoppe,' she ventured, smiling.

'Mrs Jackson, of course.' The connection clicked, aided by the tote bag and scarf and, unless she was mistaken, by the woman's attractive blue suit as well. 'I should have recognised you immediately. I'm sorry.'

'Don't be.' The older woman waved that aside. 'I'm one among very many customers, while you are only one salesperson. And, to be fair, my shopping trips are few and far between. My spare time is so limited that I tend to invest strictly in classic co-ordinates when I do shop.'

'That's an excellent strategy,' Raine acknowledged, 'and one that a great many working women follow.'

'Meg is a working *mother*, actually,' Kyle's attractive voice stressed the distinction, giving Raine the impression of some private joke between them.

'Of five,' Meg elaborated, returning his smile. 'Two boys, three girls.' She directed a fond glance towards Jenny's dark head. 'But, in lieu of dragging out my little photo book yet again, I seriously ought to get moving with Jenny. How's your arm feeling, darling?' She bent to eye level, her gentle query eliciting a quavery 'Fine.'

'Are you ready to get dressed, then?'

Jenny pouted sadly. 'I want to stay with Doctor Kyle.'

'Oh, I know, darling. But you'll be seeing Doctor Kyle again in a few weeks. He has to check your arm.'

Jenny turned enormous brown eyes to Kyle, as if to confirm the information. For answer, he laid the book aside and swung the child up on to his lap. 'Don't look so sad, Jen. I'll think about you every day.'

'Promise?' Jenny whispered solemnly. 'And you'll be here to check my arm?'

'I promise. I'll be here.'

Nodding, Jenny flung her good arm around his neck and hugged fiercely, before turning to look at her new playmate. 'Bye, Stephen. Thank you for letting me play with your toys.'

Stephen stared back, round-eyed, then reached beside him to the heap of discarded playthings the two had deposited in the corner of his bed. He selected a white stuffed kitten and extended the fluffy animal with all the sober dignity of a ceremonial offering. 'Take Kitty.' His little voice was gruff. 'You can have it.'

Jenny reached forward, managing to hug the toy with her plastered arm. 'Thank you,' she said again, in her proper, piping little voice.

'That was a very nice thing to do,' Kyle told Stephen, some of the quick rush of pride that Raine felt reflected in his own voice and eyes. 'And now, Jenny, you'd better tell Raine goodbye.' He carried the child to Raine where, to her surprise, the little girl leaned over to peck a sweet small kiss on to her cheek. The lump in her throat grew to new proportions, husking her reply.

'Be a good girl, sweetheart. We had fun, didn't we?'

'Yes,' Jenny nodded.

'Think Doctor Kyle might escort us to your room?' Meg teased the little girl and won herself a half-hearted smile, before seeking Kyle's eyes. 'I need to talk to you.'

'We'll round up one of the aides to get this young lady dressed,' he complied.

They were back in a short time, minus Jenny, although they stood outside the door talking in hushed tones long enough to arouse a chase of alarmed thoughts in Raine's head.

'Well, Stephen.' Meg started towards the little boy's bed without further preamble upon re-entry to the room. 'I have something here that belongs to you.'

Raine flashed Kyle a swift glance as Meg reached into her tote bag, but her bid for reassurance went unsatisfied. Kyle was watching Stephen intently, stealthily moving closer to the crib. Raine's pulse fluttered as Meg's hand was withdrawn, something furry in tow.

'*Boo!*'

Raine knew that she would never forget the look of utter delight that came over Stephen's small face at that moment. So this was Boo? A shabby, dingy, long-eared rabbit that wrenched an excited squeal from the child even as it brought tears stinging to Raine's eyes. The little boy's arms came up, waving ecstatically, clutched at the much-loved toy and brought it down to the small chest in a flurry of hugs and kisses and pats that turned Raine inside-out.

'His things were delivered by the police yesterday,' Meg told her quietly. 'There was some sort of oversight responsible for the delay. His clothes, shoes, things like that have been stored with the agency. And I only brought the toys that he could use at this point, the rabbit and some books. Those are in my bag. Kyle and I thought Boo would be enough for one day.'

That explained their secret conference in the hallway. There had to have been some concern about Stephen's reception of the familiar toy, in light of the loss of his mother. The reminders of his life before the accident could easily trigger a major upset, yet she cautiously judged that none was forthcoming, at least, not any time soon. Stephen was too enraptured to be upset. The sporadic kisses and pats continued, along with the frantic hugs that proved exactly how the lanky rabbit's neck had come to be limp and stuffingless. 'Boo!' Stephen crooned happily, jubilant at his reunion.

'Doctor?' Meg sent a questioning glance towards Kyle.

'So far, so good,' he said. 'Raine and I will stay until he falls asleep.'

'Fine.' Meg seemed satisfied, delving into her bag for the mentioned books. 'I'll leave these, then, and collect Jenny. Nice to see you again, Miss Jacobs. I've wanted to meet Stephen's benefactor.' She smilingly gestured to indicate the toys, posters, and books that ringed the room. 'He's always talking about his Raine.'

Whether from sheer excitement, or from exhaustion after his long day, Stephen had dropped off to sleep within minutes, his Boo clutched fiercely and irretrievably to his chest. Raine smoothed back a silvery lock of hair and tucked the blankets more firmly into place before turning a soft, slightly flushed face to Kyle.

He was propped against the wall cabinets, head bent over one of the books that Meg Jackson had left. *The Tale of Peter Rabbit*. Only, unlike the new copy that she'd bought at the mall, this one was thumbed through, corners frayed to a pulp, as if it had been read every day. Kyle was staring almost sightlessly at the inside cover, deeply absorbed, and he hardly glanced up when Raine moved to his side. She looked over his shoulder, seeing the small gold block that was printed inside the front cover. On the line that said 'THIS BOOK BELONGS TO:' someone had written Stephen's name. 'Stephen Russell Thompson,' Raine read softly aloud.

'This story must have been his absolute favourite. Look how worn the book is.' Kyle didn't respond, and she surreptitiously studied his taut expression, feeling uneasy, somehow. 'No wonder he was reminded of Boo,' she ventured again.

Kyle shook his head slightly, as if forcibly chasing some incomprehensible thought. 'What?' For just a moment his eyes seemed dark and unfocused. Then he passed the book to her and moved towards Stephen's cot, sharply alert. 'Sorry. I was miles away.' His look encompassed the resting toddler and the strangled stuffed rabbit, and softened. 'Asleep already? He's had quite a day, hasn't he?'

'Yes,' Raine agreed, telling herself to relax, although a remnant of her unease persisted. 'We all have.'

Kyle bent broad shoulders over the crib, one forearm resting on the railings, to stare into the child's composed face. He was silent for so long that Raine felt more apprehension rising. Without warning, he tossed her a glittery sideways look. 'Have dinner with me?'

'What?'

The handsome mouth twisted. 'It's a social invitation, Raine. Is that so difficult?'

'I suppose you startled me. Is it wise to leave Stephen alone?'

'He won't be alone when there's a staff of eight on the floor. I'll ask that a close watch be kept over him, although in my professional opinion he's out for the night. We have to eat. Now would seem the logical time.'

'Then I'd better give in gracefully.' Some slight inner masochism pushed Gavin into her mind. Her briefcase, dispatched neatly to a shelf, came into her wandering line of vision. But she determinedly tamped down the sense of obligation that each evoked. Tonight would be soon enough to face her inconsistencies.

Once inside the Porsche, that shivery air of danger enfolded Raine again. Kyle was leaning over the ignition, and she studied the clean, strong lines of his profile, summoning up a nervous smile when he turned and caught her at it. 'I'm dressed too casually to eat out,' she told him ruefully.

'I find jeans and a ponytail very appealing on you,' was his easy response. 'And I'm casual myself.' Hardly that, Raine thought, admiring the well fitting grey cord trousers and muted-patterned sweater. They'd stopped by his office on the way out, where he had exchanged the cotton lab coat for a charcoal-coloured suede jacket. He looked handsomely, carelessly elegant. Beside him she suddenly felt like a jittery teenager. 'Regretting the fact that you said yes?' he mocked with uncanny accuracy.

'No.' The small white lie was told as much to convince herself as to appease her sense of etiquette. 'Just hoping that you'll choose someplace low-key.'

'Women!' Kyle grinned darkly. 'I suppose you're afraid one of your customers might see you looking a little less the fashion-plate than usual.'

'Something like that,' Raine relaxed enough to return. 'Do you mind?'

'Not at all.' Putting the car into gear, he expertly backed it out of the reserved parking spot. 'There's a family-run Italian place not far from here. Does that appeal to you? Or,' he sent her a considering glance, 'we could do steaks at my place.'

Raine's smile went a little stiff on her face. 'I don't think...'

'Forget it,' Kyle said drily, his expression hardening just enough to reveal his irritation. 'It was only a suggestion, Raine. An offer of food, nothing else. Or, at least, nothing we hadn't both agreed upon.' His mouth twisted. 'But, after that shocked reaction, I think it's just as well that I retract. We'll eat Italian.'

He'd driven out to the exit gates before she found the courage to lay a restraining hand on his arm. 'Kyle, I'm sorry. We'll go to your place, if the offer is still open.'

'It's not.' But the olive branch seemed to partially appease him. 'It was probably a bad idea,' he reflected darkly.

'Why?'

Lord, she was a glutton for it! His face showed a glimmer of like sentiment. '*Why?*' he repeated, paused, then flexed his shoulders in a self-deprecating shrug. 'Because, easy as it was to promise you no seduction, there's always the chance that the temptation would prove too great.'

'Maybe the same thing applies to me.' She said it without looking at him, before she lost her nerve. 'Maybe that's why I objected.'

'That's quite an admission coming from you, lady,' he drawled roughly, throwing her a burning blue glance. 'Do you mean it?'

'Yes.'

There were moments of silence, then his slow, lazy grin. 'Well, being the gentleman that I am, I'll stick with the other arrangement.'

The restaurant was charming, if totally unpretentious. They were seated at a traditionally red-chequered table with a shaded candle flickering at its centre, menus brought and orders taken. Kyle asked that a bottle of red wine be brought beforehand. Raine settled back after the waiter poured, toying with the slender stem of her glass. 'Tell me about Jenny,' she said softly, her eyes dark with unconscious emotion.

'She really got to you, didn't she?' He brought his glass to his mouth, features gradually tightening as he thought about her request. 'Jenny was made a ward of the state several months ago...taken from her parents on grounds of neglect, and placed with foster parents while the couple underwent counselling. As I understand it, the results have been less than satisfactory. Jenny may soon be a candidate for adoption. Meanwhile, there's the problem of finding her a new foster family who will take their responsibility towards her a little more seriously.'

'Are you referring to her fall?' Raine asked, frowning. 'Accidents happen, Kyle.' She hadn't thought of the way that statement applied to herself until he reached for her hand.

'There are extenuating circumstances,' he explained, mouth grim. 'Jenny was totally unsupervised when she fell from that tree. Luckily, a neighbour heard her crying and went to investigate. She found Jenny alone. The foster mother had apparently gone shopping.' He broodingly played with Raine's fingers, voice harsh. 'Suppose she had fractured her skull instead of her elbow? There wouldn't have been any cries to alert help.'

'I know from experience that most people in the foster programmes are decent and reliable,' she commented. 'Mrs Jackson must have been terribly upset.'

'Meg?' Kyle grimaced. 'You'd better believe it. She took Jenny's accident as a personal affront.'

'You know her very well, don't you?'

'And like what I know,' he admitted. 'Meg is a remarkable lady...totally dedicated to her cause. She gives one hundred per cent every day, and can't conceive of anyone doing less. Then she goes home to mother her own five.'

'Kyle——' Raine sipped briefly, keeping her eyes on him '—I have the impression that Stephen and Jenny aren't isolated cases. Are you involved with many of Meg's charges?'

'Several,' he told her matter-of-factly. 'She helps oversee a special needs programme, consisting in part of children with debilitating bone or muscle conditions. Most of them are on crutches or in wheelchairs. Some are beyond any real help, but some are still within the range of treatment or correction.'

'So that's where you come in,' Raine assimilated. Yet she didn't fully understand. The fact remained that Physicians Hospital was privately owned and run, but she didn't intend questioning the financial aspects. 'You're a surprising man.'

'Why surprising?'

Raine faltered a bit, barely aware that she'd voiced the observation aloud. 'Different character traits at odds, I suppose. The first night we met, you were so fierce and arrogant, so determined to upbraid me for my carelessness. I could scarcely credit the tenderness that you showed me later.' She lowered her eyes, flushing slightly. 'That you still show me. Seeing you with Stephen and Jenny...talking with you, I've come to realise that you're really a very caring and compassionate man.'

Kyle grinned a little when she trailed off, eyes intent on her face. He still held her hand, turning it wrist-down against the table so that their palms touched. Very firmly, he laced his fingers through hers. 'That must have been very difficult for you to admit. I don't believe you've had much faith in my gender up to this point.'

He was too clever, touching so deeply on the truth that some long-established corner of her mind shut down hard. 'I don't want you trying to figure me out.'

Kyle held tight to the hand she was trying to extricate. 'Isn't that what you were doing with me?'

Their meal arrived with excellent timing, giving Raine a moment's respite as the waiter unobtrusively arranged plates and cutlery. Mockingly handsome, Kyle only cocked a brow at her comment on the delicious appearance of their food. 'I'd like an answer to that question,' he drawled, once the slight, moustached man had made his exit from their table.

'Is it so important?' She picked up her fork with nervous fingers and laid it down again.

Blue eyes blazed. 'I think it is. You seemed ready to trust me there for a while. Then I got too close, and you fell into the same trap of deciding to push rather than to hold on. Well, *I'm* holding on, Raine. What does it take to make you accept that?'

Her hand, on the wine glass now, trembled. 'I'm not sure what you're saying.'

'The hell you're not!' He leaned close, voice slow and emphatic, and tantalisingly gravelly. 'I'm saying that I won't let you get away with this evasion. Is that plain enough? We have something between us that might be worth building on.'

'*Might* being the key word.'

'Take a chance, lady.' The words fairly grated over her.

He was asking her to step out of a safe, ordered existence, where she knew and trusted all the boundaries, because she had been the one to set them. 'I don't have time for an involvement,' she heard herself saying. 'I'm starting a seven-day work week beginning tomorrow. I have Stephen to think about, and the shop. What you're asking is impossible. Kyle, I . . .'

'So what's the real reason?'

His look was so piercingly blue that she couldn't avoid it. She swallowed on a throat that felt dry as parchment, her voice when she found it shockingly insubstantial. 'I'm just not sure that I have anything to give.'

'I don't believe that,' Kyle came back with quiet conviction. Raine bowed her head, struggling with her fears, and when she looked up again there was an odd glint in his eye, suggesting that he'd found something in her reactions to satisfy him.

Back at the hospital, they checked and found Stephen still sleeping soundly. The car park was deserted when Kyle walked Raine to her car afterwards. She made no protest as he drew her full-length into his arms, his mouth covering hers with a possessive thoroughness to which she instinctively responded. Pressing closer into his hard, muscular body, she could feel all the contours of it through the double layers of their heavy clothing. He made a low sound in his throat, a primitive groan, and tore his mouth away, both hands coming up to hold her face steady for his probing stare. She saw pure electric flame in his eyes, and knew that his passion cost an effort to master. Swallowing convulsively, she focused on a small muscle that jerked alongside his jaw, peripherally seeing his mouth twist in faint self-mockery. 'Maybe we should have gone to my place, after all.'

'Maybe,' she agreed, breathless at his low, husky tone.

His soft laugh brushed the side of her neck. 'You're brave when you think there's no chance of having your bluff called.' He trailed a fingertip with devastating slowness down her cheek. 'There's always next time, lady.'

Raine shuddered and, against all her better judgement, lifted her mouth again. Kyle's responding hunger nearly consumed her, yet her own emotions shook her more. The sweet passion flowing out to him. And the elation that the words 'next time' evoked.

# CHAPTER FIVE

THE following days were unbelievably busy. The mall was open an hour earlier and later each day through Christmas and, as sales figures rose at the shop, Raine's morning routine lengthened.

Felicity would arrive between nine and ten, wound up to a fine tension and ready to sell. Thank goodness for Kim Landon, who cheerfully rang the cash register keys over and over, her smile never fading.

Raine got away by six most evenings, the frequent guilt pangs that she felt upon leaving the others usually assuaged by Stephen's gratified little face once she'd reached the hospital. Her time with him was rushed at best; his eyes would be drooping by half-past eight. But she did her best to provide the quality attention that was rightfully touted by most child authority sources, and he seemed singularly trusting in her nightly promise of 'see you tomorrow'.

Kyle made a point of sharing the bedtime ritual. They usually had a late supper afterwards, on Kyle's insistence that it was the only way he could trust her to eat anything at all. His eyes were too shrewd, easily noting the slight weight loss that had fined her already delicate bone structure, and deducing the reasons for it. Doctorlike, he had delivered one brief lecture on the evils of overwork, stress, and poor nutrition; after that, he simply took matters into his own hands.

That male solicitude was a new experience for Raine, and one that she almost guiltily began to enjoy. Kyle, aware of the briefcase that awaited her attention, rarely kept her more than an hour. Afterwards, he would return her to her car, give her his brooding smile, then duck his head into the window for one last, frighteningly sweet kiss.

He was pacing himself; Raine recognised the restraint and felt a mixed gratitude for it. Half-wanting, half-fearing a sexual confrontation from Kyle, she was instead shown understanding, companionship, and a controlled desire that left her wondering dazedly what the full effect of his passion would be.

Raine came into Physicians Hospital one evening to find Meg Jackson admiring the enormous spruce tree that had been erected in the lobby...a dazzling display of ornaments and lights that stood a good twelve feet high.

'This is gorgeous!' she breathed appreciatively upon joining the older woman.

'Yes, isn't it?' Meg agreed. 'The volunteers put it up today. And not a moment too soon. What is it now...two weeks?'

'Sixteen days,' Raine offered, well versed by the shopping-day countdown that was broadcast throughout the mall several times daily. 'Have you come to see Stephen?'

'I saw him this morning. Actually, I was waiting for you,' she admitted after a pause. 'I was told that you come about this time each evening, and I was hoping to talk.'

Raine searched the pretty features quickly, seeking an explanation for the rising disquiet she felt. Pleasant, but carefully bland of other emotions, it was a professional face. Calm and authoritative. 'Is something wrong?'

The shining honey-coloured head dipped for an instant, then blue eyes locked back into place, a wry glint behind them. 'I'm really not sure.' She touched a hand to Raine's arm. 'Let's find a cup of coffee, shall we?'

Installed in a booth inside the ground floor coffee shop, with steaming cups in front of them, the social worker finally came to her point. 'The truth is,' she began, after taking the first hot sip, 'I've found myself in an awkward position. I'm afraid I'll have to ask what your intentions are towards Stephen Thompson.'

'My intentions?' Raine set down her tea, jarring the serviceable crockery. Somehow she hadn't expected that. The gravity of the request shook her so that she was a long moment forming a reply. 'I hadn't really thought about my *intentions*, as such.' She forced her eyes to make contact and remain steady. 'I can't explain what I feel for Stephen, other than to say that I understand what's happening to him, and I want to help him feel less afraid. I've tried to make him as happy, as secure and comfortable as I can, that's all.'

'Even if, in doing so, you've allowed him to become so attached to you that he could well be devastated upon separation?'

'That's a powerful assumption to make, isn't it? You've seen us together once.'

Meg sighed, not a defensive sound as much as a troubled one. 'I've been closely affiliated with Physicians Hospital for some time, Miss Jacobs. I know most of the paediatrics staff. By interviewing Stephen's caretakers and visiting him often myself, I think I've formed a fairly clear picture.'

Raine stared numbly, a flush beginning to creep up her cheeks. 'Someone's come to you complaining about the time I spend with Stephen? Is that it?' A horrible, sick suspicion began to grow inside her. 'Who?' she demanded flatly, while the voice in her head mocked, *who else*?

Meg looked blank for an instant, then gave a slight shrug. 'Does it really matter how my conclusions were drawn? This isn't meant to be a personal attack. I simply feel it's my job to warn you that a precarious situation may exist. There can be a very thin line between offering care and comfort to a child and fostering his dependency. Stephen may have come to think of you as the mother he lost. If that's true, then in effect he'll be losing her again when he's dismissed from the hospital, when you stop being there for him.'

'What are you asking me to do?' Raine got out, eyes dark with agitation. She couldn't...wouldn't think about Kyle. Not yet, if she wanted to hold on to some kind of dignity.

'Only to examine your emotions.' The other woman leaned forward, clear eyes very direct. 'Decide how much of what you feel is a result of your part in Stephen's accident... Yes, I know about that and, believe me, I'm not condemning you for it, just asking for an honest assessment. If you are saying goodbye to that child at the end of his stay here, then wouldn't the more humane thing be to ease away gradually? Save him anything abrupt or traumatic? You'll still be his friend, but not his world.'

Raine was struck with a very vivid mental picture of the little boy and all he meant to her. For just a moment, fear swam in her eyes. She bent her head, concentrating on stirring a spoon around her teacup, and came up with a less vulnerable face. 'Are you telling me that I should have just left him alone?'

'No. I'm telling you that a danger exists,' the social worker repeated gently. 'What you do about the situation is largely your own choice at this point, but I do hope that you'll take my professional advice into account. Think about what I've said. Will you do that?'

Kyle's office door was locked. Raine learned from the switchboard operator that he had been called to the surgical unit only moments before. 'But you can't go down there!' the startled attendant exclaimed as she pivoted away from the desk.

Despite the warning, Raine took an elevator back to the ground floor, and with the use of directional graphics located the correct seemingly endless corridor. She was in a totally antiseptic area, with no colour or decoration to counter the looming white sterility. The smell of disinfectant and the blank walls closed tight around her, making her breath harsh and uneven. Small-girl fears rose inside her, adding to the fury of disillusionment that filled her head.

Of course it had been Kyle. By his own admission, he knew Meg Jackson well enough to provide a sufficient rapport. And hadn't Kyle warned Raine often enough against her growing attachment to Stephen? *You want to replace his mother.* Memory threw his harsh, low voice at her from the night he'd heard Stephen call her 'Mama'. That very image left Raine no doubt, though she desperately wanted another solution to come.

So she had been an utter, ridiculous fool. She gritted her teeth as the dream that she had subconsciously fostered collapsed around her feet. The three of them together...that little illusion of family...was only a sadly misplaced fantasy, and one that Kyle had never shared. How else could he have done this to her? And to Stephen?

She came to double doors, wrenching them open with complete disregard for the sign that said '*Absolutely No Admittance Except To Surgical Staff*'. She had stepped into what looked to be a supply room, ceiling-high metal shelves stacked with surgical equipment, and immediately green-gowned figures came running in outrage. Raine pressed her back rigidly to the door when it swung shut. 'Get Kyle Benedict,' she said through clenched teeth.

Kyle was there almost instantly, gripping her shoulders with hands that hurt. 'Raine, what is it? What's wrong?' He shook her, blue eyes dark with foreboding. 'Stephen?'

'Stephen is fine.' She glanced over his green scrub suit, tunic ties loose to indicate that he had just been dressing. Beyond him, curious faces were watching. 'I don't think you want an audience for what I have to say.'

Her tone was taut and quivering, leaving no way for him to misread her mood. She saw his vivid eyes narrow, watched an answering dark anger seep into his handsome face. Iron fingers clamped around her wrist.

'Five minutes,' he said, tight-lipped, to one of the nurses, before dragging Raine into a small side room where he forcefully closed the door. She jerked against the hard fingertips digging into her fine-boned flesh, only to have him push her flat to the wall, face shoved close enough for her to feel the deepened pressure of his breath. She concentrated everything she was feeling into returning his stare, her eyes grey as storm and shimmering wildly. 'What the *hell*,' Kyle spat out with ominous control, 'makes you think you can behave like this? We're in *surgery*, lady.' She actually heard him grit his teeth, the words thrust with harsh force of his tongue. 'I can't even think of a reason that would be good enough.'

'Try this one, *Doctor Benedict*! You spend days supposedly trying to gain my trust, then you go behind my back to sabotage everything that I hold dear? Well, you can't keep me from Stephen! Do you understand?' She was half sobbing, oblivious of the furious tears glittering on her face. Her anger lashed back into her past, mingling with another betrayal until it had reached unreasonable proportions. She saw Kyle's clenched jaw, and a guttural small sound escaped her. 'No, I can see that you don't. Maybe this will put things into focus for you. You know that my father abandoned me when I was five? Let me tell you the rest of that miserable little story.' She continued glaring, eyes flashing amethyst fire. 'I was admitted to a hospital with acute appendicitis. My dad tucked me in with an ice pack and my teddy that first night. And I never saw him again. He couldn't pay the bill, so he gave them me as collateral. He never came back. Just like Melanie Thompson is never coming back for Stephen. Does that shed any light on my position at all?'

Kyle remained stern and silent, as if she were a trembling neurotic who needed careful handling. No, that wasn't quite fair. She thought she glimpsed a glinting pain in his eyes. 'Raine, I don't know what you think I've done. I want to help, but there is a kid out there who needs my help worse than you do.' He sighed harshly. 'You have to go. Now. We'll talk later.'

Raine wrenched away and past him, sick now with the irresponsible way she'd burst in, sick with the callous way she'd told him about her father, as if four or five terse sentences could cover the way her life had been moulded by that rejection. 'I'm going,' she said flatly, pausing by the door just long enough to wipe her face. 'But there's nothing else to say, Kyle. I just want you to leave Stephen and me alone.'

Stephen was asleep. She sat by his side for only a few minutes before returning to her car just to drive. The night was very cold, the sky clear dark blue overhead, with stars as hard-edged as diamonds. Raine rolled down her window part-way and drew painful breaths of the icy air in an attempt to calm her shaking body, while she found a residential area and distractedly drove the Mustang around its shadowy streets. After reaction came numbness. She could not have said how long she was in the car, but presently she passed a phone booth and some inner dictate made her park beside it and get out. She ran a fingertip down a page in the thick plastic-covered directory, found the name that she wanted and noted the address. Then she got back into her car.

She found the house in one of the older suburbs, a white clapboard dwelling with french-blue shutters and a porch swing. there was a ten-speed bike chained to the railings. Half-way along the bricked pathway, an orange cat came to wind its rangy body around Raine's legs, purring throatily.

She rang the doorbell twice in succession, unconsciously holding her breath as rapid footsteps approached. The porch light flared in her face, the lace curtain that covered the glass lifted, then the door swung open. 'Can I help you?' The boy was about sixteen and dark-haired, but his friendly face and light blue eyes made him very much Meg Jackson's son.

'Is Mrs Jackson home?'

'Sure. Come on in.' Raine had scarcely stepped into the living-room before he yelled *'Mom!'* at the top of his lungs, then proffered an apologetic smile. 'Sorry. You'd better have a seat ... I think she's putting the little kids to bed. I'm Jason, by the way.'

'Raine Jacobs,' she responded, shaking the hand that he extended. Spots of colour caught her eye all around the old-fashioned room: a yellow dump truck parked beneath an end table, Lego blocks scattered on a tray flanking the fireplace, a lavender windbreaker that had been tossed across the seat of a chair. The furniture was dark gleaming wood, cherry mostly, and the upholstered pieces of a pretty, but slightly faded brocade.

Over to one side sat a girl of about twelve. Raine took in the serene brown eyes and blonde ponytail first, the blanket-covered legs and wheelchair after. 'Miss Jacobs, I'd like you to meet my sister, Tara,' Jason offered, and the girl put down her book with polite interest.

'How do you do?'

'Hello, Tara. I'm happy to meet you. Your mother said there were two sons and three daughters,' she commented lightly. 'Are the others all younger?'

'Yes,' Tara answered, her smile sweet. She pointed to a row of photographed faces propped on the mantel. 'Pam is eight, Kirsten is six, and Ben is five. They're upstairs. Bedtime is eight-thirty for the younger three, but with Jenny spending the night the baths and everything ran into overtime.'

Raine shot a swift reflex glance at her watch to find that nine o'clock was well past. 'I had no idea it was this late,' she began, only to be interrupted by Meg's pleasant voice.

'Don't let it worry you.'

She was descending the staircase, where Raine could see an adjoining ramp mounted, presumably for Tara's wheelchair. The immaculate businesswoman image had disappeared at some point during the past few hours, to be replaced by that of relaxed mother. Raine swept a glance over the other woman's warm caftan and slippers and cleansed face, feeling again the extent of her intrusion.

'I should have called first,' she apologised immediately. 'I went for a drive and lost all track of time.'

'You've been thinking about our conversation,' Meg guessed shrewdly, an almost rueful appeal in her light eyes. 'Any hard feelings?'

'No,' Raine denied and realised that it was true. All her bitter resentment could be rightfully heaped on Kyle's head. He was the one who had put her position with Stephen in danger, not Meg. The social worker was simply doing her job.

'I'm glad.' Ruffling Jason's hair in passing, she gestured for Raine to follow her lead. 'Come into the kitchen and I'll make you a cup of tea. Have you two introduced yourselves to Miss Jacobs?'

'Yes,' the pair said in unison. 'Little kids in bed, Mom?' Tara asked as Jason moved to flick on the television set.

Meg flashed a weary grin. 'They are, finally. How's the homework coming? Sorry, Tara, I see your history book there on your lap. Jason?'

'I did mine in Study Hall,' the boy said, flopping on to the sofa with lanky grace.

'I'll take your word for it,' Meg grimaced fondly.

The kitchen was big and comfortable, obviously the heart of the household. The kettle was already on, and Meg set out cups and saucers while Raine studied some crayon drawings held by magnets to the refrigerator door. She gathered an image of trailing green vines, scrubbed pine cabinets, and warm brick walls that felt pleasurable around her. The soft sound of Tara's laughter came through the door.

'You have lovely children,' she commented sincerely.

'Thank you,' Meg turned briefly from her task. 'They've been a great joy and comfort to me, all of them. Jason's father died when he was three,' she explained. 'I met Tara when I went back to work. She and my other three are adopted. Tim and I had planned a large family, anyway, and I saw a way through the agency to pursue that dream.' Something flickered oddly in her eyes and voice. 'Up until now, I've always been able to make room for one more.'

Raine looked at her comprehendingly. 'Tara told me that Jenny was spending the night.'

'Yes.' Her hostess turned back, adding instant coffee to one cup and a teabag to the other. 'I expect that we'll place her with new fosters in a few more days. She was feeling lonely, so I brought her home for the evening. She and Kirsten, my youngest daughter, are already fast friends.' She brought the drinks to the table, a soft sadness in her pretty face. 'I'd like to give Jenny a permanent home, actually. But I'm afraid that neither my resources nor my house will expand any further.' She met Raine's silent empathy with a small resolved smile. 'So... what about Stephen?'

There was no point and, as instinct told her, no need to prevaricate. Even then, Raine's hand shook a little, spilling a few grains of sugar from a teaspoon in transfer. Distractedly, she put the spoon back into the china bowl. Her eyes were very grey and, once making contact, didn't waver. 'It seems I've been very dense with myself these last few weeks. After all the warnings I've received about my eventual separation from Stephen, I've finally come to a realisation. It wasn't the advice so much that bothered me... it was the very concept of the separation itself. I know now that I don't want to say goodbye to Stephen,' she swallowed visibly, hands clenched tight in her lap, '...not ever. I want to keep him. I want Stephen to be my child.'

'Well,' Meg said simply, a gentle and oddly complacent light in her pale eyes.

'Is it possible?' Raine pressed huskily. 'I apologise again for intruding, but once I knew what I wanted to do, I had to know whether the idea was feasible. I don't know how adoption laws work. I'm single and I have a career...'

'I'm widowed and I have a career,' Meg interrupted reasonably. 'But have you given enough thought as to how a small child would change your life-style? I'll have to admit that, from the standpoint of Stephen's welfare, your idea pleases me, but it's my duty to make sure your eyes are completely open. Children are hard work. They're time-consuming and at times they can be complicated, even difficult. From a more practical side, have you considered the expense? Things like childcare while you work?'

'I have the means to support Stephen——' Raine waved a conciliatory hand '—and there is an excellent daycare centre in the mall where I work...or else I could have someone come into my home. I know I couldn't be with him that much, but I would hardly be alone. Most households today are run by working parents, often single.'

'You're right,' Meg conceded, 'and, although we prefer adoptive couples, the fact that you are unmarried won't be held against you, providing you can prove means of support and a suitable home environment. There is something else we should discuss...' She bent her head briefly, as if broaching a precarious subject. 'Stephen's health. Although we are all praying to the contrary, there is a possibility that Stephen won't walk normally again. Can you cope with the thought of a handicapped child?'

'My God, what kind of question is that?'

Meg settled back in the chair, her smile suddenly easy. 'My reaction exactly when the question was put to me regarding Tara. In fact, all of my adopted kids are special needs children,' she admitted. 'They've offered a lot of extra challenge, perhaps, yet the truth remains that they are children, just like any others, who want to love, to be loved, and to belong. But, understandably, not every prospective parent is suited to an exceptional child. It's best to find out immediately...our goal is to make appropriate matches, after all.'

'Do you consider Stephen and me to be an appropriate match?'

'Personally...yes. But you'll have to realise that, although I can make recommendations, a decision wouldn't be in my hands. The process of application is rather involved. We'd need complete background and financial information. You'd be assigned a case worker who would have to be free to inspect your home at several undetermined points...interview character witnesses, that sort of thing. Are you willing to give up that much of your privacy?'

'For Stephen's sake?' Raine raised her chin. 'I'll do whatever you require.'

'Good.' Meg drained the last of her coffee with a perky smile. 'Then do this. Go home and think about what we've discussed. If you're still completely sure, call me Monday at my office, and I'll take the initial application. The rest could be pushed through fairly quickly, at least enough to get you temporary custody if everything is in order. If it means less shuffling around for Stephen, we'll move double-time.'

'I won't change my mind.' Raine stood up and returned the smile, her hopes taking cautious wing. 'I want Stephen. I love him enough to build a life around him. I ought to thank you for making me realise that.'

Bearing in mind that the situation with Meg could have gone either way, the adage of all's well that ends well just wasn't enough for Kyle's redemption. The betrayal shook Raine all over again when she found several terse messages from him waiting at home. Hands trembling, she hastily erased the tape in her answering machine, slamming the device back on to the table afterwards with uncharacteristic force. The phone began ringing again almost immediately. Raine stood beside it unmoved, hearing the machine engage upon the fifth ring to play her pre-recorded message. Kyle's voice crackled from the speaker in a way that couldn't be blamed on the wiring. 'Raine, dammit, if you're there, pick up!'

She refused to comply and he left no further message. The phone rang intermittently for the next two hours, and when Raine finally abandoned the book-keeping to drag herself into bed, the sound of an angrily slammed receiver seemed to echo in her ears.

A confrontation was inevitable. Kyle was waiting in Stephen's room the next evening, making some pleasant excuse to the little boy and dragging Raine off before she had even properly said hello. She bitterly resented his tactics, and fiercely rounded on him to tell him so. The look in his eyes stopped her, bringing her back defensively against the wall. A hand came up hard on either side of her, trapping her there. His glower was frightening, in spite of the ridiculous way he'd turned the tables. She was the one who had been wronged, yet Kyle looked as if he might eat her for dinner if she made the slightest peep.

'What's going on?' he ground out, the doctors' lounge dangerously deserted.

She found the courage to be flippant, holding his burning gaze with a fine contempt. 'I'm being manhandled by an egotistical, manipulating fraud, for starters!'

'Say that again,' he invited, so menacingly that she blinked back her answering retort. She stared at his clenched jaw, wisely electing to drop the sarcasm from her tone.

'Let go of me, Kyle,' she said flatly.

'Kyle? So it's Kyle again? What happened to the utterly scornful *Doctor Benedict* that you were using yesterday? And while we're on the subject...what happened yesterday, Raine?'

'Nothing you weren't expecting, I'm sure.'

'I didn't expect you to burst into surgery. The move was totally lacking in class, lady.'

'I agree.' The impulsive way she'd walked into that surgical suite filled her with shame in retrospect, not because of any discomfiture on Kyle's part, but rather for the simple reason that she had violated the sanctity of a medical institute in that way. She might even have endangered a life with the interruption. 'Let's just say that I was too furiously disillusioned to take responsibility for my actions.'

'Let's just say you were,' he repeated tersely. 'I'm entitled to an explanation. *Now*,' he insisted when she didn't speak.

'You really think you can stand there and snap out orders?' Raine flared, colour rising. 'You are entitled to nothing from me, Kyle Benedict. If I'd wanted to speak to you, I would have answered the phone.'

His expression said that she had been extremely unwise in revealing her hand. 'You really ought to be thankful that my patient kept me here all night.' Hard fingertips bit into her jaw. 'After the third message, I was ready to strangle you.'

'Like you're doing now?' He wasn't at all, but the conversation had degenerated disgracefully. Raine saw his eyes darken, yet she refused to cower. 'Let go,' she said thickly. 'I can't bear you touching me.'

'Oh, no?' The dangerous insinuation warned her, too late, of his intention. His mouth came down, hard, and forced hers open. Her sharp protest was muffled in her throat, her breath cut off completely. Pinpoints of light swam behind her eyes, while her body twisted ineffectually against him. She was caught to the wall beneath his weight, heart hammering frantically into his chest, like a separate creature, frightened and fluttering. His mouth and tongue were doing unbelievable things to her, so that when the pressure eased a fraction she forgot to use the resulting breath to scream, forgot to struggle, the sensations in her body temporarily overpowered her mind. Kyle seemed bent on devouring her, heedless of shaking limbs. Keeping his lower body moulded close, he slid a hand over her heart to lift the warm weight of her breast between them. Raine shuddered with the sensation, feeling the imprint of his fingers through the thin silk of her blouse and straining towards the erotic caress.

'You aren't trembling with *revulsion*,' he mocked in her ear, and she despised herself for the additional shudder the warmth of his breath evoked.

'Kyle, don't *do* this to me!' Her voice broke and she shut her eyes tightly, dreading the hot tears that seemed imminent. Kyle would have a field day if she cried. He'd tormented her enough already, drawing a response from her untried body that caused her shame. Gritting her teeth, she thought of Stephen and willed her red rage to return and replace this feeling of mute tragedy.

'Tell me what's wrong, Raine.' There was a rough sound to her name, as if it had been dragged unwillingly off his tongue. 'You can't make some kind of wild accusation, then refuse to discuss it.'

She stiffened then, the previous day's pain coming back in full force. 'Do you really intend to try and bluff your way out of this?' she asked, outraged. 'You've been opposed to the time I spent with Stephen all along. Did you think I wouldn't make the connection when Meg Jackson asked about my intentions? Don't insult me further by pretending, Kyle.'

The fine bones of her shoulders felt pressure, his hands biting into her as if physical violence might give him intense satisfaction. 'What the devil are you talking about?'

Just for the smallest instant, Raine's conviction faltered. 'Tell me you've never discussed me with Meg Jackson,' she challenged flatly.

A muscle tensed in his jaw, seconds ticked away, but the denial didn't come. That was it then, all the proof, or lack of acquittal that she'd needed. Pride came to her rescue, drying up the tears before they'd spilled and making her back painfully straight as she stood before him. Pride lent a calm unemotionalism to her tone. 'Ironically, Kyle, things didn't happen the way you intended. When it came to facing a future without Stephen, I discovered that I couldn't. Instead of driving me away from him, you pushed me closer. I'm applying for adoption on Monday. Meg thinks I have a good chance of getting Stephen. I want him to be my son.'

'Am I supposed to display some negative reaction now?' Kyle eventually said, low-toned. 'Well, I don't feel it. I have no doubts concerning your ability to mother Stephen. But your inadequacies as a woman boggle my mind...'

'My inadequacies?' Raine broke in furiously. 'For weeks you've talked about my barriers, my fears, my lack of trust. You almost had me there, Kyle. You really did. For a while I came dangerously close to forgetting a lesson I learned when I was five years old. That you can't trust anyone. That moment you let your heart out-shout your head, you're inviting disaster...because it's only the people with any emotional power over you who can destroy you.'

'Of all the warped, crippled outlooks on life!' he gritted, actually shaking her a little. 'And are you going to teach that philosophy to Stephen...make him emotionally disabled, too? Maybe you aren't fit to mother him, after all? If I'm as adept at manipulating Meg Jackson as you seem to think, that should give you reason to worry. Suppose I want Stephen for myself?'

Wanting to believe that he'd only made the threat out of spite, Raine instead glimpsed a hard element of truth in the blue eyes. He did want Stephen. And supposing he made a counter-suit for adoption, who would be the likely winner? Having already proved that he felt no qualms in using his influence with Meg, Kyle seemed the logical and imminent choice. He was a wealthy man, with a position in the community, an excellent reputation with the agency which might well prejudice them in his favour...while she could only offer Stephen a moderately comfortable life and her love. She glared up with tears in her eyes, her body gone ice-cold. 'Do you mean that?'

'That I want Stephen?' He betrayed an odd watchfulness. 'Yes.'

Raine's head jerked back as if he'd struck her. 'I'll fight for him, Kyle!' Swallowing hard, she flung him a glittery stare. 'After what you've done to me, I can hardly see you as perfect father material, either. I'll admit that you're starting out with every financial and social advantage, but that just means that I'll have to fight doubly hard. I love Stephen…nothing you do or say can change that.'

He made a move towards her, then abruptly checked the motion, a white ring of anger around his mouth. 'No, I've had enough. You've got some idiotic misconception in that pretty head of yours and a redhead's stubbornness to compound it.' She actually heard his teeth gritting behind the clench of his jaw. 'But I'm not going to add to the confusion by retaliating…badly as I want to do just that.'

'And what would you do?' Raine taunted bitterly, maddened into the provocation by his condescending air.

'What wouldn't I do?' he drew out savagely. 'Teach you some realistic expectations, for openers…such as the possibility of having that little-girl mentality treated as such, in the rudest imaginable way. You need *someone* to help you grow up, sweetheart.' The endearment was no endearment at all, his face dark with leashed fury. 'I realise your dad didn't stick around to fulfil the obligation, and I am profoundly sorry for that, but I won't treat you with kid gloves because of it.' He drew a harsh, controlled breath. 'You've overlooked something in your hurry to make accusations, lady. Where's my motive? What possible reason would I have for going to Meg with…I can only guess what information, since you refuse to discuss it rationally?'

Raine had gone very still, unable to stop doubt from haunting her, but then he was an eloquent man…perfectly capable of playing both ends against the middle. Right? No sound came from her mouth and she jumped at Kyle's soft jeering laugh. His blue eyes burned with contempt, making the role of injured party complete. But was it only a role? Temples pounding with confusion, Raine could only stare helplessly.

'Think about it,' he grated. Then, flicking her cheek insultingly, he stalked out, leaving her to find her own way.

# CHAPTER SIX

CHRISTMAS shopping reached a new peak on Saturday, as the shoppers who had been restricted by weekday jobs flocked into the stores in response to the remaining two-week time-frame. Raine, in spite of four years' experience leading up to this point, had never worked so hard. The pace was all but overwhelming, the crowd a retailer's dream. But RaineBo Shoppe's success didn't keep her back from aching after hours, or prevent the throbbing pain in her head. She knew she was unaccustomedly silent in Stephen's presence, even zombie-like as she sat by his bed and let the childish chatter flow. He found nothing amiss, discounting his puzzled references to 'Doctor Kyle' for which Raine had no possible answer. She hadn't seen Kyle at all during the past two days, and could only assume that she wouldn't see him in future. He could easily spend time with Stephen during the day, thereby avoiding her altogether.

She didn't want to think about him, and Stephen's immature probing was totally uncooperative. If she thought about Kyle, then she was afraid that she'd admit to herself that she had misread him. Worse, that she cared about him. She'd gone over that scene countless times, baffled by his stance of injury, yet no plausible explanation came to mind. She knew what Meg Jackson had said and she knew what Kyle claimed, and stubbornly the two stories failed to mesh. Only someone privy to her closeness with Stephen could have gone to Meg with enough conviction to make the woman act. Who else but Kyle? her head prompted again. Sadly, she found no way past the implications, his challenge to her to name a motive the one outstanding point. And even that fell against him in the end. What better motive than a desire

117

to alienate her from Stephen, when he'd admitted to wanting the child for himself?

But when she met with Meg Jackson on Monday, no mention was made of any other applicant who wanted to adopt Stephen. Meg seemed genuinely pleased that she had followed through with her decision, filling out a lengthy questionnaire herself before turning Raine over to her assigned case worker. Standing in front of Louise Stacey, with her beaky nose and prim, thin mouth, Raine was glad that she had chosen a conservative dress suit for the meeting. Miss Stacey released her after asking a few tight, dry questions, leaving a nervy disquiet in Raine's chest. The woman was plainly by-the-book, and of an era when single adoptions and working mothers were hardly common. Raine came away from the office fighting a jittery impulse to go and ask for someone else. That would hardly put her in a favourable light with the agency, rather as if she might have reason to doubt her case.

The following week made vast inroads into her reserves. Herself estranged from Kyle, it was a further shock to her system coming home one evening to find Felicity in a state of tragic dishabille before the fireplace, brooding into a half-emptied brandy snifter while streaks of mascara dried on her face. No overnight parting this time; her break from Brian had stuck. Raine got one word in answer to her concerned query. Nola. If the luggage piled inside the doorway, with shoes protruding upside-down from side pockets and bright material spilling out around the zippers, revealed impulsive haste in her leaving, then Felicity's morose refusal to discuss her argument with Brian had added the weight of finality.

Not that she wasn't hurting. Raine watched her now, flirting outrageously with the mall manager's assistant across the room, and thought that she had never seen her partner so gaily brittle, almost at splintering point. All this...the staff Christmas party that had somehow become a different affair...was in aid of convincing their immediate circle of friends that Brian Keaton didn't matter. No little get-together this year, Felicity had invited upwards of twenty guests to the party that was being professionally catered at the apartment.

Feeling more like an uninvited guest than co-hostess, she slipped away to her room for a moment's reprieve, only to find the noise level permeating that area as well.

After freshening the colour on her mouth, Raine stood there unseeingly, weighing the joint reaction if she were to say her goodbyes now and go to Stephen. This being Sunday, she had spent the morning with him, but he was unusually fractious and clinging when she'd left for her afternoon stint at the store, making her long to drive over now for one more cuddle. If propriety dictated that she remain at the party, her heart certainly wasn't in it. She'd give it another half-hour. If the spirits kept flowing at their current steady rate, then her absence would scarcely be noticed.

A loud burst of laughter shook her out of her dark musing and sent her rapidly to the door, the proximity of upstairs and next-door apartments leaping to mind. All they needed was to have the police alerted by some irate neighbour! She wouldn't like explaining that this raucous free-for-all was actually a business function.

Felicity and her date were the culprits. In a remarkably short time, the furniture was pushed to the outer perimeters of the room, and the couple took the floor, deigning to show the college students a turn or two. Winding her way through a series of pretzel-like movements, red silk dress billowing, Felicity looked as if she were having the time of her life. Responding to his partner's flushed cheeks and laughter, Bill Sanders was as oblivious to the dull look in her eyes as Raine was aware of it. But then, she was no stranger to restless energy herself. At least she had Stephen to counteract it, while Felicity had to burn off her own frightful supply as best she could.

Applause smattered up and deepened, the laughter escalated, and that same inexplicable uneasiness had Raine jokingly calling a halt. 'Could we hold it down, please? If we're all arrested, who'll mind the store tomorrow?'

'Ease up, Raine,' Felicity whirled by, her smile oblique, 'you'll have it all to yourself soon.'

Raine subsided unhappily, understanding the remark, if no one else did. The subject of the apartment had been reluctantly broached and discussed not three days ago. Felicity would be staying through the end of the month only. Unenthusiastic about sharing a home with a small child, she had vetoed point-blank Raine's offer to consult her case worker. As soon as normal business hours resumed, she would begin looking for a new place.

So tonight was to be the grand culmination of not only the holiday season, but of Felicity's life-style, as well.

Jill Cassidy passed by, dimpled and astonishingly pretty in a silk blouse and satin trousers, her good-looking husband grinning in tow. 'Could you keep this for just a sec?' she laughingly held out a half-finished glass to Raine. 'Ian and I are going to show you all how it's done.'

Raine looked down helplessly at the champagne glass, then back at the married couple as they began to twirl, their routine surprisingly superior to any exhibited thus far. Even Felicity and her date had to exchange a rueful look, realising they'd been bettered. 'We both minored in Dance,' Jill imparted breathlessly as Ian flung her over his arm in a final dramatic dip.

Shouts for an encore nearly drowned out the door-bell's insistent ring. The next number had already started up before Raine picked her way over shifted furniture and discarded shoes, dread instinct leaping in her breast. Has Mrs Flannery upstairs actually called the police to complain? Or suppose Felicity had invited more guests? Where on earth would they put them?

She had far greater reason for worry. Flinging open the door, an enquiry coolly set in her eyes, Jill's drink in her hand and a virtual riot at her back, Raine came face to face with Louise Stacey, her case worker.

'Oh!' Her mouth formed the word soundlessly, so acute was her shock and distress. Not tonight, of all nights! But it was happening. Miss Stacey's small, birdlike eyes flicked for a long moment past her, then back, lighting with distaste and disapproval on the sparkling liquid in the glass she held, as if just daring Raine to try passing the champagne off as ginger ale. Raine didn't try anything. She went tragically numb, certain that her fate and Stephen's had been decided during that one accusing glance. All the rest was mere formality.

'Good evening, Miss Jacobs,' the woman said tightly. 'It appears that I've come at an inconvenient time.' The schoolmarm tone thoroughly rattled Raine, the thin, set mouth completing the job. 'May I ask who are all these... people?'

Voice strained, Raine delved about for some non-condemning way to present her case. 'RaineBo Shoppe employees.' She made a small, helpless gesture with one hand. 'Also some mall personnel and fellow merchants. We have a staff Christmas party annually... as a way of thanking our people for their hard work.'

'I see,' Louise Stacey clipped, leaving Raine in little doubt as to what she actually did see.

'Won't you come in?' Raine offered a bit desperately. She had no idea how to proceed, when she'd envisioned her home study visit so differently... a placid tour of the apartment, a meaningful chat about Stephen, and perhaps a shared pot of tea. Now all her well intentioned plans to charm the woman before her were irrevocably mislaid, replaced with a nightmare of misconception.

'Oh, no!' Miss Stacey shook her head, lips stretching grimly over small white teeth. 'No, I don't think that will be necessary. I've seen more than enough to suit my purposes.'

'How can you say that?' Raine began, softly shaken, just as her peripheral vision showed her Felicity's flame-coloured figure floating towards her. She half turned, attempting to signal her friend to silence, but the older girl had her eyes fixed curiously to the thin, bundled woman in a knit beret and sturdy shoes who stood in the entry hall.

'I don't believe we've met,' Felicity said to Louise Stacey, her voice not slurred, but just controlled enough to suggest a degree of intoxication. Raine groaned inwardly as her partner stuck out a beringed hand, wrist wreathed in gold bangles. 'I'm Felicity Boian, Raine's room-mate. Who are you? One of the neighbours?'

Miss Stacey dragged her offended gaze from Felicity's plunging neckline to the scarlet-tipped hand that she made no move to take. 'Hardly,' she got out, before sending an icy, meaningful look to Raine. 'I was unaware you had a room-mate.'

Felicity leapt into Raine's silence, making an obvious effort to assimilate. 'It's only a temporary arrangement,' she volunteered, black eyes narrowing and her scorned hand dropping to her side. Raine felt too sick at heart to intervene, but when Felicity ventured on in a less charitable tone, she fervently wished that she had. 'My partner and I are entertaining a few friends. I hope the noise hasn't bothered you. We're usually a very upright bunch...'

'I doubt that,' the other woman interrupted quite rudely. As if to support her theory, Bill Sanders chose that moment to appear at Felicity's back, half sliding an arm around her narrow waist and outrageously nuzzling the side of her neck.

'Where'd you go, sweetheart?' His friendly, slightly flushed face swivelled then to Louise Stacey, teasing laughter in his eyes. 'What's this, a gatecrasher? Well, aren't you going to invite her in?'

'Don't bother. I was just leaving!'

Had there been time, Raine might have prayed for the floor to swallow her. But, as it was, only her heart plummeted while the social worker shut her mouth tightly, fixed a hard glare towards the group, then turned and stalked away. A sarcastically muttered 'Goodnight!' was snatched back on the draught from the slamming outer door.

'Who was *that*?' Felicity and Bill asked almost in unison.

Raine leaned her back against the door, tears of dismay and frustration already welling. 'That,' she said thickly, as she stared at the ceiling in an effort to arrest the gathering teardrops, 'was my case worker. I think we blew it, kids.'

'Oh, God, Raine!' Felicity was aghast. Around them, the commotion had barely dropped a decibel, and now Raine was grateful for the noise. At least, if the others were preoccupied, it meant that her humiliating exchange with Louise Stacey had gone largely unnoticed. Sensing undercurrents that he didn't understand, Bill Sanders' exit from their small tableau was far more discreet than his approach had been moments before. That left Raine and Felicity, the older girl gravely astonished and prepared to say so, except that Raine was beyond listening, beyond everything except escaping to her room before she began to cry in earnest.

She waved a detaining hand at Felicity, making her way around the edge of the group as best she could. Safe in the privacy of her bedroom, then, she threw herself down on the bed, perversely wishing that Kyle was there to hold her. He became part of her tears instead, his betrayal no longer kept rigidly at bay when her whole future seemed to be collapsing. She was angry at the issue that had come between them, furious with Felicity for mutilating their agreement to keep business affairs businesslike. And she was appalled that Louise Stacey had taken such a rigid, self-righteous attitude. But most of all, she was afraid. Stone-cold afraid. She knew instinctively that the case worker was going to block her attempt to adopt Stephen with every ounce of professional power that she possessed.

Eventually, she sat on the edge of the bed, dried her face and reached for the phone. Meg Jackson answered on the third ring, her cheerful tone fading drastically as Raine poured out her dilemma. The pause afterwards lasted ominously too long. 'Raine, I have no idea what to say. I know you called me for reassurance, but in all honesty I just can't give it. Lou Stacey is as strict as they come. In a situation like this, where leniency and under-standing are needed, you frankly don't have a hope in heaven of getting a reasonable report out of her. She just doesn't work that way. She'll put down exactly what she saw, in black and white. Period. There's no room in Lou's mind for the benefit of the doubt.'

'Then I've lost Stephen,' Raine said flatly, numbly. She couldn't let herself think about it yet, only be-ginning to brace herself for the tearing hurt.

'There may be a way...' Meg said hesitantly, as if mentally weighing pros and cons. 'It's a little un-orthodox, but if you're willing to try it...'

'Anything!' Raine agreed fervently.

'Well, I'm sure you know that a psychiatrist is oc-casionally called into an adoption case to evaluate the feasibility of matching a child with the prospective parent? What I'm thinking is this...I know he isn't a psychiatrist, but he has come to know Stephen very well...suppose Doctor Benedict made a recommen-dation on your behalf?'

'Oh, Meg, no!' Raine could have wept her frus-trations all over again. 'I don't...'

'Wait. Hear me out,' Meg insisted. 'Kyle is Stephen's doctor, therefore any recommendation from him would be considered seriously. As an added bonus, he is highly respected and admired by everyone on staff at our branch. Without Kyle donating his time and skills, a lot of our kids would miss out on the corrective treatment that they need, simply because our budget is limited and the most severe cases always take priority. Kyle has made a difference to a lot of little lives!' The glowing accolade continued, Meg totally oblivious to Raine's stunned si-lence. 'As I understand it, he was also responsible for setting up the Katherine Benedict Memorial Fund that his family continues to support. The Fund is paying for Stephen's stay at Physicians...I doubt that you knew...and also Jenny's, and several others each year.

So you'll agree that if there's one person who can counteract the damage Lou Stacey is likely to do to your file, it's Doctor Benedict. Will you ask for his help, Raine? Just ask...and I'll do anything I can to back you up.'

Raine drew a frightfully shaky breath, realisation adding just one more thick layer to her depression. How she had misjudged Kyle! Would she ever fight her way out of the confusion to see clearly again? She asked the question because she was afraid to trust in what her common sense told her; her powers of deduction had led her astray too many times. 'Meg...I thought...didn't Kyle complain to you before about Stephen and me?'

'Kyle?' Now Meg seemed to be the one who was stunned. 'Good lord, no! What gave you... Raine——' she halted in mid-sentence, her voice gradually taking on a soft consternation '—I'm afraid I owe you an apology. I just didn't realise how big an apology it needed to be. Kyle had nothing to do with our talk that evening at the hospital. He's been nothing but complimentary about you and what you've done for Stephen.'

'Then you did discuss me?' Raine asked, conscious that she'd asked Kyle that same question, and he had made no move to deny it.

'Well, yes...but not in the way you'd imagine. Whenever I'd see Stephen, he would chatter on about you. Raine this and Raine that. And there was always a new toy to admire. Curiosity... and a personal interest, too...got the better of me. So I asked Kyle about you, but believe me, nothing derogatory was said.'

'Then what prompted you to question my intentions?'

'That's where the need to apologise comes in...' Raine could hear the rueful smile in her voice. 'What I did, plainly put, was to run a gambit on your emotions. I'd seen you interact with Stephen, I had heard Kyle's opinion, which I value, and I came to feel that you belonged with that child. I decided to supply a small threat of separation, hoping to make you realise that Stephen had a permanent place in your heart. I justified myself by rationalising that if the bond wasn't strong enough it was time to wean Stephen away from you anyway. In retrospect, that's known as manipulation, a word I despise. At the time, I preferred to think of it as professional licence. I hope you can forgive me? The only thing I can say in my defence is that my instincts were good.'

Yes, Raine thought later as she replaced the receiver, but her own instincts were all wrong, or maybe it was her thought process that had gone awry, making an enemy of Kyle, when it seemed he had been her best friend instead. No, her instincts weren't at fault, just her unwillingness to trust them. She could see that now. She'd let her perception of Kyle suffer because of something her father had done almost twenty years ago. And his tolerance of her skittish behaviour had waned. The insult of the accusations she'd made took on new proportions after what she'd just learned. Kyle performed surgery on Stephen without a fee, admitted him to the hospital under a charitable fund that he had helped found, and Raine had the audacity to suggest that he'd used the little boy as some kind of pawn in a power play? No wonder he was furious with her! She was sick just thinking of the mistakes she'd made.

There was only one answer. Somehow, some way, she had to see Kyle, apologise and try to explain. For now, an overwhelming desire to see Stephen overtook her. She repaired her make-up with a slightly lighter hand, but didn't bother changing. The black dress was perfectly suitable for a hospital visit, and the colour suited her disheartened mood. She felt as if everything dear had been taken from her. And she had no idea whether she could fix any of it.

# CHAPTER SEVEN

STEPHEN had obviously cried himself sick. Sweat dampened his normally shining hair until it clung to his small skull in flat ringlets. His face was flushed, his body limp and listless. There was no movement aside from a great tear that squeezed past screwed-up eyelids and the pitiful quiver of his jutting lower lip. Even Boo had failed to comfort him, the woolly rabbit haphazardly lodged against the steel railings of the cot. Kyle, sitting on the edge of the mattress, rubbed a rhythmic palm over Stephen's tummy and murmured something soothingly incoherent. His head came up sharply when Raine entered the room, blue eyes boring into her, but Stephen didn't stir.

'What happened?' she mouthed silently, meeting only with Kyle's shrug. She walked close, reaching down a tender hand to stroke a few clinging wisps off the little face. 'Stephen? Look at me, sweetie,' she coaxed, gentling with both voice and touch. 'Tell me what's wrong. Why are you crying?'

His eyes opened part-way at that, brilliant blue beneath the standing tears. 'Stay me,' he cried huskily, small chest heaving with exhaustion. 'Ho'd me.'

'Sssh, it's all right.' Raine struggled with the bedrail until it clicked into a lower notch and gathered up the child as best she could. He had both arms around her neck in a strangling embrace, fists tangled in her hair, straining the pins that held it. Sliding a hand under each shoulder, she hugged back, hampered frustratingly by his cloth restraint. Poor little boy, he was trembling like a drenched puppy, the kisses she dropped to his cheek and chin of virtually no comfort value. The whimpers gave way to piteous sobs. He was so miserable and ill that Raine had to fight the need to join in.

Shuddering convulsively, the toddler turned his face into her neck. She could feel his hot tears against her skin as he hiccuped violently. 'W-where m-my...'

'Boo's right here, sweetheart,' Raine anticipated. Kyle untangled the rabbit and passed it over, Raine tucked it firmly into the crook of a little arm.

'No!' Stephen startled her by shouting, his small body twisting to free itself. Raine sat back just a bit, enough to see Boo flung unceremoniously to the floor. 'Don't w-want Boo!' The little face crumpled afresh. 'W-where my mama?'

Pain twisted inside her. She hadn't seen that coming, and was totally unprepared. Eyes darkened, she stared down at the sobbing child. 'Oh, Stephen,' she whispered numbly. 'Darling, I'm so sorry.' Just forming words hurt her throat unbearably, but drowning blue eyes were locked on to her face, trusting her to explain, to make everything all right. 'Your mama... Your mama loved you very much, darling... But she had to go away.'

'Why?' he quavered, chin wobbling.

'Oh, darling, I don't know why.' Her throat closed completely then; she could scarcely draw breath. She flung a shimmering glance to Kyle, begging for help as the small arms clenched tightly around her neck again.

Kyle's voice was husky with emotion as he carefully found words and catered them to the two-year-old's level. 'Your mama didn't want to go away, Stephen... Not ever. She just had to. That's why she left you with Raine and me... so we can take care of you... so you don't have to feel sad or afraid without her.'

Very slowly, the sobbing child seemed to relax. Raine held tight for a long time, finally aware of Kyle's arms pulling her away. Stephen, utterly exhausted, had fallen asleep, his fingers still gripping her hair. Kyle came to her rescue again, releasing the fine strands and tucking the small, relaxed fists under the blankets. His beautiful man's face hid whatever he was thinking or feeling, while Raine was vulnerable, the tears drying on her face. 'Do you think he's going to be all right?' she asked thickly. 'I didn't know what to say.'

'You did fine.'

He seemed to mean it. Raine stood up, swaying, and struggled to put the safety railing into place. Kyle stepped close to her back, reaching around her to manoeuvre the stubborn catch, and it was just as well, because her hands were shaking too badly to manage. 'I should never have left him today,' she confessed, blinking at the sleeping child. 'I knew something was wrong this morning...he just doesn't get that cranky without good reason. But I was due at the shop.' She passed a hand over her eyes, voice breaking. '*Damn* the shop, anyway! Why couldn't I be here when he needed me?'

She brushed past Kyle, fluttering around to the other side of the bed, putting distance between them. She felt wildly upset, too upset to cope. What she really wanted was to fling herself into his arms, put pride precluded that particular urge...Kyle's pride, not her own. She owed him a grave apology, yet his features were set against her, a little angry, a little cold, so that the words wouldn't come. What could she say that would be good enough?

Shuddering, she wrapped her arms across her narrow ribcage, staring distractedly at Stephen. She'd failed him, too, poor baby! He had counted on her to right his small world and instead she had done the one thing that everyone warned her against. She had let him learn to love her. And now she had to walk out of his life, knowing that the memory of her leaving would take far greater position in his young mind than any of the good times they'd shared. If he remembered her at all in a few years' time, she would simply be another adult who had let him down. So that meant she'd lost both of them...irretrievably.

Kyle's gravelly voice cut softly across the small space, his brilliant eyes compelling her to raise her face, to look at him. 'Kids are resilient, Raine. He'll be just fine.'

'I don't know,' she responded flatly. 'Was it fair to give him false hope? You told him we'd take care of him...as if you were promising for ever.'

'Maybe I was,' Kyle said broodingly.

'You don't understand,' Raine insisted, eyes agonised. 'Kyle, I'm not going to be approved for adoption. They won't let me have Stephen.'

'Why?'

She gave a bitter laugh, but told him about the party that had got out of hand, about Louise Stacey's untimely visit. 'So you see,' she added despairingly, 'it's all but certain that my application will be rejected.'

Kyle made no response, and she closed her eyes, fighting for control of her ravaged emotions. 'I guess that leaves you a clear road,' she said croakily, voice bitter-sweet. 'Why wouldn't they approve of you? You're the finest man that agency has ever seen. Just as I'm the greatest fool . . . Meg told me, Kyle. I know about the surgery you do. I know about the fund that's supported Stephen's care. And I know that all the accusations I made were unfair and unfounded. I don't know what else to say except that I am very, very sorry for the way I distrusted you.'

'Apology accepted.' She hadn't heard him move, but when she opened her eyes he was standing barely two feet away, blazing intensity in his handsome face. He was unbearably, broodingly attractive, and oh, how badly she wanted to bridge the gap between them!

'I chose a lousy way to repay your kindness,' she said softly.

He laughed, a dark impatient sound. 'Kindness had nothing to do with it.' He put out a hand, studied a stray red-gold tendril, then let it drift back on to her cheek. 'Raine . . . you make me just a little crazy sometimes. Then I tell myself that you aren't being *deliberately* obtuse.'

She stared at him, hurting. 'Did you have to avoid me? Why not just explain . . . make me believe?'

'No way,' he said grimly. 'There are only so many times I'll hit my head against the same brick wall. I told you once that you were mistaken, the next move had to come from you.' Grimacing, he cupped both her shoulders in his palms, as if he longed to shake her. 'I'm still waiting, lady.'

'I missed you,' Raine whispered, eyes enormous and storm-grey.

'Oh, yeah?' Kyle drawled, his face alive with passionate challenge. 'Show me.'

He'd really meant what he said about the first move. Sighing, feeling an oppressive weight dissolve around her, Raine stood on tiptoe, wrapping her arms around his broad neck. He stood completely still, not helping, but the glint in his eyes gave her courage to follow through. She stared into their blue depths for a long moment, her body pressed lightly against the full length of his, a silent communion passing between them. Then, with a small shadow-smile playing about her lips, she kissed his firm male mouth, nuzzling softly until the contact was moister... fuller. Even then, it was essentially a chaste kiss, yet he made no move to take charge, simply linking his hands in the small of her back when she drew away, smiling down enigmatically.

'What am I going to do with you, Raine?'

'Not much, given our present surroundings,' she teased. Her expression changed almost immediately, as she glanced at Stephen asleep in his crib. How could she have forgotten the little boy for even a minute? Kyle followed her look. When she caught his eye again, she was full of worried consternation. 'Kyle, what about Stephen?'

'Don't look so guilty.' He searched her eyes and the sweet vulnerable curve of her mouth, his own mouth twisting. 'There's a solution.'

'Meg seems to think my only hope is to have you give me a recommendation,' she told him quickly, before she lost her nerve. Somehow, she didn't feel in any position to ask favours. 'I didn't intend to mention it,' she explained tautly, 'then I realised that I'd do almost anything to keep Stephen.'

'If you mean that, then you've just given me the perfect opening for what I'm about to say.' His beautiful mouth quirked again, his blue eyes very intent, watchful. 'I wasn't lying when I said I wanted Stephen, but at the same time I had to be realistic. What adoption board would grant me single custody of Stephen, with the hours that I work? I couldn't give him much of a homelife on my own. He needs a mother, too. He needs us, Raine, both of us. Now more than ever. Let's adopt him together... give him two parents and a home.'

'What?' she breathed, mouth gone dry.

'I'm asking you to marry me,' Kyle clarified, so attractive, so stunningly male that her first reaction was to recoil.

Marry him? The concept of marriage to Kyle and all it entailed made impact, and fear rose in her throat. Fear of the unknown. Fear of living with him in that capacity. Or did he intend their marriage to be strictly a shelter for Stephen? The idea seemed dubious, but she asked anyway, voice hesitant, 'What... what kind of marriage do you have in mind?'

'A good one,' he said immediately, dark amusement in his eyes. 'Something much better than average. We have what it takes, don't you think?'

'Sexual attraction?' she moistened her dry lips, the quiver starting up again.

'Yes, sexual attraction!' he blazed huskily. 'And every other kind with it. How else did we get this far this fast? I'll admit that Stephen has been the main focal point, but he isn't the only bond between us.'

'I don't know,' she swallowed nervously. 'I need to think...'

'No.' He shocked her with his insistence, both hands coming up to clasp her head. 'You do too much thinking, and it only sets us back two paces for every one we move forward. So don't think. Just give me your gut reaction, and we'll go with that.'

The fierce stark blue of his eyes arrested her, bullied her. She couldn't speak and, with a self-deprecatory twisting smile, he let his fingertips find the few pins in her hair, removing them. 'Kyle...' she whispered uncertainly, but he ignored her, loosing the tumbled mass over her shoulders, sifting through shimmering tendrils with his fingers.

'You are so incredible,' he gritted huskily, almost as if her beauty pained him. 'I don't think you have any idea how badly I want you. And you want me, too, Raine...you're just too cautious to admit it.' And she did. Her entire body was suddenly flushed and burning, a throbbing pulse urgent at its centre. 'Come here.' Kyle lost patience. Excitingly, endearingly arrogant, he tipped up her face, kissing her open mouth with a possessive ferocity that stole all the substance from her limbs. 'Tell me.'

She could no more imagine a future without Kyle than a life without Stephen. She knew that with a certainty, and deemed it the gut reaction he'd wanted. 'That wasn't fair——' softly shaken, she leaned her face into his shoulder '—but yes.'

Felicity was alone when Raine came back to the apartment, her red dress exchanged for a warm terry robe, a cup of black coffee in hand. The kitchen and living areas were devoid of party clutter, all the furnishings put back into place. 'You must have sent them away hours ago to accomplish all this.'

Felicity arched a thin shoulder. 'It suddenly seemed to be in poor taste. My fault,' she owned tersely. 'The kind of proper celebration we normally have would hardly raise an eyebrow.'

That admission, along with the meticulous clean-up, was the closest thing to an apology that Felicity could manage. Seeing no reason to press for more, Raine simply nodded, curling into a chintz armchair near the fireplace while she cast about for a neutral way of saying what had to be said. 'It's difficult socialising on one level and supervising on another,' she finally ventured. 'But I doubt that any lasting damage was done. If we're both very professional tomorrow, I dare say the working relationship will fall back into perspective for the others.'

'So that's one problem solved.' Felicity shook a slender cigarette from a pack, picking up a ceramic table lighter afterwards, motions jerky. 'What about you? Have I ruined everything, or can it be fixed?'

Not expecting to be confronted so soon, Raine froze for a moment. Doubts at her own wisdom...disbelief at Kyle's mastery assailed her. She balked at explanations, realising that just Kyle Benedict's existence would be news to the friend who had shared her education, her home, her partnership...and who had once known nearly every detail of her life. 'I've found a solution, too,' she got out softly.

The telling took only a few minutes; Felicity's silence lasted much longer, her expression, once the initial shock gave way, a study in flat scepticism. She drew nervously on her cigarette, watching the thin blue stream of smoke as it cut through the air, her black eyes shadowed. 'Well...I'm not usually so dense,' she finally commented, 'but would you believe that the idea of another man never occurred to me? I even invited Gavin to our party this afternoon, thinking that the two of you might need an opportunity to work things out. I had no idea he'd already been replaced. At least that explains his blunt refusal.'

'Felicity,' Raine all but winced, seeing how her partner's thoughts were travelling, 'it wasn't like that. Not really. Gavin and I were never right for each other. I'll admit that we enjoyed being together in the past, but it could never have evolved into anything deeper. We were only marking time.'

'Until a ready-made family came along to take Gavin's place? Maybe Brian has made me cynical, but I just can't see it.' She shrugged almost ruefully. 'Aside from the fact that I get to keep the apartment...I hope you weren't expecting any ecstatic reaction?'

'I wasn't.' She had to admit, though, that the blatant aversion hurt. 'I wasn't expecting total rejection of the idea, either.'

Felicity's full mouth twisted. 'Do you blame me? I'm not some uninvolved bystander in this. What about RaineBo Shoppe?'

'Nothing changes. As I told you before, a working mother is no phenomenon...Well, neither is a working wife.'

'That's what you say now. What about later...when the pressure of being Superwoman gets to you? Don't tell me I won't be the first to go. A partner is much more dispensable than a husband or a child, we both know that!'

'Why are you taking this attitude?' Raine groaned, totally perplexed. 'Other than hiring Jill Cassidy to work my evening hours, I've done absolutely nothing to upset the routine!'

'True enough,' the other girl conceded tightly. 'But, until recently, just the idea of doing that would have horrified you.'

Sighing, she made an attempt to re-focus, to defuse the situation. 'Look...don't let's do this. We never used to argue, and it certainly isn't getting us anywhere. Can't we just talk?'

'You want to talk?' Felicity echoed huskily, grinding out the cigarette before it was half-finished and drawing a shaky breath. 'OK, what have I got to lose? The bottom line is...I'm terrified. There's been too much change, too fast. I'm not in control any more. I might have...just might have handled this thing with Brian if the business weren't closing in on me, too. Until this year, taking time off during the holidays would have been incomprehensible to you. You were a rock, someone I could always count on. Now you've gone off on this substitute mother tangent and, frankly, my trust is shaken. Because, as the shop becomes less important to you, more and more of the responsibility will fall back on me. And I don't know whether I can go it alone. I *sell*,' she laughed shakily, 'and I'm damn good at it! But that's *all* I do. I'm not a book-keeper. I'm no financial planner. Without Gavin to guide me, I couldn't even muddle my way through the advertising decisions! If you decided to bow out, who would take your place? The business could very well falter. I could lose everything...all that I have left. So you see,' she glanced away at the last moment, trying to hide the fear in her dark eyes, 'I have a right to worry.'

'A right maybe,' Raine said with conviction, 'but no *reason*. Felicity, I have as much a stake in that business as you have. I worked the same part-time jobs during school. I made the same sacrifices. So believe me when I tell you that I have no intention, now or in the future, or bowing out. I'll admit that my personal life might make some juggling necessary, but that's as far as it goes. And, when it comes to the point, neither of us is bound to absolute loyalty. As I understand it, most professionals do rate some kind of private life...even me.'

'I suppose I deserved that,' Felicity said tautly, after a while. 'I'm sorry. But I thought I had guarantees with Brian, and look how that turned out.'

'Just don't judge me by Brian's example,' Raine said, mildly now. 'I think I've proved that I can deliver what I'm promising.'

'So, can this Kyle Benedict do the same?' Felicity changed tack with disconcerting swiftness. 'I know you well enough to understand his motivations,' she elaborated, the compliment characteristically backhanded, 'but how do you benefit from the arrangement?'

'It isn't anywhere near as coldblooded as you make it sound,' Raine protested, sighing. 'And I'm getting a chance to be Stephen's mother.'

'Something you would have had anyway, except for my dramatics. But is that basis enough for a marriage?' Her laugh was low and entirely humourless. 'I know I'm no expert on relationships, but one thing I've realised is that you can't use a child to cement one together.' She paused to light another cigarette, hand visibly trembling. 'Raine, I'm mortified just admitting this, but not so long ago I considered having Brian's child, becoming pregnant. I suppose you could call it a last-ditch effort to hold on to him, but in the end I couldn't follow through. I'm not the maternal type——' the joke came out hollow '—and, anyway, how could I introduce an innocent child into a relationship that had already gone wrong? It would have been so unfair! Children should be created because they're wanted, between two people who love each other. Having a child out of desperation, as the means to cling...that's such a risky decision.'

Raine sat motionless for the moment, an aching empathy rising as she realised the emotional distress it must have taken to drive Felicity to that precarious a brink. So many things became clear then. Felicity's brittle, burning tension. Her impatience and short-fused temper during recent weeks. 'I'm so sorry,' Raine murmured, thinking the phrase woefully inadequate. 'I had no idea things had become so difficult for you. Why didn't you tell me?'

'Probably for the same reason you didn't tell me about your doctor...because we've grown apart. Or maybe because I couldn't picture you getting into the same position. You disapproved when I moved in with Brian...oh, not verbally, but I knew. And I hated proving you so completely right.' She shrugged, attempting to be philosophical. 'The point is that I learned something, and I'm trying to pass that on to you. Is what you're planning so different from what I almost did? Forming a marriage strictly for the sake of a child?'

'That isn't the only reason.' Realisation set in and she lifted eyes that had darkened as the knowledge formed in her heart. 'I'm in love with Kyle. I think I have been all along.' She drew a deep breath. 'Maybe it isn't so different, after all, because I don't know how he feels about me. There's physical attraction...and there's Stephen. Kyle needs me. I'm hoping it will be enough.'

In spite of a shopping force that rose to fever pitch at the mall, the next few days were still an exercise in waiting and self-doubt for Raine.

Then suddenly it was Christmas Eve, and almost closing time. Raine glanced around at the nearly empty shop displays, the dwindling line at the cash register, and allowed herself the luxury of exchanging a relieved and congratulatory smile with her partner.

Felicity was with the one remaining customer, a small, flustered man who had put off buying his wife's gift until the last moment. Raine didn't envy her the job of suggesting clothing for a woman sight-unseen, whose mate hadn't the presence of mind to find out her size beforehand. She saw him making measuring gestures with his hands, and shook her head consolingly as Felicity glanced up again over his shoulder. The black eyes glinted with amused exasperation, then flickered with something less easily definable as they moved towards the front entrance. Expecting to encounter a straggling customer, Raine turned and instead saw Kyle.

He looked incredibly handsome in a brown tweed sports coat with suede patches at the elbows, wool trousers, Oxford shirt, handknit tie.

'Hi!' Raine's voice, husky-soft, seemed scant competition for the heartbeat that had become almost painful in his presence. She felt inordinately glad that Stephen wasn't around to push a stethoscope at him and say 'you listen', or else her secret would be lost.

'Hi,' Kyle returned mockingly, easily, one lean hand coming out to cradle her elbow. 'The sign says you're closing shop at six. Like a ride to the hospital?'

Raine glanced at her watch, glad for any small distraction from what was fast becoming a mesmerised stare. 'Five more minutes,' she murmured, forcing her pulse under control in the process. 'You didn't drive all the way over to give me a ride?'

'No.' He flashed a look around the store interior, smiling at and, Raine suspected, dazzling Felicity, whom he must have known by the photograph he'd seen in the apartment. Raine hazarded a glance that way herself, only to intercept a look that said roughly, 'This is your doctor? He's gorgeous!' Blushing slightly, for goodness knew what reason, she locked in quickly to Kyle's husky voice. 'Very impressive place, lady... Is there an office, someplace we can talk?'

'A stockroom,' she got out, struggling to read his inflection.

'OK.' His firm mouth twisted, giving nothing away. 'You lead.'

Raine did so, conscious of the female eyes—four pairs of them, all widened in appreciation, if not downright envy—that followed their progress across the carpeted floor. The double doors had barely swung shut behind them before Kyle leaned against the edge of a packing crate, drawing her unresistingly between his knees. Pressing one palm lightly in the small of her back and cupping the other to the back of her bright head, he pulled her in to his lean body and slowly, fiercely kissed her open mouth.

'What was that for?' She drew away, breathing unevenly, her legs shaking.

Kyle didn't answer immediately, his brilliant blue gaze passing over her flushed face to the slender, curved body sheathed in its cowled sweater dress, the cashmere a lovely wisteria colour that seemed to reflect in the grey of her eyes. 'That was for my beautiful fiancée,' he paused, smiling, 'and for the future mother of my future son.'

Speechless, Raine stared...until his look told her everything she needed to know.

'Oh, Kyle,' she breathed giddily, instant emotional tears springing to her eyes. 'He's ours? He's really ours?' Unable to contain herself any longer, she closed the small distance she'd put between them, both arms thrown about his neck.

'Going to be,' he corrected gently. 'Meg called. We've been issued temporary custody. Stephen's going home with us just as soon as I get him out of traction and into a cast, which means that we'd better talk about a wedding date. I thought New Year's Eve.' He held her away a little, amused indulgence in his face. 'You aren't crying, are you?'

'No, but only because I have to go and help thank our employees for their hard work.' She sniffed delicately, a brilliant smile on her mouth and in her eyes, and no thought at the moment of hiding any of it. 'Then can we tell Stephen?'

'I'm counting on it.' He turned practical then, standing her upright with obvious reluctance. 'Meanwhile, our five minutes are up. You'd better go do your thing, boss.'

'No, come out and meet everyone,' she said impulsively, fingers twining with his to urge him to his feet, her spirit soaring with reckless abandonment.

Half-way to the doors, Kyle stopped her again, snaking an arm about her waist and tipping her head back against his shoulder so that her mouth was upturned for his kiss. Trembling, melting, Raine had barely seconds to conceal her reactions afterwards, before he pushed at the swinging panels.

'*That* was for me,' he drawled softly in her ear.

Stephen was a priceless addition to Raine's Christmas, his eyes growing more blue and more enormous with every gift he opened. Pushovers, both of them, Kyle and Raine had given way at the first childish plea, seeing no discernible difference between eve and morn when the recipient was two years old and pouting adorably. The shreds of colourful paper grew yet again as a pair of Disney hand-puppets were extracted. Kyle and Stephen put them on, exchanging a nonsensical ad-lib conversation as Mickey Mouse and Donald Duck that had Raine shaking her bright head in hopeless amusement. Then, adding the puppets to his other booty, Kyle presented Stephen with the last gift. 'This bi-i-ig,' the little boy enthused wide-eyed, tearing at the wrappings that covered the largest box of all. Raine put a steadying hand on the package, pinning it firmly to the mattress beneath Stephen's onslaught, while sending Kyle a quizzical glance. He was responsible for this one, fetching it up from his office at the last minute, and she was almost as curious as the child. Paper gradually fell away from the box, but not before Raine heard the first small scratching sounds that revealed the nature of its occupant. Kyle lifted the lid off, light shining through the small air holes that she hadn't noticed, and Raine gasped simultaneously with Stephen, when a pair of enormous chocolate-brown eyes peeped out. With a whine, a tiny sneeze, and a shake of long curly ears, the most beautiful golden cocker spaniel sprawled across Stephen's small chest, his clumsy soft paws scrambling furiously.

'A doggy!' Stephen squealed, no further evidence needed of his delight. The puppy blinked soulfully, then swiped a soft pink tongue across Stephen's rounded cheek, nuzzling his chin exploratorily. 'Hi, doggy!' Stephen chuckled riotously, patting and hugging in immediate fond acceptance, while floppy paws gingerly trod over his shoulders and chest, tail crazily thumping.

'Kyle, I hope you know you've completely upstaged me,' Raine whispered, Stephen's delight infectious. 'What a fantastic gift!' She reached over to stroke the silken, honey-coloured fur, adding aloud, 'Does he have a name?'

'Stephen gets to choose one,' Kyle announced, eyeing the little boy with quiet enjoyment. 'What do you say, sport?'

'Doggy!' Stephen insisted promptly.

Raine grinned as Kyle grimaced. 'OK, Doggy it is…at least for now. But there's something I have to tell you about your pup, Stephen. He can only stay in your room for a while. After that he's going home to my house. And in a few more days, as soon as you're better, you're coming to my house, too. You're going to be my little boy. I'll be your daddy.' He gave Raine a reassuring glance, catching up her hand. 'And Raine will be your new mommy. Would you like that?'

Stephen's pout was disheartening. Then his gruff small voice made its reason known. 'I want Doggy stay me.'

Relaxing, Raine reached over to tickle his chin. 'Sweetie, he can't. Dogs aren't allowed to stay in the hospital. But he's going to wait for you at your new home. Then you can play together any time you want.'

Stephen swivelled a solemn, considering blue gaze from one adult to another, finally breaking into a grudging smile that grew bigger and brighter by degrees. 'OK.' He put a careful palm against the animal's gleaming neck, patting as gently as a child of two can manage, suddenly matter-of-fact and confident. 'You stay, Do'tor Kyle.'

'Kyle.' Raine glanced up, softly accusing, as he put the lid back on the box an hour or so later, the newly christened Doggy inside and Boo restored to his position of honour, sprawled across the sleeping child's chest, 'you aren't supposed to have that puppy up here. You smuggled him, didn't you?'

'I confess,' he mocked softly. 'Planning to turn me in? Or are you going to help me get him out to the car?'

'I'll help,' she smiled, fishing about under a chair for one of the shoes she'd slipped off, 'but if we're caught, I know absolutely nothing.'

They gained access to the Porsche without a whimper to give them away, a quick glance into the box showing them a furry bundle that had grown sleepy and content during transit. 'What are you going to do with him?' Raine asked, after Kyle saw her settled. 'Is he house-broken?'

'He'd better be,' Kyle said glibly, 'because you're holding him on the way home.' He scooped the puppy up, big paws dangling, and passed him over, tossing the empty box into the back. Laughing, Raine nuzzled the warm, drowsy body, feeling a contented lethargy of her own. She couldn't remember a happier time than the hours she'd just spent with Kyle and Stephen. She didn't want the day to end.

Kyle had started the engine, but made no move to put the car into gear. Raine glanced sideways to find him staring at her with an expression that had gone oddly still. 'Are you hungry?'

'A little, yes.'

'Come home with me?'

Something in his eyes made her mouth go dry. Raine's heart gave a jolt, then began thudding against her ribcage. 'Why?' she got out shakily, aware that he was waiting.

Kyle sighed. 'Because we have things to talk about... Because you should see the place where you're going to live... Because it's Christmas Eve, and we're both hungry, and Doggy here wants his basket.' A glint of mocking humour lit his eyes, only to disappear just as quickly. The shrug that followed was attractive, brooding, dismantling the protest on her lips. 'But, mostly, because I want to be with you.'

She was an age forming her answer, the seduction of his request heating the blood in her veins. A moment ago she'd been wishing this time didn't have to end. Felicity would have left for her mother's house in Allentown; all that awaited Raine if she refused was an empty apartment and another lonely Christmas. While, if she accepted...well, Kyle had left her no room to misinterpret the invitation.

Clearing away after the steak and salad dinner they'd prepared, Raine was getting a taste of what domesticity would be like with Kyle. Easy companionship, underscored by the inevitable pulse of sexual tension. Loading the dishwasher, as he rolled up his shirt sleeves to rinse items at the sink, she could hardly believe that they had just planned their wedding over the informal meal. That in less than one week, Kyle's beautiful glass and cedar house was to be her home, the handsomely masculine bedroom upstairs a shared domain, with Stephen sleeping just across the hallway.

The odd bemusement stayed with her as they carried hot drinks to the den. Kyle went down on his haunches before the massive stone fireplace to light the ready-laid wood, grinning indulgently when Stephen's puppy lifted its head to emit a sleepy yap-yawn. 'How are you doing, fellow?' He absently rubbed behind the long curly ears.

Raine watched the first flame catch and grow, watched the firelight flicker golden across his downbeat head and his muscled forearms, and on to the animal's gleaming coat. The puppy's discordant yap had become a contented little growl.

A smile was still soft on her face when Kyle straightened abruptly, taking her unawares. 'Don't stop now,' he mocked gently, the intensity in his eyes a mismatch for the surface ease. Raine swallowed visibly as he lowered his lean frame on to the sofa beside her, the buttery leather crinkling beneath his weight. Purposefully he removed the teacup from her hand and set it on to the antique trunk that served as coffee-table. 'I have to do this,' he said quietly, tipping up her chin. He drew the kiss out unbearably, teasing her with the feather-light brush of his lips before parting her mouth to the slow thrusting exploration that he had taught her to crave. Raine kept her eyes closed afterwards, blood hammering hectically in her temples and throat as he dropped a line of smaller kisses along her jaw, stopping provocatively near her ear. 'There.' She heard the husky satisfaction in his voice. 'Whenever you start looking at me as if I were a stranger, there's only one way to set you straight.'

'This is your answer to everything,' she murmured, only provoking soft laughter.

'It's my favourite answer, anyway.' His fingers sifted through her hair, feeling the fine, silken texture. His tone deepened. 'I want you, Raine.'

The dark urgency got to her, causing her to open her eyes and moisten her mouth. 'Kyle...' She paused there, unsure what she had meant to say. The emotions coursing through her were unendurable, a surplus of sensation that swiftly converted to panic. 'I'm not...ready for this. I need time.'

Kyle cupped her face with both palms, his gaze burning into her. 'When *will* you be ready?' he probed huskily. 'There isn't that much time left.' She dipped her head, and with a low groan of forfeit, he let her go. 'What you have to realise, Raine, is that whether it happens tonight or a week from now, you *are* going to be my wife...in every sense of the word.' His sensuous tone rasped over her, igniting her senses afresh. 'I probably ought to wait for a more tender moment,' he dipped into a jacket pocket and drew out a small silver-bowed box, 'but I suddenly feel a frustrated male's need to have my mark of possession on you.'

His rueful expression stripped most of the offence from the statement. Raine accepted the package, prevaricating apologetically, 'But your gift is in my car. I didn't think we'd exchange them until tomorrow.'

'It doesn't matter. Mine can wait.'

Nodding, Raine tore off the paper, slowly lifting the lid of the velvet jeweller's box she'd uncovered. Bedded inside was the most exquisite diamond that she'd ever seen, surrounded by amethysts and delicately set in gold. Wordlessly, Kyle took the ring out and slid it on to her finger, where she turned it gently to reflect the firelight. 'Kyle, thank you. It's lovely.'

His mouth twisted attractively and she was seized by a painful need to placate him, to erase the shadow that she'd put in his eyes. Impulsively she laid a palm along his polished jaw and touched her lips to his. His response was brief and controlled, not at all what she wanted, and blindly she deepened contact, moaning when he caught both her wrists to fend her off. 'Raine,' his voice was low, exasperated, and perversely she revelled in the sound of it, 'don't start something you have no intention of finishing. My self-control isn't up to the challenge.'

'It doesn't have to be.' She flung up a shimmering, intense glance, besieged by a sudden and nearly primitive ache to *know* him, to impress her love upon him in a purely physical sense when, unless substantiated by him, the words couldn't be said. Her tone was raw and scarcely recognisable. 'I won't ask you to stop.'

Kyle stared into her face for an age, then he was moving her on to his lap, fitting her into his side as if his had been the rib to form her. She shuddered at the violent sweetness, his thighs hard beneath her, his hand lifting the warm weight of her breast. Sighing, she curved her fingers into the hard bones of his shoulders as the hand wandered, gliding across her ribcage... moulding her taut belly and the swell of her hip. The blood beat erratically at all her pulse points, her breath laboured under the sensuous assault, then she was forgetting to breathe altogether, because Kyle had sought the hem of her dress. She felt the slightest tremor in him as he moved the soft cashmere, traced the lightly muscled length of her thigh. He stopped just short of further intimacy, his fingertips pressing a subtle emphasis into her silken flesh.

Raine understood the unspoken question. Feverish with need, she arched her body and urged him on.

A moment later, the touch that had been subtle changed. Consumed by the fire of his kiss, she felt him lay his hand upon her, setting the seal to his right of imminent possession. Her body stiffened for barely a heartbeat, then melded completely into molten sensation, accepting a touch more intimate than any she'd known. Time blurred at the edges, then dissolved, some unknown interval passing before Kyle turned his face into her throat and, mouth hot with passion, said again, 'I want you.'

Three small words, and Raine's heated blood somehow began to cool. Want. Not love...not even need. The wondrous rush of her own love and need ebbed, and immediately she mourned the loss, her eyes closed tightly against Kyle's responding tension, her body gone oddly wooden in his arms. How could she make him understand that, loving him, she was casting about desperately for more than his desire? Just a simple acknowledgement that he cared, even a little. The word *want* reverberated through her again, and her throat clamped tight, leaving her capable of no more than faint sound. 'I'm sorry.'

'So am I.' With painstaking deliberation he withdrew his touch, straightened the dress that he'd tangled. Then he lifted her bodily away from him and back into her own seat. 'At least you kept your word...you didn't ask me to stop. You didn't have to.'

Raine flinched from the dark irony in his face, and hated herself for having put it there. She raised both hands to her pounding temples, willing him to understand. 'What we're doing suddenly seemed so cold-blooded.'

'Lady, we were about as far from cold-blooded as two people can get.'

'But a marriage based on convenience?' she stammered, flushing. 'On...lust?' *Without love*, she added only silently, when uttering the word would amount to a kind of self-betrayal.

Fire flickered briefly in the blue eyes, and Raine realised that he had lost patience. 'You couldn't handle anything else without going on emotional overload,' he mocked harshly. 'Why complicate things?'

Raine asked herself the same question, reflecting on the speed at which everything had gone wrong. She knew that he had every right to be angry, shame and uncertainty burning fresh in her cheeks. There was no way she could defend her hot-and-cold responses without revealing the depth of her involvement. And without that defence, she could only imagine what Kyle thought of her. That she was a cheat. Or worse. Seeing no way to redeem the desolate situation, she succumbed to the escape urge, her tone stilted and raw, 'Please take me home.'

She had decided that Kyle intended to ignore her when he finally moved from his rigid position, hooking up his sports coat from the back of a chair and impatiently shrugging into it. 'I'll take you home, Raine,' he agreed tautly. 'But this is the last time I allow you to run away. Nothing has changed between us. The wedding arrangements still stand. I'm sure you'd be the last one to withdraw the security we've offered Stephen, once your injured sense of morality... or whatever the hell this is... falls back into proportion. In the meantime, you might take another look at that little word we've been batting back and forth.' His mouth quirked sarcastically at one corner. 'Trust is an empty concept without the commitment to back it up.'

# CHAPTER EIGHT

'I HOPE Kyle hasn't made you uncomfortable, leaving you here with me?'

Raine immediately turned her head from the horseback figure she'd been watching, to smile a bit self-consciously at the man by her side. Looking at his father, Raine thought she could see Kyle as he would be in another twenty years. There was a great deal of physical resemblance between the two, although David Benedict was shorter by perhaps two inches and a bit slighter of build. He was athletically fit, wiry and compact, evidence of the weekend tennis and handball that Kyle had told her he relished, and she knew that his recent skiing trip was responsible for the contrast of tanned skin against the pure silver of his hair. The eyes alone were identical, father and son sharing that same stark, brilliant blue, although the older pair held a world-weariness in their depths. Not surprisingly, this was a handsome man. And a charming one, although possessed of a rather cynical wit that would take some getting used to.

'Not at all, Mr Benedict,' Raine responded to his question, and meant it, disallowing the fact that he had caught her staring with brooding fascination after Kyle. 'I was just thinking how lovely this all is.'

From their chairs in the sun-room they had an almost panoramic view of the attractive stables behind the massive German-style house and the blocks of Pennsylvania farmland that stretched as far as Raine could see. The acreage hadn't been farmed by the Benedicts for several generations, Kyle had told her during the drive up here, although ancestors had made a good living at it in times past. Now the outside tracts were leased to neighbouring farmers, while David Benedict's only agricultural venture lay in the rough winter-

148

coated cattle that could be seen speckling the brown horizon. The horses that she'd seen earlier this afternoon—several saddlebreds and thoroughbreds, including the impressive black stallion that Kyle had mounted not ten minutes before—were kept strictly for pleasure.

This beautiful family home, like so many vintage Philadelphia dwellings, was something of a historical showplace, resplendent with its antique pieces, rich old tapestries and carpets, and a fireplace in nearly every room. Nothing if not tasteful, the sheer size and opulence of it none the less overwhelmed Raine. She was glad that Kyle didn't expect her to live here once they were married. He'd moved out years ago himself, to be nearer his work, which meant that David Benedict had been on his own long enough to have his routines and life-style well patterned. Raine wasn't anxious to bring a new marriage and a small child under his roof, in spite of the offer he'd extended to that effect only minutes after meeting her today.

Raine had to wonder if physical resemblance was all the two men shared a moment later, when, apparently gleaning her thoughts, David gave her a wry grin. 'Sure you won't reconsider moving in here? We could have one of the upstairs wings converted into a living suite. There's more room than I know what to do with, plenty of places for a child to play, and I keep enough staff to make an outside babysitting service for the boy completely unnecessary.' He held up a conciliatory hand at her disconcerted look. 'I know, I shouldn't have brought up the matter again. My son made it clear when he phoned last night that his house will be the point of residence. But you can't blame me for wishing that you'd chosen differently. I'd like to have family around this place again.'

'And you will have,' Raine told him. 'Just not every day. You're going to adore Stephen,' she added with absolute certainty. 'Everyone does.'

'I can see that you and Kyle are in agreement on that point. He may have been involved with countless children in his work, but none of them has meant to him what this boy apparently does. You can imagine my surprise when I got back from Vermont last evening to hear that Kyle had found a fiancée and a son! He's promised that I'll meet my intended grandson in a few days. With the changes the boy's already been through, I can understand Kyle's caution at springing a new grandfather on him, too.'

'He just learned that he's getting a new mommy and daddy three days ago.' Raine smiled faintly. 'Your son can be a very persuasive man, Mr Benedict. It took less than a week for him to have temporary custody of Stephen granted. The adoption process itself will be more involved, but we don't foresee any problems other than the time it will take.'

'That's just time you can use to your advantage. Come to know each other as man and wife. Learn to be parents...In your case, learn to juggle motherhood with your business. Kyle tells me you co-own a shop and that you intend to keep working. I admire that. A woman needs an interest of her own.' He smiled at her with dry approval. 'And make it David, by the way. I won't ask you to call me Dad, since you probably reserve that term for your own.'

So Kyle hadn't told him. 'I don't have any family, David. I was raised in foster homes.'

The blue eyes narrowed slightly, shrewdly. 'Then that accounts for it.'

'Accounts for what?'

'That small edge of reserve you have about you. A *mystique*, if you will. And before you take offence, let me tell you that I find that quality very attractive. And, I dare say, so does my son.' The rather cynical smile was back. 'He's seldom had to do the pursuing in a relationship up until now.'

'And what makes you so sure that he had to with me?' Raine asked, taking a sip from the iced drink in her hand to cover her discomfiture. David Benedict was every bit as direct as his son tended to be, if not even more so! What would he say if she told him that, in spite of reaching a reconciliation of sorts, their marriage was to be based almost solely on a desire to give Stephen a home?

'Because it was the same with me when I married his mother. She was the only woman who evaded me continually. I found her maddening, frustrating, and completely irresistible. When I finally pinned her down, it was with a proposal I'd had no intention of making, but one that I never regretted. Katherine made me a happy man.'

'That was her name...Katherine?' Then the fund that supported Stephen and children like him had been established in memorial to her. 'Kyle spoke about her once. He loved her very much.'

'They adored each other,' David agreed, only the most subtle of edges to his voice to indicate that the thought somehow rankled. 'Both of my children might have resembled me physically, but Kyle was largely his mother's son. Not that I can fault any of the traits that he inherited from her. Strength, sensitivity, vibrancy...that incredible presence...all those things drew me to Katherine in the beginning. It was only fitting that she should pass them on to Kyle.' He shrugged eloquently, giving Raine a self-effacing smile, in light of his faults, that looked identical to a gesture she had seen many times from Kyle. 'Russ was just a small boy and Kyle barely starting high school when my wife's bone disease was diagnosed. She died some eight years later. She was a wonderful woman, incredibly strong and brave. Kyle drew closer to her during those years, and as a result he spurned my plan to take him into the business, going on to study orthopaedic medicine instead. If he couldn't save his mother, then he'd damn well save others from her fate. And, betrayed as I felt at the time, I'll be the first to admit now that I admire and respect my son's choice.'

He met her look squarely, as if judging her reception of his revelations. 'Russ has been another stumbling block that we've had to get over. Did Kyle tell you about his brother?'

'Only that he was killed a few years ago.'

'Three years this April.' Expecting to hear the details, Raine none the less understood when the older man lapsed into an introspective silence instead. Like Kyle, when speaking of his younger son David had become taut and bland of expression, a good indication that the grief of loss was yet too strong to permit easy discussion. Giving him time, Raine found her glance drawn to the windowed wall again to pick up the diminishing horse and rider. The black stallion was awesome, really, even more frighteningly impressive in motion than he had been towering over Kyle in the paddock earlier.

'I don't know much about horses,' she commented lightly, 'but Kyle seems to be handling that one very well. He looks so big and menacing that I can't help thinking the name Deuce suits him...It means "the devil", I believe?'

'That's one definition,' David agreed, 'and the one Kyle had in mind.' Surprised by the odd tone, Raine turned just as he jerked his head towards the field where Kyle was riding. 'Deuce was the horse that threw Russ.' The admission elicited a shiver of foreboding from Raine, taking her eyes back very swiftly to the galloping figure. 'I wanted to have him put down afterwards,' David continued flatly, 'but Kyle stopped me. No one else has ridden him since...no one has been permitted. Russ was rarely allowed to, if it comes to that. Deuce belongs to Kyle.'

'Is he dangerous?' Raine got out, justifiably fearing for Kyle's safety. But he seemed to be in total command of the powerful beast, the two leaping a rail fence at that precise instant as if in demonstration, the technique smoothly controlled and disciplined.

'Under normal circumstances, no,' David grimaced. 'But, like any stallion, he's spirited and high-strung. Russ knew that. He wasn't himself the night the accident happened, or else he would never have driven the animal so hard.'

'You'd argued?' Raine prompted gently, acting on an impression that Kyle had given her once in saying that his father held himself to blame.

'Very perceptive.' David's mouth twisted, again reminding her of Kyle. He took a long swallow of his drink, staring into the contents of the glass afterwards, as if contemplating where to begin. 'I've told you that Kyle was his mother's son,' he said finally. 'Well, Russ was *my* son. Even as a small child, he had this incredible knack for figuring things out: puzzles, riddles, numbers. Anything that challenged his mind. I should have realised early on that he was the candidate to carry on my business; he started asking me about my day, my work, when he was still in footed pyjamas. But I had my sights set on Kyle for the job. I suppose Russ was in eighth or ninth grade before all those excellent maths scores, those commendations on his report cards began to sink in. Kyle had almost entered his internship by then, so I certainly had no hope left there. I latched on to Russ with a vengeance. He was fourteen years old when I started him weekends and summers at the office. He was a natural, even then.' He smiled in bitter-sweet memory. 'So I ignored Kyle's warnings that I was stealing Russ's youth away. Sure, he didn't date much or play sports in school, but with those grades I argued that we had to be doing something right. He was accepted at Harvard,' he told her proudly. 'I was on top of the world for the first two years.'

'Then?' Raine asked, visualising the young prodigy that Russ must have been.

'Then he drove home one spring evening to tell me that he'd met a girl. He was getting married as soon as possible and wanted my blessing.'

'Was that so terrible?'

'Now…no. Then, yes. I saw it as the end of his future, the end of that supreme dedication I'd been so accustomed to having from Russ, the loss of another son. I blew my temper when mere reasoning failed to change his mind, told him he was cut off from further support...tuition, the company, all of it...unless he gave up what I thought to be an idiotic idea.'

'He refused.'

'Yes. He said he loved her. I said that she must have been a hell of a...' He grimaced painfully. 'Well, you can imagine. Russ was outraged. Strangely enough, only when he stood in front of me yelling in defence of this girl did I realise how much she really meant to him. I was too angry to back down. I let him storm out. I watched him mount Deuce from these very windows...and that was the last time I saw him alive. The stallion came back alone within the hour. We found the top rail broken from a fence that was higher than anything he'd taken before, and beside the fence we found Russ. His head hit a boulder when he was thrown. Even Kyle couldn't save him.'

They sat for a while in silence, Raine knowing that whatever words of sympathy she offered would not be enough. The tragedy touched something deep inside her, leaving her saddened. Saddened for the father and brother who had been left behind, but also for the girl Russ had loved. Raine's eyes misted, but she controlled the moisture by re-focusing on some point far beyond the windows. 'What became of the girl?'

'There's no way of knowing.' David's tone was harder. 'She didn't attend the funeral...never even contacted us. My son's death was publicised both on and off campus. She must have known.'

'You never tried to trace her?'

His mouth twisted. 'I didn't even have her identity. Oh, I'm sure that Russ mentioned her Christian name that night, but I'd let so much time elapse before I considered the notion of locating her that the name eluded me. I had nothing to go on. And what was the point, anyway? She showed me just how much she cared about my son by her silence.'

He didn't know that for sure, but Raine stopped herself from saying so. There was no point, as he'd already stated.

'So now you know all the family secrets.' The joke was mildly sarcastic, aimed more towards himself than her. 'Still want to be a Benedict? I'll say this for you, you're easy to talk to. I rarely discuss what happened to Russ with anyone other than Kyle...I rarely see any need.' He paused to toss back part of his drink. 'Care to venture an objective opinion?'

'It may not be what you want to hear,' Raine obliged slowly, 'but I think you're taking too much blame on yourself. When it comes down to fact, Russ was the one who took Deuce out ill-advised. Russ drove the animal to jump a fence that was too high. If anything, his anger caused the accident.'

'Anger that I, in turn, provoked.'

'But he was ultimately responsible for his own reckless behaviour. You can waste your life brooding that you drove him to it, or that you didn't stop him, but what will that prove? Will your misery bring him back?'

She saw him bristle, and thought that she had gone too far. David reached for his glass again, swallowing deeply, then turned back, considering her drily. 'That makes two versions of the same opinion...yours and Kyle's. I've turned an impatient ear to my son these three years, but hearing it fresh from you adds weight.' Introspection gradually gave way to a reluctant wry amusement that spread a slow grin on his face. Seeing Raine's puzzlement, he immediately let her in on the point. 'There's another trait of Katherine's that Kyle inherited...an uncanny skill for guiding people and situations to a desired end. It just occurred to me that we've been set up, you and I,' he elaborated further. 'But for once I don't mind that Kyle's accomplished what he intended. Welcome to the family, Raine.' Restored to good humour, he lifted her hand to brush the back of it with his lips. 'Kyle's instincts are excellent. I'm going to enjoy having you for a daughter.'

The glow of acceptance that Raine felt began to dim once Kyle came in from his ride. Going upstairs to change from faded jeans and his worn leather jacket, he was an inordinately long time in joining them afterwards, some odd tension gripping him in the meantime that was almost as tangible as it was inexplicable. Barely going through the motions of drinking the coffee that Raine had poured, he refused his father's invitation to dinner for both of them, and contributed only cursorily to their conversation otherwise, leaving Raine to fend off David's questioning glances, when she had no inkling as to what had gone wrong. Half an hour later, she was seated beside Kyle in the Porsche, goodbyes said.

It was all surprisingly abrupt. Doubting her right to question him, while battling the urge to do so, Raine watched several country miles eaten up beneath the powerful vehicle before her curiosity got the better of her. 'What happened back there?' she asked low-toned, nervously arranging her soft challis skirt over her knees.

Kyle threw her a dark, preoccupied glance. 'What do you mean?'

'I would have thought it was obvious. What happened to put you into this mood?'

The blue gaze locked in, irony and impatience apparent. 'Isn't it a little presumptuous of you to be questioning my moods?'

'Sorry.' She was hurt, and her voice conveyed the fact before she could do otherwise. Mouth set, she turned to look out of the passenger window, while furiously reading herself a reprimand. Kyle might be the man she was going to marry on Friday, but he was still entitled to private thoughts and feelings, any probing on her part—however well-intentioned—unwarranted.

'No, *I'm* sorry,' Kyle amended. Raine turned, studying his impassive face, and he sighed heavily, muscles tensed in neck and jaw. 'I opened up my mother's room. It always seems to do this to me...too many memories, I suppose. One day I'll take you there and you'll see for yourself. For one thing, my mother was a great believer in family photographs. There are framed pictures on every surface in her bedroom. School pictures, formal portraits, plain old snapshots...even the charcoal drawings she had done of Russ and me once at some fund-raiser or another. I was about fifteen, hating it...and Russ was more like two...' His faint, reminiscent smile faded. 'When I saw that drawing, I could almost believe...'

'What?' she asked, not understanding the nuances of emotion she intuitively picked up. Mere sentiment could not account for his mood. There was an underlying note that seemed out of place, as if something weighed very heavily on his mind.

'Nothing.' He'd shut her out so completely that it could only be by conscious decision. The eyes that he turned on her were brilliantly blue, coolly shuttered to hold nothing now of uncertainty. 'Still feeling doubts about the marriage, Raine?'

'No.' She accepted the change of subject slowly, a familiar barb of panic pricking her consciousness. 'We're doing this mostly for Stephen,' she went on, as much to convince her errant heart as to appear unshaken to Kyle. 'Since neither of us could easily get custody of him on our own, the intelligent thing is to make the best of our situation.' There was no mistaking the way Kyle's face had hardened when Raine looked up from beneath her lashes. She expected one of his rasping remarks suddenly, her eyes going warily dark.

Kyle didn't disprove her instincts, the vivid gaze he angled her a-glitter with some unreadable emotion. 'Justify it any way you want, sweetheart. The end result will be the same to me.'

The wedding passed by in a beautiful, bitter-sweet blur, and Raine stood beside Kyle in her romantic Chantilly lace dress afterwards, somehow feeling a fraud as she accepted best wishes from male guests, misty hugs from the women. Meg, looking lovely and chic in her blue suit, embraced Raine and Kyle in turn, her face a study in warm pleasure, 'I'm so thankful that Stephen has the two of you...this is like a fairy-tale come true!' A dimpling Andrea voiced similar sentiments, but Felicity, who knew the true situation, was more circumspect, carefully studying Raine's beautiful, still face before delivering a silent hug.

Raine ventured a troubled sidelong glance at her husband, to have it met by a darkly attractive look that could have meant anything and did very little to still her fears. The barrage of congratulations had nearly ended and Jenny came running up to steal Kyle's attention, complaining that the ribbon holding the small wicker basket to her casted arm had a knot in it, and could he get it off please, because there weren't any rose petals left. Grinning indulgently, Kyle went down on one knee beside the little flower girl, deftly dealing with the ribbon while Jenny turned adoring brown eyes his way. Raine looked at his blond head, bent close to the silky dark one with its wreath of baby's breath, and felt a melting tenderness stir. Jenny had been enchanting, a miniature replica of Felicity in rose-pink satin, all big solemn eyes and speechless wonder.

In fact, the entire ceremony had been enchanting, considering the short time allotted for arrangements. The reception followed suit in a small room adjoining the hospital chapel, the wedding cake only two-tier, but elegant and—according to several of the guests—delicious. Raine's own piece threatened to choke her; aside from the bite that she traditionally exchanged with Kyle, she actually got no more of it down. She felt terribly relieved when David Benedict, nearly as handsome as Kyle in his dark suit, eventually came to her rescue.

'I have never seen a lovelier bride,' he declared sombrely, placing a warm kiss on Raine's cheek, before gripping his son's shoulder. 'It was an honour standing up with you, Kyle. And it would be an even greater honour,' his blue eyes twinkled, 'if you'd take me upstairs to meet my new grandson.'

'I'd like to change first,' Raine demurred. Felicity went along to help her, and in a few minutes they'd returned, Raine feeling less unsettled in a china-blue silk dress, her ivory satin slippers replaced by matching pumps. It was expected of her to throw the bouquet, and Andrea caught the cascade of pink rosebuds and white baby's breath easily, lifting the fragrant mass to her flushed face, green eyes sparkling secretively, in a way no doubt connected with her attractive escort.

Goodbyes exchanged with the others, Raine walked between the two men to the elevators, allowing them to carry the conversation during their brief ascent. Stephen was delighted to see them, but grew a little subdued at the unfamiliar elegance of Kyle's suit and Raine's silk dress. His engaging grin slipped even more when he caught sight of David, a stranger. His thumb strayed betrayingly to his mouth.

'Stephen,' Kyle walked over to the bed, taking a small hand in his large one, 'I'd like you to meet my father. He's your grandfather now, so you can call him Grandad, if you want.'

David's reaction to the child both surprised and pleased Raine, his blue eyes growing fractionally more brilliant... if not actually misting then coming perilously close. His voice had roughened slightly, confirming the notion. 'How do you do, young man?' He solemnly held out a hand. Stephen removed the thumb, still uncertain, although his interest had plainly been captured. Finally he gave in and stretched his arm up for the handshake. 'Nice cast you've got there,' David added.

Stephen proudly patted the white plaster, already partially obscured by doodling from the Magic Markers Kyle had given him. The cast was called a Spica, extending from under his arms all the way to the ankle of the fractured leg, and to mid-thigh of the other, and judging by the variety of scrawls she saw, Raine deduced that the entire fourth-floor staff, if not its occupants, had each been invited to autograph it. Now Stephen awkwardly grasped a bright red marker from the bedside stand and held it up to David. 'You draw!'

'Where?' David moved closer, bending his silver head over the spot where a tiny pointing finger had landed. The pen made a scratchy sound. 'There... it says David Benedict.'

'No!' Stephen pouted instantly. 'Grandad!'

David was startled . . . and gratified, dipping his head again to add the requested title in quotation marks beneath his name. That betraying gruffness was back. 'Whatever you say, son.'

Raine couldn't resist looking at Kyle, only to find him studying his father with dark absorption, and why not, since he naturally wanted the man and boy to develop an affection for one another? The two were apparently well on the way, Stephen effortlessly charming David with his whimsical grin, so that she had to wonder whether the toddler was in danger of being hopelessly spoilt. 'I had two little boys like you once,' David was saying.

'Where'd they go?' demanded a round-eyed Stephen.

'They grew up.' The older man almost involuntarily twisted around to share a complicated and emotional glance with Kyle. Raine couldn't stop the moisture from gathering in her eyes and Kyle pressed a lean hand to his father's shoulder. 'In a lot of ways, you remind me of them.' David turned back to Stephen, his voice firming determinedly. 'It will be nice having a little boy to play with. We'll go to the zoo one day, how about that, Stephen? Or the Philadelphia seaport to tour a submarine?' He went on at the child's vigorous nod, naming all sorts of fun adventures the two of them might have, finally waving Kyle and Raine out of the room without him some time later, with the protest that he had a grandson to get to know.

They had driven up in front of Kyle's house, and he swung the Porsche into the driveway, pushing the button to his garage door opener and pulling inside before he cut the engine. He turned to face Raine, studying her pale features in the light that had automatically come on over the car. Finally he put out a hand, tucking a stray tendril behind her ear, yet the tenderness in the gesture didn't soften the severity of his expression. 'Home,' he said tautly, reaching for the door latch.

Raine was half-way out of her seat, struggling to extract the case containing her wedding things from the back, when he came around. 'Leave that. I'll get it tomorrow,' he told her, waiting until she complied before closing the car door and lifting her into his arms. 'Tradition,' he said simply, stilling her questioning upward glance. Heart pounding, Raine forced herself to relax, to let him carry her over the threshold of his—no, *their* home. He put her down just inside, his hand warm against her waist for balance. 'I think I'd like a drink. You?'

Raine refused, but followed him into the den. The assembly of covered warming dishes, cutlery and china immediately caught her eye. A single note sheet was propped against the silver ice-bucket where a bottle of champagne was chilling. Striding across, Kyle unfolded the page, a faint smile touching his otherwise sombre mouth. 'It's from my father,' he explained. 'Best wishes to both of us...He had the meal catered. I believe this is the first time he's ever used the key that I gave him. I thought it might come in handy some time when he was in town, but he always prefers to drive back to the farm.'

Raine clung to the note of normality, distractedly shrugging out of her coat and hanging it away in the nearest cupboard. 'Whatever it is, it smells lovely,' she declared, coming back to the coffee-table to lift a lid. 'Duck in orange sauce,' she pronounced lightly. 'Acorn squash, baby snow peas...'

'And white chocolate mousse in the refrigerator,' Kyle tacked on drily, 'according to the note. Champagne, Mrs Benedict?'

A small thrill travelled the length of her spine, arresting her motions, and darkening her grey eyes. 'Yes, thank you.'

Kyle popped the cork and poured, handing her a glass with an air of dry challenge about him. 'To us,' he toasted briefly, 'and to our soon-to-be son.'

Stephen. Suddenly everything that they were trying to achieve came home to her. Creating a stable, happy life for the little boy. Being parents to him. How could any of it work as long as she and Kyle were behaving like wary adversaries? Stephen was far too perceptive of adult undercurrents. He'd sense that something was wrong immediately. He probably already had. And the blame would mostly fall to her, if she were honest with herself. Because she was too inhibited...even too frightened...to step whole-heartedly into the relationship. It was a sobering thought, and some of it must have shown in her expression. Misinterpreting, Kyle tossed back an impatient drink, looking for all the world as if he were at the end of his endurance.

'Kyle,' she said thickly, needing to do something, anything, to salvage the moment. It was hard getting past that point, her eyes riveted to the inquisitive brow he raised. Hand shaking, she set her glass on the low table. A couple of tentative steps brought her close enough to lay her hand on his sleeve, to feel the warmth of muscled flesh beneath her palm. His male scent drifted sensually to her nostrils, causing the pulse in her throat to drum relentlessly.

'Yes?' He wasn't helping her, but the swift blazing glint in his eyes gave her courage.

'I want this marriage to work.'

'For Stephen's sake?'

'Of course, for Stephen's sake,' she agreed huskily. 'But also for my sake, and yours.' Her eyes turned beseeching, locked with quiet fascination into his blue, blue gaze, a sudden wonder striking her that this overwhelmingly attractive man was her husband.

He moved then, linking his hands in the small of her back, a new severity in his face, unlike the taut displeasure that had gone before. 'I asked you to be my wife, Raine. I'd like to think that means something to you, if it's reassurances you need.'

'I probably will need them sometimes,' she admitted, eyes momentarily troubled. 'I've spent most of my life avoiding serious relationships of any kind. It seemed the wisest thing to do. The safest thing, I suppose.'

'Yet you were involved with Stephen from day one.'

'That was different. Stephen was innocent, helpless. And abandoned.' She half shrugged, her expression suddenly shadowed. 'I'd been there myself, remember?'

'I remember.' Kyle drew her close to his chest, hands moving slowly up and down her back. His breath stirred her hair. 'Tell me about your father.'

'Kyle, no,' she moaned into his shoulder, loath to give up the comforting spell that he was casting over her, loath to delve into painful memories again. Sighing, she closed her eyes, but it was too late now to avoid the issue. 'If I gave you the impression that he was an insensitive man,' she began slowly, 'then I was wrong. He was a kind man, incredibly gentle. I can understand now what my mother's death must have done to him, how hard it must have been to try raising a small child on his own. He drank, and he must have had trouble holding a job, because I remember that he was at home most days. When he did manage to get work, there was only a neighbour to check in on me. I was hungry sometimes,' she shrugged, feeling Kyle's arms tighten around her, 'not often, but sometimes. I imagine my getting sick was a blessing in disguise for him, a way to make sure I was fed and cared for, while taking the burden from his shoulders. He never came back. It took me, maybe, three years to stop waiting.'

'Then?' Kyle asked huskily, still cradling her body.

'Then I had to accept my lot. And I got angry. Because I began to understand that he could have fought harder to overcome his problems...that I should have been reason enough to make him fight. But I wasn't. It was as if I didn't matter to him at all.'

'Maybe you mattered most of all,' he suggested gently. 'Suppose he believed that just about any life was better than the one he'd given you up to that point? It may have been an act of sacrifice, rather than abandonment.'

She thought about that, but the concept differed so greatly from what she'd always believed that she couldn't accept it. 'Raine,' Kyle's hand presently cupped her nape, tipping her head back so he could see her face, 'do you have any idea how I felt when you walked into the surgical suite with that story...and there was nothing I could do? I was furious afterwards, when you refused to answer my calls.'

'You had every right to be furious,' Raine said ruefully.

'Now I only want to take care of you. Protect you.'

Her eyes instantly filled with tears. 'No one ever said that to me before.'

'You little fool!' Kyle laughed huskily, pressing a hard kiss to her mouth. 'What else have I been telling you all these weeks?'

'That you want me?'

Her soft, shaken tone arrested him, drawing the laughter from his eyes and replacing it with pure intensity. Desire, hot and pulsing, threaded itself through his deep voice. 'There's that, too.'

His kiss was scorching, making her skin burn against the fine material of his formal clothes, turning her bones almost instantly to water. Raine responded in kind, feverishly obsessed by a need to know and to be known that had her clinging to Kyle's hard frame, moulding her soft woman's body to every taut angle. This was flashfire, a searing, melting sensation that went beyond mere passion. A commitment of lives and souls...and one heart...Raine's.

Just as she felt unable to stand any longer, Kyle swept her up into his arms, a fierce sort of mastery in his beautiful, hard face. He carried her upstairs, and stood her beside the big bed, while he slipped open the tiny covered buttons that ran down the front of her dress. She thought inconsequentially that the blue silk exactly matched the colour of Kyle's eyes, blazing so passionately as, inch by inch, her skin was revealed to him. He dipped his mouth into the shadow between her breasts and cut short any half-formed musings, leaving no room in her mind then beyond the sensation he created.

He freed the buttons at her wrists, glided the soft fabric over her shoulders, and the blue cloth created a pool about her feet. She couldn't think what had happened to her shoes. It didn't matter, because Kyle was kissing her, lifting her silky camisole over head, groaning as she shook her hair free and he watched her firm breasts settle voluptuously into his hands. He tasted the pale, gilded flesh and then it was Raine who groaned, thinking that no sensation would ever be that exquisite again.

But Kyle proved her wrong, endlessly. She was sheened with a fine perspiration and quivering before he'd even undressed, lying unashamedly naked on top of the spread. His mouth, his hands had melted away her inhibitions, and she watched, grey eyes smoky, as his dark suit went the way of her dress. He was unbearably attractive, muscles flexing smoothly in back and shoulders, his hips and thighs lean, and equally taut. With lithe male grace, he stretched full-length beside her, turning her slender body sideways into his. She went eagerly, shuddering at the first searing contact of skin on skin, then growing feverish as supple fingertips began a slow-motion dance across her flesh. It became unbearable, too much, and she told him so, but he only laughed softly into her hair, then covered her mouth with his own while the room shivered and shimmered about her.

He dropped a slow line of gentle kisses along her damp forehead, waiting for her breathing to steady, waiting until her heavy lashes drifted up. Only then did he turn her beneath him. Raised on one forearm, he stared into her eyes for an age, his look enough to start her trembling all over again.

'I need you, Raine,' his gravelly voice nearly made time stand still, 'more than I've ever needed anyone.'

Raine drew in her breath, a slow, fierce glow unfurling in her breast. 'Then you'd better have me,' she whispered.

# CHAPTER NINE

A PALE semicircle of light shone from Stephen's lamp, illuminating the little boy in his favourite sleeping position: knees tucked to tummy and bottom in the air. And in the bedside rocking-chair watching him was Kyle. Raine had lost track of him when the phone rang earlier; sensing that the call had been private, she'd excused herself to go and fill the bath. Now she stood unnoticed in the doorway, idly sifting fingers through curls that had gone a little wild from the steam of her bath, content to play voyeur.

But Kyle caught her at it, emerging from his own thoughts with a familiarly sensual grin. His vivid gaze touched the bronze halo of her hair, slid along the pale pink fabric that clung to skin still faintly damp. Raine followed the look down and, with a wry little grimace for the revealing nightdress, belted its matching robe about her waist. 'Nine weeks of marriage,' Kyle's mouth tilted gently, 'and my wife's still shy.'

'Not when it really counts.' She flung him an unabashedly smouldering look, but spoiled the effect at the last minute by laughing. Kyle's blue eyes crinkled in answer, doing strange things to her pulse until, as always when she was in danger of conveying too much, she changed tack. 'Will you look at this child!' Sighing indulgently, she crossed to the narrow bed. Stephen rarely got through a night under the covers, and this night he was already in disarray, his pyjama top unsnapped from its counterpart and rolled up about his chest, undershirt with it.

'I'd rather look at his mother,' came Kyle's soft drawl. He proceeded to do just that while Raine gently fished down jammies and T-shirt and re-fastened snaps. Settling the little boy on to his side, she dealt with bunched

166

Snoopy sheets, then rescued a pillow that had somehow ended up on the floor. Stephen slept angelically throughout. As a final touch, Boo went into the crook of his arm and a featherlight kiss into the nearest dimple. The surge of love came from deep inside. Savouring the scent and feel of baby skin, she wondered whether she could possibly love a natural child more . . . or even quite so much. Undeniably, the idea of Kyle's baby appealed to her.

She was unaware of the almost fiercely maternal look that had played over her delicate features, of the quiet wistfulness that touched her now. Stephen was compensation enough. She was continually delighted by her charismatic small son. The cast had been off a mere month and he'd impressed them all by re-mastering his walking skills. There was still a noticeable sideways limp to his left leg, owing to muscles that had grown stiff from immobility and trauma, but every therapy session made him stronger. His confidence was following a direct parallel. They had bid a fond and tearful farewell to his private nurse Frieda, and he now attended playschool at Spirits Mall. He was learning to fingerpaint. And befriending the other children. Strictly Big Boy stuff.

Raine turned back and flung out an unconsciously intense smile, pondering Kyle's quiet mood. He hadn't changed out of the clothes he'd worn to work, sleeves rolled up his forearms, his shirt unbuttoned over a muscled chest matted with golden hair. His eyes were startlingly blue, and as alert as ever, yet he seemed bone-tired, filling Raine with a sweetly protective ache, not unlike the feeling she had for Stephen, tucked up defenceless in his bed. 'Have you been here all this time . . . watching him sleep?'

'Guilty.' His smile was faint and crooked. 'Want to join me?' Raine took the hand he held out, loving the warm, hard feel of his fingers tangling with her own. Kyle drew her on to his knee and she curled up gracefully, her curves to his hollows, a perfect fit. She nestled her bright head closer, irresistibly tasting the warm skin that was taut over his collar-bone, and his arms tightened. 'Can't you behave?' The husky taunt ruffled her hair.

'Do you really want me to?' she breathed softly, exulting in the heartbeat that thudded faster beneath her ear.

'Only for a while.'

Raine subsided obediently and let him cradle her, her thoughts going off into private avenues as they sat listening to Stephen's rhythmic puffs of breath. There were times, like now, when Kyle made her feel cherished and wanted and inexplicably soft about the edges, as if the old Raine, so painfully brittle and wary, had all but ceased to be. But, of course, she hadn't. If it was the new softness in her that teased and shared and made love with perfect abandon, then caution lay just beneath the surface, conducting the usual self-torture. Does he care? Does he not? Will he ever? Not knowing, she shied from verbal admissions. Otherwise, she poured her whole self—mind, body, and spirit—into loving him, as if by sheer absorption she might possess his heart.

Responding to some tension in him now, she slid her arms around his torso and hugged. He held her tight in the embrace, and, dropping a light kiss atop her head, cast down an abstracted smile. 'What was that for?'

'To be used as needed.' She stared into eyes that were dark blue with an unreadable emotion. 'I was hoping *you'd* tell *me*, actually. What's bothering you, Kyle? You've been very quiet since that phone call.' A thought occurred to her and she drew a palm along his lean cheek. 'You didn't lose a patient?'

'I lost,' his mouth twisted and she felt the muscles move rigidly under her hand, 'but, no, it wasn't a patient. There are some problems with a project of mine, that's all. Nothing for you to worry about.'

The reply was dismissive, but stubbornly she longed to probe, to comfort. 'Maybe I can help.'

'I don't think so, baby.' The endearment softened his refusal. He turned her hand and kissed the palm, evoking a kind of sweet pain. Reading the shadow of rejection in her darkened eyes, he groaned under his breath and cupped her face. 'Try to understand.' He delved gently into the kiss, the slow thrust of his tongue creating instantaneous heat.

Raine was quivering when he released her, dipping her head into the hollow of his shoulder, lips brushing the warm flesh. She understood perfectly: Kyle's feelings in no way ran as deep as her own. She was not everything to him, and probably never would be. But there was one level where she satisfied him explicitly, and they had crossed into its sphere via that one exquisite kiss. Even as Raine deplored her limitations, her body was responding to the fire in Kyle's look.

'I think you *can* help,' he murmured, the soft mockery for himself alone. Deliberately, he slipped the knot that secured her robe and laid its folds aside. Sliding one narrow strap off her shoulder, he exposed a perfect taut breast to his touch.

'Stephen...' Raine breathed an unwilling warning, not wanting him to stop.

'Is sleeping.' He cupped her breast in his palm and lowered his mouth to taste it, reducing her to a state of raw need in a pitifully small amount of time. His free hand wandered, warm and firm, along the inside of her thigh. Then he was lifting her, like a quiet conqueror, carrying her languid body to their bed. Raine stared up as he settled her, unconsciously searching the vivid eyes for something more. But Kyle was already moving, dispensing with her nightclothes in passionate haste. Then he was running his hands over her slender body, an intense and oddly reverent aura about him, so that wonder struck her at what she could make him feel. But only physically, something inside her lamented. And his possession, when it came, was bitter-sweet.

She awoke to a depression that lasted throughout the day. Even Stephen's rambling account of what he'd done at playschool, delivered en route to therapy, failed to revive her. Andrea Cummins, waving from the first-floor elevators as they passed, was a welcome distraction. 'Hi, you two!' She immediately left the lift to join them. 'Going to therapy?' She laughingly scooped Stephen's bundled little figure into her arms and danced him around, kissing cheeks that were apple-red from the first March wind. 'I've missed you, Stevie Boy!' Stephen chuckled and puckered his lips, smacking a hasty reciprocation on to her chin.

'Wanna walk, Andy!' An impatient struggle punctuated the demand.

'Well, I don't blame you,' the nurse complied in good humour. 'Show me what you can do, then. You know the way.'

Stephen strutted ahead, showing off, and Raine exchanged an indulgent smile with the blonde. 'He's terribly proud of himself.'

'Unless I miss my guess, so is his mama.' The green eyes crinkled. 'Family life must agree with you. You look terrific. So does Kyle, for that matter.'

Raine's pulse did a painful little skip-stop and she smiled faintly to offset the moment. 'I was just thinking how terrific *you* look, actually.' And it was true. There was an indefinable edge to Andrea, a new sparkle.

'No more so than I feel,' she said simply. 'Come have a Coke with me while Stephen is in therapy. I'll tell you about it.'

Andrea's news turned out to be the diamond on her left hand. 'Mark Walters . . . my escort at your wedding. He's a lab technician here at the hospital, and the most hopeless romantic. Can you imagine proposing on Valentine's Day?' But the glow in her eyes was anything but cynicism. She stretched her hand across the table to give Raine a closer look, dimples in evidence. 'I owe it all to you, Mrs Benedict, for tossing me your bouquet.'

Raine listened to Andrea's plans for a June wedding with outward enthusiasm, yet a familiar dispiritedness gathered inside. What would it be like entering into a marriage for no other reason than love? Mutual love, with no doubts, nothing unsaid? She wanted that with Kyle. Desperately, she wanted it. But she could hardly go about attaining it single-handedly. Without Kyle's love, any declaration from her could only be categorised as an emotional trap. And she wouldn't do that to him. Her pride wouldn't let her.

Andrea chattered on, oblivious to the doubts that she had fed, and Raine forced the mask of attentiveness to remain on her face. But the afternoon had gone flatter than ever. She parted company with the nurse outside the therapy facilities, aware of an unprecedented reluctance to keep the promise of a visit to Kyle's suite. Stephen, however, was enamoured of the ritual and wouldn't be diverted from his plan to 'see Daddy' no matter how hard she tried.

Kyle's secretary, Emily, smiled and waved them on to the private office, where he joined them a few minutes later. 'Feed fish, Daddy,' Stephen demanded instantly, his eyes bright and round as he stood in front of the lighted aquarium.

'OK, but you can't pollute them,' Kyle warned drily, hoisting the little boy to waist-level and handing him the food canister. Wisely, he kept his hand covering the small fist, restraining Stephen's impulse to shake too vigorously. Mouths began gulping immediately, drawing a delighted chuckle from the child. He didn't protest when Kyle stood him down again, content to watch the feeding frenzy from below.

Raine had moved to the window meanwhile, adjusting the narrow blinds so that she had a view across the side lawn where the tips of green daffodil shoots had bravely emerged to ring a massive oak tree. She sensed rather than heard Kyle come up behind her. He made no move to touch her and she wondered despairingly how to proceed.

'Do you want to tell me about it?' He took the decision away from her, his handsome face sombre as he purposely entered her side-vision. 'What's wrong?'

Here was her chance to tell him. To say 'I love you, Kyle', and end the tension of keeping it concealed. But at what price? 'What makes you think there's anything wrong?' she stalled huskily.

'Body language?' Kyle suggested, taking in the stormy dark grey of her eyes, and the rigidity of stance that even the fluid line of her dress couldn't disguise. Her hair was held back on either side with tortoiseshell combs, the irrepressible few tendrils escaping to further soften her fine-boned face. She looked vulnerable somehow. Uncertain. 'Instinct?' he murmured, mouth twisting faintly. 'Whatever it is that married people share.'

*I asked you to be my wife, Raine.* The words came to her so vividly that they might have been spoken moments earlier instead of weeks. The word trust was there, too. Reminding her of all he meant to her. And, stubbornly, she refused to risk what they had together by asking for more. 'I've had a difficult day,' she made her choice, 'that's all.'

'Is there anything I can do?'

Raine hesitated, then gave in to longing. 'Put your arms around me?'

She saw his handsome mouth quirk at the smaller version of her voice. Then he was pulling her close, moulding her body against his hard side and cradling her silky head to his shoulder. She wilfully surrendered dark thoughts to the warmth and security that his arms provided, wondering in that instant whether it might not be enough.


'Raine?' Kyle's husky voice drew her back from the exotic darkness where she'd been drifting. Stirring, she felt the skin of his shoulder against her mouth, its warmth and texture tingling across over-sensitised lips.

'I'm awake,' she murmured faintly, surprised that she could think or speak coherently. Memory came back in sketches: another phone call . . . Kyle's brooding and unconfiding absorption. Her whole body suffused with heat when she remembered the way she'd kissed him once he finally came to bed. There could have been no doubt in his mind as to the invitation in that kiss. And when his mouth and body had hardened to passion, there could be no doubt either in her response. She'd clung to him more fiercely, returned touch for touch more feverishly than ever before, a reckless need in her to believe that she was necessary to him. For a while she'd succeeded, caught fast at the centre of Kyle's brilliant concentration. He'd tapped off every ounce of energy that she could ever hope to possess, and she lay exhausted in his arms for long moments afterwards, believing that he belonged to her, that something almost spiritual had passed between them. Now he'd made her surface, and the edges of her contentment involuntarily began to fray.

Kyle curved his arm about her waist, pulling her closer, as if sensing her withdrawal and purposely forestalling it. She was lying half-way on top of him now, her body as naked as his, and for the first time in ages, she felt shy of him, grateful for the darkness pierced only by narrow slivers of moonlight escaping the closed blinds. His fingers gently played through her hair, and after a moment she relaxed again and laid her head against his chest.

'How do you do that?' he asked presently, a palm warm over her shoulderblade, slowly massaging. She heard the attractive rasp in his voice, the soft incredulity. 'Just when I think we can't possibly get any better together, you prove me wrong.'

Just words, Raine told herself lightly. But she didn't really believe that. Not with the thud of his heart uneven beneath her ear, his arms firm around her. Still smiling to herself, she missed his subtle shift in mood, so that the next comment took her unawares. 'I have to go out of town for a couple of days, Raine. I'll be leaving tomorrow afternoon from the hospital and staying at least until Sunday morning.' There was a pause. 'Don't worry about making arrangements for Stephen. I'll give Dad a call in the morning. I'm sure he will take over for me Saturday. As a matter of fact, he's been hinting for a chance to take Stephen out.'

Although David had been to their home on several occasions and they to his, he had never supervised Stephen on his own. But Raine certainly saw no reason to protest. 'If David is willing to have Stephen,' she said tentatively, thinking aloud, 'then suppose I went along on your trip? Just the two of us? Jill could cover my hours at the shop.'

'A kind of belated honeymoon?' he mused, the smile there. 'I like the sound of that...and soon.' His hesitation made the refusal low-key. 'But this is business.'

'I understand.' Raine prayed that her voice didn't convey how instantly lost she felt. Aside from the occasional night when he'd been called out to the hospital, they had never really been apart.

'If the trip goes the way I hope, I'll explain everything,' he promised gently, making her realise that he had absorbed more of what she was feeling than she might have liked. Yet he gave her no time to question the enigmatic statement. She felt his fingertips trickle a slow suggestion down her spine, his palm following with heated pressure. Then he was moving over her, as if some store of restless vitality had been released. He sought her mouth in the darkness, the warm rasp of his tongue evoking slow-motion shudders from somewhere deep inside. When he raised his head there was humour in his low voice, but mostly the rough catch of passion. 'There's no reason why we can't make up for lost time...in advance.'

Friday passed slowly. It was Raine's regular day off but, in spite of a dozen household chores that needed doing, she couldn't seem to accomplish any of them once she'd helped Kyle pack that morning. Finally, she gave up on the laundry and the swatch books she'd borrowed for the living-room upholstery, and bundled Stephen up for a day at the park instead. The cocker spaniel puppy, who was becoming used to the new name that Kyle had coaxed from Stephen and answered to just plain Cocker now, went along on his leash to make a threesome, and in spite of herself Raine had a good time.

Saturday was not so easy. She got through the morning by concentrating on her paperwork, then left Amy to man the cash register as she set up a complicated new swimsuit arrangement. She was still working on the display when Felicity began her shift. The dark-haired girl came over almost immediately, black eyes too shrewd by far. She picked up a *maillot* that Raine had just clipped to a hanger and held the bold turquoise wisp at arm's length, scrutinising the newer geometric line.

'I'd look like a maths equation in this,' she quipped drily, 'all angles.' Reaching for a violet suit with softer lines, she levelled a sympathetic look. 'You seem down today. Is something wrong?'

'Kyle's away for the weekend,' Raine imparted.

'I see,' Felicity said so understandingly that Raine felt worse. 'That means Stephen is at daycare,' she brightened with the next breath.

'Sorry, Kyle's father has him for the day.'

'Oh, I wanted to go down there and play with him during my break.' She flashed a rueful grin at Raine. 'I just adore the way he's starting calling me "Aunt Lissie". Are you sure you didn't coach him?'

Raine couldn't stop a faint smile. 'He thought of it on his own, honestly.'

'You should have introduced me to Stephen sooner, actually, and saved yourself a lot of grief.' Felicity grew wistful. 'I understand now why you went to such lengths to keep him. He's absolutely precious. He makes me want one of my own...' Both partners stilled for an instant, then Felicity gave a short, sudden laugh. 'After that inopportune lead-in, I almost hesitate to tell you, but...I had dinner with Gavin last night.'

In spite of the laughter, Raine sensed that the other girl was closely watching her reaction. 'How is he?' she asked evenly.

'Carrying a torch.' That was imparted with a rueful shrug. 'I hope you don't mind, but I'm trying hard to put it out.'

'Then Brian is completely passé?'

'Completely.'

'I'm glad,' Raine said truthfully, pairing Felicity with Gavin in her mind, and somehow sanctioning the match. The two had always felt a grudging approval of one another; she'd been aware of that from the beginning. Gavin admired Felicity's sass, and she his respectability, although she might have cringed to hear Raine say so. It would be strictly a case of opposites attracting, granted, but Raine liked the thought of two people she cared about getting together.

She was at home again, mulling over Felicity's revelation and sorting laundry, when the phone rang.

'Hello, Raine.' David's voice caught her off guard when, of course, she'd wanted to speak with Kyle. 'Listen, how about Stephen spending the night here at the farm? We've had a great day together, and don't want to see it end.'

'What about pyjamas?' Raine stared helplessly at the dial. 'A toothbrush?'

'We keep spare toothbrushes around,' he sounded amused, 'and I dare say I can rig up some kind of makeshift sleepwear. You wouldn't be guilty of over-protecting your little chick, would you?'

'Stay Grandad, Mama!' Stephen piped up unexpectedly over the line. 'Please?'

Raine couldn't keep a woebegone note from her voice when David recovered the receiver. 'He isn't in the least opposed to staying away from home. I think I'm just a little bit jealous.' She sighed. 'But I know he's in good hands. You'll bring him home tomorrow, then?'

'Right after brunch.' She could hear his smile. 'You won't be too lonely?'

'Not lonely enough to deprive you and Stephen of your fun.'

But she *was* lonely. Puttering about the house, feeling dejected, she found it hard to believe that she had once welcomed—even needed—solitude. Now she found herself wandering from room to room, surveying the progress that the decorators had made in the diningroom, flicking through the fabric swatch books again, taking an armload of Stephen's clothes from the dryer, and all the while trying to keep dark thoughts at bay.

Carrying a fresh pile of little jeans and shirts upstairs, she could hardly bear the inanimate silence in Stephen's room. Even poor Boo was lacklustre, his wool matted and his limbs dangling, that rip that she had mended twice already starting to gape again. She couldn't understand Stephen's passion for unravelling threads, but she made up her mind to try one more time. Boo's stuffing—of which he already had a deficiency—would be tumbling out at this rate.

So she found needle, thread and scissors, and as an afterthought went to her lingerie chest for some stockings that had ripped. There was no harm in making Boo a little less limber while she was performing surgery. Providing she didn't change him too radically, Stephen wouldn't notice. And he could do with a wash, too, if she was to make the most of her opportunity.

She took the unfortunate toy and her repair materials into the den, made herself a cup of tea, then curled up to begin cutting the damaged stockings into lengths that would be soft and manageable enough to serve as bolstering material for Boo's wobbly neck and arm sockets. That done, she pulled out the remainder of the previous mending thread in order to utilise the ripped seam as an opening.

Taking a handful of the cut silk, she carefully pushed her fist through the back of the animal, reaching into the head with the idea of repairing the neck first. Almost immediately, her fingers brushed something papery. Initially, she thought it was a label attached to an inside seam, but then it moved, and there was weight inside it.

The object dropped into her lap. She didn't want to retrieve it right away, a feeling of the most terrible foreboding clutching at her throat. But there was an equally terrible curiosity. This little paper bundle was something significant; the very way that it had been wrapped and hidden told her that. And it was obviously meant for Stephen, secreted in his most cherished possession.

Boo had somehow landed face-down on the thick carpet at her feet, and Raine picked him up, righting him beside her in the sofa corner, all renovation plans on hold. There was nothing else to draw her attention from the fascinating object . . . now in her palm. With shaking fingertips, she turned back a paper fold, then another. The glint of gold spilled out, a delicately thin chain that webbed across her skin. It was attached to an asymmetrical heart shape inset with one tiny diamond. A locket.

She opened the catch, closing her eyes against a wave of haunting sadness as she glimpsed Melanie Thompson's smiling image. She looked at the other photo and saw the face of a young man: blond, very attractive, his mouth curved in an easy grin. The face was familiar, and yet not familiar. The blue eyes were almost Stephen's. Was this a photograph of the child's father? Given its place opposite Melanie's picture, and hidden inside the favourite toy, she could draw no other conclusion. She looked closer, convinced now, seeing more of Stephen in the adult expression, the bone structure.

She became aware of the paper still in her hand, at some point became aware of writing inside. This time she was longer in gathering courage, but finally she began to smooth the crumpled page. 'My darling son,' she read at the top of the sheet, and tears immediately scalded her eyes. The letter was meant for Stephen, a letter from Melanie Thompson to her son. And it was dated the day of the accident.

Blinking fiercely, she began again to decipher the rounded, sloping hand.

> My darling son,
> You were a smart boy to remember where Mama put the letter. Maybe you are a big boy now, or maybe someone else is reading this for you. If you have the letter at all, then it means that we are apart. And that's what I wanted to write about. To tell you that I never wanted to leave you...that I will always love you, no matter what happens. But you are a special little boy, and one day you'll be a special man, just like your daddy was. You should go to school and learn about the world. You should have things that I can't give you. Because you are a Benedict. No matter what anyone might tell you, Stephen, you are. Your daddy wanted the three of us to be to-

gether, but he died before that could happen, and even though I spent a long time running away, I see now that you have a right to know his family and they have a right to know you. If you have this letter, then it means that they couldn't let me stay with you, but I don't want you to feel sad or angry about that. Just be a good boy, and be very, very happy. Remember what I told you. Your daddy and I will always stay with you in your heart.

Raine could not have said how long she sat there, watching a tear that had splashed on the crinkled paper dry, while an older spot of diluted ink told her that Melanie Thompson had once done the same. The words 'you are a Benedict' shimmered crazily before her, slowing the beat of her heart to a painfully eratic thud. At some point she got up, still clutching the locket and the letter, and climbed the stairs, shocked memory making her seek some bridge for the fantastic gap her thought processes had to leap. Her fingers fumbled over the books on Stephen's shelf until she found the one she wanted... the well-worn copy that had caught Kyle's attention so forcibly at Thanksgiving. She folded back the front cover, staring again at the small gold box on the inside, reading what she now recognised as Melanie's gently sloping script with new significance dawning. *Stephen Russell Thompson*... Russ Benedict's son... Kyle's nephew.

Feeling utterly boneless, Raine stumbled to the master suite, curling her body into a protective ball on the bed. She could scarcely absorb the radical way events had swung out of balance. She and Kyle had started as equals with Stephen, yet the proof in her hand shed an entirely different light on the adoption process they'd initiated together. Kyle was a blood relative, Stephen's uncle. He didn't need her any more to gain custody of the child... *her* child... *her* son. Now, even the possessives no longer applied. God, she no longer had any claims to Stephen at all! And, with the little boy removed as a deciding factor, she had even less claim to Kyle.

Take away Stephen, and her marriage was founded on one premise. Passion. And, while she once might have put a great deal of faith in Kyle's physical attraction to her, she now had to wonder how much of what he felt stemmed from a desire to make the marriage work. How much was sheer relativity? She felt as if she had been leaning very heavily on a support and had had it kicked cruelly away.

She spent an hour just staring at the wall, unconsciously tracing out the pattern of flowers and stripes in the wallpaper she'd chosen. Of burgundy and navy on a neutral background, it co-ordinated nicely with Kyle's walnut furniture. She had hung several well chosen prints about, filled the deep window sills with green plants and, as a result, the master bedroom had lost its solely masculine flavour to a softer state of co-existence. Evidence of Raine's tastes had sprung up all over, in fact. The house that had once seemed so alien now felt very much her home.

Appreciating the possible irony in that, she forced herself to leave the bed, pacing about a while before finally going to run a hot bath. Distractedly, she added bubbles and scent, letting the large tub fill amost to its rim. She turned off the taps with automatic movements, walked back into the bedroom to undress and lay out a robe. Then, piling her hair on top of her head, she slid into the deliciously scented water and soaked. She had nearly succeeded in making her mind a blank when sound penetrated from the stairs. She recognised Kyle's footsteps before the shock took its toll. But still there was the shock of facing him with what she had learned.

'In here,' she called huskily, seeing no reason to prevaricate. He appeared in the doorway, looking flat-out tired, but contrastingly alert. Blue eyes brilliant in his drawn face, he surveyed her slender body against its backdrop of green potted ferns, soap bubbles concealing all but head and shoulders as she reclined in the bath.

'I didn't expect you tonight,' Raine murmured, self-conscious, her throat aching.

Kyle shrugged tiredly, something in her tone striking an odd note. 'I accomplished all I needed,' he said. 'And I wanted to get home.' At some earlier point, that admission might have filled Raine with warmth, but now she could find no response. Kyle stood there for a moment, stripping off his tie with repressed impatience, unbuttoning his shirt. She recognised a super-charged quality about him suddenly, a dark restlessness to match her own. He moved inside without haste, carelessly pitching the tie on to the tiled countertop and lowering his taut frame to sit on the wide edge of the tub. Involuntarily, Raine recoiled, water lapping about her shoulders. She saw Kyle's face harden. 'Why do I get the impression that you would have preferred another night on your own?'

Raine couldn't answer, tipping her head back, grey eyes looking almost bruised in her pale face. She could see Kyle searching, delving for the explanation that she wasn't ready to give. Deliberately, he reached for her hand, indifferent to the water that sluiced off her skin on to his. 'Raine?' Impatiently, he tangled their fingers together. 'You'd better tell me what's wrong.'

She closed her eyes tight, shutting out his beautiful male face before she poured out all her pain, her betrayal. 'Will you please bring me my robe?'

She felt him freeze for a long moment, his grip tight on her hand, but she wouldn't look at him. 'No, I will not bring you your robe,' he ground out at last. 'You want another barrier, you get it on your own.'

Raine nearly sobbed at his choice of words. If he hadn't insisted on stripping away at her barriers, she would be safe now. Immune from loving him. And he powerless to hurt her. 'Kyle . . . *please*.'

Her hand made a small, abrupt splash in the water when he released it. She heard him stride into the other room, her heart shuddering with alarm as she remembered too late that her robe was lying across the bed, the locket and letter beside it, within easy sight. He was gone too long not to have found them, and she pictured him reading Melanie's letter to Stephen, fitting the pieces together just as she had done earlier.

His expression was nowhere near as incredulous as she expected. Having lifted a cautious face, Raine went still at the quiet acceptance in him. He had the letter in his hand, along with the open locket...and no robe, although it scarcely mattered now. He stood leaning in the doorway, displaying none of the shock that Raine still felt, voicing no surprise at all. 'Where did you find this?'

'Hidden inside Boo. I was going to mend him with some extra stuffing...' She trailed off, grey eyes baffled. 'Don't you understand what it means?'

'Russ was Stephen's father.' He said it matter-of-factly, gazing thoughtfully into the locket before snapping it closed. There was a sombre smile in his eyes when he looked back at Raine. 'That makes me his uncle...at least until the adoption is final. And,' he hesitated, mouth rueful, 'it tells me once and for all that I am not insane. There were times when I had to wonder.'

'You sound almost as if...as if you've known.'

'I didn't have any real proof until now.'

Raine shivered in spite of the warm water. 'I don't understand.'

'That's my fault,' he admitted, moving forward. 'I chose to keep my suspicions to myself, I suppose because there was always a chance that they were wrong. Almost from the beginning, though, I've had this unshakeable feeling that Stephen was no stranger. I couldn't even pinpoint it at first, but later it amounted to a kind of recognition.'

'You thought you'd seen him before,' she remembered.

'I was convinced. But hospital records proved that I'd never treated him, so I had to drop that theory. Then Meg brought Stephen's things, and I saw his name written inside a book. The Russell seemed an odd coincidence. I told myself it was *only* a coincidence, but it didn't quite work. When I opened my mother's room and saw that drawing of Russ again...done when he was just about Stephen's age...I started to see the physical resemblance. I suppose Stephen has enough of his mother in him to make his likeness to Russ nothing obvious, but it crept up on me, little by little.' He smiled faintly, reminiscent. 'Dad, on the other hand, probably still doesn't know what hit him. But seeing my father drawn to Stephen, just as I had been, was ultimately what convinced me to take action.'

He leaned back against the double sinktop, turning the locket over in his fingers. 'What I wouldn't give to have found this earlier.' He didn't notice the way Raine stiffened. 'I've had a private investigator checking into Melanie Thompson's background for weeks. He finally traced her to Massachusetts, to a little restaurant just outside Cambridge. She was working as a waitress there three years ago. The owner recognised a photograph of Russ. I talked to the man, Melanie's boss, myself. That was this morning. Then I spoke with a couple of class-mates of my brother's who still live in the area. Their stories confirmed that Melanie and Russ had been seeing each other... so the timing was right. My own instincts told me the rest.'

Raine shifted warily, wrapping her arms around her knees. 'You've been to Massachusetts?'

'Massachusetts was nothing compared to the territory that investigator covered.' Kyle grimaced. 'The man has called me from parts of three different states. There were times when he lost Melanie's trail altogether. Stephen's not quite three, and he's lived more places than I care to name. The way Melanie moved them around, they might have been fugitives.' The letter rustled in his hand. 'She had absolutely no reason to be frightened.'

'She couldn't know that, could she?'

'But living like that, Raine?' He glanced up, eyes shadowed. 'Taking whatever job that was available, leaving Stephen with any decent babysitter or neighbour she could find? All because we might just be inhuman enough to separate a child from his mother? Why base a whole life-style on assumption?'

Something seemed to snap in Raine's head. 'Maybe I can explain,' she said intensely. 'When you are raised in one foster home after another, like Melanie and I were, something happens. You become wary. Slow to indulge in optimism. You learn to guard your possessions jealously. And you never, ever trust a stranger to treat you fairly.' There was a bitterness in her lovely curved mouth. 'That makes it difficult to trust at all. Because even if you try to get close to someone, how can you ever be sure that you really know him? That he hasn't just shown you the part of himself that he wants you to see?'

Kyle made an impatient movement, searching her face, then he went still. 'We aren't just talking about Melanie,' he said tautly. 'Are we, Raine?'

'Just tell me something, Kyle. You have Stephen.' She fought a perilous battle with her choking voice. 'Isn't that enough for you? Do you have to take my pride, too? I can't bear the way you're pretending nothing has changed. Stephen is yours now. I know that. You can *say* it. You don't need me any more. So if this marriage is only teetering between your sense of integrity and my self-respect, then, for God's sake, leave me *something*!'

Kyle drew a harsh breath, looking startled, explosive. *'What?'*

'Get out!' Raine lost control. She was going to cry her heart out any minute now, and she didn't know what possessed her still to be in the tub, so completely vulnerable to his flashing gaze. 'Is that plain enough? Just *get out*!'

Kyle thrust a hand through his hair, indecisive for the briefest moment, then he was jerking open a cabinet door, withdrawing a thick, folded towel. He turned back to Raine, violently whipping the bath-sheet flat and holding it up. 'No *you* get out.'

Raine glared at him with hotly brimming eyes, and he took a menacing step forward. 'Don't think you're going to cower in there where I can't touch you. Either you come out, or I'm coming in.' Raine slid to the farthest corner of the massive tub, stunned that he wasn't even allowing her the privacy of her tears. His mouth thinned grimly at her disbelieving look. 'I've already proved that it can be done. Very successfully, in fact.'

Raine whitened, unbearably insulted that he'd use their lovemaking as a taunt. Biting her lip savagely to hold back a sob, she stood up, fluttering into the towel and away from him so wildly that she nearly unbalanced on the slippery tiles. Her feet left damp prints on the bedroom carpet, her arm nearly sliding out of his gasp when he caught at her.

'No, you don't!' He spun her around, hauling her dripping form against him, entirely oblivious to the wet patches seeping through his clothes. 'You're going to explain yourself.' She stared up in mute pain and defiance, and after a long moment he gave a harsh groan. 'Oh, what the hell? There's only one way I've ever been able to reach you.'

Expecting punishment, Raine went weak beneath the treacherous touch of his mouth. He wouldn't even fight fair. A hard, controlling kiss she could have easily spurned. But this? This soft fire? She moaned deep in her throat, and Kyle pressed her closer, the heat of his body encompassing her chilled flesh. His hands were moving... stroking... gentling. She felt his fingers over her breast, slipping the knot, and then the towel was slipping.

'No!' She tore her mouth away, wrenching free of him with all the strength she could summon to her already lethargic limbs. 'You can't do this to me!' She backed away, groping into her robe, her eyes locked with terrible fascination on to his taut face. He angrily tossed the towel aside, moving, and she flung up her head, delicate nostrils flared. 'Damn it, Kyle, *no*!' She shuddered uncontrollably, prepared to follow Melanie's example, her father's example, because she had found something in Melanie's letter to help her understand. But she couldn't maintain her resolve if he *touched* her. 'I'll leave if you want,' she swallowed, tone gone fierce, 'but you can't have everything.'

Raine thought she counted a full ten seconds while he stood there, blue eyes blinking warily, handsome features tensed with the effort of restraint. 'I have to hand it to you,' he lashed out finally, 'you're one lady who won't wait to be had. You've got it all figured out, haven't you? Stephen is mine. You've served your purpose. And I'm supposed to be cold enough to end it all, just like that. Only you'll go one better and save me the trouble. You'll walk away. Noble Raine.' The smile was utterly grim, humourless, then, flash, it was gone. *'Like hell!'* he gritted emphatically. 'Melodramatic, I'll give you. And distrustful? Well, you win that one hands down. But noble you aren't, sweetheart. If you were, you'd stay and fight.'

Raine blinked wet lashes, unbelievably tormented. 'You're angry with *me*?'

'Hell, yes, I'm angry! If I haven't proved to you by now that I love you...that I can be trusted...then what's the use? I'll be damned if I'm going to grovel! You believe what you like.'

'What did you say?' He'd just told her the one thing she'd prayed to hear, and he was walking away? 'Kyle, wait.'

'I *said*, believe what you want.' He didn't even turn around. 'I won't defend myself to you.'

'Kyle,' she husked urgently, wonderingly. 'Oh, darling, *please*!' She took a step forward when he stopped, searching the hard, handsome profile that was all he would allow her. He looked disgusted, fed-up, and uncertainty crept over her in sick waves. It might be too late. 'Kyle, I...did you mean that?' She could scarcely speak. 'You love me?'

He turned full-face, looking totally impassive. 'I meant it.'

'Oh, Kyle!' She stood there, eyes luminous, until unsmilingly he removed a hand from his pocket and held it out. Suddenly Raine was in his arms, crushed against him, body shaking with emotional force. 'I love you, too,' she drew out on a tortured breath. 'Desperately. I didn't think I'd ever be able to tell you.'

'You mean you had to hear it from me first,' Kyle chided, his voice as rough as his hands were gentle, 'while I, on the other hand, was holding back, trying not to send you into an emotional tailspin.' His eyes lost the faint spark of humour. 'Raine, how could you? You read that letter and drew the worst possible conclusion, that I no longer needed you. Haven't I told you...'

'No,' Raine interrupted huskily, blinking the leftover moisture from her lashes. 'The only thing you really told me was that you wanted me.' Her eyes unguarded, she allowed him an unwitting glimpse of the uncertainty she'd endured, and he pulled her tight to his chest with a rueful frown.

He was changing subtly, tense muscles easing, yet his voice still sounded gruff. '*You* could have saved a lot of misunderstanding by telling me you'd fallen in love with me. Was it so hard to do?'

'Yes.' The word was muffled in his shirt, her palms moving convulsively against the fine material. 'I didn't want you to feel trapped by a commitment that wasn't part of our bargain.' She gave a small, helpless shrug, and felt him gather her even closer. 'I guess I wanted to salvage my pride.'

'My poor, sweet, cautious lady,' he sighed into her hair. 'Why do you make everything so difficult for yourself? Don't you know that what we have is incredibly rare? *Think*, baby.'

Raine raised beautiful, shimmering eyes, absorbing the fierce sweet look of him, seeing her rising passion so vividly matched in his blue gaze. Slowly, deliberately, she linked her hands behind his head. 'I'd rather *feel*,' she whispered.

Kyle's arm was warm and heavy across her waist, his palm idly stroking over the fine flesh, when Raine finally drifted back to conscious thought. She lay musing for a while, content to be near him, to have been *with* him so completely, but inevitably, the questions surfaced. 'The phone calls you've been getting,' she succumbed, 'they were about Stephen, weren't they?'

'The investigator,' Kyle admitted ruefully. 'I had him checking in constantly.'

'Then Stephen was the project that had you so pre-occupied. It hurt that you were unable to confide in me. Why couldn't you?'

He sighed, brushing her temple with his mouth. 'Because, as I said earlier, I might have been wrong. But also because I know how you tend to think. I couldn't trust you not to see my obsession with Stephen's parents as a desire to change our situation. As it happened, you added two and two on your own and got the wrong answer anyway.'

Exactly as if on cue, the bedside telephone rang. Raine couldn't stop herself from stiffening slightly; she'd dreaded those phone calls for too long. Kyle stretched across her, flicking on the lamp, scooping up the receiver. 'Hello.' But his eyes were on her, lazily perusing her smoky gaze, her softly swollen mouth. She heard him laugh huskily, murmur 'No problem,' then replace the phone. 'That was your harassed father-in-law.' He stared down mockingly, making no move to change his position. 'It seems that Stephen is no longer so sure about spending the night. I could hear him howling in the background, as a matter of fact. Dad is bringing him home.'

'You mean he missed me?' Raine half smiled.

'Don't look so happy about it,' he advised drily. 'This means our honeymoon plans are shot to hell.'

'Why take it so hard?' She reached up to stroke the dark blond hair back off his brow. 'We have a lifetime for honeymoons, right?' They shared a secret, complicated smile, then Raine grew thoughtful. 'Maybe Stephen is becoming too dependent on us,' she admitted sombrely, hesitating. 'How would you feel about another child? A sister for our son?'

'A baby?' Kyle went still, considering, blue eyes dark with feeling.

'Your baby?' she breathed, drawing her palm across his lean cheek. 'I'd love that . . . some day, when the time is right.' She paused, searching his face closely. 'Actually . . . I was thinking of Jenny.'

The look in his eyes in no way diminished. She watched as the idea grew on him, sensed his acceptance. Without breaking visual contact, he slid lower, settling his muscular body to every soft line and curve. His voice was a quiet, grating caress. 'Have I told you how much I adore you, lady?'

'No,' Raine drew an unsteady breath, lifting her mouth for the gentlest of kisses, 'but it takes a while to drive out from the farm.'

# ATTRACTIVE, SPACE SAVING BOOK RACK

Display your most prized novels on this handsome and sturdy book rack. The hand-rubbed walnut finish will blend into your library decor with quiet elegance, providing a practical organizer for your favorite hard-or soft-covered books.

**Only $9.95**

**Approximately
16" x 8"
when assembled**

**Assembles in seconds!**

------------------------------------------------

To order, rush your name, address and zip code, along with a check or money order for $10.70* ($9.95 plus 75¢ postage and handling) payable to *Harlequin Reader Service*:

Harlequin Reader Service
Book Rack Offer
901 Fuhrmann Blvd.
P.O. Box 1396
Buffalo, NY 14269-1396

*Offer not available in Canada.*

BKR-1A

*New York and Iowa residents add appropriate sales tax.

*Exciting, adventurous, sensual stories
of love long ago*

**On Sale Now:**

Harlequin Historicals

### SATAN'S ANGEL by Kristin James

*Slater was the law in a land that was as wild and untamed
as he was himself, but all that changed when he met
Victoria Stafford. She had been raised to be a lady, but
that didn't mean she had no will of her own. Their search
for her kidnapped cousin brought them together, but they
were too much alike for the course of true love to run
smooth.*

### PRIVATE TREATY by Kathleen Eagle

*When Jacob Black Hawk rescued schoolteacher
Carolina Hammond from a furious thunderstorm, he
swept her off her feet in every sense of the word, and she
knew that he was the only man who would ever make her
feel that way. But society had put barriers between them
that only the most powerful and overwhelming love could
overcome...*

*Look for them wherever Harlequin books are sold.*

_Temptation_ ™

# TEMPTATION WILL BE
# EVEN HARDER TO RESIST...

In September, Temptation is presenting a sophisticated new
face to the world. A fresh look that truly brings Harlequin's
most intimate romances into focus.

What's more, all-time favorite authors Barbara Delinsky, Rita
Clay Estrada, Jayne Ann Krentz and Vicki Lewis Thompson
will join forces to help us celebrate. The result? A very special
quartet of Temptations...

- **Four striking covers**
- **Four stellar authors**
- **Four sensual love stories**
- **Four variations on one spellbinding theme**

All in one great month! Give in to Temptation in September.